THE CLANDESTINE QUEEN

WHAT OTHERS ARE SAYING ABOUT THIS BOOK

The Clandestine Queen will keep you on the edge of your seat as you root for a girl learning that she can be much more than she ever dreamed of and for a villain who is searching for redemption. With storytelling similar to C. S. Lewis and Andrzej Sapkowski, Brandon masterfully manages to create complex characters that have to learn to work together, all while a demon is out to ruin everything good in the world. *The Clandestine Queen* will certainly leave you aching for the next book!

—Elizabeth Drysdale, author of *Out of Time*

Greer has woven an intricate, fantastical world filled with witches, demons, and an eclectic cast of characters. *The Clandestine Queen* is fast-paced, suspenseful, and surprising. Maggie Abernathy's journey had me hooked!

—Frank L. Cole, author of the Potion Masters trilogy

BRANDON J GREER

THE CLANDESTINE QUEEN

SWEETWATER BOOKS
AN IMPRINT OF CEDAR FORT, INC.
SPRINGVILLE, UTAH

The Clandestine Queen was previously published as *Loravain's Gamble*.

ISBN 13: 978-1-4621-4171-5

Published by Sweetwater Books, an imprint of Cedar Fort, Inc.
2373 W. 700 S., Springville, UT 84663
Distributed by Cedar Fort, Inc., www.cedarfort.com

Library of Congress Control Number: 2022930092

Cover design by Shawnda T. Craig
Cover design © 2022 Cedar Fort, Inc.
Substantive by Rachel Hathcock
Edited and typeset by Spencer Skeen

Printed in the United States of America

10 9 8 7 6 5 4 3 2 1

Printed on acid-free paper

To my wife, Laura. You inspired me in
more ways than you can possibly know.

PROLOGUE

Deafening silence enveloped her as she crouched, hidden in the tall underbrush of autumn. She was keenly aware she was being tracked but waited to discover who her pursuers were.

Frozen plumes of breath escaped through her pursed lips as she exhaled. She watched it rise into the air in front of her. Peering into the surrounding trees, she listened for the sounds of pursuit: a crunching leaf, a snapping twig, and whispered conversation. She assumed it would be the villagers. Who else would it be?

Knees creaking in protest, she forced her legs to stay bent beneath her. Her gaze darted wildly as the whispering echo of a crack found her ears, desperately searching for the source of the disturbance. She knew she would not have to wait long.

Ignoring her instinct to flee, she held fast, wiping the sweat from her palms on her thick pants. When she finally saw them, a measured sigh of relief flooded from her lungs. She'd been right; it was the men from the village that she had been skulking around.

She crouched lower, almost to the point of lying down. Swiveling her head, she planned out the best possible escape route before leaping out into the open. She knew she could easily defeat the lot of them, but she sought another way. A peaceful way. She wasn't like other witches who hated humankind but she had learned to fear them. It wasn't for their hatred of her kind, but their ignorance and numbers.

Happy with the route she'd chosen, she backed away from her cover and, turning her back to the men, darted for the morning shade of a large oak tree. Its branches reached high into the air, their brightly colored leaves hanging in such a precarious way that even a sneeze might send them spiraling to the ground. The wide trunk offered ample space to cower behind while waiting to make her next move.

As she scanned the forest floor, the villagers once again caught her attention. Something had changed. A loud murmuring rose from the group. She twisted her body so she could peer around the tree. The men had crowded together and were watching something out of sight. They seemed excited. A voice in the back of her mind screamed at her to flee, to put as much distance between them as she could, but suicidal curiosity won out. She cursed herself for not running when she'd had the chance.

The villager's voices rose and fell for almost a minute before their conversation ended abruptly. The crowd parted around a solitary figure. A nervous tension flooded her body as she pressed her back flat against the trunk of the tree. She felt the blood drain from her face, leaving her already fair skin ghostly white. Her breath came in ragged gasps as panic set in. The villagers were not on their own. They had enlisted the aid of a hunter to help them. A hunter that rumor whispered was not entirely human.

She pushed her lithe body away from the tree as she stole one last glance behind her. The hunter was no longer alone. A massive black wolf stood at his side, sniffing at the air. She had precious little time left. Keeping the tree between them, she bolted, knowing that caution wouldn't make the slightest bit of difference now. Speed would be the only thing keeping her alive today. Sprinting through the woods, she vaulted over fallen logs, swung from low-hanging branches, and dodged brambles and boulders.

Surprising herself, she laughed as she crashed through a large, thorny bush. Her clothes ripped, her skin bled, but her mind whisked her back to a time when things had appeared just as bleak. She'd been in plenty of tight spots before and had always come out on top.

"Stop it, Sarah," she said, chiding her thoughts. Thoughts like that would only ensure her capture. She couldn't risk pride right now. Yes, she'd had a rough go of things in the past. Yes, she'd barely made it at times, but this wasn't like those times. This "man" and his wolf were legendary witch hunters.

Picking up the pace, Sarah pushed herself harder. A large gully sped into view. Quickly judging its distance, she readied herself to jump. It was broader than any human man could ever dream of jumping, she thought, then prayed that it would be too wide for an "almost man" to jump as well. Glancing over her shoulder, she was horrified to find that the hunter was nearly keeping pace with her. No man had ever been able to run as fast as her, which cemented the rumor that the hunter was something more than a man. She was the only witch she knew that could run down a deer, not that she knew many anymore. Yet this man, this hunter, was gaining on her.

She shifted her attention back to the gully just in time to jump. She planted her right foot on the lip of the drop and pushed her body out into the open air above a shallow, meandering stream. Time seemed to slow down as she glanced back, realizing how close she'd come to being captured. The hunter was seconds away from the drop. His wolf was en route to join him, sprinting in from another direction. They had been trying to flank her.

Landing hard on the dirt and dead grass of the far side, the witch rolled out of her fall and leapt lightly to her feet. She spun around and faced the hunter. The distance was too great to make out his features, but their eyes locked. She shuddered and forced her gaze away from his, focusing on his body instead. He was tall, lean but muscular, and favored dark, shadowy colors. The wolf standing at his side was completely black except for a streak of silver fur that ran across its left eye and over its ear. If she didn't know any better, she would have thought it a scar.

A smile crept up her face at her good fortune. Her hopes of an easy escape soon vanished when the hunter dropped into the gully and gracefully bounded over the stream. The wolf, on the other hand, bolted off in another direction.

"Of course," Sarah cried as she turned and ran.

She sprinted as fast as she could, but the sound of pursuit quickly followed. She could almost feel the twigs and leaves crushing behind her. She didn't dare look back. Pushing aside a branch, she vaulted over a fallen log.

"It's now or never," she whispered to herself as she weaved around slender, tightly grouped aspen trees. A glance to her side revealed the hunter closing ground. She pushed harder. Knowing her body's limitations, Sarah knew she couldn't keep this brutal pace up for long. Frantically searching for an escape route, her gaze fell upon a low-hanging branch. It was too high for an ordinary human to reach, but not for a witch. She only hoped it would be too high for him as well. Leaping off the ground, she practically flew to the limb. Stretching out her arms, she panicked when her momentum slowed and gravity began pulling her back towards the hard, unforgiving earth.

The branch, mere inches away, felt more like miles as she fell. With a final stretch, she felt rough bark against her fingers, and she grabbed onto it with all her might. Her descent came to a sudden, jarring halt. She wanted to take a moment to calm her ragged breathing but knew that would put her at too much risk.

She pulled herself higher up the tree, climbing as swiftly as she could. With every passing second, she felt the fear in her chest release its grip on her heart. But she knew that if she faltered now, it could mean her death. To escape, she needed to get high enough to jump to one of the neighboring trees. The treetops were now her best chance of survival.

The hunter had lost sight of his target. His last fleeting glance of the witch's shimmering blond hair had just whipped behind a tree. The magic that had allowed him to keep pace with her was waning. Even though he was forcing himself to stay behind her, it wouldn't last much longer. If he didn't catch her soon, she might evade him and then he wouldn't be paid.

When he rounded the tree and came to a stop, the witch was gone. Spinning around, he waited for his monstrous wolf to catch up. Padding close, the wolf panted slightly.

"Don't lose her scent," the hunter said as if the wolf could understand him. "We cannot allow this witch to escape."

The wolf bobbed its large head in acknowledgment and bounded forward. The hunter, on the other hand, was not so sure of himself.

Dropping to one knee, he examined the earth. He scooped up a messy clump of dirt and moss and carefully sniffed it.

"Nothing." He tossed the worthless debris back to the ground. "She has to be here."

He studied the forest floor, moving back to where he'd lost sight of her. There were her footprints, imprinted deep and clear in the muddy grass. Three more steps forward and they disappeared. They had been so easy to follow up until now.

"Can this one become invisible?" he asked himself as he glanced around. "No, that would be impossible. Only my master would have that ability. And that wouldn't hide her footprints."

Making a renewed effort, he inspected the footprints again. There was something different about the last one. He chuckled when he figured it out. Taking a step back, he looked up into the trees.

"Thanatos," he called.

The wolf ran back to his side and gazed up into the tree branches as well.

"We have her now."

Scrambling higher, Sarah surveyed her prospective routes. A slender pine tree shot skyward not far from where she was clinging. It was a wide gap, more than ten running paces, but she thought it was possible. A shorter, more stable oak grew to her left. It was closer, but the top branches looked more brittle. Both jumps were risky. Taking a chance to peer below her, she was surprised that she couldn't see the hunter nor his wolf. She froze. Could he have somehow passed her? Was she free? She considered waiting in the tree for another hour then climbing back down instead of making an insane leap to either of the trees.

A short crossbow bolt impaled itself into the trunk directly below her. Doubt fled from her mind as she breathlessly pulled her body up the last few branches she could reach. There was no time left to debate her options. She shimmied out along a thin branch, which almost snapped under her weight. The cracking of wood hurried her on.

Sarah sprinted nimbly down the branch and stepped out into open air. Willing herself to glide into the branches of the pine tree she was now plummeting towards, she readied herself for a painful impact.

The small twigs and shoots of the branches were almost in reach when blinding pain blossomed across her abdomen. Her body folded into the fetal position as she fell, her weight snapping limbs on the way down, bruising her legs, arms, and ribs as she went. Her only saving grace was the years' worth of pine needles, decay, and autumn leaves piled up on the forest floor.

She hit hard; her breath ripped from her lungs. She gasped painfully for air, but no relief came. Fighting against her body, she inhaled again and again until her lungs responded and she moaned out in agony. More than one of her ribs had broken.

Tears flooded her eyes as her vision began to sharpen. Curled up in a tight ball, Sarah glanced around, cursing her good fortune that she'd survived the fall. She knew what was coming and didn't want to give the hunter the satisfaction of his bounty.

A shadow fell across her face as a thick pair of legs obstructed her view. Through gritted teeth, she rolled onto her back and glared at the man who had done this to her. He aimed an enormous crossbow at her. When she didn't move, the hunter shouldered it.

Gingerly touching her body, Sarah found neither bolt nor wound. She continued to poke and prod until her finger brushed against her ribs and she flinched at the pain. There was no trace of blood or broken skin, but the bolt had worked as intended. She knew she wouldn't be walking away and fell back onto the leaves to await her death.

"Don't count yourself out of this life just yet, witch," the hunter said, his voice higher than Sarah pictured it would be. "Had I meant to kill you, you would be dead. Consider yourself lucky I was not paid for that."

The hunter walked around to her backside and yanked her hands together, binding them with coarse rope.

"This is not the gentlemanly thing to do, and I apologize for the situation I will be leaving you in, but you must understand. Business is business. I trust you will not try to run?"

Debilitating pain flared through her body as she fought against him. When she realized she couldn't win, she collapsed onto her side.

Her only reply was a shake of her head. No, she wasn't even capable of running.

"Good," the hunter said. "I know you will not be able to move for some time, but since I can't have you struggling and injuring yourself . . ."

He placed a rag beneath her nose. She held her breath for as long as she could but finally gave in, inhaling the aroma of snap willow blossom. Her eyelids began to droop as the overwhelming urge to sleep flooded her body. She fought it for a moment but failed.

The hunter stood up and looked down at her face. He wiped the sweat from his brow and whistled. The wolf sauntered into view, his back reaching the hunter's waist.

"One of these days I will be done with these cursed tasks, but until then, there is gold to collect. Come, Thanatos."

He turned his back on the sleeping witch and disappeared into the trees. He never glanced back, only continued west, his wolf trailing behind him.

CHAPTER 1

Early morning sunlight filtered through the treetops of the Eastern Woods as a shrouded figure paused beneath the slanted roof of a dilapidated barn. The village of Lakes Hollow was beginning to rouse from its slumber and the new day was about to be rung in. Unaware he was being watched, the blacksmith readied his hammer. Unlike the rest of the sleeping villagers, he had been up for hours stoking the fire and preparing his tools. Metal, which had been heating since before the first light of dawn broke the sky, was now bright red, brilliant with heat.

It was a near-perfect fall morning. The air was crisp and clear and not a cloud could be seen in the sky. It had been the same over the last few days, easing the burden of the harvest. The rays of the sun began to brighten the beaten path leading from the blacksmith's forge to the commons at the center of the village. The first resounding clang of the hammer echoed off the buildings, ushering in another productive day.

The figure slipped in and out of the dying shadows, keeping out of sight while she continued to watch the blacksmith work. With the rising sun, shadowy hiding places were disappearing, and better cover would be needed. Ensuring that the blacksmith's attention was elsewhere, his stalker stepped out of the darkness, only to disappear behind the barn.

Maggie Abernathy kept her back to the worn wood of the wall as she shuffled her way to the back of the barn. She pulled her black cloak tighter to her body, afraid the blacksmith might recognize her if he looked up from his forge. A heavy hood nearly covered her eyes, but she knew the way by heart. Maggie had followed this path countless times before and knew exactly where she was going. Even so, she gasped when her ankle rolled on a rock, nearly sending her to the ground. She glanced over her shoulder in time to see him lift his head. Before their eyes could meet, Maggie slipped around the backside of the barn and fell to her knees.

"Clumsy oaf." Her eyes filled with tears as she rubbed her ankle. It didn't hurt but had almost given her away.

"Is someone there?" The blacksmith's voice sounded closer than Maggie thought it should be. "Hello?"

"Oh no," Maggie cried as she pushed herself to her feet, tripping as she ducked through a small hole in the barn wall. Her heart beat wildly in her chest as she scrambled for a place to hide. She breathed easier when she heard the hammer strike the anvil again. When she was sure it was safe, she moved out from behind a pile of old wagon parts, ripped saddles, and bags of rotten potatoes.

The barn was one of the oldest and most dangerous buildings in the village. As hazardous as it was, the town council had not yet decided to pull it down, and Maggie was grateful since it worked perfectly for her needs. It provided her with a private place to spy on Jacob, the town's apprentice blacksmith. His father was the real blacksmith, but the fever had taken his leg, so he left Jacob to manage in his stead.

Jacob's hair was usually golden blond but with all the ash in the air from working the forge, it was grayer than anything else, giving him an aged and distinguished look even though he was only a teenager. His arms were large and muscular, one of the benefits of swinging a hammer all day. He wasn't tall, but his shoulders were broad, giving him the shape of a barrel. A desirable barrel, Maggie thought. His eyes shone blue in the sun, which reminded her of the cool, deep lakes her village fished on. In short, Jacob was the man of her dreams, and she loved watching him.

Maggie was the opposite. She was tall, lanky, and agile. Her hair, almost entirely black, matched her eyes and was shoulder length and ragged as if someone cut it with a pair of dull gardening sheers. She considered herself pretty but had never had a wide range of suitors to agree with her. At least no one said anything to the contrary. That was understandable though as she was just now reaching the age of marriage. In three months' time, she would turn sixteen and her parents would start preparing to marry her off. The only thought that brought her any comfort about that was that Jacob wasn't married either. Would he ever consider marrying her? The idea tickled her stomach.

Inside, she shimmied up a questionable-looking ladder to the loft above. She'd done it many times before, so she had learned which rungs would send her plummeting back down to the hard floor below and avoided them. On the far wall of the loft was a small knot in one of the planks of wood with a tiny hole carved into it. When she lay down on her belly, she had a clear view of the forge. Closing one eye, she peered out the slight opening and watched Jacob take a drink of water. She was in luck. He'd been working hard and was already sweating. When he had finished drinking, he poured a ladle of water over his head. The thin fabric of his shirt stuck to his chest. It was almost more than Maggie could bear.

She rolled onto her back and stared through the gaps in the roof. She lost herself in a waking dream. Jacob stood in front of her, gently taking her hands in his, then slowly fell to one knee and proposed. Her parents were there as well, beaming with pride at the prospect that she would accept. The dream shifted to a wedding scene where she wore a beautifully tailored dress. The entire village was in attendance and all eyes were on her. The flowers that lined the crowded streets were stunning with bold and agreeable colors. The food was delicious, both sweet and savory, and lively music filled the air, encouraging everyone to dance. It was the biggest party the village had ever seen. When her lips were moving to form the words "I do", the smile faded from her face.

"Jacob Prescott. You know I can't concentrate with you pounding that hammer all morning."

It was the voice Maggie despised most of all, and it pulled her harshly back to reality. It belonged to Katie Levinston, the butcher's daughter. She was wealthy, according to Lakes Hollow standards, and beautiful. Her mother had passed on a few years back from the same fever that had taken Jacob's father's leg, and since then her father had attempted to raise her all alone. With a bustling shop to manage, he let his daughter do whatever she wanted. Like Maggie, Katie was close to marrying age and her father was doing everything in his power to attract a long line of suitors for her. He was a little blind when it came to his daughter because Katie didn't need help when it came to finding suitors. Without his help, the line she could garner on her own would be even longer. No matter the disdain Maggie held for her, she thought Katie was stunning, which made her sick. Her hair alone was enough to entangle any man within a hundred miles of Lakes Hollow. It was rarer than diamonds in these parts. It was curly, long, and red. Her father had black hair and her mother's had been light brown, so no one knew where the red had come from but a few wicked rumors had floated around the village. Her eyes shone like emeralds, a brilliant breath-catching green, which was another rarity. All the boys swooned over her and all the girls hated her while secretly wishing they were her. Maggie loathed her, just like the rest, but for another reason. Jacob liked her. They were always flirting and playing around in the streets, putting on a show for the entire village. This morning was no different.

Flipping back to her stomach, Maggie pressed her face to the wall. Katie looked magnificent as usual. She wore a gorgeous new green dress that matched her eyes and accentuated her figure. A tight ponytail hung down her back that showcased her slender neck and hypnotizing gaze. The morning sun glistened off her exposed skin, displaying her next-to-perfect complexion. Like any other boy his age, Jacob could not help it and dropped his hammer when he saw her. Two inches to the left and he would have lost a toe.

"K-Katie," he stammered. "You look amazing today."

"Thank you," she beamed, almost touching his arm but pulling back at the last second.

"Who would wear something like that this early?" Maggie huffed. "She's on the prowl for sure."

It was easy to see why she didn't want to touch him. Katie was elegant and proper but most of all, clean. Jacob was hard-working and dirty. The harder he worked, the more he sweat. The more he sweat, the more the ash would cling to his tantalizing body. After two hours of hammering, his arms, hair, and clothes were indistinguishable from the ground around him. He noticed Katie's hesitation and played off it.

"Katie, my dear, you're almost old enough to be taken as someone's wife. You know I've thought about that. If you hug me now, I'd run to your father and make all the arrangements this instant. I've received more jobs lately and could afford the kind of wedding I know you want."

With open arms, he jumped at her, threatening to ruin her perfect dress. A wide smile crossed Maggie's face. *Do it*, she thought. *Pull that smug look off her face.*

Katie stumbled back, just out of reach so Jacob moved closer than she was comfortable with. She squealed in fright and skipped down the path.

"If you do that, I'll make sure you never marry me, ash boy," she fired back. "You have no idea how much this dress cost. Father would be upset with me if he knew I bought it, but he would kill you if you ruined it."

"I'm not scared of your father," Jacob countered. "What is it going to be? A dress or the wedding you've always dreamed of? Dirt is momentary, marriage is forever."

"You don't know what you're talking about," Katie said. "This dress cost twice what you could afford for a wedding."

"Do you really want to gamble on that? Business has been good," Jacob said.

He lunged at Katie again, but it was too much for Maggie to stomach. She pulled away and sat up cross-legged in the loft. The last thing she heard was a kiss. It was a quick one but enough to tie a knot in her stomach and push the tears from the corners of her eyes. Katie could not hide her bluff and folded.

"Why can't that be me?" she asked the empty space in front of her.

That one kiss, just a simple thing like lips touching, made her imagined future with Jacob evaporate in front of her. He would choose Katie, and Maggie would be left with someone else if she got married at all. Tears flowed as her thoughts turned dark and traumatizing. She imagined herself marrying the tanner's son, Fredrick. He was about as attractive as a boar's behind and just as smart to boot. The prospect of marrying him made her consider the life of an old spinster, shunned by the village to live as an outsider. And the candidates only got worse from there. So much so that they weren't even worth thinking about.

Hopping to her feet, she stepped to the edge of the loft. She considered using the ladder but instead stared down at the landing below her. It was at least a twenty-five-foot drop; however, she felt careless with the mood she was in today. She jumped out as high as she could and lifted her arms above her head. Her fingers grazed the ceiling, which was another ten feet above her, then she fell straight down.

Her hair whipped around her face as she plummeted. With a single thought, her body slowed just before her feet touched the ground. For a moment, she felt weightless, held motionless in the air by her will alone. A grin played across her lips as she relished the sensation of landing lightly on the packed dirt floor. Glancing over her shoulder, she looked back up at the loft and through the missing planks in the ceiling. She was still amazed every time she did that. Besides spying on Jacob, freefalling from the loft was one of the only things that brought her joy. If anyone found out what she could do, that joy would be ripped away from her. The thought of that happening stabbed at her heart and made her sick. No one could find out. Her secrets needed to be buried deep and locked away.

Maggie brushed away the loose hay and dirt clinging to her clothes and ran out the same way she had come in. She kept to the backs of the buildings until she was well away from the forge, forcing the thoughts of Jacob and Katie from her mind. Turning up the collar of her cloak, she stepped out into the open and disappeared into the crowd congregating around the market stalls in the village center. The booths were portable and could be moved around when needed, but the buildings behind them were permanent. They housed the more established businesses and shops for the baker, butcher, and cobbler, plus a small eatery that was too expensive for Maggie or her parents to visit. The smell of sweet pan bread and thick syrup tickled her nose, reminding her that she had not eaten breakfast yet. When she had awoken that morning, her thoughts had only been of Jacob.

The communal well, sitting in the middle of the center, was said to have been the first structure built in their village. William Pickler dug the well nearly a century ago when he settled near the deep lakes. The stone work of the well wall may have been more elaborate then, but now it was nothing more than a pile of moss-covered stones rising a few feet above the ground. The village had sprung up around it, now complete with homes, farms, a thriving market, and a small tavern that hosted most of the village's entertainment. Most families in Lakes Hollow had a market stall, including Maggie's parents, though it was seldom used. They grew herbs and plants used primarily for healing and medicines and only purchased by a few people who went directly to their home to get them. They only used their stall when they had an abundance. When they needed money, they sold spices for cooking and leaves for tea. The other stalls in the market were used daily and were full of warm bread, fresh cuts of meat, and thick, creamy milk. Things like tools, clothing, fabric, and weapons could be found in shops elsewhere in the village.

Lost in depressing thoughts, Maggie wove through the crowd, trying to ignore the morning bustle as best she could.

"Watch where you're walking," a voice cried after Maggie bounced off yet another shoulder. "I almost dropped my bag."

"Sorry," Maggie said shyly as she looked up into the wrinkled face of the village's councilwoman. A grimace crossed her face when their eyes met.

"Magdalena Abernathy," said councilwoman Vega. "I should have known. Don't you have something better to be doing?"

"Yes, Councilwoman. I was just on my way there now," Maggie said as she backed away.

"I doubt that. You forget that I know you. If you can get out of an honest day's work, you will. You are a disgrace to your parents. They work so hard to provide for you and this is how you repay them? If I were Ruth, I would have left you on the stoop the day I found you."

The words stung, but Maggie brushed them off. It wasn't the first time the councilwoman had said them, and it would not be the last. The only thing Maggie could do was nod her head until the councilwoman grew bored with her, then she would be off to find the next delinquent who irritated her.

"I'm sorry," Maggie repeated.

The councilwoman huffed as she turned and walked away. When she could no longer be seen through the sea of bodies between them,

Maggie pressed on with more care, doing her best to avoid anyone else.

"Maggie," a voice called out, eliciting a small cringe.

Maggie slowly turned around when she heard it but smiled when she saw her friend. "Good morning, Victoria."

Victoria was Maggie's only friend, and she ran her parent's honey stand. They were beekeepers. It was one of the more popular shops as honey was used in everything from medicine, to cooking, to drinks.

Victoria had always been as sweet as the honey she sold. She was well off, like Katie, but the two girls couldn't have been more different. Victoria dressed more down-to-earth and was happier in general. Her long brown hair was braided into an intricate ponytail, which hung to the middle of her back. Her dress was neat and pressed but used. Most likely a hand-me-down from her mother.

"What was that about?" Victoria asked.

"Oh, you know Vega. She is always looking for someone to yell at but this morning she found her favorite target. Why doesn't she leave me alone? And why does she always have to bring up that I was abandoned?"

"I wouldn't call it being abandoned," Victoria countered. "You just weren't born into the family you needed to be with, and destiny intervened."

Maggie smiled at her friend. Victoria always said exactly what she needed to hear. However, from the way she was bouncing on her heels this morning, it look like she was dying to talk about something else.

"What is it?" Maggie asked.

"Did you *see* her?" she asked. Maggie knew exactly who she was talking about. They rarely called Katie by her name. "And that dress? You'd think she was getting married today."

Gossiping was Victoria's favorite hobby.

"Don't get me started," Maggie said, distracting herself by browsing through the bottles of honey for sale, knocking two of them over, then picked up a small honeycomb. "Everything looks good this morning."

"Were they together again?" Victoria was the only other person who knew of Maggie's infatuation with Jacob.

"I just don't know why he likes her," Maggie cried, breaking the honeycomb in half. Victoria carefully took the two pieces from her and placed them back on the shelf. "Okay, I get why he likes her, but if he looked past her body and hair for ten seconds, he would run."

"Straight to you?" Victoria finished.

"What's wrong with that? Why shouldn't he?"

"Have you talked to him yet? Does he even know who you are?"

"Everyone knows who I am," Maggie said, nearly knocking over the jars of honey again as she threw her hands around. "The village isn't that big."

"You know what I mean, Mags." Victoria gently pulled Maggie away from the jars of honey and the boxes of honeycombs before she could do any more damage.

"One day he'll notice me, I promise," Maggie vowed

"Then you have to do something soon," Victoria said, placing a hand on her shoulder. "You're running out of time."

"I know," Maggie said, backing into the crowd. "See you later."

"Remember what I said, Maggie. Make your move or Katie will do it for you."

Maggie nodded as she was swallowed up in the rush of people. The market was usually only busy during the morning. After that, everyone went back to their daily routines: farming, cooking, hunting, and all the other things Maggie hoped she would never get stuck doing her whole life. Leaving the commotion of the shoppers behind, she cut off into the woods where she could find some peace. Her house was farther away than most as the herbs her parents tended grew best in shadowy, quiet places.

Her thoughts were still dark and depressing, even with the distance she'd put between herself and the blacksmith. She did her best to turn them around but failed. When she tried to think of something positive, like telling Jacob how she felt, her mind quickly turned it sour. Instead of reciprocating her feelings, he would laugh at her, walk away, or start screaming. Even in her imagination she could not envision them together.

Stomping her foot, she clenched her fists and screamed. The release felt good but didn't ease her emotions. She wanted to hate Katie for being so close to Jacob. She tried to hate Jacob for liking Katie, but

Victoria was right. Maggie had done nothing about it and watched their relationship bloom from a distance hoping that Jacob would somehow choose her instead.

"It's never going to happen," she yelled.

Her face flushed as tears began to burn at the corners of her eyes again. Why did she have to feel this way? Why couldn't she muster the courage to walk up to Jacob and profess her undying love? She closed her eyes and ignored the thoughts that were spiraling out of control and ran blindly into the underbrush of autumn. She didn't know why she did it, but she regretted it instantly. Searing pain shot through her arm as she crashed to the ground. She'd run right into a pine tree that stood in the center of an aspen grove. All its branches stretched out well above her head except one. A mangled, broken limb jutted out at shoulder height, creating a sharp, wooden dagger ready to stab anyone dumb enough to run into it. It glistened with fresh blood.

"Why am I so stupid?"

Frustrated, she threw her back to the ground and lay in silence. With only the trees and birds to witness her, she broke down and sobbed. Giant tears streamed down her face, leaving tiny trails of salt on her cheeks. She cried until she was tired, until she didn't have the strength to continue. When her eyes refused to produce more tears, she sat up, crossed her legs, and willed the sounds around her to fade to nothing. She wanted to be alone.

CHAPTER 2

As a child, Maggie learned she could do things that she assumed everyone else could do as well. It wasn't until she talked with her father about it that she realized that she was the only one with those gifts. One of her gifts, as her father called them, was closing off her mind, shutting out all the sounds the world could produce. All that remained was utter silence. The more she practiced, the more she could do. In addition to silencing the world, she could single out sounds she wanted to hear, increasing their volume while everything else faded away. She could pick out the chirping of a single swamp toad at night through the cacophony of the marsh. She could listen to her mother's heartbeat from the next room. Sometimes, she thought that if she listened hard enough, she might be able to hear someone else's thoughts. Though try as she might, she had never accomplished that.

But right now, all she wanted was silence. She wasn't interested in what the world had to offer, so she turned it off.

The world went quiet, but it didn't happen all at once. The loudest noises faded away first: the wind, the birds, and then her breathing. Then the quieter, unnoticeable sounds disappeared: her heartbeat, the sounds of insects scurrying around beneath her, and the gentle scratching of blades of grass as they rubbed together in the breeze. She didn't know how long she sat there. It could have been minutes, or it could have been hours. All she knew was that she was rocking back and forth slightly. Carefully opening her senses, she slowly let the sounds back in. Letting it all in at once could be dangerous. She'd learned that the hard way.

Opening her eyes, she saw her father crouched down in front of her. He wore a worried expression on his tired, wrinkled face. She half-smiled as she took in his familiarity. His gray hair, crooked nose, and warm, inviting eyes. His smile was what stood out though. Everyone in town knew it because he never stopped smiling. He was always ready with a good joke and the whole village liked him.

"Dad? Is everything okay?"

"You tell me. How long have you been sitting like that? You weren't listening to a word I was saying."

Stretching out her cramped legs, Maggie leaned back to ease her throbbing muscles. As she did, her spine snapped and cracked, relief thundering through her lower back.

"I guess a bit longer than I thought," Maggie said.

Her father set down a bundle of rags, most likely filled with leaves and flower petals, and sat down beside her. His arm found its way around her shoulder and Maggie let herself fall into him. Life had rushed back in with the sounds and the tears began to flow again.

"Oh, honey," her dad said with a kind laugh. "What's going on?"

"Why am I so different?"

Her father positioned himself so he was looking directly into her eyes. "Tell me everything."

As Maggie recounted the events of the morning in detail, the sun continued across the sky. The birds, animals, and insects moved on with their lives, and the world moved on. But for Maggie and her father, time froze while she was consoled. When she was done, her father stood up, then pulled her to her feet as well.

"The day we found you, your mother and I, we were confused. We knew everyone in the village, and no one was expecting a child. We didn't know where you had come from. To this day, we don't know why you were sent to us. All we know is that you were the child we were never able to have. Your mother and I have talked about this day for a long time."

"What day?" Maggie asked.

"The day you started to question your place here."

Maggie thought for a moment about what she could do. She thought about her shyness, and her inability to make friends or talk to Jacob. Maybe this was fate's way of telling her not to get attached to anything. Except for Victoria, everyone seemed to be wary of her. Perhaps life was pushing her towards something else.

"You're right," Maggie said. "Maybe I need to find out where I come from."

Throughout her childhood, the fact that she was orphaned wasn't new to her. Her parents had been open about that. They referred to her as their miracle child. The baby that fell from the heavens. Knowing that she had been abandoned was enough to keep her where she was. However, now that she was getting older, maybe she should learn about who she really was.

Maggie's mind mulled everything over as they walked. She paid no attention to where she was going, allowing her father to guide the way.

She was surprised to see her home in front of her when she looked up. It wasn't much of a house, but it was perfect for her parents' occupation as herb farmers. It was small and built into the side of a hill. The roof was covered in earth, a grassy mound that gently leveled off around back. A brown door stood in the center with only one window to the right. The glass was thick and only allowed diluted light to enter.

In front of the house was a small well. Her mother was there now, drawing up a bucket. Like Maggie's father, her mother's hair was grayer now than the black it once was. She did an excellent job of hiding it, though. She wove her hair into a tight bun and usually wore a shawl or bonnet over it, though today it cascaded down her back to her waist. Her arms and legs were muscular, but despite that, she was thin and agile. She was one of the most intelligent people Maggie knew, though not that attractive, in her opinion. She was stern, hard-working, and incredibly generous and loving, in her own way. She perfectly evened out her husband's giddy and carefree attitude.

When the water was up, her mother dumped it into a large clay pot used for washing. Dropping the bucket when it was empty, she stood up straight, finally noticing them.

"Where have you been all morning, child?" her mother asked, scolding her. "There is work to be done." She carried the pot over and handed it to her husband, who took it gracefully. "Take that around back and get washed up. Tabitha will be here shortly to pick up her order and we must be ready for her. As for you, young lady, you are filthy. Just look at the state of your . . . What happened to your arm?"

Maggie glanced down at where the stump had struck her. Her sleeve was covered in dried blood and a long tear in her dress exposed the gouge on her shoulder. She fingered it gingerly, wincing as she touched it.

"It's nothing, Mother, just a scrape."

"Just a scrape?" her mother repeated. "Do you know how many people have died because something was thought to be just a scrape? No, this needs to be treated. Sit."

Maggie's mother pointed at a large, flat stone they used as a makeshift worktable. At the command, Maggie sat and watched her mother rush back to the house to grab her few medical things. She wasn't a healer, but she had picked up a few things working with them as much as she did. She knew which herbs would bring down a fever, ease an upset stomach, and ward off potential infection.

She jogged back to Maggie, a small bag held tightly under her arm along with a wooden spoon and a kitchen knife.

"Don't just sit there," her mother cried. "Take off that jacket."

Again, Maggie did as she was told, shivering as the cold autumn air enveloped her skin. Fresh blood poured from the wound as a drying scab ripped from her flesh.

"I really wish you would be more careful. That is more than just a scrape, my dear. And I believe this the third time I've had to patch you up this month," her mother said as she set to work. "Now, tell me, what were you two discussing out there?"

Maggie told her everything. They talked until the wound was properly closed and bandaged. A bright red leaf covered the imperfect stitching and a clean, white cloth was wrapped around that. The leaf would help the swelling go down and prevent infection.

"Sounds like you've had a busy morning," her mother said as she put her tools away. "Come with me into the kitchen. We'll have some bread and tea, and I'll tell you how your father and I met. I love him dearly, but that man was as slow as a stubborn donkey when he was younger."

A faint smile appeared on Maggie's face as she picked up her jacket and followed her mother into the house.

FINISHED WITH HER breakfast and with images of her father she would never get out of her mind floating at the front of her thoughts, Maggie sat on her bed and hugged her pillow. Her arm, stomach, and attitude felt better. She could always count on her parents to help her feel rejuvenated. In a way, they were more than just her parents. They were her confidants and friends. She had no trouble confiding anything in them.

She was still laughing at the stories her mother had told as she lay her head on her pillow. It had been an emotional morning, which had left her feeling drained. All she wanted now was sleep. Closing her eyes, she tried to imagine her father dancing the slow, steady marriage waltz. She had never seen him dance before and according to her mother, he moved like a duck stuck in the mud. She chuckled to herself once more before falling into a relaxing sleep, though it didn't last.

It was the voices that roused her. They were quiet but persistent. Opening her eyes, she glanced around her room. Sunlight fell through the open, barred windows. Bars? Windows? Her sleeping room had neither.

Rather than lying on her comfortable bed, she noticed she was on a cold, stone floor. The room around her was not her own. She quickly sat up, fully aware that she wasn't alone. A small, occupied cot was pressed into the far corner. Behind her, bars rose from the floor to the ceiling. She was in a jail cell.

"How did I get here?" she whispered.

She didn't remember getting out of bed and she definitely would have remembered being arrested. Nothing about her situation was familiar but the voices that had woken her were getting louder. Backing up, she hid in the corner opposite the cot and its sleeping figure. She crouched, making herself as small and insignificant as possible.

A door opened somewhere in the jail, and she could finally make sense of the voices.

". . . Be ready in about a week's time."

"For now, keep your distance. There is no telling what she might be capable of."

"She didn't cause too much trouble when she was brought in."

"If you want to risk it, be my guest, but don't go putting the rest of us in danger to cure your curiosity. Witches are evil, tricky creatures. Once they get you, you're lost."

Maggie glanced over at the person on the cot. Could that be the witch they were talking about? She'd heard about witches before. Her parents told her stories about what witches did to those they caught. Bolting from her corner, she ran to the bars and screamed out for help.

"Let me out of here! I don't belong here."

There was no response. The voices disappeared as the door slammed closed, taking any chance of rescue with them.

"Please," she pleaded in a whisper.

"Don't bother with them," a voice said from behind her.

Maggie spun around and watched a beautiful blond woman emerge from the covers. She tried to wriggle through the bars to get away from her.

"Help," she screamed.

"They can't hear you, nor would they help you if they could. They don't trust our kind."

Maggie stopped struggling and slowly glanced over her shoulder. "What do you mean, our kind?"

The woman stared at her. "You have no idea who you are, do you? What you are."

Maggie let go of the bars and slipped to the ground, terrified of what this woman, this witch, might do to her. She closed her eyes, hoping that when she opened them again, she would be back in her own room. No such luck. She was still in the cell.

"I'm not going to hurt you," the blond witch said, sitting back down on the bed. "You can stop thrashing around like a fish out of water."

Taking a deep breath, Maggie tried to calm her breathing. "Okay, who am I?"

"You are like me, a witch."

Maggie almost started laughing at how impossible that would be. She had never even met a witch before.

"How?" Maggie asked. "How could I be a witch? I don't know any witches. How could I be a witch if I don't know any?"

The blond witch stood up and crossed the cell. She bent down and stared into Maggie's face, her piercing gray eyes burning through her as if they could see something Maggie could not.

"You don't become a witch by knowing a witch," she said. "You are born a witch."

"How?"

"One of your parents would have to be a witch or a child of a witch. All witches are female, but a witch can give birth to a male child. That offspring wouldn't have any gifts, but he could still give life to a witch. If you don't know any witches, then it would be safe to assume that your father is the child of a witch."

"But I don't even know who my parents are," Maggie said.

"Interesting. Now, are you going to help me out of this cage or not?"

"How am I supposed to do that?" Maggie asked. "I'm stuck in here with you."

"Actually, you're not. Only your consciousness is here. Your body is still wherever you left it."

"How did that happen?" Maggie asked, reaching down and touching her body. It felt real.

"I brought you here. Or at least I called for you and you came."

"Witches can do that?" At her question, Maggie pushed herself away from the bars and scooted closer to the cot.

"Not all witches. What a witch can do or cannot do depends on her ancestry. Her genealogy."

"What does that mean?" Maggie asked.

The blond witch sighed. "It means that the powers a witch will have depends on what her mother or grandmother could do." She stood up and began pacing the cell. "Are you going to help me or not?"

"I don't know how," Maggie said. "Why are you in here?"

"So, these stupid, ignorant men can ignore common sense and reason. They are full of fear, hate, and spite and want to kill me."

"Why?"

The witch looked down at her. "You have no idea what's going on, do you? Humans hate witches. It is what they do. If they don't understand something, they feel the best course of action is to destroy it."

"Why come to me for help?" Maggie asked. "If you could bring any witch here, why not bring one who could actually help you?"

"You're the only witch I've been able to find. There are not any other witches close enough, and it took me time to find you," she said, looking Maggie in the eyes again. "Whether you like it or not, we are sisters. We need to stand together and help one another."

"I don't know how to do that," Maggie said.

"If you can't find a way, I'll die. If you can, then I can teach you about who you are and what you can do."

The room began to fade around Maggie as darkness crept in at the edges of her vision. Maggie panicked. She wanted to know more about who she was and how to help.

"No, wait. How will I find you?" Maggie cried out as her vision started to distort.

The witch smiled as she crouched down beside Maggie. "I've enjoyed our chat. If I could keep you here longer, I would, but I don't have the strength. And don't worry about finding me. If you agree to help me, I'll take care of that on my end, but you must hurry because I don't have much time left."

The vision faded from view, and Maggie woke up in her own bed. Not knowing if what happened was real or not, she stayed where she was, eyes open, staring at the cloth barrier separating her bed from her parents.

CHAPTER 3

Charred logs cracked loudly in the fire pit as the long, amber flames cast eerie shadows on the surrounding trees. The stars shone brightly in the cloudless sky as the temperature quickly dropped. This was not a problem for the hunter. The cold didn't bother him in the slightest. Cupping his hands together, he blew into them. A faint, glowing ember rushed out on his breath, instantly warming his chilled fingers as it ignited against his skin. His roaring fire had been started the same way. His breath had easily ignited the dry kindling. Because of this, some had begun calling him the Dragon.

"This life is getting less and less appealing," he said to the darkness.

"Yet you willingly continue to follow the commands of your master," came a reply from the cover of night.

"I thought it would get easier after all these years. I thought my conscience would be silenced and I would be allowed to work and earn my freedom in peace."

"You know that will never be the case, Loravain," the voice answered. Bright yellow eyes reflected the firelight as the hunter's wolf, Thanatos, padded closer to him. "You never were the kind to kill needlessly. You should not have fallen prey to that demon's twisted lies."

Loravain regarded his companion with the same interest he always had. Even after nearly twenty years, the hunter did not truly know who or what Thanatos was. He had interrogated him on many occasions only to be met with an impenetrable wall of silence. However, no matter how uncooperative the wolf had been, Loravain had gleaned a few bits of information. First was that he was ancient and nearly impossible to kill. They had fought side by side in enough battles for mortal wounds to occur, but the wolf never succumbed to death. Secondly, Thanatos held knowledge that had been lost to the world. He always seemed able to provide a hint or trick in the heat of battle that enabled Loravain to come out victorious when the odds were piled against him. The hunter often faced opponents he had never heard of or encountered before, but the wolf always knew their weaknesses.

"What other choice did I have?" Loravain asked. "I was desperate."

"You could have said no. Now the weight of your commitment is crushing your soul."

"Like always, you know just when to apply pressure to the wound. With you around, I may never heal."

"With me around," the wolf growled. "You may finally give in to reason and turn your back on that demon and live your own life. You will find no satisfaction in hurting the innocent and serving evil. Regrettably, I once had to learn that same lesson and it nearly cost me everything. Trust in my words, Loravain. I speak from experience. Get out while you still have life to do so."

"I am not in the mood to be having this conversation again."

Thanatos dropped to the ground near the fire and rested his large head on his paws, but he didn't press the matter. The hunter hung his head in shame, regretting what he had done and who he had become. He knew the demon's offer had only held empty promises, yet his desire to be with his wife again clouded his judgment. Since that day, he had committed unspeakable acts which he was immensely ashamed for. His only solace came from knowing that one day he would die and he would be free from his obligations as the demon's hunter. Guilt coursed through him as he reflected on the last few days. He knew he should have refused the offered gold for his latest quarry. It was just another tally mark in his long list of mistakes. That witch had done nothing to earn what the villagers were going to do to her. They were scared and angry and could do nothing about her on their own. They were after blood. Loravain wished he could have turned a blind eye to their offer, or better yet aided the witch, but helping them was part of his contract. His demon master loved the mentality of men. They feared what they didn't understand, which made them easy prey. Loravain had been no different. He had been just as easy to twist and manipulate as the next fool.

"What's next then?" Thanatos asked.

"We head west, towards the coast."

"Hoping to make a quick stop at home on the way?" the wolf questioned.

It was foolish of him to think Thanatos wouldn't guess his intentions. They had traveled together for far too long for that. Glancing up, Loravain starred into the wolf's eyes.

"I miss her. I miss my old life. Do you blame me for wanting to remember what I once had?"

"No, I do not blame you, but you know it is not wise to go there. Going home will only resurrect horrible memories, and your nightmares will inevitably return. The last time was bad enough, and sleep eluded you for weeks after. I say we go south. I want to get out of this cold for a change. Winter is near and the ocean air only makes it worse. I'm not like you. I do not have a spring of fire living inside waiting to warm me whenever I call to it. The chill is beginning to creep beneath my fur."

"You speak the truth, but it's not the memories I go there for. I will have those regardless. I want to be somewhere familiar. They may not remember me there, but other than you, they are the only family I have. Anyway, Cape Charles holds more than just bad memories. I would like to visit my parents' grave and pay my respects. I was not there when they died nor when they were buried," Loravain countered.

"I am aware of that," came the wolf's reply. "But the heartache and confusion that brings serve only as a distraction. If you do not wish to heed my recommendation of willingly leaving your master's service, you need to stay focused on your goal: restoring your freedom through servitude."

Loravain leaned against a fallen log and covered his eyes with his wide-brimmed hat. He understood Thanatos's point well enough. Freedom was the ultimate goal, yet that never seemed to come. It had been twenty brutal years since that fateful day, and he seemed no closer now than he was then. Closing his eyes, the memory flooded back, bringing the painfully beautiful face of his young bride to his mind.

"How was the hunt today?" Camila asked in her sweet, reassuring voice.

"It could have been better. The game was skittish. Something has them spooked. Maybe a storm is coming?"

Camila shook her head. "Mother would have checked in by now. She can always tell. Are we going to be okay?"

Loravain closed the door behind him, crossed the room in three strides, and wrapped his arms around his beautiful bride. "We have enough for now and tomorrow is sure to be better."

They had been married for three months and life seemed like a dream. They were expecting their first child, and their one-room home, which Loravain had built with his own hands, was as sturdy as it was small. The rough log walls kept the cold ocean air out and held in the heat from their cast iron stove while the tightly woven thatched roof kept them dry when it rained. Loravain would remove a section of thatch on clear nights to allow moon and starlight to bathe them as they slept on hot summer nights. Their home reflected their marriage, cramped at times but full of love.

Built at the edge of the village where they had grown up, their small cabin was nestled at the base of a towering, snow-capped mountain. The ocean was near enough that they could smell the salt in the air when the wind was just right.

A small trail cut through the woods from their humble home to a bustling village of seventy-four sea-hardened souls. Seventy-five when their child arrived. Loravain's family still lived there, along with Camila's. His father was a skilled tracker, trapper, and fisherman and had trained Loravain from a young age. However, the young hunter wanted more action than that. He relished the chase and weaponry of hunting. He was especially deadly with the crossbow.

Camila was a seamstress, taught by her mother. When he brought home game, he would skin it, and Camila would create beautiful clothing and blankets from the hides for the villagers. They all worked hard, every family contributing whatever skills they could to survive.

But the simple life they worked so hard to have and maintain was torn apart in a few horrific moments.

"You are so beautiful," Loravain whispered to his wife, pulling her tighter into his embrace.

Face to face, his lips inched closer to hers. Her eyes urged him on as she slowly closed them. Her breath was warm on his skin as his lips caressed hers. Pushing his body against hers, they were thrown to the floor when the walls of their home blew apart around them.

A violent force ripped through the single room, shattering the door and windows, hurtling shards and splinters inward. Using his body as a shield, Loravain threw himself between Camila and the danger threatening them. Nothing could be seen through the gaping void that had once been the front wall of their cabin. Lunging for his crossbow, he snatched it up and aimed at the darkness.

"Your bolts," Camila cried.

He looked down the stock and grunted. It wasn't loaded. He quickly searched the room, but the destruction made it impossible to find anything, let alone his quiver. Instead, he picked up a slender sliver from the mutilated wall and placed it in the groove meant for his dart.

The night fell silent around them. He moved towards the hole and glanced outside, first to his left, then to his right. There was nothing there. When he felt sure there was no immediate threat, Loravain turned and faced his wife. She was still lying on the floor, eyes wide, her gaze darting back and forth.

"What happened?" she cried.

"I have no idea," Loravain answered as he lifted her to her feet.

"Magic?" Camila suggested.

Loravain shrugged his shoulders. As far as they knew, there were no magic users in their village. No witches, magicians, or gifted.

They struggled to their feet and began to assess the damage. Not only was the front wall gone, but the cabin had been ripped in half. There was so much debris scattered around, they felt lucky to still be in one piece. All the furniture they had managed to squeeze inside was either kindling or missing. Another hole glared at them from the back wall, though smaller. Whatever had caused the damage had exploded through one wall and gone out the other.

"What are we going to do about this mess?" Camila asked.

Ignoring her question, Loravain walked back outside. The woods around their home hadn't fared much better. Trees were uprooted, and large patches of earth had been gouged out of the ground. Plumes of smoke rose from the village, illuminated by the fires burning below them.

"The village is on fire," Loravain called back. "I have to help."

"NO!" Camila screamed.

Loravain stopped cold. That wasn't a scream of protest but one of fear. He spun around and choked down a cry of his own. A gigantic bear was standing between him and his wife, larger than any he had ever seen before. How had that gotten there without him noticing? The expression on Camila's face was frozen horror. She scrambled back into the far corner, trying desperately to escape the beast but was trapped. Taking careful aim with his crossbow, Loravain fired the shard. The shot went wide. It missed its target but got the bear's attention.

Rearing up on its hind legs, the monstrous brute pushed aside what remained of the roof. Opening its maw, it roared so violently that the ground shook, forcing Loravain to his knees. Never in his life had he encountered a beast like this. He had hunted bear before, but nothing came close to this monster in front of him. It stood over twelve feet high and brandished razor-sharp claws the size of daggers on its paws. Black, rotting fur covered its muscular body, and bleeding, oozing scars crisscrossed its exposed belly. Evil intelligence shone in its eyes as it studied him. An unnatural smile grew across its muzzle. With a glance back, it viciously attacked Camila.

The fear and hesitation Loravain had been feeling drained away, leaving only pure rage. Grabbing the nearest thing to him, he dropped his useless crossbow and attacked. Loravain swung a gnarled pine branch and beat the creature's legs and back until the limb broke. Picking up another, he continued his assault, trying desperately to pull the beast's attention back to him. He struck it over and over until his arms were too tired to continue. No matter what he tried, the bear paid him no mind. Dropping the branch, Loravain resorted to pounding his fists against the rock-hard body of the bear, working his way slowly to Camila. With a lucky punch to the ribs, the bear let out an annoyed growl. It turned its head, baring its blood-stained teeth. A massive paw swatted at him, trying to squash him like an insect, but he ducked under the attack and fell to the ground next to his wife. She was somehow still alive but horribly injured and disfigured. Her breathing came in ragged, uneven gasps and her face was as white as snow.

"Please," Loravain pleaded. "Leave us be."

The bear reared up once more but made no move to attack. It seemed to be waiting for something. Taking a chance, Loravain turned his back on the beast to attend to Camila. Tears streamed down his cheeks as he embraced her. She gasped out in pain and he released her. His hands, moving up to caress her face, were covered in her blood.

"No," he sobbed, crying uncontrollably.

With a final gasp, Camila's body shuddered, then fell still. Loravain cradled her broken body against his, rocking her back and forth. She was gone. He put his hand gently on her cheek then slowly closed her eyes. His anger was now entirely directed at the bear towering at full height behind him.

"You did this," he bellowed, fury overtaking his body.

He rushed at the beast, throwing punch after punch, hoping a killing blow would befall him and send his spirit to be reunited with his love.

"Your rage is impressive, human," came a guttural growl of a voice.

Loravain glanced around the room. "Who's out there? Help me! This beast has killed my wife."

Bellowing laughter filled the air. The bear dropped down to all fours, knocking Loravain to the floor.

"You have courage, small one, even if it is misplaced."

Shock replaced anger as Loravain realized that the speaker was the bear. Rolling to his side, he grunted as he tried to crawl away. Pain erupted through his chest when the bear pinned him to the ground with a deadly paw. It was shaking its head.

"Learn your place, worm," it growled. "If you can do that, you will be rewarded. Serve me and earn your place in this world."

Loravain shook in anger and fear. He ignored the command and faced Camila's body, refusing to reply to the demon.

"Agree to serve me and I will bring back your mate," the bear said, removing the paw holding Loravain down.

"You can do that?" Loravain asked, desperation dripping from his words.

"I can do whatever I wish. There is none more powerful than I. If I say I can bring her back, then I can do it. What say ye, human? Will you serve me?"

Loravain hesitated. He stared at Camila and shuddered. He could already feel the crack in his heart spreading. He knew he shouldn't trust the bear. Could it really bring a soul back from death? If he could, servitude would be worth it. If he did nothing, there was no chance of getting her back.

"I will serve you," Loravain said with a nod. "Now bring her back to me."

The bear laughed. "Humans are ignorant to the ways of magic. It is not that easy, worm. First, you must prove you are willing to serve me. Once I am sure of that, then, and only then, will I bring her spirit back. Now, get to your feet and repeat after me."

Loravain struggled to his feet and waited for the bear to speak.

"I will serve my new master in body and spirit until such time as I have outlived my usefulness."

Loravain repeated the words. "I will serve my new master in body and spirit until such time as I have outlived my usefulness." He spat out the last two words as if they burned his tongue.

The bear nodded when he finished. "Excellent. I accept your oath. You belong to me now."

Loravain stared at his wife. "I have done what you have asked now bring her back."

"You have not proven yourself to me. Come, worm, we have much work to do."

CHAPTER 4

"They've never seemed so real before," Maggie said after telling her mother about the dreams.

After the curious dream the day before, Maggie had stayed in bed for a long time. Her parents thought she was sick when she never came out to complete her chores. She had briefly come out for supper, then gone right back to bed. Later that night, she'd had the same dream.

"Having the dream once would be just a dream," Maggie said. "But twice in a row? Mom, it was so vivid. There has to be more to it."

"Have you ever seen this woman before? Maybe from the village?"

"Never. And she called me a witch. Could I be a witch?" Maggie asked.

"My daughter is not a witch," her mother said, focusing intently on her task, her gaze quickly flitting from her hands to Maggie's face then back again.

"But I'm technically not your daughter. You don't even know where I come from. You don't know who I am."

Her mother dropped the satchel she was patching and looked up from the table. "I know exactly who you are. I may not have given birth to you, but you are my daughter. Witches are evil creatures who steal people away for their own sick pleasure."

"How do you know that is what witches do? Have you ever known a witch, Mother?"

"Good heavens, child, what has gotten into you? Two dreams and you think you're a witch. Stop it with this nonsense and get your work done. I will hear no more of this witch talk. Now scoot." Her mother flicked her with the end of a rag to get her moving.

When Maggie left the room, having to be told more than once to go, her mother slumped to the floor. Ruth's emotions were on the verge of overflowing but she was proud of herself for staying as calm as she had.

"I knew this day would come, I just knew it," she mumbled, covering her mouth with a shaky hand and fighting back tears. "Francis," she yelled.

Finding the strength to pull herself up, she staggered to the door and peered outside. Maggie sat at the grindstone sharpening spades. An herb farmer needed plenty of sharp spades and a family of herb farmers required even more. Over the years, Maggie had learned to use the grindstone well. Francis, her father, had taught her all his techniques and tricks.

"Francis?" She yelled for her husband again then sat down in a rocking chair.

Coming in from the garden, encrusted with grime and mud, Francis sauntered through the door. His hands were filthy from preparing the vegetable patch for winter. It was hard work and he would be picking mud from under his fingernails for weeks.

"What are you yapping on about now, Ruth?" Francis asked, laying his dirty tools on the table.

"It's time," she whispered.

"Come again?"

"It's time," she fired back impatiently.

"Time for what?"

She pointed outside. "We have to show her."

Francis looked out the door then nodded. "I guess you're right. She has the right to know everything. Seems now is as good a time as any to be telling her. She's not a child anymore."

"That she is not. Better for her to know something about where she comes from before she's married off. Go and fetch the box, will you? I'm going to talk to her."

"Be easy on her. This could be hard for her to take," Francis said.

The morning was cool, but the autumn air held the promise of a few more warm days. The leaves around the house had changed to brilliant reds and yellows, which complimented the dying grass. The birds were singing but were cut short by Maggie's cursing when her hand slipped free of the spade and hit the spinning grindstone. The spade fell to the ground with a thud.

"That's going to leave a scar," she said after regaining her composure and dabbing up fresh blood with a dirty rag.

"Language like that does not become a woman," her mother said as she stepped up beside her.

"Sorry, Mother," Maggie said, lowering her eyes.

"Sorry you said it or sorry I was here to overhear you?" The hint of a smile crept up her mother's face.

"Both?"

"You are just like your father. You take after him more, you know."

"It's that cursed blade. It has a nick in it that doesn't want to smooth out, no matter what I do." Bending down, Maggie scooped up the spade from the dirt and brushed it off. A small drop of blood glistened on the handle.

"Sometimes life can be like that," her mother said as she took a seat next to her, taking the spade from Maggie's hands. "Seems no matter how hard we work at something, it wants to do what it wants to do. And it's not always about blades."

"What are you talking about?" Maggie asked, snatching the spade back.

"I mean that we can't be too sure about things sometimes. Take that spade for example. When you picked it up and saw that nick, you thought you would be able to grind it out and it would be as good as new. That's not always the case. We don't always see what is really causing the problem. And sometimes life can view you like you do that blade."

Maggie eyed her mother suspiciously. "Are you trying to tell me something?"

"Your father and I . . . ," she began but was interrupted by her husband stumbling from the house, a massive bundle of rags held tightly in his arms.

"Confounded ax handle. Why in blazes are you in my way?"

Maggie started to laugh. "I'm not the only one who needs to get caught saying things they shouldn't."

Finally getting himself untangled, Francis made his way over. Maggie waited for him to trip over something else, which was a good bet as the bundle he was carrying blocked his view.

"I thought laundry day was next week, Dad," Maggie called.

"Laundry day? What are you talking about? Has your mother not told you anything yet?"

"She might be trying to tell me something, but I don't have the slightest clue what that might be."

"Ruth, you always were a jabber box," Francis said as he stepped on a rock and rolled his ankle. He fumbled forward until he caught his balance then limped the rest of the way to the grindstone.

"Oh, put that thing down before you hurt yourself for real," Ruth cried.

Maggie's father dropped the mysterious package on the ground, put his hands on his hips, and stretched his back. Maggie stared at the odd mashup of blankets, clothes, and other rags that had been collected over the years. A strange odor wafted off it.

"What is that?" Maggie asked, covering her nose as the breeze shifted in her direction.

"This is what I want to talk to you about," her mother said.

"This better not be your idea of some pre-marriage gift or a dowry. If it is, I might die right now. Anyway, I don't even have any potential suitors."

"Remember what I said about the spade?" Ruth asked, taking the spade from Maggie again.

"How can I forget?" Maggie answered with an eye roll. "You've never been more eloquent."

"Joke all you want," her father said. "This could change your life."

Maggie shifted her gaze to the bundle of laundry at her feet. She kicked it gently, secretly hoping it would grow legs and scamper away. She wanted nothing to do with it.

"How is a pile of dirty laundry supposed to change my life? Are you saying I should become a washerwoman?"

"Listen to us, honey. The clothes aren't important. It's what's on the inside that matters," her mother said.

"Again with the cryptic wisdom? Please, just tell me what you're talking about."

"Open it," her father said.

"Open what?"

"Your mother was telling the truth. It's not the clothes that matter but what is wrapped up inside that's important."

Maggie looked at her parents skeptically then grimaced as she began to shed away the top layers of moldy clothes.

"If I get through this and find a dead animal, I'm running away from home. I promise."

Her joke fell on deaf ears. Neither of her parents replied. They sat in silence while she continued to unwrap the bundle. After all the clothes, blankets, curtains, table clothes, towels, and rags had been ripped away, a single piece of silk remained. It was wrapped around something hard. Maggie carefully removed the handkerchief, uncovering a beautiful handcrafted box. Pictures had been etched into the wood, expertly carved. The clasps holding it closed were pure gold. It was breathtaking.

"What is this?" she asked.

"We don't know," Ruth answered. "It was with you the day we found you. We never opened it but knew the time would come when you would need to see what was inside."

Maggie's fingers traced the carvings across the lid as she stared at the container. A picture depicted a beautiful woman holding a crown above her head. The wood was dark red and the carvings had been painted gold. The contrast was mesmerizing. With its clasps and paint, the box was the most expensive thing Maggie had ever held, let alone owned.

"What do you think is in it?" she asked, almost to herself.

"We'll give you some privacy," her mother said, holding back tears. "But no matter what you find in there, we will always be here for you. We will always be your parents."

AS HER PARENTS walked away, Maggie's mind filled with the possibilities of what lay before her. Anything could be inside this box that fit so perfectly in her hands. Once her parents were inside, she stood up and walked into the woods, knowing exactly where she wanted to open it. There was a place she went when she wanted to be alone, think, or practice doing the things only she could do. Nestled a short distance from their farm was a small, enclosed clearing. It was only accessible by squeezing under a large rose bush. Tall hedges ran around the perimeter, strengthened by vines growing throughout them.

She'd discovered it when she was chasing a rabbit. She remembered the day clearly. It was a cold summer and the herbs hadn't been growing well. Hunger had a way of making you do things you usually wouldn't. Her parents were trying their hardest to provide but the cold weather had been hard on everyone. Game had either been picked off or scared away by the constant commotion of the villagers foraging in the woods.

Pulling herself into the clearing had been easier when she was smaller. She'd followed the rabbit through the small gap, finding the clearing full of dead trees, bushes, and other debris. Over the following months, she cleaned it out. For the next few years, she tended it. Now it was beautiful. She had even planted a few berry bushes. Those were the benefits of being raised by herb farmers. Maggie knew how to care for the earth.

Maggie sat on a rock in the center of the clearing, box in hand. Glancing around her, she admired her handiwork. The grass was still green but covered in dry, autumn leaves. Her berry bushes had done well over the summer but were now barren of any fruit. This had been her life for the past fifteen years, but the contents of this box could change everything. Was there something inside that would link her to the life she had come from or was it confirmation that this was the life she was supposed to be living? She could make as many guesses as she wanted to but that would never ease her anxiety.

Quickly undoing the golden latches, which stuck from years of neglect, she opened the lid. She closed her eyes, wanting the moment to last. The box was cool to the touch. She stroked it like a long-lost friend. Breathing out slowly, she opened her eyes and looked inside. A small white cloth covered the contents. She carefully removed and folded it. When she looked inside, she found it mostly empty. Only two small items sat at the bottom.

The first was beautiful, almost beyond compare. A bright, jewel-encrusted hairpin glimmered in the light of the afternoon sun. The pin itself was white, as if made from bone but smoother and softer. It had five teeth, which curved slightly as they extended. Four jewels of different colors ran along the top: green, blue, pink, and purple. Picking it up, she held it to the back of her head. It sat perfectly against her scalp as if it had been made specifically for her. She pulled up her hair and inserted the pin to hold it in place. It felt natural.

Turning her attention back to the box, she found a worn and folded piece of parchment. It was ripped at the edges but was still intact. With cautious fingers, she began to unfold it. She was afraid that after so many years, it would fall apart before she could see what was written on it. Carefully pulling at the pages, she opened it. It was a letter. The ink had faded in places, and a few of the words were hard to make out, but she read through it as she held her breath. The letter was from her mother. Her birth mother. Hands shaking, she shifted her body so the words would be legible in the sunlight.

My dearest daughter,

It breaks my heart to do this but my options are limited. You are, and always will be my greatest joy. I have struggled for days on end, pondering about how to write this letter to you. You must be confused about who you are, where you come from, and why I did this to you. Please know that it was for your protection, as well as ours, that this was done.

As you read this letter, know that this moment has been foreseen. It was done so at great cost, as glimpses into the future are dangerous. Much suffering and death came of it, but it was for the greater good.

Daughter, as you have grown, you have undoubtedly found that you are not like those surrounding you. You have greater power than even you realize. This is why you had to be hidden away. I hoped that we would never be separated, but I must do what is best for my people. For our people.

As for who you are, you are what humans would call a witch, but you are, and always will be, my daughter. As my daughter, you are the rightful heir to the Coven Seat, or the crown of Priama, and it is your birthright to rule over the clans and covens with wise judgment. You are the future Queen of Priama. You alone can undo what has been done and I now call you home to fulfill your destiny.

Struggles will find you but you will not be alone. Others will assist you. Trust in yourself and your instincts. They will never lead you astray. Be strong as the enemy is ever-present. Now that you are beginning to understand who you are, he will be watching. Be swift and I will hold you in my arms once more before I take my final breath.

With all the love in my heart,

Your mother, the Queen.

Reading the letter through twice more, Maggie tearfully reflected on each word, folded it, and placed it back in the box. Closing it, she put it on the ground, stood, and paced the clearing. She really was a witch. She wasn't too surprised but the most shocking revelation was that she was the daughter of a queen. A witch princess. Or at least that was what someone was claiming. How could she be sure that this wasn't someone's idea of a cruel joke? No one knew her well enough other than her parents, and they would never allow something like that.

When she'd had enough time to organize her thoughts, she scooped up the box and left the clearing the same way she had entered it. She took her time getting home. It wasn't because she desired to delay telling her parents but because her mind was racing with so many different possible futures. At first, she daydreamed about what life would be like to be a pampered princess. Then she thought about what life might be like had she lived among witches instead of the villagers at Lakes Hollow.

She made it home as the sun was setting behind the trees. She stared at the grindstone where everything had started. Her chores were done, along with a few other things that needed to be completed before the first snow came. Her parents must be as anxious as she was, if not more.

Not wanting to talk about the letter yet, Maggie sat down at the grindstone and thought about the one thing she'd been trying to ignore. If the letter was true, she would have to leave home. She owed it to herself to find out who she was. How would she tell her parents? Like always, her thoughts took her to the worst possible outcomes. She pictured them forbidding her from going then locking her in the house. Or they might become overly excited and admit they'd never wanted her in the first place. In reality, she knew they would understand. They were probably already preparing for it.

Maggie took a few deep and calming breaths to settle her nerves before going inside. She lingered at the door before pushing it open. Her parents were sitting at a large table that took up most of the living area. They were preparing a medicine bag for delivery. When they saw her in the doorway, they stopped.

"Well?" her mother asked.

"What was in the box?" her father asked, almost at the same time.

"Before I say anything, you have to promise me something."

They nodded. "Of course, honey. What is it?" her mother said.

"Promise me that no one has opened this box and what is in it is really what was left for me."

Her father nodded. "That box has remained untouched, wrapped up in those blankets for fifteen years. The only change was the extra layers we added over the years."

"You have our word on that," her mother added.

Maggie joined them at the table and placed the box between them. Reaching behind her head, she pulled out the hairpin, freeing her hair to fall back into place around her shoulders. She set it on top of the box.

"It's beautiful," her mother gasped, seeming almost relieved.

Her father whistled. "That right there could make you the wealthiest person in the village."

"I don't care about wealth," Maggie said. "There's more."

"More jewels like that?" her father asked with a wry smile as he set down a vial he was labeling.

"There was a letter," Maggie said, hanging her head.

"And?" her mother asked carefully.

"It was written by my mother. My birth mother."

Silence followed the announcement. The mood had gone from tense to relieved, then back again. When the silence became too much for Maggie to stand, she broke it.

"Aren't you going to say anything?"

"I think it's best not to. Whatever you need to do now, you need to do it on your own," her father said. He stood up from the table and walked to a bucket of water and doused a rag.

"So that's it?" Maggie cried. "After all these years, I finally found out who I am and you're going to turn your backs on me?"

Her mother slid next to her and wrapped Maggie in her arms. She rubbed her hands up and down her back, shaking with emotion as she began to sob.

"Of course not, child. We would never turn our backs on you. But you're nearly an adult now and you have the right to make your own decisions. I just hoped you would have known who you were without having to read it in a letter written when you were a baby. You have a life here and we love you for who you are."

A heavy tear slid down Maggie's face as she embraced her mother. She glanced at her father, who stood by the door, shifting his weight from leg to leg.

"What is it, Dad?" Maggie asked when her mother released her.

"What will you do?" he asked.

Looking at both her parents in turn, she smiled briefly then dropped her gaze to the table. "I don't know. There's a lot to think about. I know this is my home, and it's all I know, but my birth mother is calling me home."

"Calling you home? What do you mean?" her mother asked.

"That's what the letter said. It said this time had been foreseen and it was time for me to return," Maggie said.

"How is that possible?" her father asked

"Can we talk about this a little later?" Maggie asked. "I think I want to be alone right now."

"Of course," her father said. "We'll be here when you're ready."

Maggie pushed herself away from the table and walked into her bedroom, which was no more than a small nook in the living room cordoned off by a thick blanket. She pulled it shut, plunging herself into darkness. Falling onto her bed, she began to silence the world around her, one sound at a time. When she was satisfied, she began reciting the words of the letter in her mind.

CHAPTER 5

The smells and sounds of the mountain tavern were precisely what he needed to rouse his spirits. Loravain sat on a wooden bench in the middle of the dining hall and eyed the plate in front of him. One large potato, a soft and steaming roll, and a thick cut of venison. This was a feast compared to what he had been eating. The roaring fire that burned in the hearth livened the spirits of the other patrons as well. Winter had crept in early and warmth was sought by all. Lifting his goblet to his nose, he savored the aroma of the honey mead he'd ordered. It was a bit thick but what wasn't in the cold mountain air?

Loravain had finally relented and admitted that seeing his old home wasn't the best idea. Instead of going south as Thanatos had wanted to, they went north into the highlands. There were fewer chances Loravain would be given a contract when everyone around him wanted nothing more than to stay shut away indoors all the time.

The tavern was crowded and a lively group of musicians had begun playing an invigorating tune that enticed even the most weatherworn patrons to dance. Those present were warm, content, and drunk and soon became boisterous and belligerent. Loravain chose only to become warm as he needed to keep his wits about him. He'd made far too many enemies over the years to get lazy.

He broke his bread into parts and dipped them, one by one, into his drink then chewed slowly. Unlike the others, his attention wasn't only on his plate. Loravain ate with care as his eyes flitted around the room, but he enjoyed the music. Ever so slightly, he tapped his boot in time with the rhythm, the hint of a smile playing at the corners of his lips. He sat facing the door, looking up each time it opened, sizing up any newcomers before resuming his meal.

For what seemed like the hundredth time, he glanced around the tavern. The walls were thick pine trunks and covered in massive animal heads, skins, and antlers. The gray stones of the hearth and floor had most likely been quarried from the surrounding mountains where imposing granite cliffs were abundant. He counted eleven tables scattered around the room, including the one he sat at. Each table sat ten men in total, five to a side. Most were full while a few of the other patrons wandered around the hall, aimless and drunk, making conversation with anyone near. Loravain deflected every question thrown at him with a stern gaze and a quick flash of his crossbow. Along the back wall, a serving table sat laden with full mugs of mead. Beyond that was a small kitchen where the meals were prepared. That he could see, there was a single door providing his only means of escape if needed. Chances are that there would be another exit through the kitchen, but Loravain would never risk getting cornered like that.

This was how the hunter spent all his indoor meals. He anticipated the worst, yet it rarely happened. They were usually spent in peace without as much of a hello from anyone else. Loravain hoped that tonight would be no different.

When his plate was empty, he took his drink and found an open seat near the crackling fire. It was the safest place to be if a real fight broke out. Most were just drunken brawls that were quickly quelled. The few times it was something more, it was wise to be away from the tables.

Time passed and the music began to crescendo. This is when the people looking for a fight usually found one. Tonight was a drunken brawl: quick, clean, and disappointing.

"Do you mind?" a man asked, motioning to the empty seat next to him.

Loravain shook his head and slid down a little, giving the man more space to sit.

"Quiet night, huh?" the man asked, clearly looking for conversation.

"Yes."

"You know, I was in here the other night when a real fight broke out. One man was tall, wide, and extremely drunk. He couldn't hold his tongue or his liquor for anything. The other . . ."

"Do I know you?" Loravain asked, cutting him off.

"Not yet. The name is Zane, and I believe we have a common acquaintance."

"I very much doubt that."

"And why is that?" Zane asked. "You and I are not that different."

"I don't have time for this. Excuse me," Loravain said, standing to leave. He pushed his way past a shirtless man with a tattoo covering most of his chest when a hand found his shoulder from behind.

"Oh, I think you're going to want to hear what I have to say, hunter."

Loravain looked Zane in the eyes then slowly sat back down.

"Good choice. Getting back to our mutual friend. We might not view him in the same light, but we both know him. I see him as more of a teacher. You, on the other hand, most likely see him as a warden."

Loravain did not like where this conversation was going. He leaned over and extended a hand to Zane, who took it. Loravain pulled him closer while squeezing his fingers.

"Zane, do you know who I am or what I do?"

Zane gave a good-hearted laugh even though Loravain could see pain behind his eyes. "I'll tell you one thing. I am certainly not in the habit of wasting my time talking to strangers in forgotten, out-of-the-way taverns. You do try to make yourself hard to find, don't you?"

Loravain dropped Zane's hand and scanned the room. Could there be others here who knew him or would it be innocent people dying so he could escape? As if sensing his discomfort, Zane reached out and placed a hand on his shoulder.

"My visit is nothing to get riled up about. I am just the messenger here."

"And what is this message, exactly?"

"The master wishes to speak with you. Personally."

"About what?" Loravain asked.

"A job, most likely. That wasn't for me to know."

Loravain looked at the man in earnest for the first time. He had never been summoned to speak with the master before. All the jobs he had received since his first encounter had come from other sources.

"How do I know I can trust you?" Loravain asked.

Zane slid over and whispered in his ear. "Do it for your wife."

Standing up, Zane walked across the tavern, wading through a sea of bodies, then stopped at the door. When he turned around and saw Loravain still sitting on the bench, he returned, a look of disdain on his face.

"What are you waiting for? The master does not like to be kept waiting."

"We're meeting him now? He's here?" Loravain surveyed the tavern, searching for anything or anyone that might be hiding a demon.

"For being one of his favorites, you sure don't know much about him, do you?" Zane asked. "Now get up and follow me. I'll take you to him."

They walked out of the tavern together, slipping into the frigid night. Zane pulled his fur coat around him tighter, shivering in the wind while Loravain shrugged it off. The sky was clear but clouds threatened to cover the moon from the north.

"Hurry up," Zane said through gritted teeth. "It's not far from here."

The road leading away from the tavern turned into a series of switchbacks. Zane led the way halfway down the slope to a narrow path hidden behind a small copse of trees. The trail was dark, rocky, and dangerously steep.

"Follow this trail," Zane said. "Once you reach the other side of the hill, look for a circle of standing stones. Walk into the middle and wait for him to call for you."

"You're not coming?" Loravain asked.

"Are you kidding? It's absolutely wretched out here. I'm going back for a drink. Anyway, the master does not wish to meet with me tonight."

Without another word, Zane spun on this heel and retreated to the tavern. Loravain stared at the path that would take him to his meeting. Had he not been shown where it was, he would have overlooked it. The truth of the matter was that it wasn't even big enough to be considered a game trail. Blowing into his hands to warm his fingers, he stepped off the road. A gust of wind hit him hard from the back, driving him forward faster than he cared to go.

"Good luck," Zane's voice said, riding on the back of the wind.

Loravain pushed on, fighting against the howling wind that had appeared out of nowhere. The force of it knocked him off the trail every few steps causing him to backtrack several times to find it again. With no trees around him for protection, he took the full brunt of the incoming winter storm.

"What are you doing out here?" a lonely voice asked.

The hunter had learned long ago not to be startled by questions coming from the darkness. Thanatos was silent, choosing to be heard only when he wished. Even Loravain could not sense him.

"My master has summoned me."

"Are you sure it is wise to go? He is only going to assign you another task you will have a difficult time completing."

"What other choice do I have?" Loravain asked. "You know what I am trying to achieve."

The wolf appeared out of nowhere, blocking his way. "From what I know of your master, his promises are as empty as his presence in your life."

"What would you have me do?"

"Live your own life. Go and do whatever you want to, just do not be a slave to him any longer."

"If I do what you are suggesting, do you realize how short the remainder of my life would be?" Loravain asked.

"At least it would be your own," the wolf growled.

It was an argument they had on many occasions, and the frequency was increasing. Similar conversations occurred before each of his assignments. Yet this time, looking over the rise to the approaching storm, Loravain almost gave in.

"I have to do this," he said, breaking free from the path to skirt around Thanatos. "Something tells me this time will be different. The master has never summoned me before. It will be the first time since my . . . It will be twenty years since we were last face to face."

Loravain stepped past the wolf and continued up the rugged mountain path. The moon momentarily broke free from the cover of the clouds that had quickly blown in, illuminating the standing stones to his left. Thrown back into darkness, Loravain stepped off the path, crunching through frozen bushes impeding his way. Thanatos padded silently behind him. Once at the stones, the hunter faced the wolf.

"I don't know what will happen or if I will see you again, but I want to thank you for your companionship. The life I have lived has not been an easy one and you have always been there to offer your friendship and guidance."

"Stop talking as if you were walking to your death," Thanatos scolded. "This is not the end. I will be here when you return."

With a nod, Loravain turned and felt his way around the first stone. As soon as his fingers touched the cold rock, humming power began to emanate from it. A faint blue glow pulsed from deep within its cracks. The other stones, five in total, shimmered to life as well. The light bathed the frozen ground in muted blue, giving it the appearance of cracking ice. He stepped closer to the center of the ring, an invisible force pulling at him from every direction at once, growing more intense with each step he took. Though it caused him no pain, the sensation was discomforting. When his feet touched the center mark of the circle, the light from the stones flared brighter. Far beneath him, deep vibrations rose from the earth, shaking him to his core. The quaking throbbed in tandem with the pulsating blue glow, lifting the hunter into the air. Suspended above the ground, the light flashed a brilliant white, blinding Loravain as he fell hard to the unforgiving earth.

The flash had done more than temporarily blind him, it had changed the air. No longer frigidly cold, the next breath Loravain took was warm and moist. The aftereffect of the light still burned his eyes and blurred his vision, but he could see well enough to know he was no longer in the center of the standing stones.

He waited until the remnants of light faded from his eyes then stumbled along with outstretched arms through darkness so thick, he could feel it. The ground was hard and flat and each step he took echoed around him. He couldn't explain how, but the light had transported him somewhere else entirely.

"How . . . ?"

"I told you once before, worm, I am powerful enough to do whatever I like."

Though soft and quiet, the voice shook him deeper than if someone had yelled in his ear. He had not heard that voice in a long time.

"Master," Loravain said, falling to one knee, afraid of what might happen if he didn't show the proper respect.

"You remember your place. Good. Now stand and come forward."

Loravain did as his master commanded and continued to stumble blindly ahead. The same dim, blue light that had radiated from the standing stones began to pulse around him, illuminating a colossal chamber. Gigantic columns, wider than five people stretched out arm to arm, made from coarse, black stone, rose into the space above him where the blue light did not reach. Ahead of him, the light grew brighter, guiding the hunter to a narrow corridor hidden among the folds and cracks of the cave wall.

He followed it away from the entry chamber and was eventually deposited into a smaller cavern. A large, rocky throne sat empty at the far end with a fire burning in front of it. Billowing smoke was channeled away through dozens of tiny holes lining the ceiling.

"You were not the first, nor will you be the last," the voice of his master said, echoing through the stone cave. "You have done well in my name. I believe it is time to set you free, if you complete one last task for me."

Loravain's legs shook as his strength fled. He slumped to one knee to steady himself.

"Thank you, Master. What must I do?"

"There is a child; a witch who has the power to change things for me. She must not be allowed to live. If you do this for me, I will allow you to live your life as you see fit. Your days as being my hunter will be over. I will make a deal with another, though you will be missed. You have served me like no other before."

"Thank you, Master," Loravain said, bending lower.

"Secrecy is of the utmost importance. No one must know of this task. It must be done swiftly and quietly before the child grows into her power. You will find her in a village called Lakes Hollow near the deep lakes in the south. If she is allowed to reach adulthood, she will be the undoing of years of accomplishments, if not worse. Will you do this for me, hunter?"

"I swear it shall be done."

"Go. Fulfill this final task and you will be rewarded. Fail me and you will suffer eternal torment at my hands."

Loravain struggled to regain his footing. The announcement of freedom was almost too much to fathom. When he managed to rise, he stumbled back to the cavern he had arrived in. The room was still bathed in a bluish glow but he paid it no heed. His mind was occupied with thoughts of his freedom. When he completed this contract, his life would once again be his own, which he could scarcely believe. No more missions or obligations to hunt down witches and other nightmarish creatures. He would be free.

When he reached the end of the chamber, the lights flared, plunging him back into the freezing mountain air. The momentary shock of the sudden change awoke him from his stupor. The standing stones surrounded him again but were now dark and natural as ordinary rock. The ground was quiet and steady. Stepping out into the open, he saw Thanatos sitting in freshly fallen snow.

"How long was I gone?" he asked.

"Long enough. I was about to seek shelter when the stones began pulsing again. What happened?"

"I was offered my freedom."

"And what have you been asked to do to receive it?" Thanatos asked, skepticism heavy in his voice.

"I must complete one final contract. I must kill a witch who poses a threat to my master. Once she is dealt with, I will have what I have sought for so many years."

Thanatos cocked his large head. "There must be more to this that you are not telling me. Tell me his exact words."

Loravain recounted what he'd been told about the witch, which had been next to nothing. She was young, untrained, and dangerous enough to undo many of the master's deeds if she were allowed to reach the age of sixteen. The age of adulthood.

"Something does not sit right," Thanatos said, shaking his mangy head. "There must be more to this that your master has kept hidden.

How could an untrained witch be of any consequence to a being so powerful? Why would he offer you freedom for such a simple task?"

"Simple or not, this is my chance to be free, to be my own man," Loravain replied.

"But at what price?"

Thanatos struggled with the idea of this being a simple contract. Loravain, on the other hand, thought only of his freedom. In his mind, the life of a single witch could not compare to that.

"You can't do it," Thanatos said suddenly, all his attention on the hunter. "There could be more risk here than you know. Don't forget what happened in the beginning. This demon is not one for keeping his word."

Thanatos' words struck a memory hidden deep within Loravain's mind. It whisked him back to a month after he had first struck the bargain with his master. Back to when he first discovered the demon could not be trusted.

Lightning flashed, illuminating the interior of the destroyed cabin. Loravain sat on the log he'd dragged in with him next to a disfigured corpse. He knew it was his wife but nature had had its way with things and he could no longer recognize her. Crashing thunder reverberated off the remaining walls. Rain would soon follow.

"Bring her back to me," he yelled, knowing his master could hear him. "You promised."

He had done what the demon had asked him to do, even though it went against everything he believed in. He'd been forced to take his first life; the price he was told must be paid to revive another.

"One life must be taken for another to be given back. A fair trade," his master had told him.

It was love and desperation that had pushed him to do it. The chosen man was innocent. He had done nothing wrong, but the demon insisted. When Loravain hesitated, pain as he had never known washed over him. In the end, he had relented and killed the man. Now he wanted what was due to him.

"Bring her back!"

He reached down and touched his decaying wife's hand. The ring he'd given her was still on her bony finger. He rubbed it affectionately. The ring she'd offered him was still on his finger and he vowed it would never come off.

The sky whitened as another flash of lightning streaked through the clouds. Waiting, he listened for the thunder he knew would follow. When it did, another sound was mingled with it. Deep laughter, full of malice and evil. As the thunder subsided, the laughter continued.

"Fulfill your promise," Loravain shouted.

"Humans are so easily manipulated. Take away something they want and they will do almost anything to get it back."

"You gave me your word!"

"I promise many things."

Standing, Loravain let his wife's hand slip from his. The clouds finally opened, soaking him to the core. He held his hands over his eyes to shield them as he glared into the tempest.

"Bring her back or I swear I will never do what you ask me to again."

"You insolent worm." The words were spoken with such force, the storm felt like a calm breeze afterward. Thrown back into the wall, Loravain crashed to the ground. He covered his head as the rest of the logs crumbled around him. "You fail to realize the position you put yourself in when you agreed to serve me. I. OWN. YOU."

Lightning sliced down from the malicious clouds, striking his wife square in her chest and reducing her body to dust. The intensity of the impact sent Loravain hurtling into the forest. Laying in the wet mud, he fought against the fear and anger threatening to overtake him. Tears welled up in his eyes as he began to understand the consequences of his actions but they were washed away by the torrents of rain now falling.

Loravain cried out in anguish, knowing he would never see his wife again.

"Your desires mean nothing to me," the demon said. "You are a weak and naive man. You cannot deny me the services that are rightfully owed. Your wife will remain in this state forever. Even when you die, if I allow that, you will never find her. You will be cursed to wallow in your guilt and failure for eternity because of your rebellion. I will not let this be soon forgotten."

Loravain lay motionless in the mud until he was sure his master was gone. Only when the storm had faded into nothingness, he crawled back to where his wife had once been. Now there was nothing. The rain had washed her away. There wasn't even enough left to bury.

Sitting back, his head rested against the broken wall. How had it come to this? He had been so sure his wife would be with him again. Grief spread through his veins but he pushed it away, locking it deep inside himself. He refused to give the demon the pleasure of seeing him suffer. He would learn to show no emotion. He would steel his nerves, become impossible to read. He wouldn't give his master another reason to be disappointed in him. Perhaps with perfect service, he would be allowed to be with his wife in the end.

Opening his eyes, the memory faded away. He was still standing next to the circle of stones. Stepping out, he made his way towards a large pine tree that promised protection from the worsening storm. Following behind, Thanatos turned his face from the brutal wind.

Snow weighed down on the great tree's branches, forming a living cave around the lower trunk. Wriggling through the boughs, Loravain instantly felt warmer and dryer. The wind couldn't penetrate through the snow or needles, nor could the warmer air escape. Thanatos dropped to the ground, happy to be out of the open. Loravain did likewise, leaning against the tree trunk.

"I have a lifetime ahead of me to make up for the things I have done in the service of my master," Loravain said.

"I hope you get what you're looking for," the wolf replied.

Not another word was spoken as the two drifted off to sleep, lulled by the sound of wind rushing by on the other side of the branches.

CHAPTER 6

Silence lulled her to sleep. She fought it, trying to find any forgotten memory of her birth mother in the dark recesses of her mind. Would she look like her? How old would she be? Could they do the same things? As the questions raced around her mind, she drifted away.

She didn't know how long she'd been asleep; but the sound of coughing roused her. When Maggie opened her eyes, she was back in the jail cell with the blond witch.

"Have you decided to help me?" she asked.

Maggie glanced around the cell. Nothing had changed since the last time she'd been there. It seemed the witch had had no luck in escaping. The hint of a smile crept across her face as she realized she could use this to her advantage.

"If I help you, will you do something for me?"

"That depends on what you need," the witch said.

"Do you have any other options?" Maggie asked, running a finger over the dirty stones of the wall.

The question went unanswered for long enough that the silence became awkward. Thinking the witch had fallen asleep, Maggie shuffled closer to the cot. Reaching down, she tried to touch the witch's shoulder but her fingers passed through her skin.

"You aren't really here. You can't do anything except hear and see what I do. But you're right, I have no other options. What do you need?"

"I have to go home. I need someone to take me there and I think only another witch would know the way."

"So," the witch said, sitting up. "You've finally come to terms with what you are?"

"I know I'm different, but I don't know if I'll ever fully come to terms with it."

The blond witch stretched her arms over her head then turned and faced Maggie. Maggie gasped at her appearance. She looked terrible. Her skin was pale and sickly, and her hair was greasy and matted to her head. A few bruises showed around her neck and cheeks.

"What have they done to you?"

"Nothing compared to what they have planned for me if I don't escape. If we're going to help one another, we might as well get to know each other. My name is Sarah and I would like to live."

"I'm Maggie. Why are you here instead of with your family?"

Sarah threw the covers off her legs and stood up. Putting her hands on her knees, she bent forward until her head was between her shins. She stayed like that for nearly a minute then slowly stood back up. Next, she lifted a leg behind her, grabbed her foot, pressed her heel into her thigh, and repeated the process with her other leg. "They don't let me out much," Sarah said when she caught Maggie staring. "I'm not sure you're ready to hear my story yet."

"Why not?" Maggie asked.

"Because I don't know you," Sarah said then bent over backward until her spine popped. "But if you get me out of here, I'll tell you whatever you want to know."

"Why then and not now?"

With a bounce, Sarah threw her body back onto the bed. "Call it a trust issue. I've played with fire too many times before and been burned. Until I know you're different, I better keep that to myself."

"But you'll trust me enough to save you?" Maggie asked.

"Like you said, I don't have any other options about that. I still have a choice about how much I say. Anyway, you want my help getting home? Where would that be, exactly?" Sarah asked.

"Have you ever heard of a place called Priama?"

Sarah's eyes widened. She pushed herself off the cot and circled Maggie, appraising her in a new light.

"How would you know about Priama? You've been raised by humans your whole life and just recently discovered you are a witch. What don't I know?"

"I think that is where I'm from," Maggie said.

"I've gathered that much. Why do you think that?"

Maggie was afraid to answer the question. Like Sarah, she didn't know how much she should reveal yet. "Until I get you out of here and you agree to help me, I can't tell you."

Sarah smiled at her. "I can tell that we are going to be great friends. If you can free me from the hideous end I face, we'll talk. Then I will take you to Priama."

"How much time do we have left?" Maggie asked.

Sarah climbed on the bed and gazed out the window. "From what I've been able to overhear, maybe four days. Less if they can muster up the bodies to build the gallows quicker."

"They're going to hang you?" Maggie cried.

"That is what they do with witches around here, generally."

"What can I do to help?"

"Find me as soon as you can. The more time you waste, the closer to death I get."

"Do you have any idea where you are?" Maggie asked.

"No," Sarah said, hopping down from the bed. "I could be anywhere. Once you start searching for me, I'll be able to guide you in your sleep. Or at least I'll be able to keep you on the right track. When you get close enough, I might be able to communicate with you while you're awake."

"That's amazing. Will I be able to do that?" Maggie asked.

"I doubt it. By your age, your powers should have already manifested. What can you do?"

Maggie sat on the floor and thought about all the things she was capable of.

"Sometimes I feel like I can fly. I mean, I know I can't fly, but I can jump really high. If I run fast enough, I can jump even higher. I've been in the air for close to a minute before. Oh, I'm fast, too."

"Most witches have some sort of heightened agility, to an extent. It is a useful ability that helps us gain an advantage over most threats. I haven't heard of any witch doing exactly what you're saying you can do. That is a lot of time to be airborne. If it's true, we'll have to practice when we meet. I'd love to see it. What else can you do?" Sarah asked as she started jogging in place.

Maggie was about to answer when a door behind her opened. Spinning around, she saw nothing. The door in front of her was still closed.

"Don't worry about that," Sarah said as she stepped up to the bars. "Guards come and go all the time. They only come back here when they bring me food once a day and I've already eaten. They're scared of me. Please continue."

Maggie eyed Sarah for a moment before speaking again. If the guards feared her, did that mean she was dangerous? She didn't look threatening. For the moment, Maggie decided to comply. "I can turn sounds on and off in my head. I can make the world go completely silent or I can listen to one sound at a time, only hearing what I focus on."

"That could come in handy," Sarah said. "What else?"

"There is this other . . . What's that sound?" Maggie asked.

"What sound?" Sarah said, tilting her head.

"Someone is crying."

"I don't hear anything. It must be coming from your end."

"What do you mean, my end?" Maggie asked.

"You're hearing someone near your body. I should release you. Please, find me soon."

Darkness crept in at the edges of Maggie's vision and rapidly engulfed everything else until she couldn't see. Her body tipped sideways, leaving her floating weightless in the air. Then she felt the softness of her bed embrace her, the cool comfort of her pillow under her head. She was awake. Opening her eyes, she listened to her mother crying in the workroom. Sitting up, she rubbed the lingering sleep from her eyes and slipped through the curtain. A fire was burning in the kitchen stove.

"Mother? What's wrong?" Maggie asked.

Startled by her voice, her mother dropped the doll she'd been cradling in her arms. Bending down, she scooped up the fallen toy and hid it away in a small box on the shelf in front of her.

"Nothing. Did you sleep well?"

Maggie nodded and stepped up to the window. It was still dark out.

"How long was I asleep?"

"A few hours."

Wind howled outside. Maggie pulled open the door, regretting it instantly. A storm had blown in and torrents of freezing rain attacked her. She slammed the door shut, but the damage had been done. She was wet and shivering.

"Come sit by the fire. Your father is out in that right now making deliveries. I do hope he returns soon. That weather is sure to be the death of him. It wasn't like this when he left. Are you hungry?" her mother asked. "I made your favorite."

The table had been set but it was cluttered with things from her childhood. Old toys were strewn around the plates and pictures she had drawn on tree bark and leaves littered the floor. There was a small pile of dolls she'd made when she was younger. They were her attempt at making money at the market. She'd failed miserably.

"What have you been doing, Mother?"

With a sad smile on her face, she joined her daughter at the table, picking up a particularly ugly doll. She held it against her chest.

"I'm remembering. I want to bring all the memories I have of you to the forefront of my mind so that I'll remember you when you're gone."

"What do you mean when I'm gone?" Maggie asked.

"You talk in your sleep," her mother said, putting the doll back with the others. "You've been talking for the past few nights. The things you said didn't make any sense until now."

"I'm sorry. I didn't know I was going to leave. At least not all of me did. I'm scared, Mom." Maggie's mother pulled her into a tight, rib-cracking hug.

"So am I, but you are a strong, intelligent woman. You can do things I would be too afraid to try. If anyone can do this, it's you."

Her mother had always had perfect faith in her, even when she was in trouble. Yes, she would be punished for her wrongdoings, but the words spoken by her mother were ones of love and deep understanding.

"Oh, where is that man? His dinner is going to get cold, and then where will he be? Sick in bed with the fever again, that's where," her mother said as she pulled free from her hug.

Setting her face, her mother snapped her emotions shut as tight as a lake clam, like usual. When she didn't want her feelings to show, they wouldn't. Maggie was lucky to have witnessed her shell crack open. Seeing that was a rare thing indeed.

"I'm leaving in the morning," Maggie blurted out before she could stop herself.

"So soon?" her mother asked.

"There is something I need to do, and it can't wait."

"Your father won't be happy about this at all, especially with the dragon leaf harvest coming up. I wouldn't be surprised if he tried to keep you here. Always an emotional wreck, that one."

With a sack in her hand, her mother began filling it with bread, cheese, dried meats and fruits, and a bit of butter. She hid it near a pile of cloth so it could only be seen if you know where to look. Then, working together, they gathered the things Maggie would need for her journey. Not a word was spoken but there were plenty of sighs and sniffles to be heard over the wind and crackling fire. When all was collected, they sat in front of the fire and waited for Father to arrive.

Laughter rang out through the small room. Knowing Maggie was leaving in the morning pushed her parents to be more lively, upbeat, and happy. Maggie knew they were doing it to support her, and she thanked them for it, but she could see the sadness in their eyes. But no amount of sorrow could prevent them from celebrating.

". . . And when we came outside," her father reminisced, snorting so loud through his laughter he began to choke. He only continued once he'd composed himself. "You were sitting on the house and that little friend of yours was limping away, holding her rear end."

Maggie couldn't contain the sip of milk in her mouth as she tried to hold in the laughter. Failing, she spat milk out all over the table. She remembered that day as clearly as if it had been yesterday

"I can still see the look on her face," Maggie said.

"Her father came running up the hill about an hour later yelling about how his daughter had been attacked by wild demons. When he saw us, all working in the garden as if nothing had happened, he just scratched his head."

Maggie tried to keep a straight face while she cleaned up her mess. The rag was sodden and dripped with milk as she carried it to an empty bucket in the kitchen.

The wind outside was still howling and she could hear rain splashing in puddles as it fell. She worried about the beginning of her journey. If the rain kept up, she might be in worse shape than the milk-laden rag. Nevertheless, she couldn't help but be uplifted by the stories her parents were sharing.

"Do you remember the time you froze up the well?" her father asked with a chortle.

"That wasn't my fault," Maggie complained but still looked forward to the story. Her father was a wizard with words.

"We'd just finished gathering the leaves covering the garden. It was early spring and the sun was giving us a hint of summer. I was so upset when it happened. Little Mags decided to dump the whole lot of wet, stinky leaves on the fire. It had taken me all morning to find kindling dry enough to start it and there you'd gone and nearly smothered it. But then the smoke turned thick and dark."

Her mother failed to control the fit of laughter that had taken over her. It was so contagious that it spread through the room like wildfire. When she could breathe again, her mother continued the tale.

"When the leaves burst into flames, sending that fireball into the sky, you almost jumped out of your pants and fell head over heels straight into the dung pile."

That earned another round of howling laughter.

"You were so scared," her dad said, wiping a tear from his eye. "You ran to the well and dropped the bucket. You wanted to douse the flames."

"All we heard," Mother said, interrupting her husband. "Was a hollow thump when the bucked bounced off the ice."

"That's not fair," Maggie said. "How do you know it was my fault? It was early spring. It could have still been frozen."

"It wasn't," her father said. "I'd already drawn out at least five buckets that morning."

"Well, I had no idea what had happened. I just thought I was going to burn down the whole village."

As the moment wore on, silence fell over them as they each remembered different memories that brought them joy. The joviality that had prevailed began to fall away as the seriousness of the situation came rushing back. No one wanted to talk about it. No one wanted to ruin the memory they had just created, but it was inevitable.

"Well, Magdalena," her mother said, breaking the mood by using her full name. "If you really are planning on doing this, then you need to get some rest. Run off to bed now and tomorrow we can say our proper goodbyes. But for one more night, you are still my baby. Now scoot."

Maggie kept her complaints to herself and slowly shuffled off to bed. She glanced back at her parents before closing the curtain, shutting them off from her presence. It felt symbolic, Maggie thought. Her life was going to change in the morning. She had no idea what would happen or if she would ever come home again. But her mother was right. She needed to sleep.

When Maggie woke up the following morning, she lay in bed for a moment, memorizing the feeling of her bed against her back. She looked around, trying to burn the image of her cramped room into her mind. She was scared and nervous for what lay ahead, but more than that, there was a sensation at her core pulling her away. She knew she had to go now or she would somehow convince herself she didn't need to.

Working up the courage to push aside the curtain, she found the house empty. She quickly changed into clean clothes and wrapped a large blanket around her shoulders. Her mother had fashioned it into a coat for her journey. Outside, the morning looked clear but the storm had made way for cold autumn weather. The first snow would be falling soon.

She went to the kitchen and picked up the satchel she had hidden with her mother the night before. Placing it over her shoulder, she looked around her house for what might be the last time. Before she knew it, tears slid down her cheeks. She never imagined she would have to leave her entire life behind. Her happiest memories had been made here, in this room. Her knees wobbled as she slumped against the wall. Was she capable of abandoning everything she had learned to love? Taking a deep breath, she held it in her lungs and dried her face with a sleeve. There was no time for tears, her mother would say. There was work to be done. With a determined push, Maggie stood up straight and gripped the strap of her bag tightly.

From beneath her bed, she pulled out an empty pack. In it went the few things she would take. The box from her birth mother, along with the letter and hairpin, two pairs of pants, a heavy shirt, three pairs of socks, a jacket, and one thin blanket. Her satchel of food went on top. Without looking back, she stepped outside.

Standing near the grindstone, her father held a small dagger in his hands. She could tell it was newly sharpened by the way the sun glinted off the edge. She recognized the handle.

"I want you to have this," he said as she came closer, presenting it to her. "I wanted to give it to my son but that will never happen. You are my only child so it belongs to you now."

"Dad," Maggie cried, tears once again flowing freely. "I can't. It's been in your family for generations."

"And it will stay in the family. It would mean more to me knowing you had something to protect yourself with out there. If you don't take it, I'll be insulted."

Humbled, Maggie reached out and took the blade. He also handed her the sheath for it. The dark, firm leather, which had been stamped with the image of an owl, fit the blade perfectly. It was incredible leatherwork.

"It's beautiful," Maggie said, sheathing the blade and slipping it into her belt.

"The owl is the symbol of our family. It will protect you in times of trouble. Remember the owl as you embark on your new life. If you need help or are in trouble, it is said the owl will come to your aid. Probably just an old superstition, though." He embraced her, pulling her tight. "I love you."

"I love you too, Dad," Maggie replied. "Where's Mom?"

"She couldn't do it. It was too hard for her. She loves you so much. You are her whole life, and she understands why you must do this, but she couldn't bear to see you walk away. She would prefer to remember last night as her final memory."

"I'll come back again," Maggie said.

"Of course, you will. I'll walk with you for a bit. Which way are you going?"

Maggie still didn't know where to go, but Sarah said she would guide her once she started so it didn't matter which way she went.

"South. I'm going south," she said.

"Then I will go with you as far as Bear Lake," he said, picking up a long, thin stick. "I found this for you this morning. You'll need a good walking stick. They're more practical than you think.

Picking up a staff of his own, they walked away from their small house, getting lost under the reds and yellows of the autumn leaves.

CHAPTER 7

The pace they traveled was arduous, but it felt good to be moving with real purpose again. Thinking only of his freedom, Loravain pushed them on as if an army was behind them and closing in. The ice and snow of the high mountains had slowed them down, but now that they were in the lower flatlands, they were making much better time. Now their only task was to find a village that neither of them had ever heard of.

"Where are we supposed to be going?" Thanatos asked, tongue flopping from his mouth.

"To a village near the deep lakes," Loravain said.

"He had to be vague, didn't he? Which lake? There are at least ten."

"We know the name of the village. When we get closer, someone will know of it."

"Is that your plan? I think the prospect of freedom has clouded your judgment."

The hunter looked at Thanatos. "What do you mean?"

"We're running straight into a situation we know nearly nothing about. We know the name of the village. What if this doesn't turn out to be as easy as you are hoping?"

Loravain opened his mouth to answer but fell silent and rushed on ahead.

"You haven't thought that far ahead yet, have you?" the wolf asked. "This isn't like you, Loravain."

"I know," Loravain yelled, coming to a halt. "The stakes have never been this high before and I have no plan. We need information, and we can't get that until we're closer. Right now, my only focus is on moving, which we are no longer doing."

Thanatos hung his head. Loravain knew what that meant. The wolf would bite his tongue for now, but the argument was not over. Turning, he resumed his brutal pace.

The two had mostly stuck to roads, which allowed them to move faster but provided less cover. They were used to traveling through woods, forests, and other less obvious paths. The trees surrounding the road leaned in, thick branches hiding the early evening sky from sight. The openness of the road left Loravain feeling vulnerable, even though they hadn't seen anyone all day.

The path they were on now meandered through a thick forest, changing directions now and then to circumvent an obstacle, but mostly continued southward. Now that the sun was beginning to set, the emptiness in his stomach was noticeable. He needed to eat. With nightfall approaching, he would also need to find a place to rest. Turning around, he wasn't surprised to find Thanatos missing. He let out a low, sharp whistle then sat down in the roots of a tree.

Sleep had nearly overtaken him by the time he heard panting. Cracking open one eye, he spotted Thanatos on the far side of the road.

"Nothing is going to happen today. I need to find food and water. We'll continue the search in the morning."

Thanatos didn't say a word.

"The silent treatment, is it?" Loravain asked. "I can deal with that."

He pushed away from the tree and stood up. Now that he had rested, the sting of hunger and thirst was more apparent. It would take him at least half an hour to gather what was needed to satisfy him.

As he stepped away from the road and into the dark shadows of the trees, Thanatos gave a soft whimper. He was looking down the road. Straining, Loravain heard it too. Wheels. The wolf trotted up to him.

"We have things to discuss, but you need information. Get what you can."

Without another word, Thanatos disappeared. Sitting back down, Loravain waited. He hoped he would be more approachable as a weary, defeated traveler than a deadly assassin on a mission. Before long he could make out the creaking of a wagon, its wheels rising and falling in the ruts along the path. When a man came into view, Loravain hung his head, trying to look as dejected as possible.

The tall, lanky man leading a petite, malnourished horse stopped in front of him. His small wagon was overburdened, and the man appeared to be in a hurry, which was understandable with night falling. The fact that he stopped was promising. Most men would have passed him without a second look. The man glanced back and forth, peering through the trees as if expecting an ambush.

"Sir, is there something you need?" he asked.

Loravain looked up into his face, shocked to see how old he was.

"I must admit," Loravain began. "I am quite lost. I'm trying to find a friend but the directions in his letter were most perplexing. I've been waiting here for hours hoping someone would come by."

Still wary, the man took a step closer, never releasing his hold on his horse's lead rope. "Where is it you are trying to go? Maybe I can point you in the right direction."

Loravain stood slowly and offered the old man a hand. "Thank you. I am looking for a small village called Lakes Hollow. It is somewhere near the deep lakes. Am I close?"

The man took Loravain's hand with a smile. "I have never heard of this village, but I have heard of the deep lakes. No end to the fish I've been told, but I have never been there myself."

"Do you know the way? I'm afraid I'm going in circles."

"It's a four-day walk to the south. This road will take you most of the way."

"Thank you. You are very kind to aid a stranger."

The old man prodded his horse and started on his way again but glanced over his shoulder. "There is a small tavern not far from here if you need shelter for the night. It was a bit crowded for my taste, but you might find a warm meal and a soft bed for the night."

"Your help is appreciated," Loravain called after him.

When the man was gone, Thanatos stepped out into the open. "We have a direction."

"That we do," Loravain said. "Four days south of here. We can make it in two."

"Before we do," the wolf said, but Loravain cut him off.

"I'm sorry, old friend. I have no excuse for responding how I did. You were right. I need to have a plan before running headlong into what could be a trap."

Thanatos nodded. "I am happy to hear that."

"For now, we continue our way south. Once we get closer, I will start making inquiries into what we might be facing."

The wolf nodded. "A good night's rest will benefit us."

Loravain agreed then ventured out into the woods to find dinner.

"Wouldn't the night house be easier?" Thanatos asked.

Loravain shook his head. "I don't want to risk running into anyone else with a message. I am more than happy to be hidden away searching for my own dinner."

"Suit yourself," the wolf said.

The hours blurred by as Loravain and Thanatos ran, pushing themselves to the breaking point. The sooner the witch was found, the sooner he would be free to start his new life. They would occasionally stop along the way to get more reliable directions. Shortly after the third day, Loravain approached a scruffy-looking man laden with hunting gear.

"Excuse me," Loravain called. "Do you have a moment to spare?"

The man looked around. "Be quick about it. I have much to do today."

"I am only looking for directions. Lakes Hollow. Have you heard of it?"

The man nodded and pointed behind him. "Half a day's walk that way."

They were closer than he thought. At the pace they'd set, they were only a couple of hours away. Loravain could feel the weight of servitude lifting off his shoulders.

"You're absolutely sure?" Loravain asked again.

"Yes, of course I'm sure. I was there yesterday." The man started walking away but stopped when Loravain asked him another question.

"You've been there? Do you happen to know a witch who lives there?"

A puzzled expression fell across the man's face. Scratching his head, he gave the question some thought.

"No. Lakes Hollow has no witches, and I would know."

"Are you certain? Maybe you are confused? There must be a witch there."

"Must there?" the man asked, shifting his gear on his shoulder. "If there were, everyone would know about it. There are no witches in Lakes Hollow."

The man turned his back on Loravain and stepped off the road, disappearing in the thick hanging branches of the surrounding pine trees.

"What do you think?" Thanatos asked.

"My master did say that she had not come into her powers. If she hasn't manifested yet, she wouldn't be known as a witch."

"Either that or she has been hiding them." Thanatos paced around Loravain as the hunter slowly walked ahead.

"We've been up against enough witches," Loravain said. "This one shouldn't be any different."

"Then why is your master worried about her?"

The question caused Loravain to pause. The wolf was right. If there was a reason for his master to worry, he would be wise to worry about this situation himself. Up until now, he only thought about the simplicity of the task, not the hidden dangers that might be waiting for him.

"The closer we get, the more reliable the information we find will be."

The two set off again towards Lakes Hollow. The scenery began to blur together along the forest path. Tall pines dominated their view, but they occasionally made way for a handful of majestic oaks decked out in their autumn colors. A deer or rabbit would dart across the road every so often, stopping to look in their direction, then bolting out of view again. After what seemed like a couple of hours, Thanatos stopped their progression.

"I smell smoke. People may be close by."

Off in the distance, a thin line of smoke could be seen rising through a break in the tree line. A small cabin was nestled a good way off the road, just visible in the morning light.

"Wait here," he said to Thanatos as he dashed into the underbrush.

Loravain slowed down as he approached the cabin. A tall, sturdy woman tended a small garden outside the front door, and he didn't want to startle her. Through the trees, he saw a waist-high fence circling the property with a locked gate. It might prove effective for small animals but would do nothing for a genuine threat. The hunter silently searched the perimeter before conceding that he would be safe approaching the woman. He saw nothing that would indicate he was in any danger. There was a small hatch and window on the back wall of the cabin and a sturdy stone chimney reaching out of the roof. No one else could be seen and no visible tracks led to or away from the house. If anyone else was hiding inside, he would deal with that when the time came. With stealth only Thanatos could match, he marched up to the gate and coughed.

"Excuse me."

The woman spun around; a short, muddy dagger held tightly in her fist. She backed away quickly, keeping the blade in front of her. "How dare you sneak up on a lone woman like that," she scolded.

"I apologize for my intrusion. I am searching for Lakes Hollow. Do you know the way?"

"Yes, I know where it is," she answered, her eyes flitting from tree to tree. "Who else is out there?"

"I am alone and mean you no harm. I just have a few questions for you then I will be on my way."

The woman pursed her lips and stared hard at him. Her hand moved towards the wooden handle of a crude hammer leaning against the door. "If you want my help then you must be honest with me. You are not alone. I can hear someone else moving out there."

"I assure you that no one else is with me. I am traveling alone with my mongrel." If Thanatos heard him call him that, he would be furious, but it was better that the woman not know that a wolf was nearby.

Her gaze fell reluctantly back on Loravain. "Fine. Ask your questions and be gone."

"Are you aware of any witches who live in Lakes Hollow?"

The woman dropped her dagger when Loravain said the word witches. "Why are you asking about witches, sir? Who are you? We want no trouble from their kind, nor yours."

"Please, this could be a matter of life and death?"

"No," the woman said, spinning around to open her door. "There are no witches in Lakes Hollow now nor have there ever been. You have asked our questions, now please be on your way."

She slammed the door behind her, leaving her dagger stuck in the mud where it fell. Before Loravain turned around, the woman peeked out her window, followed by the eyes of a small child. The hunter waved at them and then backed away from the gate.

It was more than likely that the young witch had not come into her powers yet. His master was adamant that the witch lived in Lakes Hollow and he was never wrong. Why was he so worried about this witch? That was the one thing Loravain could not figure out. As he tried to piece everything together, he joined Thanatos back on the road.

"She knew nothing about the witch, did she?" the wolf asked.

"No. The witch must not know who she is yet. I assume her powers have not yet manifested, at least not on a large scale."

His thoughts floated around his head, mingling with the words of his master. The witch they were looking for was most likely nearing adulthood. At her current age, she was too powerless to do any damage. This sounded more and more like an easy mission.

"We must hurry," Loravain said. "If all goes well, I could be free by supper."

Playing his conscience as always, Thanatos planted seeds of doubt in his mind. "How is this easy for you? If what you think is true, then you will be killing an innocent child. Will you be able to live with that?"

Loravain paused. The words had the intended effect. Thanatos had always tried to be the voice of reason in his life, and slowly over the past two decades, it started sinking in.

"It is either this or another twenty years of slavery, possibly committing worse sins," the hunter said, though his conviction was slipping.

"As I have told you before, I will not stop you from fulfilling your destiny, whatever that might be. But I promise you this. If you kill her, I will leave you. This is a child we're talking about, Loravain."

Loravain stopped in his tracks. Turning, he stared into the wolf's eyes. Thanatos had never threatened to leave him before. Of course, he didn't want to kill her, but it was better than the alternative. His freedom was worth more to him than the continued company of the wolf.

"I have to do it."

"We shall see. I will go with you until you follow through on this decision. There is still time for you to see reason."

They continued in silence. Loravain had much to think about but instead distracted himself with thoughts of what he had lost so many years ago. He thought about his young bride and the life they should have had together. His lips curled into a cringe when his memories turned dark, forcing him to witness her death once again. For the first time since he had promised his service to his demon master, a tear escaped his eye and rolled down his cheek. His life truly had been stolen from him. He would have been a father, possibly even a grandfather by now. Without prompting or warning, his thoughts shifted to the blond witch he had recently caught and how beautiful she was. He wished he hadn't been paid to hunt her. As more memories sprang into existence in his mind, it opened the floodgates for all the actions he'd committed that he regretted. There were too many to number but each one hit him hard, almost stopping his progress. He wallowed in shame and grief. He had become a monster.

Because of the words Thanatos had spoken to him over the years, and the resurfacing of his horrible memories, Loravain came to a surprising conclusion, which scared him. He had to deny his master's wishes and spare the witch. The pain he would suffer because of it didn't bother him. No, he could deal with pain. What scared him was the fact that it had taken him twenty years to do the right thing. Decades of pain swept over him, and he desperately wished he would have said no to the demon in the beginning and given his wife and unborn child a proper burial.

"If I find that the witch poses a threat to others, I will complete the task," Loravain said. "If I decide she does not, I will do nothing. No harm will come to her. I will walk away and wait for my punishment to come. In the time I have left, I will try to make penance for my many sins. Either way, I will be free."

The wolf said nothing in return. In fact, he was no longer there. Looking up, Loravain realized they had already reached the village. Thanatos must have slunk off into the foliage, becoming invisible. He had no doubt the wolf had heard what he said, though. Steadying himself, he went on alone, knowing what must be done. Today was the first day of his new life living as a free man. The wishes and commands of his former master would no longer weigh him down.

CHAPTER 8

The village of Lakes Hollow was bursting with activity. People rushed in and out of storefronts and lined up at various stalls around a center square. He could smell honey and freshly baked bread in the air. His stomach growled in response but he had no time to worry about food. When he had the information he needed, he would eat. Turning around in circles, he sized up the people around him. Many were women carrying bags of food but a few men were making the rounds as well. If he was smart about this, he would not waste his time asking more than one person. Almost immediately, his gaze fell on a grizzled old man carrying a large bundle of sticks on his back. Stepping toward him, Loravain offered his help. The man graciously accepted, dropping an end of the bundle into his hands.

"Thank you, lad," the man said. "My back isn't what it used to be. The curse of old age, I guess. I'm sorry, but I don't recognize you. Are you new here?"

"Just passing through. I'm actually searching for someone. Perhaps you can help."

"There are not many people in Lakes Hollow and we all know one another. Who are you looking for?"

"That's the problem," Loravain said. "I'm not sure. I have been charged with finding a witch and was told this is where she lived."

The man chuckled and shook his head. "You have been sent on a goose chase. There are no witches in these parts. Not anymore anyway.

Witches have fallen into something of myth here. Nowadays, parents tell their children stories of witches to make them behave. I am afraid you have come all this way for nothing."

"I can assure you that witches are no myth. The girl I am looking for is young and may not have come into her powers yet. Do you know of anyone who can do anything . . . peculiar?"

The man dropped his end of the sticks with a thud, motioning for Loravain to do the same.

"This is as far as we're going. Thank you much for your help. As for your question, I have not heard of anything like that. Not recently anyway. I do remember a rumor, but that was years ago, almost not even worth mentioning. I don't know the particulars myself," the man said as he scratched his head.

Loravain waited for him to finish, but was surprised when the man turned around and walked away.

"Excuse me, sir," Loravain said, giving chase. "What rumor?"

"Rumor? Oh, yes. You would need to speak with Tomas Rainer about that, the father of the little girl who was . . . afflicted. He may be able to help you more than I."

"Where could I find Tomas?" Loravain asked.

"That's easy enough. He would be at home this time of day."

For the second time, the man hurried on as if he had forgotten he was holding a conversation.

"Where is his home?"

"Northeast corner of the village, just past the tree line."

The old man shuffled back into the crowd, leaving Loravain standing next to a thick, two-story building. Taking a step back, he noticed a round sign announcing it as a cobbler's shop. He glanced up and down the street, surprised at how quickly the crowd had thinned. Only a few lingering shoppers rushed about. A row of shops lined the road to his left and a blacksmith's forge and a rundown, desecrated barn stood to his right. Tall oak trees surrounded the village, their autumn colors in full display. Dust floated in the air, but it was quickly settling now that the market was nearly empty.

Leaving the bustle of the market behind him, he followed the man's directions as best he could and soon found the home he was looking for. It was easy to find, just as the man had said, about a five-minute walk into the woods. A small cabin was surrounded by piles of chopped wood and felled trees. A few berry bushes grew along a small path leading away from the building. Rapping lightly on the door, he took notice of the sharp, double-edged ax leaning against the wall. Another one rested on a tree trunk not far away.

His attention was pulled back by the creaking of the door. A pair of small eyes stared out at him from knee height.

"Hello," Loravain said, falling to one knee. "Is your father home?"

Without so much as a cry, the door slammed shut. Loravain lifted his fist to knock again.

"Can I help you?" a voice asked from behind him.

Loravain stood and turned around, coming face to face with a man covered in wood chips. He wore a long, thick leather apron, was balding, and gripped another wicked-looking ax. He guessed they were about the same age.

"Tomas Rainer?" Loravain asked.

"That would be me. How can I help you? Do you need to place an order?"

"I'm looking for a witch," Loravain said, cutting right to the chase.

"Well, my friend, I'm afraid you've come to the wrong place. There are no witches in Lakes Hollow. I'm not sure how you made it to my door, but perhaps you should be moving on now."

"Yes, I will be shortly, but an older gentleman in the village pointed me in your direction. The girl I am looking for may not know she is a witch."

"And you suspect one of my daughters to be this witch?" Tomas asked, lifting his ax.

"No, not at all. I was told that something peculiar happened to one of your daughters a few years back. I would like to know more about that."

Tomas brushed his hands off on his legs, removed his apron, and sat down on one of his logs. He offered Loravain a seat next to him.

"Now that you mention it, something did happen. Nine years ago, to be exact. Ruby, my youngest, was at the home of the herb farmers playing with their daughter, Maggie. They are about the same age. One day, Ruby came running home like a pike beast on fire. Wicked marks ran the length of her backside. By the looks of them, someone had taken a willow snap branch to her. I was in a rage. She said it hurt, but what she told me next surprised me. She said it was cold, even though the day was hot. When I touched her skin, she was right. It felt like she'd been sitting out in the snow without trousers on. I marched right up the Abernathy's to demand answers. When I got there, they were all working in their garden as if nothing had happened. We talked about it for quite some time, but they seemed just as confused as I was. When I returned home, Ruby was fine. No welts, no marks, and she acted like nothing had happened at all. To this day, she won't talk about it. Claims she doesn't remember."

Loravain mulled the story over in his mind. It sounded like witchcraft, and he was positive no one in the village would understand the truth of the situation. They would have assumed it was an accident.

"Thank you, Tomas," Loravain said as he stood. "Could you tell me where to find the Abernathy's home? I would like to visit with their daughter."

"I'm afraid that would be a waste of your time," Tomas answered. "Their daughter has gone missing. No one has seen her for the past few days. Seems she's run off in the night."

"No matter. I would like to speak with her parents."

Tomas gave him directions and returned to his work. The road leading to the herb growers' farm was long and lonely. He related to the feeling. He thought back to the home he'd built with Camila, which was isolated from people as well. Loravain and his bride had always desired seclusion over company. Padding silently at his side, Thanatos had slipped out of the trees.

"What have you discovered?" the wolf asked.

"The witch is here or was not long ago. The girl in question hasn't been seen for a few days. They say she ran off in the night. I'm sure her parents will know more."

"Do you think she caught wind of your approach somehow?" Thanatos asked.

"That is yet another question that needs to be answered."

Cresting a slight rise, the herb farmers' house came into view. It was built into the hillside with a garden growing on either side of the door and a water well standing to one side for easy irrigation. A man sat at a grindstone. With a nod from Loravain, Thanatos took cover once more.

"Good day, Mr. Abernathy," the hunter said, announcing his presence.

The man turned around and faced him. "Oh, for heaven's sake, it's Francis, not Mr. Abernathy. You must be early. We have no packages prepared for today. Come back tomorrow." He turned around and went back to work.

"I am not here for a package. I have some questions about your daughter."

The shovel Francis was sharpening fell to the ground with a clang. "My daughter is not here right now."

"No, she wouldn't be. It is said she has been missing for a few days. I would like to ask you a few questions about her."

"I will not answer them," Francis said, standing from the grindstone. "I do not know you nor your intentions. I thank you for coming but I insist that you leave."

"The information I am seeking is vital," Loravain said, but Francis continued to walk away.

A short, sharp whistle filled the air. Bolting out of his hiding place, Thanatos blocked Francis' way, growling at him. The man almost fell over at the sight of the wolf.

"What is the meaning of this?" he cried.

"I mean you no harm," Loravain promised. "I am only seeking the girl."

"That girl is my daughter! You are not from the village and she is not yet of marrying age. She should not be getting called on from anyone yet, let alone someone such as yourself."

"I am not here to call on your daughter, Francis. I am here because of what she is."

"I have no idea what you're . . . what you're talking about," Francis said, stumbling over his words.

"Your daughter is a witch. I find it hard to believe you wouldn't know something like that."

The color drained from the old man's face and his knees started to shake.

"Please," Loravain said. "Let us talk like men, not enemies. I have some questions to determine if your daughter is a threat."

"A threat?" Francis cried. "How could my Maggie be a threat to anyone? She is a sweet, caring girl."

"I can only assume she is that way because of her parents. Again, I swear I mean you and your daughter no harm, but I must find her. If you assist me, I will leave you in peace. Hinder me, and I cannot make that same promise."

Loravain adjusted a strap across his shoulder, revealing his crossbow. At the sight of it, Francis nodded and motioned to a large, flat rock.

"Ask your questions and be done with it."

Loravain sat and looked the man in the eyes. "Your daughter, is she your blood?"

"What kind of question is that?" Francis shouted, then quickly calmed when Thanatos bared his teeth. "I'm sorry. That is a personal question. If you must know, no, she is not mine. She came to us as a baby, dropped off at our door stoop in the middle of the night. We have no idea where she came from."

"Were you aware that she was a witch?"

No answer came.

"So, you know. For how long?"

Francis sighed and sat down next to Loravain. "Ruth and I had our suspicions since she was a child but it was not confirmed until a few nights ago."

"The time she left? Where is she now?"

"I don't know," Francis sobbed. "I have no idea where my daughter is, or if she is even safe. The fact that you are here looking for her proves she is in danger. Please, do not let any harm come to her."

Francis grabbed Loravain by the jacket and fell apart. Tears flowed freely from his eyes and his chest heaved.

"No harm will come to her by my hand, I promise you that. One last question and I will leave you in peace. Has your daughter ever shown signs of excessive anger or distrust towards anyone in the village?"

"Never. As I told you, she is a loving, caring, and sweet girl. Yes, there have been awkward times, but such is true for anyone trying to learn their place in the world."

"Thank you for your honesty, Francis. I appreciate it," Loravain said.

Francis continued to plead with him. "Protect my daughter, sir, if you find her. She is only fifteen and I am sick with worry."

Loravain nodded but remained silent as he stood. With Thanatos at his heels, he raced away, only turning back once.

"Which way did she go?" he called out.

"To the north. I walked with her as far as the edge of town. From there, I have no idea."

As the house and gardens faced from view, Thanatos finally spoke.

"The man is lying. I can see the trail heading south. What do you think?"

"I see it as well but he is only trying to protect his daughter, who the master feels threatened by for some reason. He acts as if she would be able to undo years of his hard work. If so, that might not be a bad thing. After what her father said, I cannot kill her. We will find her and discover the real reason the master wants her dead. I will not be used as his puppet anymore."

Dedicated to his change of heart, Loravain sprinted south, knowing they had to make up for lost time.

CHAPTER 9

Nights were becoming unbearably cold. Bundled in her blanket, Maggie lay as close to her meager fire as she dared. Stocking up on twigs, bark, and broken branches, she had strategically placed everything in such a way that she didn't have to move much. If the fire started to die, all she had to do was shift her legs to push more kindling in.

Her dreams were haunted by visions of what would happen to Sarah if she failed to arrive on time. She hated the sounds of laughter that rang out when the log Sarah stood on was kicked out from under her. She cringed as the rope became taut around her neck and she dangled in the air, gasping for breath. Sarah attempted to flee in other dreams, only to be shot in the back by poisoned arrows. Maggie watched her body writhe and twitch in agony, incapable of looking away.

Between the bitterly cold nights and the dreams, Maggie was not sleeping well. Waiting for the sun to rise, she began to regret leaving home. She'd only been gone for three days but she missed her soft bed and warm food. The comforts of home called out to her, but Sarah's need won out. If she ever wanted to find her birth mother, she needed help.

As promised, Sarah gave her directions as she slept. She could sense Maggie getting closer. It would be no more than one day now before she reached her. Preparing herself for what she might encounter,

Maggie pushed herself to run faster, jump higher, and stretch herself and her abilities more than she had before.

She breathed out a white plume of air and stared into the dying embers of the fire. Dawn wasn't far away now but she couldn't bring herself to reach out from under the blanket to push more wood on the fire.

"I hope this is going to be worth it," she said, watching the sky light up with pinks and oranges.

Before the weariness of sleep had time to fade from her mind, she rolled up her blanket and slung it across her back with the rest of her things. She stamped on the remnants of her fire, spreading the coals around the dirt and grass with her boot. Hunger and sleep deprivation pushed her on. She hadn't rationed out the food she'd brought from home and had finished the day before. She'd managed to find a few berries and edible roots but they did nothing to quell the burning in her stomach. Ignoring the gnawing, Maggie focused on putting one foot in front of the other in the direction Sarah had given her.

The air warmed slightly as the sun rose, but not enough to provide any relief. She was still freezing even with two jackets on. Glancing down, she was horrified at how disheveled her clothes looked. Dirt, twigs, and pebbles had found their way into her socks, boots, and pant legs. As she walked, she pulled at her pant legs, allowing the debris to fall to the ground. Her shirt and jackets were ripped from her time spent jumping into trees and branches. She felt and looked like a wreck. She would never allow herself to look like this at home but now she couldn't do anything about it. She dreaded the thought of what her hair must look like.

Slipping past a few more trees, Maggie finally found a road. Her entire trip had consisted of pushing her way through bushes, low-hanging branches, and wading through things she would much rather not think about. Tufts of dying grass sprouted up from the middle of the road. Glancing both ways, Maggie couldn't remember which way she needed to go. She knew she couldn't afford to go the wrong way, so she closed her eyes and pushed away the fog and cobwebs that shrouded her memories. Sarah had given her new directions in her dream last night and she needed to recall what she'd said. Sorting through each moment, she found what she was looking for.

"In the morning, follow the rising sun."

The sun rose to her left. Happy to see no trees, rocks, or bushes impeding her, Maggie stretched her legs and prepared to run. She wanted to make up for lost time and running would warm up her cold, numb limbs.

"That way it is," she said.

Despite her hunger, Maggie ran for hours. She stopped a few times along the way to drink from a stream or forage berries, but she kept up a leg-numbing pace. When her shadow stretched far ahead of her, she finally slowed down. Pain gnawed at her stomach and her throat was dry. She was on the verge of collapsing but felt no closer to reaching Sarah. Discouraged, she sat down and breathed out a plume of frozen breath. Dropping her chin to her chest, she closed her eyes. As soon as they were closed, they flashed back open. A face was floating in the darkness behind her eyelids. A familiar face. She slowly closed them again. It was Sarah.

"What are you doing?" Maggie asked. "How are you doing this?"

"You're finally close enough for me to reach out like this. I've been trying all day but could never reach you. Listen to me carefully. I'm using the last of the strength I can spare to do this. The gallows are complete and they mean to hang me soon. You mustn't rest."

Sarah's face dissolved into the black void. Maggie struggled to her aching feet, though her legs pleaded with her to sit back down. Her back spasmed in protest but her spirit won out. Pushing on, she jogged down the trail. After a mile or so, the trail merged with a much larger road.

Now that evening was properly falling, Maggie chased after her waning shadow. As she ran, she heard a rumbling off in the distance. It wasn't loud but it made her wary. Without using her powers, she could tell it was getting closer. Slowing to a walk, she focused. Ignoring the rest of the world around her, she heard it clearly. The sound of metal rubbing against wood. The turning of wheels on axles. It wasn't the best construction and was laden with furs and other trinkets. It was the cart of a traveling merchant pulled by a stocky, aging donkey.

A sigh of relief escaped her lips. When she saw the man leading it, she ran ahead, waving an arm in greeting. She hoped he would have something to eat.

"Hello," the man called out as he watched her approach. "What can I do for you this fine evening?"

"Do you have any food for sale or trade?" Maggie asked.

"As a matter of fact, I do," the man said, looking her up and down with a smile.

Without taking his eyes off her, he reached down into the cart, wriggling his hand to the bottom. He withdrew a handful of dried meats and crisp fall carrots. Maggie's mouth watered.

"How much for all of it?" she asked.

"For this? Just a bit of conversation."

Agreeing, Maggie took the food from his outstretched hand and began to eat. The man watched her chew, his smile never faltering. She had an uneasy feeling about the way he was leering at her but ignored her instincts out of hunger.

"What brings someone like you to a place like this so late?" he asked.

"I'm looking for a friend of mine," Maggie said, her mouth full. "She should be close. She's waiting for me at a small outpost near here."

"Interesting," the man said, stepping closer. "There is an outpost a short distance down the road, but no women are there. Only soldiers."

"Maybe she's running late."

"I doubt that. No one should be traveling around this late in the evening. Especially in places like this."

"Why not?" Maggie asked. "Is it dangerous?"

"More than you know," he replied as he lunged at her.

"What are you doing?" Maggie screamed as the last of her food fell to the ground. The man attacked her, pressing her violently against the wagon and pinning her arms behind her back.

Fighting against his grip, Maggie realized it was useless. He was much stronger than he looked. He held her with one hand while the other fished through the cart, searching for something.

"Now you'll be able to pay me back for those morsels," he said, pulling a short length of rope free.

Maggie struggled against him, but it was no use. His grip was like an iron vice. She yanked and pulled as the rope was looped around her wrists. Kicking out, she struck the old man on the knee. Even through the pain, he was able to hold her in place. Limping as he moved, he tied the other end of the rope to the cart. When he finished, he smiled and rubbed his leg.

"You have spirit, girl," he said with a sneer. "But that will do you no good now. What I have planned for you will break you much faster than you know. I will make a good profit on you."

"You plan to sell me?" Maggie cried.

The man laughed as he prodded the donkey. With a lurch, the cart rolled ahead, pulling Maggie along behind it. Fear rose in her chest. She didn't have time for this. Sarah was in danger and if she let herself be abducted, they would both die.

"No. Let me go," Maggie screamed as she pulled against the rope.

"Those knots are solid, my pet. You will not be wriggling your way out of them anytime soon," the man said with a chuckle, not bothering to look back.

Maggie ignored him and continued to work at her knots. Throwing glances over her shoulder, she could see the light of torches being lit. She was so close but now it seemed like her adventure would end as suddenly as it had started.

As the man had said, the knots were expertly tied. With her hands bound as they were, she could not work them loose. She gazed up at the moon, which was peeking out from behind the treetops.

"Please, give me strength," she pleaded.

"What was that?" the man asked.

"You are a horrible person. Let me go this instant."

"I'm not horrible, I just take an opportunity when it presents itself. And trust me, no amount of pleading will earn your freedom. If it would, I would be out a lot of money. Get used to the fact that this is your new life. Taking orders."

With each step, Maggie felt her connection with Sarah growing weaker. From the back of her mind, she could make out a faint whisper calling out to her.

"Where are you going?"

"He's taking me away," Maggie answered silently. "He tied me to his wagon and he won't let me go."

"Remember who you are and what you can do. If you let him take you, chances are we'll both be dead by morning."

Maggie shook her head, letting the paralyzing fear loosen. The rope had already begun to redden her skin. Sarah was right, she had to do something. Deep inside, she felt a cold, prickling sensation lingering behind her heart. She focused on it, urging it to grow. The sensation was familiar, but she'd always pushed it away, fearing it would cause trouble. Now she called out to it. She needed its help. Heeding her will, the cold spread through her body. It raced through her arms and leaped from her fingertips. While she watched, the strands of rope froze and cracked as frigid air flowed from her hands. When she pulled back, she felt the rope start to give. Frozen white flakes fell from it, leaving gaps in the rough surface.

"Stop all that fighting. You're scaring Marjorie," the man said.

Contempt coursed through her body as she yanked hard on the rope. It shattered, freeing her hands from their bonds.

"What have you done?" the man screamed as he spun on her.

Seeing the broken, stiff, ice-covered nub of rope swinging from the side of the wagon, he glanced warily at Maggie. "You're one of them witches, aren't you?"

Maggie sprinted towards the outpost without a reply, tears streaming down her face and a sob caught in her throat. Relief thundered through her and she was astonished at what she had done. The icy cold of her power had destroyed the rope yet had done nothing to her skin. In fact, it seemed to heal her. The red had vanished. The air around her hands still crackled with brittleness as she flexed her fingers. Her chilling power hadn't retreated into her chest yet. Holding it near the surface, she ran.

TAKING COVER BEHIND a large willow, Maggie got her first look at the small compound. It was little more than a clearing with three buildings at the far end, five tents spread across it, and erect gallows standing in the middle. Sarah had to be in one of the buildings, Maggie thought. Half a dozen soldiers milled about between her and her goal and another two were talking near the gallows. More men loitered near the far tree line.

Maggie closed her eyes and listened, pushing the obvious sounds away, and was left only with the sounds of human breathing. She counted thirteen people total, two of whom were sleeping. When she felt confident that she'd counted correctly, she turned her attention to the buildings. Sarah would be in one of them. One by one, she silenced the breathing of each soldier until only one remained. It was light and ragged, a sure sign of anxiety. It was coming from one of the buildings but Maggie couldn't know which one for sure. Letting the sounds return, Maggie crawled through the tall weeds away from the road. She paused when two of the soldiers walked past, though they took no notice of her in her hiding spot. When they were gone, she poked her head out into the open next to the closest building. Was this the jail, she wondered? There wasn't a window on this side. The cell Sarah was in had a window. If there was one on this building, it would be on the other side.

She waited until the guards had moved on and then bolted from the weeds, pressing her back flat against the side of the building. The moon cast dark shadows around her, hiding her from sight. Inching her way to the back, she found no window there either. She poked her head around the other side. No windows. This wasn't the jail. Dashing from her cover, she rolled across the grass to the neighboring building.

"Intruder," a voice rang out, breaking her fragile cover. "Over by the jail."

Maggie scrambled to the back of the jail, hiding between a pair of wooden barrels. Crouching, she didn't notice the window above her head or the arms reaching out.

Five men rounded the corner armed with swords, daggers, and bows. They were dirty, tired, and smelled horrible. Maggie almost gagged but managed to suck in a quick breath and hold it.

"Are you sure you saw something?" one of the soldiers asked.

"Of course. It came this way."

"What was it?" another asked.

Panic gripped Maggie's heart but she managed to control her breathing. How have they not seen me by now, she thought?

"Don't know. It was big. I saw it crawling across the ground. Big as a wolf, it was."

With their backs to her, the men stared out into the woods that surrounded the compound.

"Do you think the hunter is still around? That wolf of his was big enough to tear us apart without thinking twice."

Maggie felt herself slipping. Her lungs burned for want of air, begging for relief. If she let it out, the men would be on her in an instant. With an aching chest, she reached out for one of the barrels to steady herself. Feeling out for the rim, her fingers brushed against a glass lamp. It wobbled. Maggie cursed herself for her stupidity. Throwing out her hands to steady it, it bounced off her palm and crashed to the ground. The men spun on her. Not seeing the point in holding her breath anymore, she exhaled, gasping in clean, fresh air.

"What was that?"

The men were staring directly at her but acted as if they couldn't see her.

"It was just the lantern. One of you must have knocked it over. Now keep quiet or we'll never catch what's out there."

Frozen in place, Maggie resisted the urge to flee. How hadn't they caught her? Her mind reeled for an answer but found none. She was confused. Staying put, she waited until the men had disappeared into the woods. When they were out of sight, she slowly stepped away from the building. She scratched her head and turned around. Sarah's face grinned at her from between the bars of a window.

"It's about time you showed up. I was starting to worry," she said.

"What happened?" Maggie asked. "Why couldn't they see me?"

"That was just a simple mind trick. Hurry, it will be easier to escape while they are distracted."

Sneaking back around the way she came; Maggie was careful not to break anything else or step on any of the glass she had already broken. When she reached the front, she stepped up onto a small porch. A rickety wooden chair leaned against the wall near the door and a rusty tin plate sat next to it. A half-eaten chunk of meat steamed in the cold air. Whoever had been sitting there must have left with the others. They would most likely be back soon. Darting across the worn planks, she pushed open the door and slipped through, coming face to face with the biggest man she'd ever seen in her life. He was a giant and the sword he was holding was equally as large.

"What in the world . . . ," he began. "What in tarnation are you doing here, girl?"

He reached out a meaty hand bigger than her head, grabbing for her neck. Maggie dodged it and rushed to the far side of the room, which was smaller than it looked from the outside. She quickly realized that the building was split into two rooms. The cell would be on the other side of the wall. A skinny door stood in the middle of it, blending in with the wood. It taunted her with the possibility of escape from the mountain of a man behind her. She lunged at the handle but it wouldn't turn. The guard laughed.

"I'm afraid no one is getting in or out of there without these," he said, hefting a thick chain from his leather belt. Two large keys hung from it. "I'm the only one who has them and no one gets in there without me."

An alien sensation surged through her body. It felt primal and she wasn't expecting it. When the man lifted his sword from the floor, preparing to attack, Maggie chuckled. Pushing off the door, she leapt into the air, spinning past the blade that now hurtled towards her. Slapping the steel with her palm, the sword faltered just enough to let her pass without slicing her in half. As she soared higher, she tucked herself into a tight ball. Turning in the air, she planted her feet firmly against the ceiling and kicked out, launching herself back towards the floor. At the last second, she twisted, landing lightly on the floor behind the guard.

"How did you do that, you slippery weasel?" the guard bellowed as his sword sunk into the floor where Maggie had just been.

Striking out with a tightly clenched fist, Maggie struck the man's thigh with a precise blow, pushing him off balance. Before the man could right himself, Maggie swept out with her leg, knocking the guard's feet out from under him.

He crashed hard to the ground, his head bouncing off the wood. His body convulsed then fell still as his eyes rolled into the back of his head. Cocking hers, Maggie listened to his faintly beating heart. Relief flooded through her once she confirmed he wasn't dead. She gripped the chain around his belt and pulled the keys free. When she unlocked the door, she rushed through and slammed it shut behind her. Sarah was standing at the cell door, silently waiting for her.

"Sounds like you had a good bit of fun in there," she said.

"What are you talking about?" Maggie asked, not quite sure how she'd gotten in there. "What happened?"

"What do you remember?" Sarah asked.

"Walking through the door and seeing that huge soldier."

Maggie turned around and looked out the door. The man was on the ground, groaning in pain.

"I did that?" Maggie cried.

Sarah nodded, a grin creeping up her cheeks. "Yes, you did that."

"How?"

"It's not uncommon for young, untrained witches. Your mind knows what you are, even if you don't. When it feels threatened, it takes over," Sarah explained. "But you shouldn't rely on that. It is better to rely on your skill and knowledge than to wait for instinct to take over. Knowing what you are doing is much better than waking up to see your handiwork for the first time."

Maggie was both amazed and sickened by what she had done. "I could have killed him."

"You could have, but he could have done worse to you. When he stopped being a threat, your mind returned control of your body."

"How do I stop that from happening?" Maggie asked. "That's kind of scary."

"Learn what you are capable of and train yourself. Once you've done that, you will always be able to protect yourself without instinct taking over. Now, how about you get me out of here? I don't want to waste any more time in this pitiful excuse for a prison."

When Maggie unlocked the cell door, Sarah charged from the room, leading Maggie past the downed guard, his body still prone on the ground. Sarah flung open the door and froze.

"Don't let them escape," came a shrill cry.

Peeking past Sarah, Maggie stared at a dozen men in full armor, all holding weapons, blocking their way.

"Well," Sarah said with a smile. "It's time to see what we can do together. This many men against two witches? Hardly seems fair."

Sarah jumped and grabbed the lip of the roof. Pulling herself up, she disappeared, leaving Maggie to face down the small army in front of her alone. They stared at her, swords and spears pointing at her face. A few men stepped forward. Maggie took a step back into the room.

She wanted to curse Sarah for leaving, her but her mouth wouldn't work.

"You two," a voice boomed. "Go around back. We can't afford to lose her."

The pounding of footsteps echoed above her. Looking up, Maggie watched Sarah soar from the roof, then land lightly behind the soldiers, who somehow didn't notice. They were still focused on her.

"Get ready to run," Sarah's voice said in her mind as she pointed at the two soldiers closest to her. "You'll know when."

Sarah contorted her face. One of the soldiers she pointed at turned on the other, a confused expression on his face. Lifting his arms, he pointed his sword and charged.

"Look out!" the soldier cried as he ran down his companion.

"Stewart? What are you doing?" the other man cried, barely throwing up his sword in time to parry the attack.

Moonlight danced off the metal blades as they met together in battle. The sounds of the clashing swords were enough to rip the soldiers' attention away from Maggie.

"Stop it," a voice commanded. "The witch is controlling you."

A barrel-chested man stepped towards the brawlers. The soldier Sarah was controlling turned to face him. Fear shone in his eyes. His arms were shaking, causing the point of his sword to bounce around aimlessly, keeping the others at bay.

"Take it easy," the commanding officer said. "Calm yourself."

He glanced at another soldier, an archer, giving a silent command. From the back, the archer raised his bow and pointed an arrow at Sarah's chest.

"Let my man go and I will not fill you full of holes."

Maggie was surprised to hear Sarah laugh.

"Oh, you won't kill me if I let him go? Then what were you planning to do with that?" she asked, pointing towards the gallows. "No, I think I'll take my chances with the arrows."

The archer's fingers vibrated with anticipation. Maggie's body leaped into action without her consent again, taking her along for the ride. She jumped from the porch, clearing the tallest of the soldiers with ease. The cold spark hiding behind her heart spread, racing through her. Her body sensed a threat and was doing what it needed to. She was more aware this time though. The numbing cold flowed through her arm and out her fingers. As the bowstring was loosed, pushing the arrow towards Sarah, the air between Maggie and the shaft of the moving arrow glimmered with cold. The air worked and twisted its way forward like a living being, sliding up and down the bow, sparkling as it enveloped the passing arrow.

Still soaring through the air, Maggie clenched her fist. The shimmering trail of cold instantly hardened to ice, halting the arrow before it left the bow. Flipping over, she touched down next to the archer. With a single jab to the neck, the man dropped his weapon and fell.

"Go," Sarah's voice shouted in her head. "I'll be right behind you."

Maggie sprinted between the buildings and into the trees. Glancing over her shoulder, she tripped and crashed to the ground. She tried to push herself up but was violently shoved back down.

"You're not going anywhere, witch."

The only things she could see were the grimy fabric of the man's blue pants and his muddy shoes. She felt the cold steel of a sword touch the back of her neck. She was terrified.

"Sarah," she screamed. "Help."

"No one is going to help . . . ," he said, then crumpled next to her. Sarah was standing behind him, a shovel in her hands.

"Go," she said, helping Maggie up. "I'll do my best to hold them off."

She didn't have to be told twice. She sprinted away, listening to the thundering pursuit behind her. Every few seconds, a deep moan or unmanly scream rang out through the woods as Sarah attacked another soldier with her shovel. Squinting in the dim moonlight, Maggie ran hard, desperate to put as much distance between them as she could.

CHAPTER 10

Tracking the witch had almost been relaxing. Her trail was so easy to follow, either Loravain or Thanatos could have tracked her in their sleep. The direction she was heading was clear. At times, though, she veered off course for miles before righting herself.

"It's like she's being guided by a blind beggar," Thanatos said.

Loravain agreed that the trail was odd but what more could they expect from a witch who had been raised as a human by two herb farmers?

"These people aren't used to being cautious. They have no reason to hide their tracks. They are lucky."

"Well, this one might not be if we aren't the first ones to find her. We need to pick up the pace," the wolf said.

They had walked for a day and a half since speaking with Maggie's father, and they were catching up. The trail was fresh and her scent was strong. Thanatos could find her by that alone.

Rounding a large evergreen, a sunny meadow came into view. Bright blue flowers blossomed despite the nip to the air. They moved into the open, finding a small circle of burned grass. Striding over to it, Loravain held his hand over the ashes and closed his eyes. He could sense the heat that had lingered in the coals. From what he could tell, it had been a weak fire, nearly dying more than once before being brought back to life. He lowered his hand even farther, dipping his fingers into the dead coals. He frowned as he sifted through them.

"The embers have been cold for hours, but are not yet a day old. We are getting close."

"What will be done when we find her? If you are going to go against your master's wishes, we must have a plan."

The wolf was right. Loravain hadn't decided what he would do when he found her. He only knew she was important, though he didn't know why. The pieces of the puzzle kept shifting in his head.

"We know she is young. She was raised by humans, so she does not know the extent of her powers. At the very least, she knows little. She has a good heart if we are to believe her father's words, who seemed to be a trustworthy fellow. Yet the master fears her. There are too many missing pieces. If only we had a way to discover more."

Thanatos paced back and forth while Loravain spoke. His ears perked at certain words. The hunter knew an idea was brewing in his mind.

"If we are to proceed with the information we currently possess, we could be going about this all wrong. We might assume the world would be in danger if the girl lived, and by fulfilling your mission, you are doing good. However, if she can undo the evil deeds of your master, bettering the world in the process, then by letting her live, you are doing good."

"The only way to get the information we need is by finding the witch," Loravain said.

The giant wolf shook its mangy head. "That might not be true. She may know as little, if not less, than we do. We must seek knowledge elsewhere."

"If you believe the girl knows nothing, then how . . . ?" Loravain paused when he understood what Thanatos was suggesting. "You mean the owl?"

"She may be able to shed some light on this matter. She has lived at least as long as I have, if not longer. She has many allies and connections."

"You told me she could not be trusted," Loravain said.

"When it comes to your predicament, she cannot be. She has never taken a liking to the darker practices of this world. However, we may have a good chance of her taking an interest in this."

"How long would it take you to find her?" Loravain asked.

"Not long. I can signal her if needed. You continue after the witch, and I will go speak with her. Once I know more, I will find you."

Loravain had no time to reply before Thanatos sped into the underbrush, racing back the way they had come, a single guttural howl piercing the air. Loravain remained next to the dead fire, brushing the ashes from his fingers. Glancing around the meadow, he focused on the path he would take. This would be too easy.

Thanatos charged through the forest, dodging trees, bushes, and other obstacles. He knew exactly where he was going. She could usually be found near the same place this time of year. With winter coming, the owl tended to hunt mice and maturing foxes that called the tight groves of Cauldron's Forest home.

He'd been calling out to her throughout the day and was positive she'd be waiting for him when he arrived. He had to be careful. She had been known for her fierce temper, but it had been many years since they had last spoken.

The scent he was following changed abruptly, bringing the wolf to a swift halt. He sniffed the air. The owl was close. The smell of the ancient creature was unmistakable. She would be aware of him as well. Caution was essential. Peering up into the branches of the trees surrounding him, he searched for her bright yellow eyes. His were more than capable of spotting her, even at the tops of the massive trees. But she was not there. In the owl's absence, Thanatos dropped to the ground, eager for the rest he had earned.

Moments after dropping to his haunches, a giant great horned owl glided through the air, landing lightly in the branches of a mighty oak tree. Settling in, she began to feast on the meal she had caught. Thanatos sat in silence, waiting.

"What brings you here, old friend?" the owl asked when her meal was finished.

"I am here on behalf of my companion," Thanatos answered.

"Why do you continue to subject yourself to serving a mortal human? It is beneath you and you know it."

"This life we live is a lonely one," the wolf replied. "Even you need companionship. There are some things I am not able to do in this form, so I take help where I can get it."

"And what is it you have come to ask me?" the owl asked. "You know I will not help him. He got himself into this mess, he can get out by himself."

"Things have changed, Gwendolyn," Thanatos said. "I know you are unwilling to help Loravain, but he is not the reason I am here. I may be here on his behalf, but there is something else troubling me. The Dark One has offered Loravain his freedom."

The owl stopped what she was doing and stared at Thanatos. She was well aware of what the man had been through. She knew what he'd been forced to do and whom he served. Granting the human's freedom was not something this creature would do lightly.

"What must he do? To even consider freeing a slave as productive as Loravain, this mission must be dangerous in ways that even the Dark One would not risk going on his own."

"He has been ordered to kill a witch."

"Nothing out of the ordinary from what he has done before," Gwendolyn said.

"This witch is young, untrained, and unaware of what or who she is. Until recently."

"Go on," the owl said.

Thanatos shared everything he knew with her.

"A single witch, raised by humans, threatens to undo the demon's work in this world?" Gwendolyn asked. "You are wise to seek me out. This task seems too simple to win Loravain his freedom. There must be more to this hiding below the surface. This is not something I would usually trouble myself with, especially at my age, but this bears the winds of change, for good or evil. What do you want from me?"

"If the Dark One is worried about this witch, we need to know more about who she really is. What makes her such a powerful threat? If she is as formidable as the Dark One thinks, will Loravain even stand a chance against her? This is the information I seek. Do you know where to find it?"

Gwendolyn shuffled down the branch she was perched on. "I remember hearing a rumor once, years ago. A lost child and a grieving queen. But too much has been forgotten. I must consult with Duncan, who has spent much of his time among the covens. He may have the knowledge that could aid us. When I learn something that will help the situation, I will find you. Until then, do not let any harm come to this witch."

Spreading her wings, Gwendolyn stepped off the branch and disappeared into the night, leaving Thanatos alone at the base of the tree. Lying down, the wolf closed his eyes to sleep. It would be a long journey back and he would need his rest.

An unnatural silence had fallen over the small compound Loravain walked into. There was an air of military to the scene, and he didn't like it. He'd had more run-ins with the militia than he cared to think about. They always seemed to be out for blood and didn't care where they got it from. A gallows had been erected in the center of the compound, proving his point. A jail, command post, and storage shed stood at the edge of the clearing to his right. The emptiness was unsettling. No guards or soldiers could be seen and no workers manned the gallows. Loravain strode towards the center of the compound next to the gallows and turned in circles. Tent flaps danced in the night breeze and the cool moisture on the blades of grass at his feet had begun to freeze. Glancing inside a few of the tents, he found them empty. The place had been abandoned. He examined the buildings next, finding the command post and shed empty as well. The only person he encountered sat in the guard room of the jail nursing a head wound.

"Nasty bump you have there," Loravain said, sitting down next to him.

"Speak of it again and you'll have one to match," the man fired back.

"What's your name?" Loravain asked, unaffected by the anger in the guard's voice.

The man looked at him, suspicion in his eyes for a moment, then gave into the conversation.

"Markus."

"Well, Markus, it looks like you've had a rough go of things tonight."

"You can say that again. The whole command is out there now searching for the witch that escaped."

"Tell me what happened," Loravain said. "By the look of things, there should have been at least fifteen guards stationed here."

"There was," Markus verified, wincing as he repositioned the damp rag on his forehead. "Not enough, was it? That witch knew what she was doing. Summoned another one to break her out. We shoulda been expecting that."

"Summoned another witch? How did she do that if she was locked up?" Loravain asked.

"There ain't no telling how any of them do what they do. All I can tell you is that door flew open, and I was attacked before I could do anything about it. Put some kind of spell on me, she did. Evil they are, the whole lot of 'em."

Most humans were biased when it came to witches. Witches and humans had a volatile history and pressing it would only make the situation ugly, so Loravain changed the subject. He did not want the story to be exaggerated to the point of fiction.

"What was supposed to happen here tonight?" he asked, motioning out the door towards the gallows.

"We was gonna hang her. The blond one. It would have been over and done with by now had the other one not shown up."

Loravain stood and paced the room. An itch was forming at the back of his mind, illuminating a few more pieces to the puzzle.

"How long had the blond witch been here?" he asked.

Markus looked him in the eyes. "You should know. You were the one who done caught her for us. You're the witch hunter, ain't you?"

"This was the witch I caught a fortnight ago?"

Markus nodded, acting as if the conversation had completely exhausted him. Loravain studied the room. The door to the cell was wide open. Striding over, he peered inside.

"Do you mind if I take a look?"

"It's empty in there now but knock yourself out," Markus said.

Loravain closed the door behind him. He rubbed his forefinger and thumb together, igniting a small flame between them. Slowly, and by will alone, he urged the tiny flame to grow higher until the room was cast in dim, dancing light. Nothing seemed out of place.

The door to the cell had not been forced. A bed, hardly large enough for one person, sat under the single window in the cell. Next to it was a dirty jug, most likely the toilet. Something was off about the bed though. Taking a closer look, Loravain noticed two indents in the mattress directly below the window. Someone had stood there recently. He closed his eyes, trying to remember what the witch he'd captured looked like. He pictured her standing on the bed, just tall enough to look between the bars. Something had happened outside.

He returned to the guard room and excused himself. Markus only grunted as he left. At the back of the jail, a few items littering the ground piqued Loravain's interest: a pair of large wood barrels, a small, broken lantern on one, and sacks of who knew what on the other. He picked up the lantern and turned it over in his hands. The chimney was missing and the casing was bent. He found a few shards of glass stuck between the frame and the metal housing upon closer inspection.

"Interesting," he whispered and then continued to look around.

Stepping back, something cracked under his boot. Spread around the grass was more broken glass. Someone had taken the time to pick up the lantern but didn't clean up the glass. They must have been in a hurry. Now paying more attention to the ground, Loravain noticed multiple sets of footprints. Most were larger, the size of men's feet. One was smaller and lighter. The grass next to the building had been flattened as well. Pacing, Loravain deduced that the small footprints, most likely belonging to the summoned witch, had come to the back of the building, hid between the barrels, and then ran back towards the front. Following them, he traced the trail back to the porch he'd just left.

The grass around the front of the building had been trampled. By the size of the area, he assumed a large body of at least a dozen men had congregated there. Scouring the grass, he saw what he thought was more glass. He was wrong. It was cold and wet. The night was brisk but not cold enough to form a piece of ice that big. Something unnatural had taken place.

The conversation he'd had with Tomas Rainer came to mind. His daughter had come home with cold welts across her backside. Could the same person have caused this as well? He tossed the ice back to the ground and followed the shuffle of feet into the woods. They were hard to spot amid the stampede of soldiers' boot prints, but it was clear. Two smaller sets of footprints fled into the woods while the mob gave chase. That was not a good sign. Loravain broke into a sprint, hoping he wasn't too late.

CHAPTER 11

Maggie and Sarah ran for hours. The moon traveled across the sky as they went, losing itself in the branches, clouds, and then finally the horizon. The edges of the sky were starting to glow with pre-dawn light when they stopped. Leaning against the trunk of a large tree, Sarah took longer than her usual five seconds to relax as she listened for the sounds of pursuit.

"I think that's it. We've lost them for good now."

Not caring where she sat, Maggie dropped to the ground and planted herself in the dirt to catch her breath. As she did so, she closed her eyes and shut out the world, sound by sound.

"You're right," she confirmed. "They must have turned back. How long do you think we've been running?"

"Too long. They were determined but what chance did they have in a race against two witches?" Sarah asked, a wild grin playing across her face.

"Now what?" Maggie asked.

Sarah's weary body slid down the trunk of the tree and she collapsed next to Maggie. Her breathing had gone from ragged to controlled in seconds while Maggie still struggled to keep hers quiet.

"As far as I am concerned, you kept your end of the bargain, and quite brilliantly I might add. It's time I kept mine. I told you I would take you to Priama. May I ask why you want to go there?"

Maggie glanced at her nervously, appraising her. She wanted to know if Sarah was trustworthy before revealing who she really was. Or who someone said she was. For now, she decided to keep her secret.

"My mother lives there," she said.

"How do you know that?" Sarah asked. "You've lived with humans all your life with no contact with our world."

"I always knew I was orphaned as a baby," Maggie said. "Until recently, I thought nothing existed from my birth parents beside me. Not long after I dreamed about you, my parents gave me a letter and said it was left with me as a baby. It was written by my birth mother. She told me that Priama is my home."

Sarah turned away from Maggie and stared out into the trees. "Priama is not the safest place to be right now. There is a power struggle going on. I've been told the Queen is dying."

"What?" Maggie gasped, almost shouting. "How?"

Sarah glanced at her quizzically then focused on the ground where she drew in the dirt with her finger.

"All I hear are bits and pieces. Ever since I distanced myself from that life, information has been hard to come by, but the state of the Queen and the Coven Seat is known everywhere."

"Why did you distance yourself?" Maggie asked.

"I never managed to see eye to eye with the other witches. At least not the ones I was raised by. They like to live one way, whereas I prefer another. After one too many heated arguments, I knew I had to leave."

"How long have you been on your own?"

"Nearly ten years," Sarah said.

"I've always wondered what it would be like to be on my own," Maggie commented, pushing away from the tree trunk and lying down to stare at the glowing sky. She positioned herself as comfortably as she could between the knotted roots jutting out of the ground. "But when I left home to find you, I changed my mind. I've never been so scared before."

"It was difficult for me too, when I first left," Sarah said. "Entering the world of men was hard. In the beginning, I tried to hide who I was and to deny my power, but it was a part of me. To not use my powers would be a betrayal of who I really am. You're lucky. You never had to learn how to hide what you are."

"I had to hide what I could do," Maggie said. "Even though I never knew what I was, there were still things to hide. I could do things no one else could. How old were you when you left?"

"Probably a little older than you. What are you, sixteen?"

"Fifteen."

"I was eighteen when I left," Sarah said.

"So, you knew how to use your powers before you left?" Maggie asked.

Sarah nodded. Maggie sat up, a look of determination on her face. This was the moment she had been waiting for. Too many years had been wasted by second guessing herself every day.

"Can you teach me how to use my powers? I'm sick of hiding what I know I can do. My parents were afraid that if people found out what I could do, they would do bad things to me. I don't want to live like that anymore."

Sarah glanced over then hopped to her feet. She stretched her legs behind her then bent forward and placed her palms flat against the ground. "I don't know what I can do for you, but I can try. We need to keep moving though. I won't feel comfortable until we put more distance between those soldiers and us."

With a smile, Maggie stood and stretched as well. They'd been running most of the night and she wanted nothing more than to build a fire and fall asleep. She felt slightly more energized now that she'd been granted a reprieve, but her whole body ached. Each step she took hurt, pain spreading from her toes to the top of her head. Even so, she followed Sarah towards the rising sun.

"Don't break that," Sarah said, glancing over her shoulder. Maggie was pushing aside a branch so she could pass.

"Why not?"

"The more damage we cause, the easier it is for the humans to track us. The easier they can do that, the sooner they'll find us. We need to pass through the woods as if we were never here."

"How do we do that?" Maggie asked, turning around to survey any damage she may have already caused.

"Walk behind me and do exactly as I do."

The way Sarah moved was alien to Maggie, and in the beginning it was painful, but she did her best to mimic her. Slightly bending her ankles outward as she walked, she left behind a less noticeable footprint. Sarah was also more aware of each step she took and where her foot would land. She avoided areas that would leave a deeper footprint or broken branches. Other things were easier for Maggie to imitate, such as stepping on rocks, roots, or larger logs.

"You walk like this all the time?" Maggie asked, a twinge of pain rushing up her calf.

"I have to," Sarah replied, moving behind Maggie. "When I was younger, I was too easy to find. I knew I had to make a change if I wanted to survive out here."

"How did you learn?" Maggie asked before falling. Her foot had become entangled in a system of roots as she tried to step on it. Sarah pulled her to her feet.

"It takes some time," Sarah consoled. "I wasn't always good at it either. Believe it or not, shortly after I left home, I encountered another witch who felt the same way as I did. We spent some time together and she showed me a few tricks to help me survive."

"But you probably weren't as clumsy as I am," Maggie said, reaching out for a tree branch to steady herself.

"No, I don't think I was, but it was still hard to learn."

"Do you think I'll be able to do it?"

"I have no doubt about that," Sarah replied. "I've seen you fight. You have a natural finesse about you, you just have to stop thinking."

Maggie let the conversation slip away as she focused on what Sarah was trying to teach her. Each time she fell or slipped, Sarah would gently lift her up and give her a quick word of encouragement and a few more instructions, and then they would be on their way again.

After half a morning of shadowing Sarah, Maggie felt stealthier, but it had taken a greater toll on her body than her usual careless walking. She was exhausted. Thick drops of sweat rolled down her cheeks and neck, slipping inside her collar, making her shiver.

"Do you think we've gone far enough?" Maggie asked.

Before answering, Sarah backtracked, inspecting their trail. She nodded. "Impressive. You catch on quickly. I wouldn't suggest we stop here though. We need to find a more suitable place to camp. Once we do, we can find something to eat. I'm starving. Soldiers don't feed prisoners well. Why keep the person you want to kill healthy?"

"Food sounds great," Maggie said. "I ran out two days ago. The only real food I've had since then was what that crazy man gave me."

"What crazy man?" Sarah asked.

Maggie told her about the merchant she'd met on the road outside the compound. She explained how he'd tried to trick her and kidnap her as payment for the food.

"I remember that. That is why I felt our connection getting weaker."

Maggie nodded.

"How did you get away?"

"Do you remember what I did to the man with the bow and arrow?" Maggie asked.

"What guy with the bow and arrow? The one the commander ordered to kill me? I didn't see what happened to him. I was too distracted by the sword in my face."

As they worked their way farther away from the soldier's camp, Maggie told Sarah about what she could do.

"Ever since I was a child, there has been a cold spot behind my heart. It never hurt, just a constant pressure I was always aware of. At the time, I thought everyone else had it too. As I got older, I discovered that when I focused on it, it would grow. That scared me. It slipped out a few times, but I was usually good about keeping it controlled. When the man with the wagon took me, I got so scared thinking about what would happen to me. That's when you called out to me."

Sarah listened intently. When Maggie faltered, she urged her to continue.

"He told me he was going to break me. I didn't know what he meant, but I didn't like it," she said, tears forming in the corners of her eyes. She hadn't allowed herself any time to consider what could have happened or process her emotions from the incident.

"That must have been horrible for you," Sarah said, consoling her. "But you were able to get away. You're safe now."

"What if I hadn't been able to? What if he still had me? I got lucky. I could be dead right now."

"Those are impossible questions to answer because things played out a different way. No good will come from thinking that way. Now, tell me how you escaped. The more you open up about it, the sooner you will be able to move on and the more you will understand your powers."

Maggie took a deep breath and pressed forward with her story.

"I knew I had to do something but didn't know how. The man was taking me away. That's when it happened. The same familiar feeling from my childhood spread out from behind my heart. Instead of hiding it or pushing it away, I welcomed it. It gave me hope and the more I focused on it, the faster it spread. Sarah, it was like it knew what I needed from it. My power knew I was in danger, and it flowed through my arms and into my fingers without any coaxing. The air in front of me started to shimmer and get cold, but it didn't bother me. I hardly felt it. It's kind of like when you are watching a blizzard from the warmth of your home. This was the same. When the air was cold enough, the rope began to freeze. I thought I could actually see ice leaving my wrists. Once the rope had frozen solid, it snapped and I was free. I ran before the man could do anything. When the archer was about to shoot you, the same thing happened, only that time it felt more natural."

Sarah nodded knowingly. "The more you use your powers, the more natural they become. Soon it will become second nature, like picking up a rock. You won't have to think about it, it will just happen."

As they talked, a small stream came into view and the thick trees they were walking under thinned out. The dense bushes and underbrush that had been plentiful were gone. They rushed to the water and fell to their knees. Ice clung to the dirt at the edges of the stream, announcing the approaching winter. Maggie was about to stick her face in the stream but Sarah stopped her.

"What?" Maggie cried. "I'm thirsty."

"So am I, but you have to be smart. We don't know if there are any dangers out there. We must use caution, even now. Do as I do."

Sarah immersed a cupped hand into the stream allowing clear water to fill it. She lifted it to her lips while she kept both eyes on her surroundings. Maggie mimicked her.

"That is good water," Maggie said, sipping the water as it dripped between her fingers. She dipped her hand five more times before her thirst was sated.

When she was done, Maggie stood and warmed her hands in her pockets. She glanced around the clearing. The leaves that still hung from their branches were colorful while the ones littering the ground were wrinkled and crunchy. The mountains in the distance were blanketed with snow. Even with the threat of winter lingering in the air, the sky was blue, exposing the sun which gave off just enough warmth to keep them moving.

Sarah scavenged through the autumn debris, finding enough berries and edible leaves and roots to satisfy them for now, but they would need more soon. Maggie had seen a few rabbits bounding about. The thought of hot rabbit stew turned her stomach with hunger. If she could catch one or two, it would end up being the best day since leaving home.

"Alright," Sarah said suddenly, wiping her hands off on a handful of leaves. "Let's see what you've got."

A half-chewed berry fell from Maggie's mouth and into her lap as she stared at her. "What?"

"If you want to learn to control your powers, you must use them. Get up and show me what you can do."

Maggie swallowed her food and stood up. She wasn't expecting to start training so soon.

"Okay, what should I do?"

"Let's start simple. Jump," Sarah said.

Maggie shrugged her shoulders and jumped. Not like a witch but a human. She rose about five inches then clumsily landed on the ground, almost twisting an ankle.

"What was that?" Sarah asked.

"I jumped."

"You jumped? A dying human could have jumped higher than that if they sneezed too hard. Come on, you're a witch. Jump like one. Grab that branch up there."

The branch Sarah pointed at was at least three times as high as Maggie was tall. It reached out from a tree on the other side of the creek.

"I don't think I . . . ," she complained, but Sarah cut her off before she could finish.

"Thinking isn't going to get you up there, doing is. Don't think about what you don't think you can do. If you do that, you never will. You have to try before you know what your limits are. Now jump!"

Maggie hesitated. She glanced from the water, up to the branch, then back at Sarah.

"But . . ."

Sarah charged towards her. A dagger appeared in her hand and her eyes were wild. She sped silently across the frozen dirt.

"What are you doing?" Maggie cried, worry heavy in her voice.

"JUMP," Sarah screamed as she raised the dagger above her head.

She wasn't slowing down. She was either going to stampede over her or stab her. Maggie backed up, stopping when her foot sank into the creek. The freezing water forced her into action. She spun around and jumped, kicking hard off the ground, her body speeding toward the branch. Just when she thought she was going to reach it, she fell.

"Very good," Sarah called out. She had stopped before crossing the stream. "You almost made it. I'm not sure if I could have come that close but it's always good to go big."

Frazzled, Maggie walked up to the water's edge. "What was that for?"

"What?" Sarah asked.

"The knife? The chasing? The screaming?"

"You needed motivation. Fear is a powerful motivator. I've known that for years. Let's try again. This time, try running up to the tree and kicking off the trunk. You might be able to make it that way."

"You tricked me into jumping?" Maggie asked.

"I did and it worked. Now do it again."

The two practiced together for the remainder of the afternoon. Sarah quickly found out that Maggie was much more agile than she was. She could jump higher, run faster, and react quicker. Before Maggie knew it, they were both high up in the trees, leaping from branch to branch in a high-risk game of tag. They soared through the air, landing lightly on the out-stretched limbs of neighboring trees. Maggie laughed as Sarah chased after her. When Sarah landed on the same branch she was on, Maggie would jump higher or tiptoe away, flying into the air once more. Being the more experienced witch, Sarah always caught on to Maggie's tactics and changed strategies.

The game evolved into one of cat and mouse, where instead of tagging one another, their goal became to trick their opponent into false moves that got them caught. Maggie learned that to evade capture, she had to study Sarah and adjust her tactics.

As the day waned on, they found their way back to the ground where Maggie used what she'd learned to catch two rabbits for dinner. Sarah had laughed as Maggie struggled to keep up with them. After multiple failed attempts, Sarah smiled when Maggie began to predict the rabbit's patterns. Soon after that, dinner was caught.

With a fire built, the witches reveled in the coolness of the evening. They'd worked up a sweat and an appetite. Fresh meat and cold stream water resolved both issues. The atmosphere of the night was delightful not only because they had escaped with their lives but because they could be themselves. They shared stories, sang songs from their childhoods, and built memories Maggie hoped would last for a lifetime.

"Why haven't you gone back home?" Maggie asked, taking another bite of rabbit.

"Too many bad memories there. You don't know what witches are really like, or how they treat humans. I tried to get them to change but no one ever listened to me. Our views differed on so many things that I finally decided to leave. The hardest thing about living among humans is their mistrust of witches. We've treated them horribly in the past so they see us all as threats. One day I hope we can change that and live together in peace."

Maggie nodded but didn't understand what she was talking about. "My parents tried to scare me when I was a child with stories of witches. They said if I didn't do what I was told, the witches would come and carry me off, never to see my family again. The thing was that neither of my parents had ever known a witch. I don't think anyone in my village ever had."

"Those stories probably aren't too far from the truth," Sarah said. "Think about how humans use animals. That is how witches use humans. It's not the same everywhere, though. They have a better understanding of life in Priama. More education. The same ideals aren't held or followed in the smaller, independent covens, like where I'm from. That's why I agreed to take you there. They're different. At least that's what I've been told."

"Why do you want to defend humans if they want to kill you?" Maggie asked.

Sarah sighed. "They're afraid, and I don't blame them. We've done terrible things to them. If I hurt them for what they do, then I am no better than the rest of the witches."

"Why not hide your powers and live as a human?" Maggie asked. "It might not be easy, but it has to be better than being hunted all the time."

"Because I'm a witch," Sarah snapped. "I know who I am. I will never hide that, and I'm mortified that you had to. No one should ever have to hide who they are. Witches should be proud to be witches and humans should be proud to be humans."

Maggie felt ashamed for asking the question. She'd always been torn between who she was raised to be and what she felt she might be. She knew she was different, but never knowing she was a witch, she thought she needed to hide what she could do. Her parents even encouraged it. Yet try as she might, she was always seen as different. She wasn't allowed to play with the other children because their parents were afraid of her. But the friends she did have were true.

"I'm sorry," she said. "I didn't mean the question to sound that way."

"I know you didn't. Your life was completely different than mine. But now that you know who and what you are, you should embrace it. Never hide because of what other people may think of you."

The fire crackled loudly when Maggie tossed more branches on it. It was a warm fire but she could still feel the cold creeping in around her.

"Do you know what I don't understand?" Maggie asked.

"What?"

"If the ice inside me doesn't make me cold, why does this weather vex me so?"

"I don't know the answer to that. Maybe you are only immune to the cold of your own magic?"

"Maybe," Maggie replied.

Thoughts about her powers floated around her mind until sleep started tugging them away, tempting her to close her eyes. Giving in, she let the world around her fade away. She sifted through each sound, letting them linger in her mind before pushing them aside. At the edge of the clearing, she heard a sound that didn't belong. Concentrating, the unwelcome sound grew louder until she understood what it was. Her eyes flashed open.

"We're not alone," she whispered to Sarah.

CHAPTER 12

The moon was still visible when Thanatos awoke from his slumber. He stretched his long body and yawned, his pink tongue flopping out of his mouth. Body shaking, he freed his thick, black fur from the leaves and dirt caught there. Bounding into the trees, he followed the same path he'd arrived on. He was disappointed he didn't have more information. Still, Gwendolyn had opened his eyes to possibilities that hadn't been there before.

Exhaustion was ready to overtake him when he entered a small, empty military compound. Loravain's scent lingered in the air. The hunter had been here recently. Thanatos had seen plenty of camps like this one before and knew it should be bustling with activity. By the state of it, it had been abandoned in a hurry. Tents still stood erect and smoke rose from several fire pits dotting the encampment. He couldn't see the tale-tell signs of a battle, so he assumed the soldiers who occupied the camp would be back soon.

Sniffing the air, the wolf quickly located Loravain's scent again and chased after it, leaving the hidden dangers of the compound behind. Back in the underbrush, the smells of at least a dozen others were mingled with his companions. Most were men but the lighter, sweeter scent of women was also present. He also smelled the quiet undertones of magic. That must be the witch they were pursuing. If so, she was becoming stronger. The scent was proof that she'd used her powers recently.

The sun rose into the sky as Thanatos pursued Loravain. He forced himself to go much slower than he wanted to for fear of being discovered. The sun was directly overhead when he encountered his first human. It wasn't Loravain. By the scent, it was a single man who had been cut off from the main group. Hiding out of sight, the wolf waited until it was safe to move again.

". . . Useless to keep trying."

The voice floated through the air well before its owner's body came into view. Thanatos was surprised to hear a second voice reply. He could only smell one person.

"We have to keep on. If the captain finds out we stopped, that will be the last of us. He'll use us to test out the gallows. We have to keep looking for them."

"They're long gone. We could spend all day out here, wandering around in vain, and for what? This search is going to turn up nothing."

"Do what you want, but the punishment will be far greater than you think. Trust me, it is not worth it."

"How can you be so sure? He won't even know if we stop."

"He will."

"How can you be certain of that?"

No reply came. Thanatos perked his ears to listen harder, finally hearing a sigh break the silence.

"Oh, you're probably right. Let's get this over with."

The two moved on. Now that he was getting closer to humans, Thanatos would have to be more careful. Mankind could be vicious and unpredictable. Some creatures were much more dangerous than humans, but you could always anticipate their actions, and more importantly, reactions. It was in their nature. Mankind had no such nature. One person, upon seeing a wolf, would flee. Another would attack.

Thanatos slowed his pace even more, taking time to stalk the rest of the way. When he felt sure he wouldn't encounter another human, he allowed himself a little more speed. Loravain's scent was closer now.

It was the crunching leaves of fall that gave him away. His body rubbed against a large bush as he passed, shaking the feeble branches. Ahead of him, a figure crouched down, hands gripping the pommel of a dagger. The wolf knew who it was but took pleasure in frightening him.

LORAVAIN'S LEGS WERE cramped from hiding in the bushes all morning as he tried to avoid being seen by the soldiers and witches. Startled by a sound behind him, he spun around, ready for a fight. The soldiers he'd already encountered were a mean and vulgar group. They were eager for a fight and wanted to find the witch just to make a show of hanging her. He was ashamed to be from the same race.

He lifted a hand into the air and breathed out. A faint ember floated out of his throat and found its way to his fingers and ignited, enveloping his hand in flames, only to be snuffed out a moment later.

"It's about time," he said to the wolf. "I've been waiting for you. The witches have made camp. They are amazing to watch."

"Witches?" Thanatos asked. "I thought we were only pursuing one."

"It seems the one we've been tracking was on her way to rescue another."

Loravain told Thanatos what happened and what he'd witnessed so far. He explained in great detail how they were able to soar through the tree branches and his voice revealed his envy. "What news do you bring from the owl?" he asked when he'd finished.

"She was more interested in the fact that your master is ready to release you over the death of this witch than that he offered you your freedom at all. She is worried about who this witch might be. She is searching for more information as we speak and will find us once she knows more."

"I thought she might have some insight, but I never thought she would involve herself," Loravain said.

"She feels change coming, and over the years, that is something she has become very good at. It would be wise to listen to anything she might have to say on the matter," Thanatos said as he gazed out at the witches. "Is that the witch you captured no more than a fortnight ago?"

Loravain nodded then turned his attention back to them. The dark-haired one, the one he assumed was his target, was chasing a rabbit around the clearing.

"Her form is all wrong," Thanatos said. "She's never going to catch it."

They were both surprised when the witch changed tactics, quickly overcoming the small animal. Waiting in their hiding spot, they watched the witches build a fire then skin and cook the rabbit. Even when the sun set, the two sat watching. Going up against two witches was always tricky, and when the information they had about their powers was limited, it was all the more dangerous. Loravain didn't know if he should run in and subdue both of them or turn around and walk away. Before he could choose, the choice was made for him.

"We're not alone."

The voice broke the tension and anxiety he was feeling. Both witches were now standing, searching the clearing.

"Where are they?" the blond witch asked.

"This way," their target announced, walking towards them. "I only hear two. One is human, the other isn't."

"Wait," the blond witch said, pulling the other to a stop. "Can you tell if the other one is a wolf?"

Loravain and Thanatos glanced at each other. They shouldn't have been surprised that she would remember them.

"I can't tell. It's big but smaller than a horse."

"We should go," the blond witch commanded, turning and rushing the other way. "NOW," she cried over her shoulder.

"Why?" the target asked, not moving from where she was. "We can handle two."

"Not these ones. We have to go."

"You must act now or risk losing more time. This is your freedom," Thanatos whispered.

Loravain stepped out of the bushes, hands empty and lifted in front of him, showing the whites of his palms.

"I mean you no harm," he said, confronting the witches.

The blond witch snatched a large stick from the fire and threw it at him with blinding speed and accuracy. He deftly dodged out of the way and watched it fall to the ground behind him.

"Maggie, run! Get away from him. This is the man who put me in that cell."

"No," Loravain countered. "I did not put you in that cell. I simply caught you."

"I don't see a difference," the blond witch yelled. "Had you not caught me, I never would have been locked up."

Maggie, their target, watched the exchange with interest, staying rooted where she was.

"Let's go, Maggie."

Maggie faced Loravain. "Who are you?"

"He is a killer. A hired assassin. He is here to catch us and we let him sneak up on us," the blond witch said.

"I'm not here to catch you," Loravain said to the blond witch. "I'm not here for you at all. You can leave if you wish."

"What?" Maggie asked. "You're here for me? Why?"

"To be honest, I was sent here to kill you."

The brutality of the answer knocked Maggie back as if she'd been slapped across the face. She retreated to her friend's side, hands trembling.

"Do you see now?" the blond witch said. "We should leave."

"No, Sarah, I need to know more," Maggie said, then turned her attention back to Loravain. "Why? Why would you want to kill me? I don't understand. Who are you?" The questions rolled out of her mouth unhindered. She shook so badly she almost fell over.

"If you give me a moment to explain myself, I will answer all of your questions and possibly more. You must know that even if I was sent here to kill you, that is not my intention. I am here to help you."

"Why should we believe you?" Sarah asked in Maggie's defense. "You don't care about witches. I've heard of you. You hunt and kill us for money. You have no morals. No conscience."

The words cut Loravain, but he knew they were well deserved, so he chose not to respond. He stepped back and sat down, legs crossed.

"Again, I ask you to let me explain myself. If you are still unsatisfied with the answers I have, you can leave. I promise you will not be harmed and I will not follow you. But be warned, if you leave, you will be putting yourself in greater danger than you have ever known."

"What is that supposed to mean?" Sarah shouted. "Are you threatening us?"

"I will explain everything. You have my word on that."

"What about your wolf?" she asked. "Where is it? Maggie heard it out there."

Loravain gave a short, sharp whistle, signaling to Thanatos. Seconds later, the wolf emerged from the bushes and lay next to his companion.

"Okay, now throw away your weapons. All of them."

The hunter did so. He removed his crossbow from his shoulder and placed it in front of him, followed by a long dagger tied to his thigh. He untied the belt strapped across his chest then placed his quiver next to the blade. Two small knives were fished from his boots and three more from his sleeves. Three small vials, filled with a dark, green liquid, were pulled from a pocket inside his coat, followed by a pair of iron knuckles. When he was done, he looked back up at the witches.

"Is that everything?"

"That is all."

"Fine, tell your story but listen to me first. If I think that for even a second you're deceiving us, we leave."

With a curt nod, Loravain began. "You have every reason to distrust me. I have done things that make me a less than a trustworthy person."

Sarah snorted at his comment.

"Behave yourself, Sarah. I want to hear what he has to say," Maggie said.

"The longer he keeps us here, the sooner we'll be dead," Sarah said but conceded her argument.

"I wasn't always like this," Loravain said. "I was once just a man trying to make an honest living in this world. I even tried to have a family. I was in love if you can believe that. Then, everything was stolen from me. When I tried to get it back, I was tricked and ended up serving a master who has had control of me ever since. The things I have done were not because I desired or wanted to do them. I have done them to earn my freedom. And now, I have been offered that. My final task is to kill Maggie. If I do, I will be set free, which is why you have every right to fear me. However, I cannot do as my master asks. Not yet. I need to know why he wants you dead."

Sarah was about to say something, but Maggie put a hand on her shoulder to silence her. She had questions of her own.

"Why does your master want me dead?" she asked.

"He is afraid of what you will do when you are older."

"And what is that?"

"I don't know the answer to that. All I have been told is that you will be the one to undo what he has been trying to accomplish in this world."

"Who is your master? Is he good or bad?"

Thanatos shot a glance at Loravain. The hunter knew the look in his friend's eyes. He demanded honesty.

"My master is a powerful being. A demon. And he is most assuredly evil," Loravain admitted, ashamed of himself for knowing this but still being willing to serve him.

"So that means I will do something good with my life," Maggie said, a small smile on her face.

"And even knowing that he is evil you still want to kill Maggie? Even if that means more evil will be committed?" Sarah asked.

"No, I do not want to kill her. And no, Maggie, it does not mean you will do something good with your life. You may, but either an act of good or evil could undo my master's actions if it opposes his plans. There is no telling what will be done, only that it will be done."

"How does your master know this? No man can know the future," Maggie asked.

"You are correct," Loravain said. "No man can know the future without help from a greater being. But you must remember that my master is not a man. He is a demon. I have only seen him once in my life. The day my . . . the day this all began. Since that day, I have continued to be affected by his power. I have been the instrument of his handiwork in this world and I do not doubt his power. If he says he knows what will happen, I believe him."

"Why have you not killed her then and earned the freedom you so desire?" Sarah asked.

The sigh that escaped Loravain's lips was long, sad, and full of pain. He picked at the brown grass he sat on and sifted it through his fingers. "I have questioned my actions for years and even tried to defy my master before and felt the full force of his power directly. Since then, I have not hesitated to do what was needed to secure my prize. Until now. This task is by far the easiest he has ever asked of me, and I cannot do it, even with my freedom at stake. I must find out the truth for myself first. If you are not innocent, and you may well not be, I will kill you quickly and have my freedom. But, if you are good, and you can truly help undo what my master has done, then I will aid you, standing with you against him. I will protect you. This is what I should have done from the beginning."

Maggie and Sarah leaned together and began to whisper, stealing glances at Loravain. He shared a glance with Thanatos, which was enough to convey what he was thinking. *I have laid myself out on the table, bearing my heart, full of truthfulness and honesty. What they do next, I take freely.*

"We have come to a decision," Maggie announced after minutes of hushed whispering.

"I'm listening," Loravain said.

"My friend here, who currently hates you and wishes you harm, will see if what you say is true. If it isn't, you will allow us to tie you up, without interference from your wolf, and we will leave. When you free yourself, you will not follow us but will leave in the opposite direction."

"If I was not being truthful, why would we be having this conversation? You wouldn't be alive," Loravain said.

"You may have other reasons," Sarah cut in. "As for now, I have no reason to trust anything you say. Until I can see for myself, I will believe that you are only being calm and reasonable to gain some unknown triumph over us. Understand that I am only doing this for Maggie. If you don't allow us to do as we wish, we will have no choice but to kill you."

Loravain resisted the urge to point out the flaws in her plan. "You may do as you wish. I will neither fight against you nor go against your wishes if you find me to be anything less than honest with you."

Sarah stepped closer to him but stopped when she glanced at his wolf.

"Tell your beast to go," she said.

With a nod, Thanatos stood and walked away. Satisfied, Sarah stepped behind Loravain and put her hands on the sides of his head.

"I'm going to reach into your thoughts. I will not be able to hear them, but I will be able to feel your emotions and your desires. I will be able to tell if you are being truthful."

SARAH CLOSED HER eyes and concentrated. She felt the hunter's thick hair beneath her fingertips. Pushing out, her mind slipped through her fingers and dove into his consciousness. She wasn't prepared for the tidal wave of emotions hiding beneath the surface.

Shame, sorrow, and grief were so thick she could almost touch them. Those three emotions overshadowed everything else. She couldn't imagine living like this. Somewhere deep inside she could sense a trench of pain. It pulsed through him, infecting every other emotion she could feel. It soiled any happy thoughts that tried to surface, pulling them apart until they were indistinguishable from the surrounding gloom. There was no joy, no fond memories, no sense of pride. He had been stripped down to only pain, suffering, and unbearable guilt. Floating deeper into the sea of emotions, she began to understand his driving force. He hated himself for what he'd become and wanted to undo it all. He wanted to repair the damage he'd caused. When she realized that, she felt something foreign. A dim light appeared from inside the pain. It was a small glimmer of hope. A hope that whispered change, forgiveness, and peace.

She worked her way to it, swimming through rivers of heartache. If she could reach it, she would know if she could trust him or not. It was impossible to decipher his intentions from his pain. Truth only came from a positive place.

MAGGIE STARED AT Sarah as she clung to the man's head. She was crying and her knees were shaking. The ordeal must be extremely taxing on her, she thought. Loravain, on the other hand, looked relaxed and peaceful, as if a heavy burden was lifting from his shoulders for the first time in his life. He was smiling. Sarah was not. Her teeth were gritted and exposed and sweat dripped from her brow.

When she was done, her knees buckled beneath her and she collapsed. She clamped onto Loravain's shoulders for support.

"I'm so sorry," she managed to say between sobs. "I had no idea."

No other words were spoken but it was clear that a silent bond had formed between the two. Helping her find strength, the hunter lifted Sarah to her feet and helped her to the fire. Sarah nodded slightly as their eyes met, letting Maggie know that he had passed her test.

"What happened?" Maggie asked.

Sarah shook her head, refusing to answer. She fell to the ground next to the dying embers and folded her knees to her chest. As she continued to cry, Loravain built up the fire to provide her with warmth.

"What happened?" Maggie asked again, directing her question at Loravain now.

"She knows what I've been through and what I'm trying to do. She felt my pain and anguish," he said as if it explained everything.

"What's wrong with her?"

"Nothing. She just needs time for her emotions to level out. It felt like we were one for a moment. I haven't felt that calm in years. It was an amazing experience."

The night continued in an awkward dance between the confused expressions and comments floating around. At moments it was amusing, but mostly it drained Maggie of her strength and she ended up falling asleep next to Sarah, leaving Loravain alone at the edge of the clearing with his wolf.

CHAPTER 13

Firelight danced across the slick, uneven walls of the cave. The smell of death and decay hung in the air. Bones littered the ground, some so old that the cave moss had almost devoured them. Skulls peered out of the small nooks and crannies pockmarking the walls; mouths open wide, warning any unsuspecting visitors to flee. Deaf to the silent pleadings of creatures long since dead, a small man genuflected. His long, unkempt hair fell over his face, hiding his disfigured features. His clothes were tattered and dirty. Holes showed in his knees, proof of years groveling at the feet of those he wished to serve. He waited.

"Dolan." A deep, resonating voice echoed off the polished walls.

At the sound of his name, Dolan forced his body lower, pressing his chest closer to the floor in a vain attempt to show more respect.

"Tell me, Dark Master, what is needed?"

"It pains me to call on you. You are not worthy to look upon the shadow I cast. You sneak around in the darkness, searching for ways to further your station in life, short of working for it."

A wretched smile crept up Dolan's cheeks. He knew the Dark One despised him, but he knew that by completing his tasks, he would rise. He would be great one day, feared not only by men but by all creatures who heard his name.

"Word has reached me of treachery. A crime so appalling that I must have it quelled immediately."

"Tell me, Master, what is it you desire from your humble servant?"

Malevolent darkness fell over Dolan. It was so thick that the flickering flames in the sconces along the walls nearly died. A deep shadow moved through the cave, coalescing into a hooded figure in the middle of the room. When it was fully formed, the light returned to normal. The blood-red maw of a beast protruded from under the cover of a pitch-black cloak.

"Punishment must be inflicted. This . . . situation . . . must be dealt with swiftly and powerfully. I wish to destroy one who was once close to me. A loyal servant of darkness who has been corrupted. Dolan, rise and face me."

As Dolan faced his master for the first time, he failed to hide his fear. The creature under the robe was hideous. Blood dripped from long, misshapen teeth and his eyes radiated a poisonous green. Debilitating cold rolled off his body.

The Dark One's laughter filled the air. "You must be prepared to see much worse than this if you wish to serve me."

"Yes, Master," Dolan said, lowering his head to divert his eyes.

"DO NOT TURN AWAY FROM ME!"

Trembling, Dolan forced his gaze to return to the face of his master.

"If you complete the task I give you, I will raise you up to take the place of the one who has betrayed me. If you fail, your punishment will be greater than his."

Overcome with eagerness to rise in his master's ranks, Dolan was more than willing to accept any mission he might be given.

"I am ready to fulfill any command you have to offer. Name your desire and it shall be yours."

"Do not be so sure of yourself. Only the young and immature would willingly accept a task without knowing what is being asked of him."

"What is the task?" Dolan quickly added.

"You know the price of failure. You have sworn your allegiance to me. You are to hunt the man Loravain, kill the witch he is with, and bring him back to me. Alive."

The color drained from Dolan's face as he began to understand the full depth of his commitment. Loravain was the master's most loyal and feared agent, who had served without question for twenty years, never failing in a single mission. Until now. Backing away, Dolan bowed, sweat dripping from his brow.

"Is it too great a task I have given you, oh great Dolan?" the Dark One asked, chuckling as his form melted back into shadow.

"No, no, Master. I will succeed."

The room fell silent as Dolan slunk away. One by one, the flames in the sconces flickered and died until only one was left burning. Illuminated by the single torch, the Dark One sat on his throne. Gripping a chipped bone in one hand, he scraped dirt from under his claw-like fingernails.

"You pitiful fool. Do you think you will be able to best my most highly trained hunter? He will kill you before you know you've found him, but at least I will know where he is."

Throwing the bone with all his might, it shattered against the rock of the cave wall.

CHAPTER 14

"What do you call this?" Maggie asked, greedily eating the stew Loravain had cooked for breakfast. "It's amazing."

"I don't have a name for it. I just cook what I can find."

"Well, I love it."

"When you spend most of your time on the move, you learn or you go hungry."

"You'd do well as an herb grower. My parents sometimes make money selling herbs and spices for cooking when they haven't made enough selling them for medicine."

The woods around the clearing held a buffet of edible plants, roots, and herbs. Loravain had found enough while hunting the fat and plentiful squirrels to make a thick soup. He'd started a fire before the witches were awake and started cooking. It had been only him and Thanatos for so long he'd forgotten what it was like to serve someone else.

"What's that smell?" Sarah asked, finally stirring.

"Breakfast," Maggie beamed. "Loravain cooked."

Maggie and Loravain had finally gotten around to more formal introductions that morning. Maggie told him about her life growing up in Lakes Hollow. She told him about her childhood dreams and what she wanted to do with her life, which wasn't much as she hadn't experienced too many things.

Sarah blushed when she glanced at him, then rushed to the creek to clean up. Careful not to make eye contact, she knelt down and started washing her face.

"What's wrong with her?" Maggie asked.

"I believe she may understand me a little too well now. Give her some time."

A low howl echoed through the clearing, interrupting their conversation. Dropping the spoon he was holding, Loravain grabbed Maggie by the wrist.

"Gather your things. You and Sarah need to leave. Two days to the north is a town called Raven's Nest. You'll be safe there. I'll come find you."

"What? Why? What's wrong?" Maggie asked.

"I don't know but you must hurry. The longer you stay here, the more danger you could be in."

"What's this talk about going to Raven's Nest?" Sarah asked.

"He says we have to go there because it's not safe here."

"Raven's Nest is not an option. They hate witches there. The last time I went there, I almost died."

"You'll have to lay low somewhere. I don't know what's wrong, but something is. Thanatos wouldn't have signaled me otherwise."

"Your wolf's name is Thanatos?" Maggie asked.

"He is not my wolf and there is no time to discuss this. Go."

He didn't wait for the witches to protest. He gathered the few things he had and rushed out of the clearing, leaving the witches staring at his back.

"What was that about?" Loravain heard Maggie say.

"I don't know, but we are not going to Raven's Nest."

Loravain pushed a broken branch aside and found Thanatos sitting on a large, flat rock overlooking a small but steep ravine.

"What is it?" Loravain asked, glancing through the trees, searching for danger. His crossbow was loaded and ready to fire.

"We have been summoned. Gwendolyn wishes to speak with us."

"The owl wants to see me?"

The wolf nodded as he stood up and padded away, glancing over his shoulder when Loravain didn't follow. "She doesn't like to be kept waiting."

"I thought you said your kind refused to have any dealings with man. Why does she want to see me?"

"I said that most of my kind refused to have any dealings with lesser beings. I deemed you different the day you sacrificed your freedom for the chance to be reunited with your wife. If Gwendolyn wishes to speak with you, it must be of great importance."

"Where are we to meet her?" Loravain asked.

For the first time in a long time, Loravain was nervous. This creature was rumored to be the most intelligent being in the world. He had also heard about her temper. If she was like Thanatos, the inability to be killed paired with that anger would make her a force to be reckoned with.

"Not far," Thanatos said. "We're almost there."

They walked fifty more yards before the wolf brought them to a halt.

"This is it. Wait here until I call for you."

Thanatos disappeared into a thickly grouped grove of trees. Loravain heeded the advice of his friend and stayed where he was. He didn't want to risk insulting either of them, and eavesdropping could prove dangerous. Much sooner than expected, Thanatos returned.

"It is time. You can enter."

Loravain followed the wolf, surprised to find the way in more accessible than he thought it would be. His body slid through a gap that deposited him into a small meadow on the other side. It was deceptively larger than it appeared from the outside. Growing in the center stood a stunted oak tree with wild branches reaching out in all directions. Though it was short, it was an impressive display of nature. Perched on one of the lower branches was a large, beautiful owl. Her eyes, open wide and yellow, never left him as he entered. When he stopped, her gaze turned to Thanatos.

"Gwendolyn has discovered information that makes the situation we face more dire than first anticipated," Thanatos said.

The hunter knew better than to speak out of turn. He nodded silently and waited for the conversation to continue.

"I am impressed by your restraint, human," came the sweet, almost seductive voice of the owl. "Most would not have been able to hold their tongue this long. What do you think of the situation you find yourself in?"

He showed her the respect due to her by dropping his head. "I am no stranger to things beyond my understanding. This was not the case before I encountered my mast . . . previous master. I do not suppose to know the reasons behind what I was asked to do. I have only done what I was told to gain my freedom. Yet now that I have been given a chance, I cannot complete my mission. I am conflicted. By ending the life of this young witch, I will prevent her from undoing deeds wrought years ago. I can't help but wonder what would happen if those deeds were undone. What would happen to the creature I called master? Would he continue to have power over me?"

"The questions are endless, are they not? Yet speculation will do nothing for the problem at hand. The question that remains unasked is what is so important about this particular witch?"

Loravain met the owl's gaze. "I have wondered that myself. Since meeting her, I cannot fathom how she would have the ability to undo anything as powerful as what my previous master enacted. What should I call him now that I no longer serve him?"

"You can refer to him as we all do. He is the Dark One. He is an evil influence in the world desperately trying to overshadow all the good."

"How could this witch, who has no idea who she is, be able to unravel something so dark?" Loravain asked.

"That is the question that has been causing a stir. What do you know of the girl?"

"She has natural talent. Even untrained I can see her potential. She is naive though. She wants to understand the world, but she could easily be turned, corrupted, or worse because of her upbringing. She needs guidance and training."

"And the other witch? Can she be trusted?" the owl asked.

"Her loyalty is no longer in question. She has shared part of herself with Loravain. They have formed a bond," Thanatos said.

"What bond?" Loravain asked.

"Tell me what happened," Gwendolyn said.

"This witch, Sarah, would not allow us to stay with them unless she was allowed to read his emotions. She has skill in mind magic.

When she reached inside, she got more than she bargained for. They are now connected."

"What?" Loravain said. "How do you know that?"

"How he knows will remain unanswered for now. If he says that is what happened, I will trust his judgment. The question of Sarah's trustworthiness will be discontinued. Now, we must discuss what needs to happen next. You must convince the young witch to confirm what I am about to share with you. If she does, she must be protected at all costs. This will be more important than your prior commitment to the Dark One. If I am right, the future of the world could be at stake."

Loravain tried to hide his confusion. He glanced from Gwendolyn to Thanatos. He knew these creatures were ancient and had a deeper understanding of the world, but he had no idea how much. The owl looked at him as if sensing his doubt.

"It is not an easy choice to make. You are putting yourself in considerable danger by aiding this witch. It is a great gamble, but one I hope will pay off in the end," Gwendolyn said.

"What have you learned?" Thanatos asked.

"I learned two things from Duncan," the owl said. "He confirmed that the story I heard was true. The Queen of Priama had a child. Soon after the child was born, she discovered that the baby was in danger. Though she didn't know what the danger was, she didn't want to risk it. The baby was sent away, never to be seen again. For most, the child was believed to be dead. This witch you call Maggie could be the lost daughter of the Queen, the true heir to the Coven Seat of Priama. The throne. If she is, she must be delivered directly to her mother. Troubling times are coming for both humans and witches alike. You must take the girl home. Only this can begin to restore the balance that has been lost."

"If you are correct," Loravain said.

"Yes, if I am correct. Therefore you must confirm the information with her. We must learn if she truly is the heir of Priama. The heir of the Coven Seat. She must know something, otherwise, why would she have left home? There would be no reason."

"And the second thing you learned from Duncan?" Thanatos asked.

"The Queen is dying. She does not have much time left and is currently without an heir. If Maggie is not returned in time, the Queen will be succeeded by another who does not hold the same standards or restraints as her Highness. Duncan fears that her successor has been in communication with the Dark One. If that is true, we could all be in danger. It would mean that his influence is spreading deeper than we had anticipated."

"And what would happen if this rival became queen?" Loravain asked.

"As far as Duncan was able to tell me, she would attempt to unite the tribes and covens by force. The danger lies in the possible war this would inflict on the witches. It would affect the humans as well, as a civil war would reach well beyond the borders of Priama. It would be optimistic to think that only humans and witches would be pulled into this. If the Dark One is involved, you can be certain that other, more vile creatures would come into play, throwing the fate of the world into peril."

Loravain collapsed to the ground. The weight of the world pressed down on his shoulders. How had he gotten into a situation like this? All he wanted to do was the right thing for once. He could not face something like this on his own.

"Fear not, Loravain, son of Vangor," Gwendolyn said, sensing the doubt he was feeling. "There is a way to accomplish all you are destined for. Fate is calling for you to become what you were meant to be from the beginning. When you vowed your service to the Dark One, he started a ritual that has since gone unfinished. He gave you the gift to control fire, but he limited your power to ensure you would never become a threat to him. I desire to give you the instruction you need to complete the rite and become a true Fire Mage. However, you must vow to use this power for good as penance for all the evil you have wrought in the name of the Dark One."

Loravain bowed his head. "I swear to make amends for what I have done. I will protect this witch with my life."

The owl closed her eyes, accepting his oath, then jumped to a lower branch and shuffled out until she was directly over Loravain.

"The information I give you now must be shared with no one except the companions who will accompany you. I speak of the witches you will lead to Priama. You must swear an oath to the Five that you will never speak of the location I am about to reveal to you. You must swear by pain of death. Your death as well as the deaths of any you might tell. Do you swear?"

"What is the Five?" Loravain asked.

"Once the oath is complete, I will provide you with more knowledge."

"I swear to you that I will never disclose that which you are about to reveal to me under pain of death."

"Swear it on the Five," she said again.

"I swear it on the Five," Loravain repeated.

At his words, Gwendolyn hopped to a lower branch and gazed into Loravain's eyes. A profound intelligence burned behind her golden irises.

"I accept your oath, and in so doing, I will reveal who the Five are. The Five are ancient and immortal beings who hold incredible knowledge of the world and the ways of magic. Thanatos and I are two of the Five, and Duncan, who resides in Priama, the third. The others, Heridon and Janora, are much more fierce and deadly. By swearing to us, you have put yourself at our mercy. Secrecy of the oath and the Five must be absolute. Do not bring our wrath upon you."

"What must I do?" Loravain asked as he lowered his head.

"Far to the east is a lone mountain. It is in a perpetual state of eruption. It is known as the Mountain of Fire. It is alive and will grant power over fire to any who are worthy. As you travel, follow the rising sun. On horseback, travel until the sky darkens with smoke. When you see this, your journey will last four more days. Tell none where you are going or what you plan to do, other than your companions. When you finally come to the shadow of the mountain, the setting sun will show you the Guardians of the Path. Here your worthiness will be tested. You must face these challenges alone. If you complete them, and the Guardians find you worthy, you will become a true Fire Mage."

"This is a great honor," Thanatos said. "This offer has not been extended to anyone in the last century."

"It has been much longer than that," Gwendolyn corrected.

"How will this help me atone for my past deeds?" Loravain asked.

"The gift itself will not. No gift will ever do that. You must choose to do so, and that comes from within. The gift we are offering will only provide you with the power to further your own desires."

Loravain bowed again, silently thanking the owl for her help and the information she provided. When he glanced up, both Thanatos and Gwendolyn were staring at him. The conversation was over. He backed away, leaving the two to converse alone.

Outside the grove, Loravain made his way back to the rock that he'd found Thanatos on. He was dreadfully aware that he would be asking for the Dark One's wrath by continuing down the path he was on. Despite that, he smiled.

"I'll make you proud, Camila," he whispered. "Your death will no longer be in vain. I'm going to do what I should have done from the beginning."

"Will that make a difference?" a strange voice called out from the surrounding woods.

Loravain spun around, expecting to find someone behind him. There was no one there. No matter how hard he strained his eyes or how long he looked, he saw nothing. He was still alone.

"Show yourself," he yelled.

No reply came but the message was clear. The Dark One knew about his change of heart. He should prepare for retaliation.

It wasn't much longer until Thanatos rejoined him. He didn't speak, only sat next to Loravain. They sat in silence until Loravain broke it.

"What does it mean to be a Fire Mage?" he asked.

The wolf looked him in the eyes.

"To be a Mage is a great honor, and the fact that Gwendolyn is offering it to you is unheard of. As a Mage, you will be given access to the full powers of fire. Imagine fire enveloping your whole body instead of just your hands. Imagine breathing flames instead of embers. To be a Mage is to be great, but you must respect the power you are given. There is a reason the Mages fell into myth and legend. They forgot their own limitations."

Loravain stared at his hands, trying to imagine what he would be able to do. The desire for power flowed through his thoughts. In his mind, he wielded such magnificent power that none could stand before him, not even the Dark One. Armies fell before his onslaught. It was only the words of his wife that brought him back to reality.

"The evil you served also started with similar aspirations," her voice said.

Humbled, his gaze shifted to Thanatos. He was ashamed of his thoughts. It would be easy to think you were more important than anyone else with that kind of power.

"How does one not abuse such power?" he asked the wolf.

"Never get comfortable with it," he said. "Learn to harness it, but use wise judgment."

Thanatos stood and shook the leaves out of his fur and walked away.

The campsite hadn't been cleaned as requested, nor were Maggie and Sarah gone when Loravain and Thanatos returned. In fact, it was just the opposite. A blanket hung to dry, the fire blazed even hotter, and the witches were up in the trees playing their game of cat and mouse again. When they realized they were no longer alone, they descended from the branches with poise, landing lightly on the ground. Sarah wore a determined expression on her face, ready to defend her decision not to leave. Maggie, on the other hand, looked ashamed and embarrassed to be caught there. It was clear she was not used to defying orders. She stood behind Sarah, ready to let her friend handle the battle.

"Good, I'm glad you're still here," Loravain said quickly, watching the air of defiance deflate from Sarah's face before she had the chance to say anything.

"What?" she stammered.

"There has been a change of plans," Thanatos said, shocking the witches. Maggie almost fell over.

"It talks?" Sarah blurted out.

"It has a name," the wolf said.

"How long have you been able to talk?" Maggie asked, more excited at this revelation than anything else.

"My whole life," he answered, glancing at Loravain as if the question was juvenile and didn't deserve more of an answer. "There is much to do. A trying journey is ahead of you. You leave as soon as you have collected your things."

Loravain caught on to what he was really saying. "Where are you going?" he asked.

"There is another path I must take, but I will see you before your trials start. We need more information and I must go alone to get it. Question the witch as the owl has asked. We must act before the Dark One has a chance to move against you."

Thanatos sprinted away from camp. Loravain watched him until he lost sight of him through the trees. In the last decade, Thanatos had been his constant companion. He'd stood by his side when he'd been torn between doing what he knew was wrong or sacrificing his chance at freedom. The wolf had always been there for him. Now, when he needed him the most, he abandoned him. But there was too much at stake for him to wallow in his self-pity.

"You heard him," he said when he turned around and saw the two witches staring at him. "Maggie, can we talk in private for a moment?"

While Sarah prepared to leave, Loravain led Maggie into the seclusion of the forest. He took her to a small rise where a tall, skinny aspen tree rose into the sky. He sat at the base of the hill, motioning for Maggie to do the same. He waited until she was still, took a deep breath, and prepared himself for the interrogation.

"Why did you leave home?"

The question caught Maggie off guard.

"What? Why do you want to know that?"

"You had a nice home and a family who loved you. What was so important that you would leave all that behind? What are you looking for?"

"How do you know what my home was like?" she asked.

"I spoke with your father."

Tears formed in the corners of her eyes. She tried to respond but her words caught in her throat. It took her a moment to regain enough composure to reply.

"Do you know my father?"

"When I started looking for you, I only knew the name of your village. When I reached Lakes Hollow, I was directed to him. He seems to be a good man. He thought you were in danger, and he was right. You are in danger."

"From you?" Maggie asked through clenched teeth. She glanced over her shoulder.

"No, you are in no danger from me. You are in danger from the creature I served. He will stop at nothing to see you dead. So, you must be honest with me. Why did you leave home?"

"And of all places, why do you want to go to Priama?" Sarah asked, interrupting them.

She walked towards them; a single knapsack hung over her shoulder. Loravain stared at her.

"What?" she asked. "It didn't take long to put things away. We have next to nothing."

"As long as you're here," he said, motioning for her to sit as well. "Since we're going to be traveling together, I think it's time to put all of our chips on the table. No secrets. We're going to be in enough danger as it is. We don't need anything eating away at us from the inside as well."

"What makes you think you're traveling with us?" Sarah asked.

"I am the only one who can protect you now," Loravain said. "The Dark One will stop at nothing to kill Maggie and capture me. I am fairly certain he knows I no longer serve him."

"If he is after you, maybe we would be better on our own," Sarah said.

"That is foolish," Loravain said. "He already knows about Maggie and sent me to kill her. I will not be the last. Now they will come in greater numbers. We must stick together. Maggie, tell me why you left home."

"My mother lives in Priama," Maggie said. "She wants me to come home."

"How often do you speak with her?" Sarah asked.

"I've never spoken with her."

"Then how do you know she wants you to come home?" Loravain asked.

Maggie sighed at his question. "I guess I need to tell you about my childhood first. My parents, my adoptive parents, were never secretive about how they found me. They told me what happened, how I was left on their stoop when I was a baby. When I was older, things started happening."

"Things like what?" Sarah asked.

"I would get places I shouldn't have been able to. We were at the market the first time it happened. My parents turned away for a second, but that was all I needed. The next thing I knew, I'd gotten myself on top of a two-story building and couldn't get down. I was so scared. My father had to find a ladder to help me."

"That's understandable given your natural agility," Loravain said.

"Now it is. It wasn't to a six-year-old little girl who had no idea what she was. And it only got worse from there. My parents were reluctant to let me out of the house. They loved me so much and worried about my safety. I told them that I didn't feel like I belonged there. They told me I probably didn't. Regardless, I grew up a happy girl."

"I understand you had an interesting childhood, but that doesn't answer my question. Why did you leave home?" Loravain asked.

"I'm getting to that," Maggie said. "As time went on, my parents realized they needed to tell me everything. They gave me a box that was left with me when I was a baby. My dad said it was tucked away in the basket with me. Up until a few days ago, I didn't know it existed."

"What was inside?" Sarah asked.

"I thought it was empty at first, it was so light. When I opened it, there were only two items inside. This hairpin," she said, fishing it out of her pocket. "And a letter from my mother. My birth mother."

"The Queen," Loravain guessed, already knowing Gwendolyn had been correct.

"How could you possibly know that?" Maggie cried.

"Your mother is the Queen of Priama?" Sarah shouted, leaping to her feet. "This is unbelievable. I was rescued by the heir to the Coven Seat?"

Sarah paced back and forth, kicking leaves that had piled up below the hill.

"You have to go home before your mother dies so you can be crowned queen," Sarah said.

"Maggie must become queen. Only by receiving the crown can she hope to prevent a terrible evil from spreading across the land," Loravain said.

"What do you mean?" Maggie asked.

"If you are not kept alive and sworn into power before the Queen dies, you will never be able to undo the things my previous master did. If he can't be stopped, he will become an even greater plague."

"What if I can't do it? What if I don't want to? I come from a simple life. How will I ever be able to rule?"

"Those are not the questions you need to be asking right now," Loravain said. "First, we need to get you home to see your mother. That is all that matters."

Maggie's face brightened at the statement. It was no longer about her being queen or what life would be like in the future. It was only about her meeting her mother.

"What are we waiting for?" she asked.

"That is what we need to discuss. The journey to Priama will be fraught with danger. I must be able to protect you. To do that, I must prepare myself. I have to become more than what I already am."

"What does that mean?" Sarah asked.

"When I became a servant of the Dark One, he bestowed a power on me. In truth, it was more like a hint of power."

"That doesn't make sense," Maggie said. "Either he gave you something or he didn't. Which is it?"

Instead of trying to explain, Loravain cupped his hands together and blew into them. Red-hot embers rushed out on his breath. When they touched his skin, they ignited into flames that engulfed his fingers.

"What he gave me was the means to survive. The flames inside me have kept me warm in freezing weather. It feels like I have a small fire burning in my chest. My hands are immune to the pain of heat as well. To properly serve you as I need to, I must receive the rest of that gift. I must become a Fire Mage. That is what must be done first."

"How do you do that?" Maggie asked.

"I don't know. I only know where I have to go."

"Where?" Sarah asked.

"To the Mountain of Fire. It shouldn't be a long journey from here on horseback."

"There is only one flaw to your plan," Sarah said. "We have no horses."

"I think I can help with that," Maggie said with a smile.

CHAPTER 15

The moon had already risen over the trees when they strode into the village center. Maggie was home. She glanced around, half expecting everything to look different. It felt like she had been away much longer than she had been. Reality sank in as she realized that everything was still the same. She'd only been gone for days, not years. The market stalls still lined the square, doors open and shelves empty. The barn's loft stood outlined in the moonlight, inviting her to revisit memories of her time there.

"So," Sarah whispered. "This is your home? Cozy."

Maggie smiled. "Yes, it was. Now it feels more like a prison. I want nothing more than to be gone again."

"You shouldn't throw away your past so quickly," Loravain said. "You're young and it is easy to want bigger and better things. Trust me, one day you'll look back on all this and want nothing more than to be here."

"It sounds like you're speaking from experience," Sarah said.

Loravain took a step ahead, ignoring Sarah's comment. Maggie led them past the well marking the center of town then meandered past closed shops and down a wide, dark, and dusty road. A few candles burned in windows here and there, but other than that, there were no signs of life. The village was asleep.

"The stables are over there," Maggie said in a whisper, afraid that anything louder would wake someone up.

The stables were on the far side of Jacob's forge and the barn Maggie had spent so much time sneaking around in. When she passed the barn, she let the skin of her hand brush its coarse wood. Her happiest moments had been spent here, gazing out at Jacob as he hammered or tinkered. Without realizing it, she had stopped walking, stuck in a vivid memory of a hot day and a shirtless chest.

"What are you doing?" Sarah asked, invading her thoughts.

"Yes, it is hot," Maggie answered.

"What are you talking about?" Sarah asked with a giggle.

Maggie shook her head, pushing the daydream back to where it belonged and moved on. "Sorry. I just remembered something. The stables are over here."

As promised, the stable doors stood ajar and unguarded. The horses could be heard moving around inside, stamping the ground with heavy hoofs. Loravain opened the door wider, pausing when it creaked in protest. One by one, they disappeared into the dark interior, leaving the street deserted once more.

There were seven horses in total. All of them were in good condition but were obviously farm animals. Their hooves were covered in mud and straw and their lead ropes still hung from their necks. Loravain bent down to inspect their legs.

"Not the sturdiest creatures, but they'll have to do. See if you can find any blankets or saddles."

Maggie and Sarah searched the stable high and low. The only things they were able to find were farming tools, rope, and feed sacks. None of that would be helpful.

"Are there any other horses in the village?" Loravain asked. "Without the proper equipment, the journey to the Mountain of Fire will be very uncomfortable. Especially with these animals."

Maggie tried to remember if she'd ever seen any other horses. She knew some of the villagers made trips to other towns, and the horses they rode did look a bit larger than these ones. The problem was that she couldn't recall who owned them.

"There have to be more," she said. "Some of the farmers would have their own, but I don't know where they would be. Somewhere on their farms."

"That's okay, I'm sure we can find them. Everyone back outside," Loravain ordered.

He ushered them out of the stable and back into the open. He glanced up and down the road, staring long and hard into the darkness.

"I wish Thanatos were here. He could sniff them out," Loravain said, then glanced at the sky. "Dawn is still a few hours away. When can we expect people to start waking up?"

"With winter coming, everyone tends to sleep more. We have until Jacob starts working. No one stays in bed long after that," Maggie said.

"Who is Jacob?" Loravain asked.

"The blacksmith."

The hunter fell silent for a moment, stroking his chin. "We still have some time. If we can't find anything better than what's in the stables, we'll make do with what we have. If we split up, we can search the village faster. Maggie, check the homes and farms surrounding the village. Sarah and I will focus on the village itself. Sarah, you go south, I'll go north. We can meet by the well when we're done."

With the plan set, they each set off. Maggie dashed into the trees, hoping no one would be up this early. She dreaded the thought of getting caught and having to answer all sorts of questions about why she had disappeared. She was tempted to visit her parents, to let them know she was alright, but that would just make it harder for her to do what was needed.

Maggie knew how little time she had to look and knew where she needed to look first. She picked up the pace and sprinted through the woods. Not many people lived outside the village, but those who did lived far apart from one another. Luckily for her, she was fast, and tonight she was going to push herself.

Trees blurred past her as she ran. Her parents had no horses so she would skip them entirely. It would help ease the temptation of seeing them. When she finally circled the village, she was empty-handed. Disappointed, she returned to the well, thinking she would be the first one back. She was wrong. Loravain was already there.

"No luck?" he called out when he saw her.

She shook her head. "I'm not sure where they would be. I know someone has to have some; I just can't remember who."

"All will be fine," Loravain said. "If we can't find more, we have some to fall back on. We might have more luck in another village along the way."

"I hope so," Maggie said. "I don't want to waste more time at another village. I want to get to Priama as fast as we can."

"We will," Loravain promised. "You have my word on that. Now stop all that pacing. You're starting to make me nervous."

Maggie huffed and sat next to the hunter, back against the cold stone of the well. She wanted to get a little rest before Sarah returned if she could, but her mind was working overtime. Loravain glanced at her when she started drumming her fingers on her knees.

"I've seen you two practicing in the trees, doing things I could only dream of. What else can you do?" Loravain asked.

The question came out of nowhere. It was an obvious distraction, Maggie thought. She smiled though. It was his way of helping her calm down.

"I guess something similar to your power," she said.

"You have control over fire?"

"Ice. I feel it living inside me, near my heart. If I need it, it responds. I don't know how it works, but it does. When I was younger, I couldn't control it. It would just come and things would happen. For the most part, I was lucky. When the power would come, I was usually only with my parents. But this one time . . . ," she said, trailing off, leaving the story unfinished.

"The Rainer girl?" Loravain asked, pulling her back into the memory.

"How did you know that?"

"I spoke with your father and her father. They told me what happened."

"I don't even know what happened," Maggie said. "The only thing I remember is that it scared me so much I never played with her again."

"So, you have ice powers. Anything else?"

"I can do this thing with sound," she said.

"What do you mean?" Loravain asked.

"It might be easier to show you."

Maggie closed her eyes and focused. "Do you hear those toads?" she asked.

Loravain paused for a moment. "Yes, but only just."

"There are twelve altogether: five males, seven females. I can tell you where each of them are if you'd like."

"That's incredible."

She placed a hand on Loravain's arm and began tapping in rhythm with his pulse.

"What are you . . . You can hear my heart beating?" he asked.

Maggie nodded and slowly let the world creep back in.

"Amazing. The things you could do with that," Loravain said, only to be interrupted by Maggie jumping to her feet.

"Sarah found the horses," she announced.

"Are you sure? I don't see anything."

Maggie glared at him.

"Oh, right. You heard them."

"She found two. They're much larger than the ones in the stable."

Moments later, Sarah came trotting into view leading two saddled horses. She'd already prepared them for their journey. One of the saddlebags was full of equipment. Her smile stretched from ear to ear when she saw them waiting for her.

"Look what I found."

"Great job," Maggie exclaimed, rushing up to them and gently petting their strong, muscular necks.

"There's only one problem," Loravain said, killing the mood.

"What?" Sarah asked.

"They've been shod. If we don't remove the shoes, we'll be too easy to track."

"How do we take them off?" Maggie asked.

"I'm sure the blacksmith with have all the tools I'll need."

Loravain accepted the lead ropes from Sarah and walked back towards the stables. He tied the horses to a rickety hitching post and turned to face the forge.

"All I need is some sort of chisel and a hammer."

The search around the forge produced nothing. There wasn't so much as a nail left out in the open.

"Where would he keep his tools?" Loravain asked.

"He has a small shed around back. I think he keeps everything there," Maggie said. "Follow me."

A narrow alleyway ran between the forge and the neighboring building, allowing the three of them to slip through without much trouble. A weathered set of double doors stood locked in front of them.

"What now?" Sarah asked, lifting the lock in her hand.

Maggie glanced around and saw a rock big enough to do the trick. Picking it up, she handed it to Loravain. "Let's smash it."

"Too loud," he said. "We want to do this as quietly as we can. Try freezing it."

"What is that supposed to do?"

"If you can freeze the inside, it might be enough to crack it open."

"And if that doesn't work?" Sarah asked.

"I still have one or two tricks up my sleeve."

Nodding, Maggie reached out for the lock. She took it in her hands and called out to the spark of cold lingering behind her heart. As she felt it move, she hesitated. This was Jacob's lock. Should she be doing this? The iciness receded back into a tight knot. She dropped her hands, the lock bouncing off the wood of the door.

"I can't," she said. "I don't want to be the one to do this. Not to him."

Sarah put her arm around her shoulder and leaned in close to her ear.

"I know it can be hard at first but remember what we're trying to accomplish here. We're trying to get you to Priama to see your mother. The first step in doing that and discovering who you really are is to open this locked door. You are the only one who can get us in there."

"But Loravain said . . . ," Maggie began but Sarah cut her off.

"I know what he said but you have to be the one to do this. This is your village. It needs to be you."

"You don't understand," Maggie pleaded. "This is Jacob's shed. It is his lock."

"What does it matter whose lock it is?" Loravain asked but was quickly silenced by Sarah.

"Who is Jacob?"

Maggie sighed and turned her back on Loravain so she could look Sarah in the eyes.

"He is the most beautiful boy I've ever seen."

Sarah laughed and pulled Maggie close to her, kissing her gently on the forehead. "Honey, there are men out there who could make your heart stop just by looking at them. I promise there will be more. Remember, you'd have to stay here to keep this one. You don't want that, do you?"

"I never had him," Maggie confessed. "I don't even know if he knows my name."

"Then give him a reason to remember you. Let's smash that lock and get a good look at everything he's hiding in there."

Maggie steeled her resolve and nodded. She picked up the lock again and summoned her power.

"This is for Katie," she whispered as a flood of cold rushed through her arms.

"I thought this was Jacob's lock," Loravain said. "Who is Katie?"

"The girl he loves."

"Then this will be well deserved," Sarah said.

The cracking sound from the metal casing was promising as the ice expanded but it didn't release its hold on the door. They were still locked out. Maggie held it in her hands until the whole thing was encased in ice.

"It didn't work," she said, letting it slip from her grasp.

"My turn," Loravain said, blowing into his waiting hands.

A bright ember floated on his breath into his cupped palms. When it touched his skin, it ignited. He scooped up the frozen lock and willed the fire to burn hotter. The sudden temperature change cracked the ice and metal. The lock fell to the ground with an empty thud, allowing the doors to swing silently inward on well-oiled hinges. Moonlight flooded in, illuminating a myriad of weapons hanging on walls and from the rafters, lying on the tables, and scattered around the floor. Swords, daggers, and axes were only a few of the devices of death that could be seen.

"This is the last thing I was expecting," Loravain said.

"What does he need all these weapons for?" Maggie asked, walking deeper into the shed, pushing her way between a double-edged ax and a mace.

"If I had to guess," Sarah said. "He isn't the one who uses them. With an inventory like this, he sells them."

"To who ?" Maggie asked. "I've lived here my whole life. No one here needs this many weapons."

"If there is one thing I've learned being around man, it's that men don't know when to keep quiet. They like to boast. When I was in that cell, things were said that didn't make any sense at the time. They said once they were finished with me, they would meet up with the others. One of them mentioned an arsenal package they needed to pick up first."

"What does that even mean," Maggie asked.

"Do you think this was the package?" Loravain asked over her.

"The soldier's weapons have to be coming from somewhere and I see no reason why a village like this would need so many."

"We wouldn't," Maggie said. "We're farmers and traders, not soldiers. Sure, we have some for self-defense, but this is different."

Loravain circled the room and whistled. "There's no use in wasting this good fortune. Each of you choose a weapon while I look for the tools we'll need."

Maggie paced around the room with Sarah, looking for something that might suit her. She'd never needed a weapon before other than the small spades and daggers she used to attack the dirt. She passed over the larger two-handed weapons, finally settling on a long-bladed dagger. It was similar to the one her father had given her. Long enough to do damage but short enough to conceal. It wasn't as intricate though. It looked as if it had been made in a hurry. In fact, all the weapons here looked a little sloppy.

She sliced the air with the blade, feeling foolish as she did so. She had no idea how to handle a blade this long. Glancing over at Sarah, she eyed the short sword she had chosen. It seemed at home in her hand. She danced through a couple of routines before stopping and setting it down.

"It's a little off-balance," Sarah said. "All of them are. This blacksmith of yours isn't the most proficient."

"What's going on in here?" a heavy voice boomed through the shed.

Maggie spun around, coming face to face with Jacob. He was silhouetted by the light of the moon, hiding his features in shadow, but Maggie knew that shape anywhere. He wore a rumpled nightshirt with a dirty pair of trousers underneath and held a candle in one hand and a crossbow in the other. Silence spread through the dark. Even being caught red-handed in his shed, she didn't know what to say to him. His handsomeness still rendered her speechless. Maybe Victoria was right. Even when presented with an opportunity to speak to him, to defend herself, she couldn't do it.

"I asked you a question, girl. What are you doing in here?"

Girl? The way he said it bothered her. She glanced around. Sarah and Loravain were gone. They had abandoned her, leaving her to face Jacob alone. How was she ever going to confront, or attack, the man she couldn't even talk to?

"I . . . I . . . ," she stammered.

"You what?" Jacob yelled.

"I just wanted to see inside," she finally managed to croak out.

"I don't care what you wanted to do. This place was locked for a reason. I can't let you leave now. You've seen too much."

"What are they for?" she asked, surprised by her boldness.

Jacob looked around at his weapons and lowered the bow in his hand. He almost looked ashamed in the light of the candle, but the expression quickly faded, replaced by anger. He turned around and shut the doors. Maggie backed deeper into the shed until she ran into a metal-laden table. Unexpectedly, she chuckled to herself. She was finally alone with the man she thought she was in love with, the man she had dreamed about for years, and the only thing she wanted to do was escape.

"I have no idea what they'll be used for," he said. "I get paid to keep quiet about it. Up until now, I'd done a good job."

"They're weapons," Maggie cried. "What do you mean you don't know what they'll be used for?"

"You know what I mean, Maggie."

Her body trembled. "You know my name?"

"Of course, I know your name. I know more than that, too. You of all people should know how much Victoria likes to gossip. She told me everything after you vanished. You're pretty. You should have told me how you felt."

Confused by her feelings for him, she didn't notice him inching closer. He'd set down his crossbow but held a short dagger at his side.

"We could have been great together, you know that?"

"But you like Katie," Maggie whimpered.

"I like a lot of girls."

He took another step forward and raised the dagger, the metal glimmering in the candlelight. He glanced at it with affection.

"Beautiful, isn't it?" he asked. "Before the soldiers came, I was only good at repairing farming tools, wagon parts, and horseshoes. It was hard in the beginning. I had no idea what I was doing. I slaved for months learning how to fold the metal just right. But I bet you already know all about that, don't you?"

"What do you mean?" Maggie asked.

"Victoria told me about the barn too."

Maggie cursed herself for being so open about her feelings. Then, without warning, Jacob thrust the blade at her. The attack came so fast she didn't even have time to scream. She waited for pain to explode through her body. She closed her eyes, expecting it any second, but it never came. Peering out through squinted eyes, she saw him standing rigid and unmoving in front of her, dagger inches from her abdomen.

"What happened?" she asked, stepping away.

"Loverboy here was trying to manipulate you. It was working too. He was going to kill you, Maggie," Sarah said from behind Jacob.

"What did you do to him?"

"Stopped his body from responding to his own commands. The mind can be a powerful thing, but it can be used against you if you aren't prepared."

The clinking of metal resounded from the back of the shed. Loravain stepped into the light, his crossbow raised.

"I'm glad you're faster than I am. A dead body wouldn't be the best thing for our getaway. Can you put him to sleep? We need enough time to escape without him causing trouble for us."

Sarah nodded. She placed two fingers over Jacob's temples and closed her eyes. Maggie watched in silence. She really thought she was going to die. The man she thought she loved had tried to kill her.

Anger flared through her body, breaking her free from her stupor. Leaning forward, she whispered into Sarah's ear.

"Can you take away his memories of Katie?" she asked. "After what he's done, he doesn't deserve those."

Slightly smiling, Sarah shook her head. "My power doesn't work like that. But when he wakes up and realizes he failed, he's going to panic. Who knows what he'll end up doing?"

Maggie stepped back as Jacob's body crumpled to the floor. His breath came in shallow gasps.

"How much time do we have?" Loravain asked.

"About twenty minutes."

"More than enough. If you haven't picked one, chose a weapon and let's be on our way. We need to put this village behind us fast."

Sticking with her long dagger, Maggie followed Loravain back to the forge. She watched him pry the shoes from the horses, leaving them in the dirt where they fell. When the last one dropped, he rushed into the stable. He returned with an armful of gear and three empty bags. He quickly shoved everything in the bags and tied them to the saddles. After a few minutes, Sarah stumbled into the street from the shed. She was visibly exhausted. Her arms hung weakly at her sides and her feet shuffled through the dirt. She would have fallen had Loravain not caught her.

"What happened?" Maggie asked, rushing to her.

"That boy is stronger than he looks. He started to wake well before he should have. I had to put him back under and hold him there. He has a will of fire. We should go."

Loravain nodded in agreement then scooped Sarah up into his arms and gently placed her on one of the horses. "Maggie, have you ridden before?"

"Once or twice when I was younger. I haven't been on a horse in years."

"You're going to have to ride alone for now," he said, handing her a lead rope. "With the state Sarah is in, she can't ride alone. She needs to be with an experienced rider. Whatever she did in there, it took a toll on her."

The back of the horse looked higher than ever now that she knew she would be on her own. She grunted as she pulled herself into the empty saddle. Loravain gave her a quick lesson on how to properly straddle and guide the horse.

"If you feel yourself slipping, let me know. We'll go slowly at first to give you some time to remember how to do this."

Sarah's body slumped back into Loravain's chest when he positioned himself behind her. He kicked the horse, urging it forward. Maggie followed closely behind, mimicking his movements. Soon, the horses were galloping away from the village, leaving all her bad memories behind.

With a final glance over her shoulder, Maggie became furious. She was angry with herself for liking Jacob for all those years. For trusting Victoria with her secrets. Turning back, she faced forward, towards her new life. Other than her parents, she would never think about this place. They would be the only part of Lakes Hollow that remained alive in her mind.

CHAPTER 16

Loravain set a hard pace for the horses far into the morning. After a few hours in the saddle, Maggie remembered everything she had learned as a child. Before long, she would ride ahead then cut back around, leading her horse with ease. Sarah was still asleep but had woken up a few times during the night to ask for water. Maggie trotted closer to Loravain.

"I wish I had done this more often," she said. "It's relaxing."

"It is until Sarah wakes. When she does, we'll need to make up for lost time. I want to get to the Mountain of Fire as soon as possible. I don't like the idea of spending a fortnight on this detour. The longer it takes to get you to Priama, the more danger you will be in."

"How long do you think it will be until Sarah is ready to ride on her own?" Maggie asked.

"I'm not sure. I don't know much about her magic, or many of the other types for that matter."

"What kinds of magic are there?"

Loravain rode ahead before answering. "From what I've learned, there are five base magics. It is from those that witches, wizards, and mages get their abilities. I have fire magic while you have its opposite, ice magic. Sarah uses mind magic. Aside from those, there is also storm magic, which grants power over the air and elements and nature magic. I've never seen anyone use nature magic before. It is rare and is said to be the most powerful of the five. It allows you to control nature. You'd be able to manipulate living plants and communicate with animals. There are also different abilities within each base magic. For instance, the fire magic I have allows me to breathe embers and create fire in my hands.

When a witch is born, her powers and abilities are determined by her ancestors. You have ice magic, and it is more than likely that your hearing is a part of mind magic. The most base magics I've seen a witch use is three. If I remember correctly, your mother uses three."

"You've met my mother?" Maggie blurted out in surprise.

"No. That's just what I've heard in passing."

"What else have you heard?" Maggie asked, desperate to know more.

"I've been told that she is a fair ruler. She treats everyone with a royal courtesy. However, even fair rulers can make enemies. There are some witches and humans who want control over others. They desire power. If we can't keep that desire in check, dangerous things can happen. Take Sarah for example. How easy was it for her to control the blacksmith? To many, that kind of power and control is intoxicating. If we are not careful, it would be easy to think we are more deserving of power than those we might deem to be beneath us. Then there the others, like your mother, who understand that everyone and everything has a right to exist as they see fit."

"What do you think?" Maggie asked. "Do you want power?"

"I would like to think I do not, but the mind can be a complicated thing to understand, even your own."

"What do you mean?"

"Think about your parents. They are peaceful people. They desire to be allowed to live as they see fit and respect others enough to allow them the same. They don't think about what rights or power they have over anyone else. They only do what they need to do to live. There are a lot of witches like that as well. They don't want to lord their power over anyone else. Would that change though if they suddenly received power? Or more power? I am about to become a Fire Mage. I have never had that kind of power before. I have never dreamed of it before or wanted it. I only hope I will use it in a just and wise way."

"Me too," Sarah said in a whisper. "You're human. Power seems to be especially corruptible to man. You might be different, though."

"You're awake," Maggie cried.

"Not for long. I'm still exhausted but I can't sleep on the back of this horse anymore and your incessant chattering is driving me mad. Can we stop so I can get some proper rest?"

Loravain pulled on the reins, bringing their mount to a stop. He swung his leg around the rear of the horse then lightly jumped to the ground. Taking Sarah's hand, he helped her from the saddle and carried her to a large maple tree. It was still grand enough to cast a long shadow across the dying grass even without its summer leaves.

"Thanks for the help, but I could have done that on my own," Sarah said with a shiver once she was nestled in the tree's massive roots.

"Don't talk more than you need to," Loravain said. "Exertion is only going to make this last longer."

Closing her eyes, Sarah's teeth chattered as she tried to fall asleep.

"Take my blanket," Maggie said, pulling it from her bag.

Sarah took it and wrapped it around her shaking body. Loravain made a crude fire pit, quickly filling it with twigs and dried leaves, and soon had a crackling fire warming them all. Before long, Sarah was snoring.

"Why is she still so tired?" Maggie asked.

"I can only assume that mind magic is more taxing than fire or ice. The concentration must have taken a huge toll on her. Her body needs time to recover. This might delay our journey a bit, but her health is more important. We should all take this chance to get some rest."

Despite the lack of sleep, Maggie glanced around at the low-hanging branches surrounding her. She knew she needed to sleep, but she didn't want to. Ever since she'd practiced with Sarah, she wanted to see what she was capable of. When she was in the air, she felt more alive, more in tune with who she thought she was. Picking a branch at random, she leaped into the tree and began her ascent.

The morning was beautiful. From her perch at the top of the tree, she held a commanding view. If she squinted, she thought she could see the distant spires of her village's church building. Turning the other way, she marveled at the views to the north and east. The sky was a brilliant blue with a few lazy clouds floating by on the breeze. Snow-covered mountains stood at attention in the distance, announcing that snow would soon reach them. Even though there was still the slightest hint of warmth to the air, she knew it wouldn't last. She hoped they would be in Priama by then.

Turning her attention back to the branches, she guessed at the distance between her tree and its neighbors. Each jump she contemplated was farther than she had done before, but she knew that she would never improve if she didn't risk. Taking a deep breath, she held it for a moment to calm her heartbeat, then slowly released it, readying herself. Finally picking her destination, she studied it. The branch seemed thick enough to support her weight but was a good distance below her. It would be a tricky landing.

"You can do this, Maggie," she said to herself, knowing that if she didn't go soon, she would talk herself out of it.

The hard ground mocked her from below, stunting her growing confidence. She wanted to make the jump but hesitated when she saw Loravain watching her.

"No giving up now."

Imagining herself as light as a feather, she sprinted across the narrow limb and threw her body out into the air. She closed her eyes as she soared, reveling in the sensation of the cold air on her cheeks as it zipped past. It was incredible. Opening her eyes, she quickly found her target again. The branch was close. Stretching out her feet as far as she could, she hoped for the best. She held her breath until her foot touched, then scrambled to the safety of the welcoming trunk. With ragged breaths, she looked back to where she'd come from. It was an insane leap, but she laughed as the adrenaline coursed through her body. Confident she could do it again, she eagerly pushed away from the trunk and jumped.

"You have a natural talent unlike anything I have ever seen before," Loravain said when she finally fell lightly back to the earth.

"I never knew I could do anything like that," Maggie admitted. "I never dreamed of doing this back home."

"If you keep practicing, your agility will do more to spare your life than any of your other powers. With your hearing, you could be impossible to catch."

"The problem is that I have to close my eyes to hear," Maggie said.

"For now, but look at what you did up there. You just told me you never knew you could do that. Who knows what other surprises could be waiting for you? But don't neglect your ice magic. All three will need to be developed."

"Do you practice your fire magic too? I haven't seen you use it more than a few times."

"I don't like to use it. I don't like the idea of becoming dependent on it. It is a reminder of what I have done and who I have served. But, if I am to receive the gift in full, then I do need to practice."

"How about now?" Maggie asked. "I'd like to see what you can do."

Loravain nodded. He stretched his arms and yawned before standing up. Once on his feet, he bounced on his heels.

"I need to get the blood flowing," he said, a silly smile playing across his face.

Maggie dropped to the ground and sat cross-legged to watch him. When he was ready, he drew in a long, deep breath and held it. He refused to breathe out even when his face started to change colors.

"Stop messing around," Maggie complained. "I want to see this."

At her command, Loravain released his breath. Maggie felt the heat on her face. Sparks and embers floated about, briefly flaring before dying out. Only two remained when Loravain reached out to them. They were attracted to his flesh. When they touched his fingers, they burst into flames, spreading until his hands looked like torches.

"That's so cool," Maggie said. "How big can you make it?"

The hunter smiled at her then concentrated on the fire. Before he could will the fire to grow, an arrow whistled past his hands, extinguishing his meager flames and embedding itself in the tree behind him.

"Get down," Loravain yelled as he dove for his crossbow.

Maggie found shelter behind a clump of bushes but knew she wouldn't be safe for long. Feeble twigs would do nothing to stop a well-placed shot. Rolling across the ground, she came short of the tree she was aiming for, leaving her exposed. Scrambling on hands and knees the rest of the way, she hid her body from view as another arrow pierced the dirt behind her. Frantically searching the wilderness around her, she tried to find where the arrows were coming from. She gasped when she saw Sarah still lying in the open. Her eyes grew wide as they searched for Loravain. When their eyes met, she pointed. He paled instantly.

He'd already managed to retrieve his crossbow and lead the horses to safety. He motioned towards the west, showing where the attack was coming from, then pointed at his ear. She got the message. Closing her eyes, she pushed out any unnecessary sounds. Focusing on where Loravain had shown her, she quickly found the intruder. Intruders. She could hear three heartbeats. Two calm and steady, the third wild and erratic. Signaling back to Loravain, she held up three fingers and pointed to where each of them were. He nodded then motioned for her to climb the tree. He then pointed at himself and then to Sarah.

Maggie let out a sigh of relief. She'd been so worried for her friend but didn't dare move from where she was to save her.

"Put down the weapon, hunter. You can't win this one," a shaky voice called out. It was male, small, and brittle.

Loravain remained silent. When Maggie glanced over to where he had been, he was gone. She jumped into the air, grabbing the branch above her. When she was high enough, she looked back down. Loravain was crawling towards Sarah, keeping himself hidden in the tall, dead weeds.

"The master sends his regards, but you can no longer be trusted to complete the mission you were assigned."

When Loravain reached Sarah's sleeping body, he looked up at Maggie, silently pleading for help. She understood what he needed. He wouldn't be able to get her to safety without a distraction. Signaling back, she studied the tree she was in. Her attention fell on a single branch. It stretched out into the open and came close to the branch of another tree. The jump would be easy. She would have to be quick though. Whoever was shooting was skilled. Taking a deep breath, she composed herself.

The branch she was aiming for was higher than she was but she didn't have time to climb. She would have to jump. She glanced down at Loravain, his expression easy to read. He was desperate for her help. Crouching down, she coiled her muscles like a spring and kicked out, launching her body. She shot past her target, but the distraction worked. An arrow hissed below her, barely missing her by a foot. She cursed under her breath. Reaching out for a smaller limb above her, she latched on. Before her body stopped swinging, she let go, dropping to a lower branch. A second arrow zipped past so close to her head it took a few hairs with it. With her feet firmly planted on the branch, she bolted back towards the trunk.

That was all the time Loravain needed. When Maggie looked down, they were both gone.

"Enough of these tricks," the man called out. "You're outnumbered. Give up now."

"If numbers are what you need to feel more courageous, then come out into the open and face me like a man," Loravain shouted.

"Toss your crossbow away and we'll come out."

"You do the same," Loravain countered.

"We will as soon as you do."

Loravain stepped into the open and tossed his crossbow to the ground, raising his hands in front of him. Maggie expected an arrow to pierce his chest, but it never happened. The man was true to his word. Well, true enough. Three men emerged from the underbrush. Two were large and commanding, most likely the two steady heartbeats she'd heard. They each held a bow and arrow at the ready but didn't fire. Standing half as tall as his companions, the third was a scrawny man with a disfigured face. He tried to hold an air of authority. If not for his hired goons, it would have been a humorous sight.

"You lied," Loravain said.

"Did you expect me to do any differently?" the man said. "I know who you are. I'm not going to give you the upper hand here, especially when I have you at a disadvantage. Now hand over the witch."

"The demon has lied to you," Loravain said. "He will never give you what he promised."

"That is what separates us, hunter. I gave myself to him freely. No deals were struck so there are no promises for him to keep. With this victory, I will rise to become his right hand. This is just the first step in my ambitious plan."

"Then it is a fight you're after," Loravain asked, stepping forward.

"No, I am not here to fight you, but I will if I must. I am here to kill the witch, as you were supposed to do. Once that is done, you are to be taken back for your punishment. Alive."

Maggie peered around the tree, trying to remain hidden. Jumping as quietly as she could, she grabbed the branch above her and pulled herself up. She needed a better angle for what she had in mind.

"I'll make you a deal," Loravain said.

"What do you have to deal with that would interest me?"

"Allow me to fight your men one on one, no weapons," Loravain said. "If they best me, I will stand by as you kill the witch and then go willingly to face your master."

"And if by some far-fetched chance you win, then what?" the man asked.

"You'll never have to worry about being anyone's right hand."

The two goons glanced at each other and smiled. Both were missing a few teeth and wore scars across their faces. It was clear to see that neither of them were strangers to violence. One had short hair, cropped close to the scalp, and a long red beard. The other wore shoulder-length blond hair and was clean-shaven, but they both showed off enormous muscles. Maggie immediately named them Beardy and Baby-face.

"I accept your terms," the disfigured man said. "This will be much easier than subduing you myself."

"No weapons. This fight will be hand to hand," Loravain said.

"I'll agree, but no fire magic either. I know about your gift."

When Loravain agreed, the small man nodded to his hired help. They hesitated to drop their bows but did so. Loravain slid a dagger from his belt and dropped it to the ground.

"Tell your men to drop whatever they might be concealing," Loravain said.

With another nod, the men obliged. One dropped a dagger followed by three small throwing knives, all hidden up his sleeve. He then removed a garrote disguised as a necklace. The other produced a hatchet and a pair of spiked brass knuckles.

Crawling precariously along a high branch, Maggie inched her way out over the contestants. She'd never seen Loravain fight before but she was sure he could hold his own. She knew what he did for a living. Since he was still alive, he must be good at it. Shimmying into position, she waited for the right moment.

Loravain stood calmly in the grass while his opponents stalked closer. He was waiting for them to make the first move. As they moved, the two drifted apart. She'd seen animals do that before. They wanted to attack him from both sides. However, Maggie was wary about the small man. He was either a powerful magician, waiting for the right time to strike, or he was an incredible fool.

Beardy sped forward, followed closely by Baby-face. Loravain stood his ground, waiting for the last second to counter. The first attack came in a flurry of movement. Beardy threw a right hook, which Loravain easily sidestepped, sending Beardy stumbling forward. Baby-face lunged at the hunter with a wild kick. Loravain blocked it with the bottom of his foot. Maggie almost laughed out loud. These brutes must be used to their intimidating size to win their battles for them. They didn't seem too worried about finesse.

Beardy corrected himself and backpedaled out of Loravain's reach, leaving room for Baby-face to dive at his knees. Leaping into the air, Loravain avoided the trap and landed hard on the man's thigh.

Baby-face screamed out in pain. "Get over here and help me, Tanner."

His clenched fist ready, Loravain jabbed at Baby-face's chest, forcing him the rest of the way to the ground.

"You should have spent more of your time training," Loravain taunted. "Your bulk does you no good here."

"No one hurts my brother," Beardy, or Tanner, yelled, rushing forward.

Three punches came in rapid succession but never made contact. Loravain was too fast. He circled Tanner, kicking the back of his knee, dropping him to the ground as well.

"What am I paying you for?" the small man screamed hysterically. "KILL HIM!"

"But you said . . ." Baby-face started to say before he was silenced by a brutal kick to the chin.

"You must have known this wasn't going to be easy," Loravain said, turning his attention to Tanner.

Maggie watched the fight with bated breath. Loravain was a much better fighter than she'd imagined. She had no doubt they'd be walking away from this unharmed.

Baby-face had somehow stumbled to his feet again, though his steps were off-balance. He threw a few practice punches, almost falling over in the process. "This isn't going to be easy for you either, hunter. You caught me off my guard, that's all."

Loravain shed his jacket with a smile and lifted his arms above his head, hands clasped together. He leaned back, popping his spine, then surprised Tanner with a sudden blitz as he bolted towards him at nearly inhuman speed. His first two punches were blocked, but the third hit Tanner square in the gut. The force knocked him back, but he was quickly rushing back in for more, ignoring the pain that must have been shooting through his abdomen.

"Is that the best you got?"

"You're about to find out," Loravain answered.

Loravain and Tanner fell into a volley of punches and kicks that Maggie couldn't follow. Instead, she turned her attention to Baby-face. He was crawling towards Loravain's discarded dagger. If he reached it, it could turn the course of the battle. She slipped her body around the branch, carefully lowering her legs. Holding onto the branch, she dangled in the air and waited. Baby-face was almost close enough.

When Baby-Face reached the dagger, he snatched it up and bolted to his feet, though he stumbled for a moment as he caught his balance. His head must still be spinning from that kick, Maggie thought. Not waiting any longer, she let go of her branch and fell. Focusing on the ice magic inside her, she called to it. It had been instinctual before, now it was deliberate. She landed silently behind Baby-face, frost already forming on her fingertips. Thrusting out an ice-cold grip, she caught the man's calf. The effect was immediate. Tendrils of ice spread across his leg until it had overtaken his arm and frozen him to the ground.

"What is this trickery?" he grunted, no longer able to move.

His sudden outburst distracted Loravain long enough for Tanner to finally make solid contact. He spun his body, raising his elbow as he came around. The sound of the impact was sickening. Loravain crumpled to the ground, a red welt spreading across his cheek.

"That's better, Tanner," the scrawny man yelled. "Now help Samuel and finish the job."

Before she could stop herself, Maggie launched back into the tree. She wanted to fight, but fear took over.

"Run as much as you like, darling. It won't do you any good," Tanner called after her. "With the hunter down, it's only a matter of time before we catch you and earn our money."

"What? Do you think I'd go down after only one hit?" Loravain asked, rising behind him.

He swept out with his leg, knocking Tanner off his feet before he had time to free his brother from his icy prison.

"Fire," Maggie called out from the branches. "Use your fire."

"No. I am a man of my word. They may try to cheat, but that is beneath me."

Loravain brought his fist down across Tanner's face, knocking him out cold.

"Now we're even," he said, rubbing his swollen jaw.

"What about the other one?" Maggie asked.

"He'll hold for now. Ice that thick won't melt for some time in this weather. It's time we take care of that one," Loravain said, pointing to where the man in charge had been moments before. "Where did he go?"

Maggie reached out with her mind. It was easy enough to pick out the sounds of escape as the man crashed through the dry, brittle twigs and brush of autumn.

"That way," Maggie called, directing Loravain.

"Time to see what you can really do up there," Loravain shouted. "He can't be allowed to escape."

Bounding from branch to branch, Maggie stuck to the high ground as the hunter sprinted below. The air whipped her hair around her face as she soared through the trees. She glanced down once, surprised to see Loravain keeping pace with her. The care she had to take with each step slowed her down, but she was still faster than any human should be.

"You're fast," she called out, still breathing easy.

"You're not so bad yourself. Can you see him yet?"

With each leap she took, the path the man was forging became more apparent. He was running for his life, not for stealth. She soon had the man in her sights.

"He's there, right in front of you on the other side of that fern," she called.

Taking a risk, Maggie left the safety of the branches behind, hoping to cut the man's feeble attempt at an escape even shorter. Anticipating her tactics, the man twisted to face her, hurling a short bolt at her in the process. Stabbing pain flared through her leg as she crashed to the ground. Bouncing once before skidding to a halt, Maggie lay face down in the dirt. By the time Loravain reached her, her vision was fading. Her breath came in short, ragged gasps and a burning sensation flowed through her arms and legs. On top of all that, fear flooded her mind.

Loravain flew over her and tackled the man before he could ready another dart. Colliding with the ground, the two rolled over one another, both fighting for dominance. When the tussle ended, Loravain held the upper hand, pinning his enemy in the dirt.

"What are you?" Loravain demanded.

"Your replacement."

"I doubt that. What is your name?"

"I would rather die than tell you anything, traitor."

"It may just come to that. If you wish to keep your identity a secret, that is fine. You won't live long enough for it to matter."

"If you kill me, she dies. Not that she has long anyway. Even in death, I will have accomplished what you failed to do."

"What are you talking about?" Loravain shouted.

"See for yourself."

Maggie writhed on the ground in pain, her eyes wide and unfocused. For a brief moment, her gaze met Loravain's. "Help me," she mouthed.

"What have you done to her?"

"That is another secret that will go with me to the grave," the man said with a laugh. "And so will she, incidentally."

Raising a fist, Loravain's fingers ignited into flames without the aid of his breath.

"TELL ME."

"This emotional anger doesn't suit you, hunter. And why are you holding back now? Have you turned weak since betraying the master?"

Loravain brought his fist down hard, slamming it into the earth next to the weasel of a man's head.

"There are other ways to get the information I seek."

He grabbed the man's jacket and lifted his head off the ground. "One way or another, you will tell me what I need to know."

Leaning back, Loravain head-butted the man so hard, his lopsided head bounced twice before he lost consciousness. Loravain struggled to his feet and rushed over to Maggie.

"Are you okay?"

"It hurts," she whispered through gritted teeth.

"Hang in there. I'm going to get help. You'll be okay. I will not let him win."

Maggie watched Loravain sprint through the brambles. Before he was out of sight, the strain of being awake became too much and her eyes drifted closed. Everything went dark.

CHAPTER 17

The sound of crackling fire and laughter coaxed Maggie out of the darkness. She didn't have enough strength to open her eyes, but it was easy to feel the pain and emptiness of her stomach. Her throat was dry and cracked and her muscles were sore and stiff. Everything was uncomfortable. She tried to move, but her body fought back in protest. She finally gave up trying and moaned.

"Maggie?" a cheerful, familiar voice asked. "Hey, welcome back." It was Sarah.

Water trickled into her open mouth, refreshing her parched lips. She choked when she tried to swallow but managed to keep some of it down.

"What happened?" she croaked.

"You were poisoned," Loravain answered, his voice low and somber. "You would have died had Sarah not been able to get inside Dolan's head. Once there, he had no choice but to tell us what we wanted to know."

"Dolan? Who's that?" Maggie asked.

"First tell me the last thing you remember," Loravain said.

"Running through the trees. After that, everything gets blurry. I remember the pain."

"You are a lucky young witch," Sarah said. "If we'd waited any longer, the poison would have spread to your heart."

"Dolan?" Maggie repeated. "Was he the one that did this to me? The small man?"

"Yes. He was more than willing to share that information after Sarah delved into his mind. She also got him to tell us about the antidote."

"What did you do to him after?" Maggie asked.

"Let's just say that I wouldn't like to be in his position when he drags his sorry behind back to the Dark One."

"You let him go?" Maggie yelled as best she could, though she sounded more like a wounded rabbit.

"It was the easiest and quickest way to get the information we needed to save your life," Sarah said. "If he knew we were going to kill him, he really would have taken his secrets to the grave."

"What if he comes back to finish the job?"

"He won't be able to," Loravain said.

"How can you be sure of that?" Maggie asked.

"The Dark One is not the forgiving type. Trust me on that."

Maggie nodded. She knew she could believe him. She'd seen what lengths he would go to to keep her safe.

"Where are we?" she asked, changing the subject. Her eyes were still closed.

"Two days ride from the Mountain of Fire," Loravain answered.

With Sarah's help, Maggie managed to sit up. "Why can't I open my eyes?"

"The poison weakens all your muscles until your body can no longer function. This has been the most you've moved in five days. It will take more time to recover."

"I've been asleep for five days?" Maggie asked, shocked.

"Yes, but now that you're awake, your body should heal faster. The hard part is over."

Maggie let everything sink in as she focused on a more powerful sensation. Hunger. The emptiness in her stomach was becoming more unbearable the longer she was awake, and it was screaming at her to eat something. Before she asked for it, a warm bowl was placed in her hands.

"There's a spoon in it. Let me know if you need any help," Sarah said. "Eat what you can then get some more rest."

Blindly feeling around the rim of the bowl until she found the soft wooden handle, Maggie lifted a spoonful to her nose. There was an overwhelming aroma of herbs she was familiar with. It reminded her of home, and it tasted just as good. It soothed her aching body. When she emptied the bowl, she asked for more water, which she drank with less effort this time.

"Has Thanatos come back yet?" she asked.

"Not yet but you really should try to get some sleep. We need to get an early start tomorrow. We've already lost more time than I care to think about," Loravain said.

"I don't want to sleep," Maggie said.

Her eyes were starting to crack open, and blurry, colorful visions crept in. It wasn't much, but it was better than constant darkness.

"Your body still needs time to heal. The dart that struck you had a large dose of poison. Sleep now because a full day in the saddle tomorrow is going to make you wish you were dead."

"What were you two laughing about?" she asked, trying anything to derail their desire for her to sleep.

"What do you mean?" Loravain asked.

"When I first woke up, you two were laughing about something. What was it?"

"We were just discussing something that happened a few days ago," Sarah answered.

"What?" Maggie pressed.

"Go to sleep. I promise that it is the best thing for you right now," Sarah said.

"I've been asleep for five days. I want to talk. I want to know what's been going on."

"You do realize that I can make you sleep, right?" Sarah asked.

"You wouldn't," Maggie cried.

Sarah sighed. "No, I wouldn't. But please, Maggie, this is for your own good."

"Fine, I'll sleep, but tomorrow we'll have nothing to do but talk so you'll have to tell me everything."

Accepting help to lie back down, Maggie realized how weak her body was, though she didn't want to admit it. She wanted them to believe she was fine.

Maggie relaxed her aching muscles, allowing her body to shut down again. The food and water comforted her stomach. She listened to Loravain and Sarah mumble about something as sleep overtook her.

"Wake up."

Someone was shaking her shoulder. She had no problem opening her eyes now, though it was still dark. The fire was out, and she couldn't see any stars or moon in the sky. Thick clouds rolled overhead and light snow was beginning to fall. With sore muscles, Maggie fought to sit up. Loravain was packing their things onto the horses. She stayed where she was and watched him.

"It's good to see you up on your own. I hope you enjoyed your rest. Looks like we're in for a hard ride today," he said over his shoulder.

"Why?" Maggie asked.

"These clouds are heavy with snow. If we don't get started now, it will be near impossible to get the horses moving. It will be hard enough to keep them going once the snow gets deep."

Maggie struggled to her feet. Sarah had been right; the rest had done more for her than she could believe. She was able to move much more than she could the day before. With more sleep, she would be doing even better, but she knew that wasn't going to happen. Scrounging around her, she discovered that most of her belongings, as few as they might be, had already been packed away. She picked up her few remaining items: a blanket, jacket, and her dagger belt. Forcing her limbs to follow her commands, she walked painfully over to the horses. Loravain sat astride one and Sarah climbed onto the other.

"You'll be riding with me today," Loravain said, offering her a hand.

Maggie took hold of it and let him pull her into the saddle behind him. Leaning into his back, she could feel the heat of his fire emanating from his insides.

"You're so warm," she said.

"Just part of my curse, though it will be a blessing for you when it gets colder. Now hold on tight. We need to make up for lost time."

Locking her hands around his waist, Maggie settled in for the long ride.

Loravain kicked his horse and they trotted through a fresh blanket of snow. Sarah had no trouble keeping up. As they rode, Maggie passed the time watching the snow fall. Loravain had been right. The clouds carried a lot of it. It had begun innocently enough, but once the thunder started rolling across the sky, the clouds opened and released all they had. Some of the snowflakes were almost the size of her hand. It was amazing to watch.

As time passed, the snow got deeper and deeper. Maggie had never seen a storm so wild before. She reveled in the excitement of it, but she was also worried. What if they got lost? Out of the hazy whiteness of the storm, Sarah trotted closer to them. The horses struggled with the pace their riders were trying to keep in the unrelenting blizzard.

"I don't think we'll be able to keep this up much longer." She shouted to be heard over the howling wind. Her teeth chattered as she spoke.

"What else can we do?" Loravain asked. "If we stop, we're likely to lose the horses."

"If we don't stop, we're just as likely to lose them."

A sudden gust of wind hit Maggie so hard, it almost ripped her from the saddle. She clung to Loravain's coat tightly to keep from falling. The hunter glanced back at her and nodded.

"Perhaps you're right. See if you can find some cover. We're going to need protection from this if we aren't moving."

Maggie was relieved. It seemed dangerous and foolhardy to continue.

"I'll try," Sarah yelled. "But it's hard enough to see the horse's ears in this mess."

"How much farther to the mountain?" Maggie asked, leaning in close to Loravain's ear.

"If riding conditions were better? No more than another day and a half. In this? I have no idea."

"How long will it last?"

"Heavy storms don't usually last long, but this one is stretching on much longer than I expected it to. No matter though, the damage is already done. The horses can't easily travel in this."

"What are we going to do?" Maggie asked.

"I don't know, but I promise to keep you safe."

The horses pushed on ahead, moving slower and slower with every passing moment. The snow had neither relented nor showed any signs of breaking anytime soon. It was already up to her ankles, even on the back of the horse. A feeling of helplessness washed over her. She realized how much she depended on Loravain and Sarah. Had it not been for them, she would have been dead many times over. With the prospect of freezing to death in the blizzard, she was afraid for all of them.

"I found something," Sarah said, her voice floating through the storm.

"Blasted wind," Loravain cursed. "Did you happen to catch where it was coming from?"

"No, but I'll be ready next time."

Maggie closed her eyes and pushed away the sounds of the storm. Silence swallowed her. Without the tumultuous blowing, the day seemed peaceful. She could hear the horse's labored breathing and racing heartbeat. They needed to find a place to rest sooner than she realized. The horses wouldn't last much longer. When Sarah called out a second time, the message was clearer, and she knew where it was coming from.

"She's to our right," Maggie said, then guided Loravain until she was happy with their direction.

The horse had almost completely stopped by the time they saw Sarah's outline silhouetted in the snow. She stood nearly chest-deep in it next to her steed, trying desperately to coerce the creature into a small copse of trees.

Doing likewise, Loravain dismounted, leaving Maggie in the saddle. He tugged on the reins, leading the horse through the rising snow. Stopping at a large pine tree that blocked some of the wind, Loravain pressed on to scout the area. Sarah followed him. Watching them intently, Maggie forced every other sound from her mind and focused on their conversation. She almost lost her concentration when she realized what she was doing. She'd never been able to manipulate sound with her eyes open before.

"The snow is almost as deep on the inside, but it still may offer some protection against the wind," Sarah said.

"We'll be fine. It's the horses I'm worried about. I've spent enough time surviving in weather like this. I fear that the horses will either wander off or freeze to death. Or both."

"How will we get to the mountain, or Priama, without the horses?"

"The plan is not to lose them."

Silence followed as the two pulled Sarah's horse farther into the trees. It was being stubborn and fought against the ropes but eventually gave in and slipped between the branches. Moments later, Loravain emerged and coaxed his horse through as well. Maggie was grateful that she didn't have to wade through the snow.

In the middle of the grove stood a tall evergreen. Its branches were heavy and drooping, burdened with snow. Loravain led the horse to it then stopped next to Sarah.

"How is she doing?" Sarah whispered.

Maggie still hadn't let the sound of wind creep back in yet. She heard the voices as clearly as if they'd been in a small, quiet room.

"She's strong. If we end up walking, I may have some concerns, but we're not there yet."

"Has she been asking any questions?" Sarah asked.

"No. She's been pretty quiet, though I'm sure she's curious."

"As she should be. She lost five days. She must know things have happened. We'll tell her when the time is right, but you're right, she needs to rest right now. If she knows, she'll just be agitated."

Sarah glanced over at Maggie and paled when she saw her watching them.

"We may not get the chance to wait," she said. "I think she's been listening the whole time."

Loravain turned to Maggie and smiled. He didn't appear to be ashamed or upset at her eavesdropping but there was an expression of sadness on his face.

"Stay on the horse for now," he said, knowing well enough that she could hear him. "Once I've found shelter, I'll come for you."

Maggie did as she was told and stayed put, not that she wanted to get off and wade through the snow anyway. She gently let the sounds of the storm return. Lifting her feet out of the snow, she folded her knees to her chest and watched Loravain trudge through the high snow to the far side of the tree. There, he dropped to his knees, almost disappearing in whiteness, and began pushing the snow. Maggie couldn't see what he was doing, but he was making quick work of it. After a few moments, he stood up, covered in snow, then burrowed his way through the branches of the pine tree. Emerging a few minutes later, his arms were laden with dry branches and twigs. He tossed them into the pit he'd dug then turned around and repeated the process two more times.

Soon, a small mountain of kindling and tinder rose above the snow line. Climbing out of his hole, he forged a path to Maggie.

"Help me get the horses over there," he shouted to Sarah.

As if the creatures knew there would be warmth, they followed with ease. The horse Maggie sat on trotted ahead in the path Loravain had created, coming to a stop next to the pit. Glancing in, Maggie saw the greens and browns of earth that hadn't yet had time to freeze yet in the sudden storm. It was still a wet mud but much better than the cold snow. Accepting Loravain's help, Maggie slid down from the saddle and into the snow.

"You have got to be kidding me," she screamed as the snow flowed into her boots.

"Get in the hole and take your boots and socks off before you get too cold," Loravain instructed.

Maggie did so and was joined by Sarah. They sat down on the murky ground and pressed their bodies together for warmth. Thick snowflakes fell around them, but the walls Loravain had created did an excellent job of keeping the wind out. Soon the hunter was by their side and shedding his jacket. He pulled off his boots and stood in the snow as if the cold didn't bother him in the slightest. Breathing out a plume of frozen breath into the air, a few embers escaped his lungs, blinking with heat before succumbing to the frigid temperature and fading away.

"I never get tired of this," Loravain said as he knelt next to the pile of brambles and blew.

It only took seconds for the embers to ignite the dead, dry pine needles. The rush of heat from the sudden flames was immediate and welcome. The cold, dreary landscape surrounding them didn't look so bad anymore. Maggie held her hands closer to the fire and smiled, her eyes slowly closing. She could almost picture herself camping with her father while foraging for snowberries, which only appeared during the coldest months of winter. The growling of her stomach was the only thing holding her to reality.

"Is there anything to eat?" Maggie asked.

Loravain picked up his jacket and reached into one of the pockets. He produced a few strips of dried meat and a handful of nuts and small roots he'd gathered the night before. Before giving them away, he thrust his hands into the burning fire. The aroma of home-cooked food filled the air, causing Maggie's stomach to rumble.

"What was it you wanted to tell me?" Maggie asked as she munched on her hot food.

Loravain and Sarah exchanged glances.

"We had a visitor a few nights ago," Loravain said.

"Someone trying to kill me again?"

"No, nothing like that," Sarah said, reassuring her.

"They were most likely sent by Thanatos. They brought news of the Queen and state of Priama."

"What did they say about my mother?" Maggie asked, eager for any information.

"She is not well. They expect her to pass into the next life by the solstice or before, which gives us precious little time to get there."

"I have to meet my mother," Maggie cried. "I have to."

"We know that," Sarah said. "But what we are doing now is important too. We might not make it to Priama if we don't do this. We should still have enough time to make it to Priama well before the solstice even with this detour."

"How can you be sure?" Maggie asked. "What if this is just wasting time?"

"There has already been one attempt at your life, not including mine," Loravain said. "Even though it was unsuccessful, the Dark One knows what our end goal will be. You can be sure he'll send more of his minions after us. Going this way will confuse them for now.

Once I become a Fire Mage, I will be better able to protect you. This is the safest and surest way to get you to your mother alive."

"How long will it take?" Maggie asked. "And how long is this storm going to keep us stranded?"

"We'll figure it out. But fear not," Loravain said. "I am not giving up on you. I will get you to your mother on time. That is a promise."

Maggie studied his face. She wanted to believe him. Regardless, there weren't any other options besides setting off on her own, which would be suicide. She'd probably get lost within minutes. She glared at the falling snow, silently hating it for keeping her from her mother.

"What else did they say?"

"Tensions are high in Priama. As your mother's health declines, another is trying to step in and wrestle the crown from her. If she is allowed to succeed your mother instead of you, there could be war. Her intentions are less than honorable when it comes to ruling."

"So, if we don't get there in time, I won't meet my mother and there will be war? Okay, no pressure," Maggie said with a heavy sigh.

A throbbing pressure was boiling up inside of her. All at once, a world of obligation and responsibility dropped onto her shoulders. The fate of her future was being determined by a blizzard. The cold prickling sensation behind her heart was beginning to spread. Maggie sensed that it wanted to explode out of her in answer to the frustration she felt, but there was nothing to direct it at, which frustrated her even more. She couldn't even be properly angry. Annoyed by her situation, Maggie stood up and clenched her muscles in a silent scream. When she did, the ice magic twitching inside her flooded from her skin in waves with enough force to extinguish the flames and destroy the walls Loravain had built.

"Hey," Sarah screamed when a wall of snow toppled over on her. "What happened?"

Loravain stared at Maggie, concern written across his face. But something else overshadowed it. Sympathy and understanding. Learning to deal with and understand her powers was hard. Knowing that someone could relate to her made her feel a little better. She appreciated it. He must feel the weight of the world on his shoulders too, Maggie thought. Her gaze shifted to Sarah, who was still pulling clumps of snow from her collar. She wished she could talk to Sarah about what she was going through, but she had never hidden who she was. Her whole childhood had been spent in anticipation for what she would one day be capable of, and an entire village was there to support her.

Maggie glanced around her and took in the damage. "Did I do that?"

The hunter nodded then laughed as he watched Sarah burrow free from the avalanche of snow that covered her. It wasn't a sound Maggie heard often.

"How?"

"You have ice magic. Snow is ice. It makes sense, but please try to respect others," Sarah said when her head was finally free.

"Can you do it again?" Loravain asked.

"No, please don't," Sarah cried, eliciting another chuckle from Loravain.

Maggie shrugged her shoulders. "I don't even know what I did."

"Quite a nice trick you've learned," came the unexpected voice of Thanatos, the wolf.

Everyone turned and looked into the eyes of the frost-covered animal above them. He looked exhausted.

"Come warm yourself," Loravain said, kneeling to restart the fire.

Thanatos jumped into the half-filled pit and looked at each person in turn.

"Why are you not moving? Time is short. Surely you must have received my message?"

"The snow has become too much for the horses," Maggie said.

"I thought as much," Thanatos said. "When I saw those clouds, I knew someone must be trying to sabotage our plans."

"Are you saying that someone is making it snow?" Maggie asked.

"You can't possibly believe this is a natural storm, can you? The Dark One must have witches in his service who are powerful at storm magic. We must keep moving. The situation grows more dire with every passing moment."

"How are we supposed to go anywhere in this?" Sarah asked. "The horses are stuck."

"And they will remain that way," the wolf said. "I have arranged other transportation to the Mountain of Fire."

"What will happen to them?" Maggie asked, appalled at the thought of leaving them behind.

"The fire will keep them warm enough. Once we have moved on, the storm will fade and they will make their way home. Now grab your things and follow me."

Maggie slipped her damp socks back on to her feet, quickly followed by her boots. Sarah and Loravain did their best to retrieve everything from the horses. Maggie was happy that the horses would be given the best possible chance at survival. When their tasks were complete, Loravain gathered another armful of pine needles and branches and tossed them on top of the fire.

"That should last them a little longer," he said, dusting off his hands.

Outside the grove sat two long sleds. Each had a small seat big enough to hold a single rider. Sarah hurried to arrange their gear in the closest one, then took her position standing on the back runners.

"How are we supposed to move them?" Maggie asked.

Thanatos howled in reply. The sound was swallowed up by the cacophony of the blizzard, but a wild pack of wolves heard it anyway and came rushing into view. They immediately fell into place in the front of the sleds and allowed Loravain to tether them together.

"Come sit here," he said to Maggie once he had finished tying the last leather strap to the sled.

"You know, sometimes I get the feeling you two are trying to treat me like a child on purpose. I can do things for myself," Maggie said.

"I know you can," he replied. "Now sit."

She tossed the small pack she was carrying to Sarah and strapped herself into her carriage. When they were ready, Thanatos howled again and the wolves began pulling at their harnesses. It was slow going at first, but they were soon whipping across the snow much faster than the horses would have been able to go on dry ground.

The snow stung Maggie's eyes and face as they sped on, encouraging her to practice the skill she'd discovered in the grove. Pulling at the magic inside her, she tried and failed to push the incoming snow around her. It wasn't nearly as easy as she thought it would be. She couldn't focus on an individual snowflake long enough to manipulate it. The more she tried, the more tired her body became. She soon gave up altogether. Wriggling herself deeper into the sled, she got as comfortable as she could and tried to sleep. As she did, her mind wandered back to Loravain and Sarah's desire to protect her. It could be because of who she was or her age, but at the moment, she didn't mind. She was much happier lying down, warm and bundled, safe from the cold, than standing up, taking the full brunt of the storm.

CHAPTER 18

The Mountain of Fire loomed in front of them, towering in the sky. It churned out a constant flow of ash and smoke. As they grew closer, the snow slowly gave way to ash and the air began to warm. The wolves had made quick work of the journey. They arrived much sooner than they would have on the horses. It was also a blessing that the sleds traveled across the ash just as well as the snow.

The shadow of the erupting behemoth fell across them as an uneasy feeling crept through the group. No one knew what to expect. Distracting herself, Maggie walked up to one of the wolves still tethered to the sled and extended a friendly hand.

"What's your name?" she asked.

She barely had enough time to snatch her hand back before her fingers became its dinner.

"That's not very nice," she chided, rubbing her palm as if she had been bitten.

"They won't talk to you," Loravain said, untying the last knot holding the beasts in place. When the strip of leather finally fell to the ground, the wolves bolted away, disappearing in the dying light.

"Why not? Thanatos talks to me."

"Thanatos is much more than an animal. Those were wild beasts, nothing more."

"How can you tell when an animal isn't just an animal?" Maggie asked.

"Take a look at me," the hunter said, staring up at the mountain. "I am only a man, but soon I will become something more. Will I appear any different once I'm done?"

"We're talking about animals, not you."

Loravain chuckled and rubbed her head, messing up her hair. He strode away to talk to Thanatos but commented over his shoulder. "Are we really that different from animals?"

The wolf sat still, watching the towering slope intently. It was as if he was searching for something that wasn't there. His ears twitched at the slightest sounds and his nose sniffed at the air.

"We're finally here," Loravain said. "What now?"

"Now you are to be judged. Only those the guardians deem worthy will be allowed to begin the journey up the mountain."

"And if I am not found worthy?"

"Then you will die," the wolf said solemnly.

The answer was brutally honest. Turning his gaze to the mountain as well, Loravain studied its hidden crevices and visible dangers. It was a black monster rising out of the belly of the earth. It was angry, irritable, and powerful. Lightning flashed through the clouds of ash, exposing the summit as it shook with the passing thunder.

"The owl must think there is some hope for me or else she wouldn't have suggested this," Loravain said.

"The sun is about to set. When it does, you will be on your own. We will wait here until your trials have been completed," Thanatos said.

Loravain looked over his shoulder, taking note of the position of the sun. It fell slowly, throwing light and shadow across the underbelly of the clouds threatening to hide it from view. Even though it may be the last thing he ever saw if the guardians deemed him to be less than worthy, at least he had started down the path to redemption.

"How long do you think it will take?" Maggie asked, walking up behind Thanatos. "We're still going to make it to Priama in time, right?"

"I don't know," the wolf said. "But you have my word. You will reach Priama before your mother dies. Even if we have to go alone."

"I wouldn't risk doing this if I thought we would get there too late," Loravain said.

Maggie smiled but the look on her face betrayed her.

"Look at that," Sarah exclaimed.

At the base of the mountain, a narrow, winding path had become visible. At the head stood two massive statues guarding the way. The figure to the left was a large stone man cocooned in fire, his arms stretched out in front of him. Marble robes extended to the base of the pedestal he stood on. His face was hidden beneath a dark hood. The other statue was an angry bear standing on its hind legs. It was taller than the man and much broader. Instead of a natural, animal emotion, the bear wore an expression of caution, a warning to the unworthy.

"Only Loravain is to proceed from this point," Thanatos said, stopping the others' progression to the trail. "If you cross the threshold, you will most likely die."

Head down, Loravain proceeded to the guardians alone but stopped when someone touched his hand. Turning around, he stared into Sarah's watering eyes.

"Be careful up there, okay?" she pleaded.

He squeezed her hand and whispered something into her ear that made her smile through the tears.

"I heard that," Maggie said when Sarah returned to her side. "How long has that been going on?"

Sarah shrugged her shoulders and looked away, deliberately avoiding the question.

Loravain stared up at the guardians. As he watched, the stone flames, carved so many years ago, began to flicker in the light of the dying sun. Or was it something else? Behind him, the sun was still above the horizon, but only just. He thought he could hear the faint crackling of fire as well. As he stepped closer, the flickering became more intense, the folds of the man's cloak becoming more prominent. Suddenly, the stone began to crack and fall away, chunk by chunk, revealing an actual man beneath it, wrapped in burning fire. The flames, when free from their prison, leaped to the bear. Both statues were now raging infernos. Loravain backed away.

"Glory awaits the worthy judged." A strange voice hissed through Loravain's mind. "And fire to cleanse the troubled soul. To put away the long-held grudge, the newfound hero, his story told."

The voice repeated the phrase in his head, the flames growing and falling to its rhythm. As he prepared to proceed, another voice spoke to him. A voice he knew well and longed to be with.

"Come to me. Be found worthy of this gift." It was Camila.

Loravain stepped forward, crossing into the arc of flames in front of him. Instead of heat, a cool summer breeze blew across his skin and the world behind him was silenced. More and more voices called out to him, speaking of power, glory, corruption, and death. Visions of war, blood, and carnage flashed before his eyes, followed by tranquil scenes of peace and prosperity. The voices continued, rising in volume, reciting to him his deeds. His past was played out before him, and he was ashamed of the man he had been. Yet, knowing that he had committed those sins, he took full responsibility for them.

"Yes," he shouted. "I did those things, but I am no longer that person. I have changed."

Falling to his knees, he wept for his sins, for those he had killed, and the families he had left fatherless, sonless, and parentless. When his sorrows peaked, a soft hand reached out from the bright light of the flames and caressed his tear-streaked face.

"Don't cry, my love. Your heart is noble. Your future is also being judged, not only your past."

The hunter looked up into the eyes of his beautiful bride. Her hair was brilliant, burning with fire, but her face was just as he remembered.

"Forgive me, Camila," he pleaded. "I should have done more. I could have saved you."

"You could have done nothing. You were meant to play a much greater role in life. My death has served a purpose. You are the one destined to help this witch. This is what your life has been leading you to. Had we been allowed to stay together; the world would have been plunged into darkness."

"But I have created much of that darkness," Loravain said.

"We must come to understand the darkness before we can fully appreciate the light," Camila answered.

"Will I ever see you again?"

"I am waiting for you in a place that has been prepared for us, but you still have much to do here."

"What must I do?"

"You have been found worthy. As you proceed up the mountain, you will face three challenges. They will teach you about the power you are seeking. Open your mind as you climb, for enlightenment cannot be obtained if the book is closed."

Camila stepped back into the flames and disappeared, along with the voices, the visions, and the fire. The trail appeared before him again, leading up the barren, rocky landscape of the mountain. Looking back, he saw Sarah and Maggie huddled together in conversation. Thanatos sat near the sleds. They were not watching him. They didn't appear to be able to see him. He was on this quest alone. Drawing in a deep breath of air, he held it for a moment, warming it with his fire, then slowly released it as he took his first steps to becoming a true Fire Mage.

The slope was gentle at first, and the trail smooth, but the higher he climbed, the more rugged the way became. The rocks changed from flat and rounded to sharp, ragged, and lethal. Sheer, black, and reflecting the light from the setting sun, the stone was unlike any Loravain had ever seen before. He'd encountered warriors with swords that weren't as deadly as the standing shards around him.

When dusk finally gave way to the falling night, he became astutely aware of the narrow path he was following. Dangers lay hidden on either side, mere inches away, whispering at him, distracting him in hopes that he would slip or roll his ankle. Breathing faint embers from his lungs, he caught them, igniting his fingertips. He used his hand as a torch to expose the perils hiding in the shadows. He trudged on, trying his best to ignore the calls of death around him, anxiously waiting for his first challenge to appear.

The gentle roll of the mountain suddenly turned violent, throwing Loravain from his feet. It felt as if the mountain was on the verge of a massive eruption. The precarious trail he traversed crumbled in front of him, sending the sharp stones hurtling down the mountain face. Dust and debris enveloped him as he pushed himself to his feet, but it took all this strength to keep his balance. Thunder roared in his ears, echoing off the sheer cliffs, deafening him. Unlike natural thunder, the rumbling continued to grow, becoming more unbearable with each passing second. Fire and lava spewed high into the air around him, casting a demonic red glow into the sky that illuminated the thick clouds of black ash. Yellow lightning flashed, briefly exposing the path ahead. At the sight, the hunter considered turning back. A wild flow of rocks, mud, and earth rolled like a river down the mountain. It grew wider, ripping massive chunks of semi-molten stone away with it. Fighting to keep his balance, he steeled himself against the quaking and sprinted forward. Jumping as high as he could, he landed sharply on the far side of the landslide and rolled to safety. Glancing over his shoulder, Loravain watched the trail rip free from the side of the mountain. Avoiding the razor-sharp fragments of stone, he pulled his body away from the chasm that was quickly growing wider.

As suddenly as it had begun, the mountain fell silent. The stillness that followed was eerie in the wake of the destruction that had threatened to end his life only seconds before. Leaning against a tall stone pillar jutting out of the slope, he rested in the darkness, taking time to catch his breath. Ash floated down as light as snow, attempting to lull him into a false sense of security. Had he not witnessed the destruction himself, he would have thought the mountain peaceful now.

His heart still beat wildly in his chest, but he knew he couldn't spare any more time. Pushing away from the rock, gripping its ragged edges for support, Loravain stood on wobbly legs. Taking a couple of nervous steps forward, he willed his nerves to calm. An unexpected aftershock tossed him to the ground again, dangerously close to the life-ending shards of rock. Moaning one last time in the night, the mountain shifted, leaving a gaping fissure in front of him.

Slowly crawling towards it, he feared the low whistle now rising from the deep. It grew louder, then suddenly died away, plunging the night back into an unsettling stillness. Wary of what the silence could be holding, he pushed back, narrowly avoiding the flames that shot into the ash-choked sky.

"What is this?" he cried, forced even farther back by the heat of the inferno.

Closed in on all sides now, escape seemed impossible. To his left and right, lethally sharp rocks blocked his way. Behind him, the void of darkness left by the landslide prevented him from returning the way he'd come. The only possible way forward was through the wall of flames that now towered above him. The heat rolling off it was so intense, the exposed hairs on his arms were smoking.

Loravain fell to his chest, gulping in the cooler air that didn't scorch his lungs. He covered his face with his hands. The fire at the trailhead hadn't been so hot. Maybe this was his first challenge? Did he need to master his fear of the flames? If so, all he needed to do was face it and pass through. Taking a deep breath, he stood and inched his way to the flames, only to be driven back. The heat was blinding.

"This must be a trick," he said, lifting a hand towards the wall, snatching it back as his fingertips burned. "I have never felt fire this hot in my life."

Turning his back to the fire, he stepped closer to the abyss. The air rising from the bottom was only slightly cooler than what was boiling off the wall of flames and it held the sickening odor of rotten eggs. If the wall proved to be too much of a challenge, the cliff face leading back might be scalable, but a river of lava ran below it. One wrong move would send him careening to his death. The mountain was boxing him in. Perhaps he had to think of an unconventional way to escape? He glanced at the jagged rocks around him. If he was slow and careful, maybe he could work his way back down to the bottom? One wrong move would send him head over heels and that would be the end of him. Touching one of the black shards, he gently ran his finger down the edge, wincing as it sliced through his skin like a soft tomato. Bright red blood streaked to his palm, staining his skin.

Loravain faced the wall of fire once more, realizing that was his only way out.

"I guess it's just you and me," he said, stepping forward, the skin on his face tightening in the heat.

Fighting the sensation to flee, Loravain inched forward until the flames became unbearable. He dropped to the ground hoping for relief but didn't find any.

"What am I supposed to do?" he yelled. "How do I pass this?"

At his outburst, the flames shifted, expelling a figure bathed in fire. The rock of the trail melted beneath its glowing feet.

"You wish to become a Fire Mage?" the burning figure asked, its voice flowing over him like rushing water.

"I do," Loravain answered.

"Then you must learn the true nature of fire. Without that knowledge, you will not be allowed to pass, nor will you be able to return. You will die here."

The words of his wife sounded at the back of his thoughts. He needed to open his mind. He had to admit that he knew relatively little about fire magic.

"What must I do?"

The figure placed a semi-transparent hand on his head. There was no heat to his touch, only the sensation of a gentle breeze and falling rain as the world around him was cloaked in darkness.

"Fire is the beginning."

The words came from nowhere and everywhere at the same time. Loravain only saw black but could sense there was more.

"Fire formed this world. Fire created the possibility of life. Without it, there is only non-existence. Fire is light and heat. In its absence, you will only find empty, cold darkness. Fire allows us to see what is hidden, but if one is not careful, fire will destroy what is hidden as well."

As the voice spoke, sparks of light began to appear in the distance. As the sparks grew brighter, they illuminated a foreign landscape. His attention was pulled to the closest prick of light, which turned out to be a bonfire. Ancient people huddled around it for warmth.

"Fire provides safety. Even the earliest people knew this. But as they grew, so did their arrogance. In their arrogance, they learned that fire was also difficult to control."

The scene changed to a vision of a burning city. People fled in every direction, trying in vain to escape the devastation.

"When man tries to control an uncontrollable force, death and destruction follow. Fire is a tool, not a slave; yet through proper practice, it can be harnessed."

Time reversed. The flames devouring the city shrunk away and life returned. The vision blurred and sped through the city streets until Loravain stood before a blacksmith at his forge. He was using fire to help shape his tools and weapons, while in the next building, a baker used fire to bake his bread.

"Fire is life. Like man, fire will break free of its constraints and exact retribution when forced to do something outside its nature.

When treated with respect, fire will allow itself to be guided. Every human can use fire, but a Fire Mage has a much stronger connection with it. Fire will listen to and obey the subtle desire of a Fire Mage as they are bound together as one."

Time lurched forward, hurtling Loravain through years of history. He watched as man began building a meager relationship with fire. He witnessed the birth of the first Fire Mage. She was enveloped in a cloak of flames and strikingly beautiful. As the fire danced across her skin, he sensed no hesitation or anxiety from the Mage. She knew she was in no danger. She trusted the fire not to turn on her. The Mage and the fire were two entities intertwined into one. The longer he watched, the clearer the connection between them became. Fire lived within her heart. As long as she lived, it lived. As long as the fire lived, the Mage lived.

Together, they accomplished extraordinary things. He witnessed her defeating an army, calling down fire from the sky to aid her. She summoned fire from her body, which took the form of a giant bear around her. The fire saved her from an onslaught from a horde of nightmarish creatures.

"Fire will do the bidding of its master. Its Mage. But, when forced to behave against its nature . . ." the voice trailed off as the scene melted away, leaving only a bruised and battered figure in the darkness. The Mage was on her knees, her body badly burned. She embraced another, horribly charred and disfigured. Smoke rose from their clothes. The remaining fire around her was absorbed back into her chest. She was crying.

"Fire will follow its nature. Not even a Fire Mage can prevent that. Pain will come to those who do not understand this."

Loravain bowed his head in understanding and sympathy. He felt the pain the Mage on the field was feeling. He understood her suffering.

"Fire is also life-giving. It has a regenerative nature as well. Fire brings life through what man sees as destruction."

A majestic forest sprang into view before him, only to be engulfed in brilliant flames. The trees cracked in the heat and crumbled to the ground. Both man and beast fled from the devastation. Time passed and the dark, barren landscape soon showed color. Green sprouts and saplings pushed their way through the ash-covered ground.

"Without fire, this forest would have choked itself to death, causing more damage than the fire ever did."

The new saplings melted away, giving way to a small island forming in the middle of the ocean. Deep below the surface of the waves, lava escaped from a crevice, increasing the size of the landmass. As it grew, birds landed to rest, dropping seeds from far away. Before his eyes, the desolate island became a thriving forest, providing for the animals and humans that would eventually call it home.

"Without fire, life could not exist."

The bleak, broken landscape of the mountain reappeared, and the fiery figure removed its hand from Loravain's head.

"You must persuade fire to aid you."

It waved an arm at the wall of flames. As it did, the fire faltered, briefly showing the path beyond.

"You only need to ask. Fire will never be moved by force, yet a gentle breeze can alter its course."

The figure dissolved back into the flaming wall and vanished, leaving Loravain alone to ponder on what he'd been shown. The heat of the wall, which had disappeared during his vision, poured down on him once more, but it was more bearable now.

"Persuade the fire," Loravain said to himself. "I can do that."

The flames rose high and hot as he faced them. Holding his hand up to protect his face, he stepped closer.

"Please let me pass," he said, feeling foolish as the words escaped his mouth. Nothing happened.

As before, the heat quickly became too intense, but Loravain stood his ground. He was supposed to be worthy to be a Fire Mage. He couldn't give in when things became uncomfortable. Swishing his hand in front of him, he made a feeble attempt at fanning the flames aside. When that failed, he blew on it, mixing his own fire with that of the wall. Again, nothing happened. Loravain struggled to devise new methods of asking the fire to part, and when he attempted what he could think of, they all failed. All he managed to do was burn his elbow and bruise his ego.

"Come on," he yelled at the flames, knowing full well nothing would happen. "What do you want from me? I'm trying."

After half a dozen more failed attempts, he gave in and stepped back. The heat faded and the cooler air soothed his tight, singed skin. There must be a clue he was missing. Something the figure had told him. Sitting cross-legged on the path, he concentrated on what he had been shown. He pictured the Fire Mage and how she had learned to persuade fire. She hadn't been afraid of it, or angry with it. The opposite was true. There was no apprehension in her behavior towards the fire, only trust that the flames would not harm her. That must be it, Loravain thought. The absence of fear.

The hunter faced the flowing wall again with renewed hope. Breathing out fire of his own, he caught it on his fingertips and willed the ember to burst into small flames. He had no fear of his own fire. By will alone, the flames would grow or die. He never commanded or pushed. It was like moving a muscle. When he needed it to do something, it would. It was just like using his crossbow. Letting his hands fall to his side, he stood tall and faced the wall of fire. He knew what he needed to do.

Loravain stepped forward, ignoring the heat desperately trying to push him back. The pain and discomfort would only be temporary. He stretched out his hand, allowing the fire spewing from the crevice to flow through his fingers. There was no pain, no searing of flesh as his hand lingered. He only needed to trust. The longer he stood there, his hand engulfed in the flames, the less he felt the heat. He laughed when he realized how simple it was.

Using the same thoughts and will on this wild fire as he used on his own, the flames flickered, granting an exhilarating view of the other side, if only for a moment. He plunged his other hand into the fire as well. It heeded his desires and swayed like a curtain moving in the breeze. The way was clear. Before it had a chance to close, Loravain leaped through the opening and jogged up the path. When he turned back, the fire was gone. The same was true for any signs that the mountain had almost collapsed on top of him. The trail was whole. There was no fissure in the earth, no gaping abyss left behind by a landslide that appeared to never have happened. All was as it should be.

CHAPTER 19

The summit of the mountain beckoned him onward as Loravain continued his ascent. The dagger-like rocks were few and far between now, but the way never became any less dangerous. Now, the edges of the trail plummeted hundreds of feet below, forcing the hunter to walk across narrow bridges where any wrong step would send him to his death. His progress was slow. At times he shuffled his feet at a snail's pace when the path became too slender. At a moment's notice, he had to be ready to throw his body to the ground and grip the slick, glass-like stone to avoid being ripped from the mountain by brutal hurricane-force winds. The only constant thought floating through his mind was that he couldn't see the true scope of what he was doing. He wondered if that was why the pathway only appeared at dusk. If he could see what was really being asked of him, he might have turned around and fled.

As his dark thoughts tried to console him, the stone bridge he was crossing rejoined the mountain. From here, the trail switch-backed up the steep slope of the volcano, leading Loravain up a hazardous and misleading section. Even though he was free of the danger of falling off a cliff, the trail was pockmarked with craters, trenches, fire geysers, and steam vents. At some points of the trail, he had to crawl around walls of fire, skirt dark pits, and jump over jets of burning steam that threatened to cook him alive.

The heat of the volcano also made the ground treacherous to walk across. The ground cracked and split apart where he stepped, revealing magma flowing beneath his feet. Lava breached the surface with no warning, creating impassable obstacles, forcing Loravain to backtrack to find another way through. However, he watched the summit get closer throughout the ordeal, which hardened his resolve to continue.

Offering some reprieve from his challenging climb, Loravain rounded an enormous boulder that towered above him. The trail leveled and the view of the unforgiving terrain behind him disappeared. Slick black walls of obsidian rose around him, corralling him in. It was a dead end. Running his hand across the stone, he paced the perimeter of the small alcove. The rock was so smooth, he knew he wouldn't be able to scale it. There were no gaps wide enough in the obsidian to grip and no outcroppings to step on. He searched every inch of the wall he could reach, scouring it for imperfections but came to a single conclusion. The barrier was impassable. He must have taken a wrong turn somewhere. The only way to continue up the mountain was to retrace his steps through the maze of death below.

Loravain sighed. Getting this high had been a nightmare he didn't want to repeat, but now he would have to traverse part of it again, which might be more complicated than what he had already done. Defeated, he turned and walked back into the open. The landscape was unrecognizable. In the short time he'd spent investigating the wall, the mountain face had completely changed. It had been twisted and reshaped by the heat of the lava now flowing freely down the slope. He stood, frozen, gazing at the impossible river of fire.

Spouting a string of curses, Loravain stepped away from the rising lava and back into the relative safety of the alcove. He had two options: wait for the lava flow to subside or find another way to conquer the obsidian cliff. As he considered his options, the air turned pungent. The smell of smoke and brimstone filled his nostrils. He spun around. A new fire geyser had appeared in the ground. It spewed more lava into the air and added to the flow, which was rising rapidly. Lava was only moments away from pouring into his alcove. He now had one option. He renewed his efforts to find a way up the wall.

No matter how many times he studied the wall, he found nothing. Again and again, he came up empty. Searching for a way up was useless. The maddening part was that the top of the cliff wasn't terribly high above him, maybe ten feet higher than he could reach. Maggie would be able to reach it, he thought. Or even Sarah. There wasn't even anything for him to stand on. Giving up, he dropped to the ground, folding his legs beneath him. He would have to risk waiting for the lava to subside if it didn't end up killing him first. In a moment of anger, he hit the stone ground, pain recoiling up his arm.

A resounding crack filled the air. A narrow rift appeared in the wall, running vertically from the ground up to the height of a man. The earth shook as it spread, sending rocks and pebbles cascading from the top of the cliff. Bracing himself, Loravain waited for the quaking to get worse, but it soon subsided. Ecstatic, he jumped to his feet and raced to the wall. If the fissure was wide enough, he might be able to pull himself up high enough to reach the top of the cliff. His fingers found some purchase, but he was thrown from the wall as he started pulling himself up. Rolling head over heels across the hard, unforgiving stone, he tried to right himself, ready for an attack. Once he was on his feet again, he spun around. A large stone man had stepped from the cliff, leaving a gaping hole behind him.

Like the figure of flame he'd encountered before, this figure was comprised entirely of the same stone it had come from. Shaking the earth with each step, it stomped past him and down the narrow corridor leading to the lava flow. Reaching its destination, it turned its head and faced Loravain.

"Learning about the nature of fire was your first trial. The aspects of fire are another matter entirely," the rocky figure said.

Loravain remained silent but took a step closer.

"Like humans, fire has its differences. The aspect of fire, or flame, is more subdued and visual. Being the aspect of rock and earth, I am more grounded. Of the three, I hold the closest resemblance to humans."

"What is it that I need to learn from you?" Loravain asked.

"You are to learn the aspects of fire, of which there are three. Come, stand with me."

Loravain joined the stone figure and gazed out across the devastation of the mountainside.

"What am I to call you?" Loravain asked.

"You may refer to me as the Stone Guardian, as I am from the earth," he said. "Below you will see all three aspects of fire: flame, stone, and smoke. All three are equally important. If you do not understand each of them, you will never fully live up to your potential as a Fire Mage."

Loravain nodded as he listened.

"The first aspect of fire, and the most well-known, is the aspect of flame. It is what the human world understands fire to be. Flame alone. They do not understand how fire has and continues to shape this planet. They only see it as a slave to be controlled. The first and most important lesson a Fire Mage must learn is that fire can never be controlled. If you try, it can destroy you. Flame is the most complicated of the three aspects, as it is very much alive. To grow and live, it needs food and air. Without these, it will die, much like man. And like man, it will devour anything in its path. If flame has enough food and air, it will continue to spread until nothing is left to consume. Then it will die. Flame is also the most dangerous. It does not know or understand the difference between man or plant, nor would it care. If allowed, it would wipe out whole civilizations. It has before."

"The Flame Guardian showed me this in a vision. I watched while small villages and great cities were destroyed by fire," Loravain said.

"Man was ignorant of fire in the past and continues to be so in the present. I see no reason that will change in the future. Men have never truly understood the power of fire as they only see its destructive nature. They forget that fire is as necessary to life as air is. Did the Flame Guardian also show you the life-giving power of fire?"

"It did."

"Man will curse fire for the damage it does, but as a Fire Mage, you must embrace change. From death comes new life. You must learn to become like fire. You must find the ability to change your course when needed. At times, you will burn bright, becoming a beacon to the world. Other times, you will be like stone, strong and immovable. Stone is the second aspect of fire. Deep inside the earth resides the Perpetual Forge. If you are lucky, you may venture there someday as a Fire Mage. The Perpetual Forge is the birthplace of this world. From the fire that dwells there, land was first born. As liquid fire poured out of the depths, it cooled to become stone, much like the ground you are standing on now. Long ago, this stone was deep within the earth. It will one day be used to forge tools, weapons, buildings, and many other things for man. But for a Fire Mage, stone becomes more."

The Stone Guardian hefted his large foot into the air and then stomped on the ground with enough force to send Loravain crashing to his knees. Instead of breaking apart from the impact, the stone bent to the will of the Guardian. A thin spire shot from the earth. The Stone Guardian grabbed it like a spear, snapping it from the ground.

"Stone will provide you with what you need to survive. Weapons for defending yourself, shelter when it is needed, and a means of escape when all other routes are blocked."

The Stone Guardian pointed a brittle finger at the obsidian wall it had come from. As it pointed, a small nook appeared, then another one above that.

"Unlike flame, stone can be formed and shaped, but it relies on the same principles. It cannot be forced. It must be persuaded. However, stone does not react to the same kind of persuasions as flame. Flame responds to your intelligence whereas stone responds to your instincts. To your need to survive. Your second trial will be to use the power of stone to reach the top of the cliff."

Loravain nodded and walked with the Guardian to the hole it had come from.

"There is a third aspect of fire," the Stone Guardian said as it stepped into the wall. "It is similar to flame in that it is unpredictable, but it is far more sinister. The third aspect of fire is smoke. Flame is the most dangerous of the three, but the Mage is immune to that danger. Flame is dangerous because of what it can do to the earth and man. Smoke is the deadliest to the Fire Mage. Using each type of power comes at a cost. Flames can destroy what you know, Stone can change what you know but Smoke can unmake you. Smoke can choke the life from the world, but I will leave it to the Smoke Guardian to tell you more. For now, you have received your task."

The Stone Guardian leaned back into place. As it did, the seams between it and the wall knit back together, leaving it smooth once again. The only exceptions were the two handholds that had appeared when the Guardian had summoned them. Loravain backed away and stared at the glimmering obsidian. He had no idea how to access or use the stone magic he was supposed to be capable of. He never imagined that fire magic would be anything but flames. He was perplexed.

Not knowing what else to do, he placed his palms on the stone and willed the rock to move in the same way he had done with the wall of flames. Nothing happened. He took a step back and mimicked the moves the Stone Guardian had made. He raised his arms and pointed a finger at the wall, hoping that another groove would appear. None did. Spreading his feet wider, he tried again. Nothing. Pacing back and forth between the wall and where the Guardian had stood, he contemplated what to try next. Anything that crossed his mind, he attempted. He threw rocks, yelled, stomped on the ground, and threw flames at it. Nothing worked.

Loravain collapsed to the ground and glared at the black wall. Stone magic was instinctual, and his instincts were telling him to sit down. Was it really the stone magic telling him that or his body? Did it matter? Picking up a loose rock, he tossed it from hand to hand.

"This is useless," he said. "How am I supposed to get up there?"

What had the Stone Guardian told him? Stone magic responded to his need to survive. Loravain spun in circles, glancing around the alcove. Like the guardian, he wasn't in any danger. Nothing was threatening him..

Taking a deep, calming breath, Loravain stood to try again and stepped up to the wall. He ran his fingers across the highest handhold the Guardian had created. Like the rest of the wall, it was smooth. He was expecting it to be rough and jagged. With his hand firmly pressed against the knob, he blew out a few embers, willing them to his fingers. When they were close enough, he ignited them and tried to melt the stone. His fire was nowhere near hot enough.

Anger spun around in the pit of his stomach. If something didn't happen soon, it would bubble its way through him. He wasn't sure how long he'd been stuck here, but the night was waning on. Running at the wall, he leaped up and grabbed the handholds. As he hung, a slow, deep crack resounded through the alcove. Twisting around as best he could, he watched the large boulder he'd passed when entering split in two. Lava slowly poured in around it.

Kicking the wall, he cried out for more handholds to appear, willing a path to the top. The obsidian stayed as sleek and smooth as ever.

"You have got to be kidding me," he screamed. "Did you just bring me here to die?"

Lava spilled over the top of the dissolving stone, boxing Loravain in. Kicking the wall again, he tried in vain to create an escape.

He dropped from the wall and faced the oncoming lava. It was only a quarter of the way to him, but time didn't matter. If he stayed put, it would overtake him eventually. Stamping a foot on the ground in frustration, the bare earth in front of the lava bubbled. Dust flitted into the air, blown higher by the currents of radiating heat. When it settled, Loravain saw a narrow ditch running the length of the alcove. It wasn't enough to stop the flow of lava, but it was enough to give him hope. The stone had reacted to the frustration that drove his stomp. He backed up to the wall and reached up for the first handhold again. By the time he lifted himself from the ground, lava had filled the ditch and was moving towards him.

The heat boiling off it was worse than the wall of flames. When the lava reached the wall, the strength in Loravain's arms was fading. The lip of the bluff above him was still out of reach and he knew if he reached for it, he would most likely fall.

"Give me something," he yelled, kicking the wall for the third time.

A shudder ran up the face of the stout cliff, threatening to rip him from the handholds. Now that his survival did depend on it, another handhold appeared a little higher up the wall. He grasped at it frantically, pulling himself away from the lava, which was rising faster now. By his estimation, he would only need three more handholds to reach the top.

Sweat formed on his palms, making it harder to grip the stone. He latched on to a single statement the Stone Guardian made. Stone responds to your survival instinct. Creating new handholds was the only thing that would keep him alive. To do that, he needed to understand stone magic. Taking a large, calming breath, he checked the level of lava below him. It was less than a foot away. Placing a hand on the flat surface of the wall, he pushed aside all his emotions but one. Fear. Fear was where his primal instincts came from. It fueled his desire to live. Loravain knew that if this failed, he would die. Closing his eyes, he released a long, final breath and slapped the stone. A maze of handholds, cracks, and fissures appeared on the once smooth surface.

The hunter quickly scaled the rest of the way up the wall and shimmied over the edge, narrowly escaping a harrowing end. Rolling over to his back, he stared into the dark, smoke-filled sky.

"This mountain is going to kill me," he cried out in frustration.

"Only if you let it," a voice replied. It sounded like the wind itself. "Meet us at the summit for your final challenge."

CHAPTER 20

Loravain half-heartedly glanced around the flat outcropping he was lying on. He knew the speaker wouldn't be there, but he had to be sure. It was just him, the rocks, and a faint trail leading the rest of the way up the volcano. The summit was now in view. No more obstacles were blocking him, no maze of razor-sharp rocks or rivers of lava. It was a straight shot.

His legs shook as he stood. Pushing through the pain and exhaustion, he forced his weak legs towards his goal. Trudging along, he met no external forces preventing him from reaching the top. All the challenges he faced now were internal. A myriad of thoughts assaulted him. They'd done that for years, so he was used to it, but this was worse. The closer he came to reaching the top, the more vivid his thoughts became. He saw the faces of each person he'd wronged along the way and what he had done to them. He remembered all those he'd betrayed to gain his freedom. He was ashamed of his selfishness. He didn't deserve the powers he had been offered.

When he crested the final rise, he stared into a vast, lava-filled crater. Smoke and ash spiraled skyward on a toxic breeze, mixing with the storm clouds. The air reeked of death and decay.

"I'm here," Loravain choked out.

The clouds above him rolled and twisted at his announcement. Lightning flashed, revealing the surrounding landscape below. The mountain shook violently, threatening to toss Loravain into the crater.

As the ground shimmied back and forth, a massive portion of the crater's rim broke apart and tumbled into the lake of fire. The popping bubbles reminded him of a boiling cauldron as lava spewed into the air. The scene was hellish, to say the least.

"Before you is the true power of fire," a soft voice hissed into his ear, echoing slightly as it was whisked away on the breeze.

A hazy body briefly formed in front of him, taking shape from smoke and ash. As the wind shifted, so did the figure.

"The power of fire, in its true glory, is unimaginable. Nothing can stand before it," the voice whispered. "There is nothing more powerful than the force used to create this world."

The voice came from all around him.

"Who are you?" Loravain yelled into the air, hoping to be heard over the maelstrom.

"I am the Smoke Guardian. You have learned about the nature of fire, but I am going to teach you of the power of fire."

A powerful lightning strike flashed across the sky, illuminating the outline of the Smoke Guardian floating in midair above the center of the crater. It rose and fell with the currents, then blew apart only to reform elsewhere.

"Flame is the most dangerous of my brothers," the Guardian said. "Stone is the strongest. Yet I pose the greatest threat to mankind. I have the power to change the face of the entire earth."

"How is that possible?" Loravain asked.

"I am Smoke. I am Ash. I am Death. I travel on the wind. Flame and Stone can be stopped whereas I cannot be. No weapon can pierce me, and no other element can snuff me out. I can only be moved. Redirected."

The Guardian appeared next to Loravain, zipping around as silent as the smoke rising from a flame. Startled by its appearance, Loravain stumbled back.

"How can you fight what you cannot touch?" the Guardian asked, then dissolved into nothingness.

"I can't."

"A master Fire Mage can never truly be stopped, unless by his pride and overreaching. There have only been three master Fire Mages."

"How do I become a master Fire Mage?" Loravain asked.

"Mastery of all three aspects of Fire," the Smoke Guardian answered. "Most mages will only focus on one of the three, sometimes two. Rarely will any Fire Mage consider the power of smoke. Man has always been the same. They want to show their power and strength to others. This is not done through shadow. It is not done through Smoke. Though there have been a few who followed the path of Ash. They forsook the other aspects and became like the wind. They became great, yet fell away like all the others. Smoke, like its brothers, cannot be controlled. When using smoke magic, you must be careful as you could be carried off by the winds, never to be reunited with yourself."

"Is that why most Fire Mages don't use smoke magic?" Loravain asked.

A face formed in the air in front of him. "They do not use it because they do not know about it. A man who gains power over fire thinks of fire as flame alone, never of its other counterparts. You know of what I speak. You have some power over fire, yet in your life have you ever considered stone or smoke?"

"I haven't."

"In the past, smoke magic was thought to be separate from the other five magics. It was deemed evil as only the darkest of souls attempted to master it."

"What made it evil?"

"SMOKE IS NOT EVIL!" the Guardian shouted. At his words, lightning flashed and the mountain trembled even worse. "Smoke, like flame and stone, has its nature. It is man who makes them evil. In the hands of men, all things become tainted. A tree can become a tool or a weapon. You don't blame the tree if a man kills with a wooden arrow, do you? A stone can be the means of survival or the means of death. It all depends upon the man who wields it."

"I apologize for my ignorance," Loravain said, falling to his knees in genuflection.

"Smoke magic has been used for evil purposes in the past, but so has stone and flame. In the eyes of men, smoke means darkness, betrayal, and death."

"Why do you keep referring to smoke as death?"

"See for yourself."

The smoke hanging in the air in front of him swirled together. It moved faster and faster until an image formed. The same mountain he stood on now appeared in front of him, though in another era. Trees sprouted up from the mountain and a small village had been erected around it. The smoke gave the image a hazy quality and there was no color, only shades of gray and black.

"They had reason to believe they were not safe here, yet the greed of man overpowered their senses. They came for the stones man deemed to be precious that were once abundant below the surface."

Loravain witnessed people mining at the base of the mountain. They carted away wagon loads of dirt and soil to a river then sifted through it looking for diamonds. Soon they had dug deep into the side of the mountain. Into the side of a volcano. It was too late for them now. The mountain rumbled, caving in all the tunnels that had been so painstakingly formed. When the volcano finally erupted, it rained down fire and stone from the sky, destroying all signs of life. But the devastation didn't end there. The image expanded, showing the surrounding valley. Smoke and ash flowed freely, covering the sky, and blocking out the light of the sun. Ash continued to spew from the mountain, reinforcing the shadows that grew deeper and deeper by the second. When the sky was saturated, hot ash fell like snow, suffocating and burning those unlucky enough to have survived the initial blast.

"This eruption destroyed life here for decades. No crops would grow and the river turned to poison. Those who survived fled, never to return. Even after they were gone, ash poured into the sky. The mountain sought revenge for the damage the humans had inflicted. They had dug too deep. Become too greedy."

"What about the regenerative effects of fire?" Loravain asked.

"Smoke is different from flame in that aspect. Flame will destroy the land and move on. When there is nothing left to consume, life is allowed to return. Ash will choke and poison. When it falls, it covers everything, killing it in the process. The smoke in the sky prevents the sunlight from feeding any budding plants. In manageable amounts, ash can be beneficial. It can fertilize and promote life. This explosion brought excessive amounts of ash. Too much for the earth to cope with. It took many, many years for the natural balance to return."

"What is good about smoke magic then?"

"As I have told you, smoke has its nature. It is neither good nor evil, it just is. It depends on the hands of the Mage who wields it. The use of smoke magic is different from stone but similar to flame. Like flame, smoke is not tangible. It cannot be touched but can be interacted with by will and desire. But smoke is fleeting. There is no need for smoke to be linked to a source as flame is. Flame is order, smoke is chaos."

Loravain glanced around the smoking crater. He imagined what it would be like to be part of it, floating free of any restrictions.

"Would learning smoke magic grant me the ability to take your form?"

"In theory. No man has been able to maintain smoke form, nor should he. Those who have tried have perished in unspeakable ways. It is best to never attempt such foolishness. Even I cannot hold my form for long. I exist here because I form out of the continual ash that flows from the mountain. Anywhere else, I could not be."

Below his feet, Loravain felt the deep rumblings of rushing lava. He was becoming more aware of the presence of fire around him, in all its forms.

"The ritual must be completed," the Smoke Guardian announced. "The knowledge we guard must be passed down to you."

When the Guardian finished speaking, it was joined by the others, Flame and Stone. The three circled around him, placing hands on different parts of his body. The Flame Guardian touched his forehead, the Stone Guardian his heart, and the Smoke Guardian the small of his back. As one, they began chanting.

"By the power of three, Mind, Heart, and Soul, we grant unto thee wisdom to see through the mountains last breath. Destruction and death follow behind, yet life and hope revive."

The words floated on the breeze. The Guardians rose and fell in time with Loravain's heartbeat. He could feel the steady flow of power entering his body. As it did, the mountain shook more violently, as if he were taking its life force.

"The gift of Flame, the power to burn," the Flame Guardian said.

"The gift of Stone, the knowledge to change." The Stone Guardian's voice sounded like an avalanche.

"The gift of Smoke, the ability to go unseen," chanted the Smoke Guardian.

When the words had been spoken, the Flame and Smoke Guardians flickered out of life, leaving only the Stone Guardian facing him.

"We have given you the final gift. Our purpose here is complete."

The mountain was shaking so violently now it was on the verge of collapsing.

"What now?" Loravain had to yell to be heard over the din.

"Your final task awaits you. You must be imbued with fire. Without this, you will never become a Fire Mage."

"What must I do?"

To his left, the mountain bulged out. Half of the crater rim broke free with an ear-shattering explosion and slid into the bubbling lava of the lake. Had the Stone Guardian not grabbed him, he would have been blasted off the mountain.

"You must bathe in the eternal fire."

The Guardian walked over the edge of the pit and pointed into the crater. Stomping on the ground, a narrow staircase formed along the inner wall, allowing access to the lava below.

"You must hurry. Time is short for you and your companions."

Satisfied with his warning and instructions, the Stone Guardian sank into the broken rocks, leaving Loravain to complete his final trial. The hunter stared into the pit, the tumult of the shaking mountain increasing with worrying intensity.

CHAPTER 21

"What do you think is happening up there?" Maggie asked. She'd been watching the mountaintop ever since it began quaking. Lightning strikes flashed through the clouds continuously.

"That is not for us to know," Thanatos said, stealing a nervous glance upwards as well.

Ever since Loravain had disappeared between the two guardian stones, the storm over the mountain had grown progressively worse. The wind howled and screamed through lifeless branches, whispering frantically, trying to tell them they were in danger. Thick ash fell around them, layering the ground in a fresh, sickly gray blanket. Maggie was well past being annoyed. The ash and lightning were enough to keep everyone on edge, never mind the constant trembling beneath their feet.

"Do you think it's safe for us to be sitting here?" Sarah asked. "Can't you call the wolves back? We should get farther away."

"It shouldn't be much longer now," Thanatos answered, shaking more ash from his fur.

"How do you know that?" Maggie asked.

The wolf remained silent though he was clearly agitated. He sniffed the air then flattened his ears back against his head. He knew more than he was saying, which wasn't much. The glowing fire at the volcano's summit reflected off the low-hanging clouds, adding to the sense of impending doom. The entire scene was something straight out of a nightmare.

"Well, I can't just stand around here doing nothing," Maggie shouted. "We're running out of time. I don't want to lose the chance of meeting my mother."

She stepped towards the trailhead Loravain had taken but was quickly stopped by Thanatos.

"No! Only Loravain is to cross the threshold. If you try, you will die," he growled.

"It might come to that anyway," Sarah said, pointing up the mountainside.

The volcano started to break apart. Massive rockslides flowed down the mountain like rushing water. Lava poured out of every crack and fissure running along the surface, giving it the appearance of flaming veins. The earth began to quake in earnest. It was enough to drop Maggie to her knees.

"We have to get out of here," Sarah shouted, pulling Maggie to her feet. "Now."

"You may be right," the wolf said, dropping his head in defeat. "Forgive me, my friend."

Thanatos bolted towards the sleds. "Quickly now. Get what you need and tie me up. We haven't much time."

Maggie became a flurry of movement, throwing their gear onto the sled. At the same time, Sarah strapped in Thanatos and took her place on the back runners. When everything was packed in and tied down, Maggie jumped on top and grabbed on when Thanatos started running. It wasn't a quick getaway, but they slowly started to accelerate.

"We're going to have to do better than this," Sarah shouted, stealing nervous glances over her shoulder.

"I'm trying," Thanatos replied, the weight of the sled obviously too much for him.

The view of the mountain temporarily faded from view as they passed a clump of petrified trees though nothing could silence the cacophony behind them. Sharp flashes of lightning illuminated the sky, followed by short bursts of thunder that could scarcely be heard over the tumult of the mountain.

As Thanatos ran, Maggie caught intermittent glimpses of the volcano through the trees, each one proving to be worse than the last. It was sheer chaos. The mountain was being ripped apart. In deep hues of red, lava bled from its scarred face and flaming chunks of earth began falling around them. Maggie was sure they were going to die. No matter how fast Thanatos ran, it wasn't fast enough. At their current pace, they had no chance of outrunning the destruction barreling towards them. They would be sent to oblivion like everything else. At least Loravain would have died instantly, Maggie thought. He wouldn't have to suffer through the after-effects of the eruption.

Maggie buried her face in her hands. Tears streamed down her cheeks at the thought of Loravain being gone. Not even a Fire Mage could survive an erupting volcano. Closing her eyes, she tried to drown out all the sounds clamoring for her attention. It was as if the earth was being tortured, pleading for the pain to stop. Maggie couldn't take it any longer.

"What's happening?" she screamed.

"I have no idea," Thanatos said. "I've seen volcanoes erupt before, but this is unlike anything I have ever witnessed. I would wager that Loravain has something to do with this."

"You don't think he's dead?" Maggie asked.

"That man is surprisingly resilient. If anyone could survive this, it would be him."

"I hope you're right," Sarah cried. "I'd hate to continue without him."

Thanatos pivoted sharply to avoid a burning log obstructing their path. The sled bucked beneath Maggie, tossing her over the side. Bouncing through the mud, she rolled to a stop in time to see the wolf shoot forward.

"Stop," Sarah cried, bringing the sled to a halt. "Are you okay, Maggie?"

Maggie nodded then grinned wildly.

"How much faster could you run if we got rid of some of the weight from the sled?" she asked.

"No," Sarah said. "We can't risk losing any of this. We'll need it to survive."

"I'm not talking about that," Maggie said, turning back to Thanatos. "How much faster?"

"Twice as fast, I'd say."

"That settles it. I'll run alongside you."

"Don't be stupid," Sarah shouted. "He'll leave you behind."

Maggie didn't listen to her, and neither did Thanatos. The sled bolted forward while Sarah continued to protest. Taking a deep breath, Maggie stretched her legs. If the ground was level enough, she knew she could keep up.

"Okay," Maggie said to herself. "You can do this."

She knew she could run fast but she hoped this wouldn't be too much. Sarah and the sled were almost out of sight. But this was the only way she could help them escape. It was now or never. Kicking out, she sprinted down the trail. Her hair whipped around her face, stinging her eyes. She urged herself to run faster.

"You can do this," she repeated.

The ice behind her heart began to spread through her body, cooling her burning muscles. The strain she felt in her lungs eased and her breathing returned to normal. To her surprise, she hadn't slowed down at all. She was going faster. She laughed.

The back of the sled came back into view. Thanatos was really moving now but she was catching up. Her ice magic kept her going. She sped on, leaping over rocks, ditches, and even small trees. The exhilaration pushed her on even harder.

"How is this possible?" Thanatos croaked when she overtook him.

"Just . . . keep . . . going," she managed to say between ragged breaths.

Maggie slowed down so Thanatos could keep pace with her. They raced away from the mountain, leaving the worst of the danger behind, or so Maggie hoped. Then, everything fell silent. The wind faded away, the ground became calm, and the sky ended its light show. She dared a glance over her shoulder. She could still make out the light of the lava bouncing off the belly of the clouds.

"What happened?" she asked, bringing their progression to a stop.

Thanatos struggled against his tethers but managed to twist around. A look of fear shone clearly in his dark eyes.

"The calm before the storm," he said almost to himself. "Hurry. We must find shelter."

Sarah toppled from the back of the sled, unable to hold on as Thanatos lurched forward. Clasping hands, Maggie helped her up then steadied her as they chased after the sled.

The scenery blurred past as they careened through the treacherous backwoods. Thanatos finally slowed down enough for Sarah to catch up and she jumped back on the runners, but his caution ended there. He knew something horrible was about to happen and wanted to be as far away from it as possible. Finding her pace again, Maggie fell into stride alongside him.

"Are we going to die?" she asked.

Thanatos glanced at her with his dark, piercing eyes. "Have you ever seen a mountain explode before?"

"No," she answered, shaking her head.

"Then trust me. Shut up and keep running."

Farther down the trail, Maggie spotted a small outcropping of stones. Leaping off the ground, she soared high into the air. She saw a deep ravine winding its way through a hidden glade, splitting a wide meadow in half. The outcropping overreached the ravine, possibly granting enough cover from the eruption. She watched it as she started to fall, trying to gauge its depth. When she looked up again, she was too close to the far side of the ravine to slow herself. Folding her body into the fetal position, she covered her head with her hands. On impact, her breath was ejected from her lungs and her muscles blossomed with pain. She slid through the mud to the bottom of the ravine, struggling to breathe. She straightened her spine and rolled onto her back when she found enough strength to refill her lungs. From where she was, the sky looked peaceful, but she knew it was a lie. Wheezing loudly, she gingerly sat up and cleaned herself off as best she could. Thanatos and Sarah stared down at her.

"Was that really the best way to get down there?" the wolf asked.

Maggie glared at him. "Shut up."

"Are you okay?" Sarah asked, more concern in her voice.

"I'm fine. Just a little bruised," she croaked then looked around.

From her current angle, the underside of the outcropping was deeper than it seemed from the air. It was still shallow but deep enough to provide them with the protection they needed.

"There's something here," she said with a grunt as she pushed herself to her feet.

Sarah and Thanatos joined her and stared at the indentation in the stones.

"It's not much but I think it will work," Thanatos said.

Maggie pushed her way inside then fell to the ground, exhausted. She closed her eyes, hoping sleep would take her, but they flashed back open when the ground began rocking. She held her breath, hoping it would pass without incident. From what Thanatos had explained to her, she didn't want to be anywhere near the mountain when it exploded.

"How much longer do you think it will be?" Sarah asked.

Thanatos shook his head. "There is no telling with something like this. I thought it would have happened by now. We should smile on our good fortune and get some rest while we can."

Sarah lay down on Maggie's right and Thanatos flopped down on her left. She felt safe between them. They tried to get comfortable, but the space was too cramped for the three of them. To distract her thoughts, Maggie stared out into the early morning sky. At least she thought it was morning. The sky burned orange in a way that reminded her of sunrise. The only thing telling her otherwise was the gently falling ash. When they'd first arrived here, they had escaped it. Now it had caught up to them, reminding Maggie of the danger they were in.

Not wanting a reminder of what they were going through, Maggie placed her hands over her belly, her fingers intertwined, and closed her eyes. Her feet swayed back and forth as she waited for sleep to overtake her.

"Shouldn't someone be on watch or something?" Maggie asked.

"On watch for what?" Sarah asked. "Nothing is dumb enough to be out here except for us."

"Maggie has a point," Thanatos said. "You two sleep. I'll stand guard. Maggie must be dead on her feet after that feat she pulled. I never thought I'd see the day when a witch could outrun me. You will be a force to be reckoned with once you've had time to train properly."

"Maybe that's why the Dark One wants me dead?" Maggie asked.

"I don't think he cares how fast you can run," Sarah said. "It will be something else he's after."

"I agree," the wolf said. "We'll have to keep a close eye on you to see what other surprises you hold."

Maggie tried to hide the smile that was climbing up her face at the compliment but failed. "Wake me up before too long. You must be tired too."

"Don't you fret about that. I'll wake you long before you care to be awake. Now sleep."

Thanatos sauntered off into the ash as Maggie closed her eyes. Before she'd even had time to start dreaming, she felt his wet nose nudging her shoulder.

"What? I thought you wanted me to sleep," she muttered.

"It's your turn to watch," the wolf said as he pushed his dirty body next to hers.

"I just closed my eyes. If this is your idea of a joke, it's mean."

"You've been asleep for hours already."

Maggie forced her eyes open. He was right. The sky was brighter than it had been, though it was still choked with ash and smoke.

"Ugh," she moaned. "Fine."

She crawled out of their little stone hovel, giving up her spot so Thanatos could sleep. The sled now sat next to the opening of their small indent. Thanatos must have had a hard time getting that down by himself without waking them.

As she paced, she followed Thanatos' meandering tracks as they zigzagged across the ravine. They would shoot up the slope here and there, falling from view, then reemerge a bit farther down.

Her eyelids fought against her as she walked. She wanted nothing more than to lie back down and go to sleep. She listened to Sarah's calm and steady breathing. She envied her.

"Maggie?"

The voice floated in on the ashen air. She wasn't expecting it, so she didn't catch where it was coming from. Sarah and Thanatos were sleeping so it wouldn't have been one of them. Someone was calling to her from out in the woods.

"Maggie? Can you hear me?"

Whoever it was knew her well enough to call her by name. Hesitant to close her eyes, she tried to focus her hearing with them open. If something was going to happen, she needed to be able to hear and see it coming.

"Hello?"

The voice was clearer this time. She hurried over to wake the others.

"Thanatos, wake up," she said, pulling at his fur.

"What is it?" he asked, sounding wide awake.

"Someone's out there."

"Who?"

"I don't know but they know my name."

The wolf bolted to his feet. "Where is it coming from?"

She led him into the open and pointed up the sharp incline of the ravine. "There."

Thanatos perked his ears and listened. "I can't hear anything over the mountain. Wait with Sarah. Do not move until I come back."

Maggie ran back to Sarah while Thanatos scurried up the ravine and out of sight. She pressed her back against the cold stone and slid to the ground next to Sarah, who had fallen back to sleep. She was blissfully unaware that there could be someone out there right now, hunting them. Maggie had been trying to prepare herself for another attack. If what Loravain said was true, the Dark One wanted her dead. Would he give up after one failed attempt? At this point, wouldn't it be two, Maggie thought? Loravain had initially been sent to kill her. Maggie shuddered at the thought of what her future looked like.

Her thoughts spiraled out of control as one possible attack led to another and then another. Hunters and assassins were never in short supply in her imagination.

"Wake Sarah," Thanatos called out, surprising her. "Loravain has returned."

Faster than Maggie thought possible, Sarah was up and out of the cave. A wry smile crept up her face. She had an inkling that Sarah liked the hunter.

At the top of the rise, they found Loravain sitting on a large, flat rock. His clothes were ripped, burned, and practically fell off his body. His skin was bruised, and smudges of dried blood was smeared across his face. His knees, arms, and neck were covered in open wounds that festered and dripped.

"What happened to you?" Sarah gasped.

"I became a Fire Mage," he answered solemnly.

"How?" Maggie asked.

Loravain recounted his journey. He told them that the guardians at the trail head had pronounced him worthy and explained what he would encounter on the mountain. He described the trials he had completed and retold the visions he'd had.

"As I stood at the summit, looking down into the open mouth of the crater, the Guardian of Stone formed a way for me to reach the lava. He told me that to become a Fire Mage, I was to immerse myself in the lake."

"Why?" Maggie asked, enthralled by his story. "What was that supposed to do?"

"Let him finish, then you can ask questions," Thanatos said, scolding her.

"When the path down was complete, the Guardian left, leaving me alone. I had to proceed or lose my chance at becoming a Fire Mage. The mountain was on the verge of erupting. Stepping into the lava wasn't what I expected. I was expecting it to burn the flesh from my body, but it was comforting and warm. It reminded me of home. When the lava was up to my chin, I stopped. Thinking my task complete, I turned to leave but the Guardian of Smoke stopped me. He told me that to become a Fire Mage, I needed to submerge myself and breathe deep the power of fire."

"What was that like?" Maggie blurted out, earning a glare from Thanatos. "Sorry."

"It was unlike anything I've experienced before. Searing heat rushed into my lungs. The pain was intense at first, but it soon subsided. I panicked though. I didn't know if I would drown. When I resurfaced, the Guardian of Flame stood next to me. He said the mountain would allow me to leave but I should hurry. The mountain had given me its power."

Maggie stared at him in awe. She could tell that he was different now that he was a Fire Mage.

"As I ran down the mountainside, the rocks beneath my feet were ripped apart, leaving gaping holes in my path that I narrowly avoided. When I reached the bottom, you had already left."

"How did you find us?" Thanatos asked.

"The Guardian of Smoke directed me. He was able to trace your path. The closer I got, the easier you were to track."

"I am glad you survived, my friend," Thanatos said. "But we must hurry. Time is short. I fear if we hesitate any longer, we may be too late."

Loravain nodded in agreement. He glanced around the clearing. "Where is the other sled?"

"We didn't have the means to bring it with us," the wolf answered.

"With Loravain here, we'll need to think of something else," Sarah said, chiming in for the first time. "Do you think we'd be able to find some horses?"

Thanatos shook his head. "There wouldn't be a living creature foolish enough to stray this close to an erupting volcano."

"We'll have to manage with what we have," Loravain said. "Let's get ready to move. The volcano won't hold back her wrath much longer."

At Loravain's request, they readied their belongings and loaded everything they had removed back into the carriage of the sled. The hunter searched one of the bags until he found a change of clothes. Maggie turned around as he changed.

It was an ordeal getting the sled up the other side of the ravine, but they managed it and were soon ready to depart. Sarah made a small bed on top of their bags and equipment and sat down, leaving the runners free for Loravain. The mountain had stopped quaking, leaving the ground more stable, so Maggie decided that she would run for a while. Stretching her legs, she waited for Loravain to finish strapping Thanatos to the sled.

"What do you think you're doing?" he asked Maggie when he saw her.

"Getting ready to go. The sled will be too heavy with all three of us. Poor Thanatos doesn't deserve that."

"Ha," Loravain said with a laugh. "There is no way I'm going to let you run. I know you're fast but not faster than Thanatos."

Neither Sarah nor Thanatos spoke. They watched the exchange in silence, letting Maggie handle it for herself.

"You have to trust me," she said. "With all three of us packed in that thing, Thanatos will hardly be able to walk."

Loravain turned to Sarah for help, but she only shrugged her shoulders. "She's right. It will be too heavy. Plus, she is faster than I am."

"We need to get going," Thanatos said. "That mountain won't wait much longer. I dread to think about what kind of force is going to be behind an explosion that size."

"Fine," Loravain huffed, giving in. "We only do this until we have another option."

Maggie nodded then jogged ahead waiting for Thanatos to catch up. He struggled with the weight at first but quickly fell into a rhythm. He was soon on Maggie's heels, forcing her to run faster. When the wolf finally passed her, she let him, giving Loravain a sly smile as they pulled ahead.

"You're going to have to do better than that," he yelled back at her, unable to see the smile beaming across her face.

"Are you ready for this, Thanatos?" she called out.

"Shove those words right back down his throat," came his snide reply.

She pushed her toes deep into the ash, breaking through to the mud below. Taking a deep breath, she surged forward, putting all her strength into the sprint. The path ahead was clear, providing a straight shot. Pushing with all her might, she practically flew past the bewildered look plastered on Loravain's face.

"What? How?" It was all the hunter could manage as she raced past the sled.

Sarah was beside herself with laughter as Thanatos was the one falling behind now.

CHAPTER 22

Even though the sun was hidden behind thick ash, the sky darkened considerably when the volcano finally erupted. The shock wave that emanated from the explosion blasted past them, throwing Maggie to the ground. Mud and ash clung to her body and she bounced head over feet. Coming to a jarring halt, she stayed where she was and stared back at the destruction.

Massive plumes of ash and earth rose into the air. Fiery chunks of rock and dirt vanished into the choking sky, only to return to view moments later, plummeting back down with explosive force. It was the loudest thing she'd ever heard. To save her ears, she focused on her power and silenced it, leaving an eerie void behind. What she looked at now seemed far away and harmless. The only thing reminding her of the danger now was the trembling coming from below her.

When she found the balance to stand, she searched for the others. She had escaped the blast relatively unscathed. The sled was another matter. Split down the center, it was now useless firewood. Loravain climbed down from a tree and Sarah lay flat on her back about twenty paces ahead of the sled. They both seemed to be unharmed. She couldn't see Thanatos.

"I think the Guardians held back the explosion until we were far enough away," Loravain said.

"That might be the case, which I am grateful for," Thanatos said from inside a bush. "Now help me get out of these tethers."

Maggie ran to him and pushed her way through the branches. The wolf was wrapped up in the leather straps unable to move. Pulling her father's dagger from her belt, she cut his restraints one by one until he was free.

"What now?" she asked.

"We keep moving," Loravain said. "Even though we're clear of the blast, it would be foolish to think we were out of danger."

Moving with a limp, Sarah scoured the area, searching for their gear that had been thrown clear in the shock wave.

"Can I help?" Maggie asked.

In reply, Sarah tossed a sizeable green bag to her, which almost knocked her over. "Take what you can carry. Leave the rest."

They sorted through their belongings until they only had what they needed to survive. The rest was hidden under bushes and thrown into the trees. Next, Loravain attacked the sled, snapping its runners off and turning them into kindling.

"Why are you doing that?" Maggie asked.

"If someone comes this way, they'll think a camp was ransacked. If we leave everything neat and tidy, anyone who runs across it may suspect something," Thanatos answered.

"Who's going to run into it way out here?"

"You never know who might stumble upon it," a slithering voice answered from the darkness of the forest.

Thanatos growled at the underbrush, the hair on the back of his neck standing up. Loravain had his crossbow in his hands in seconds and aimed it at a man who had sauntered into view on horseback. He was too well-dressed for someone so close to an erupting volcano to be there by chance. His face was clean-shaven and his hair was cropped close to his scalp. His hazel eyes were piercing and intelligent. He shook his head at the mess they were leaving.

"Your trick would have been much more effective had you finished and moved on before I arrived," the man said.

"And who might you be?" Loravain asked, slowly reaching for his belt with one hand, holding his weapon steady with the other.

"Oh, I wouldn't worry about that dagger, hunter," the newcomer chuckled. "And I doubt that crossbow is any condition to be fired."

He was right. The stock was cracked, and the string frayed. It would probably fire, but the shot wouldn't be accurate.

With a flick of his gloved hand, a flurry of movement flashed in the bushes around them. The stench of sulfur filled the air, eliciting a gagging cough from Maggie.

"I'm not going to waste my time with drawn-out conversations," the man said. "This will be over soon enough. If you happen to live through this, then we'll talk."

Two hideous-looking creatures ambled into the open, squinted yellow eyes focused on the man sitting in the saddle. Blood-red skin covered their scant frames and large bone-like protrusions jutted from their elbows and shoulders. They walked on their hind legs like men, but each step looked painful. Thick tusks sprouted upwards from their jaws, framing their noseless faces. Sores and boils covered their bodies, secreting a transparent mucus that smoked and popped in the open air.

Distracted by the beasts in front of them, no one noticed the identical monster creeping up from behind. With a growl of warning from Thanatos, Loravain spun out of the way, narrowly avoiding what could have been a messy and painful death. The creature lost its balance as it sped past Loravain. When it righted itself, it feigned another attack but fell back, obeying a silent command from its master.

"What is the meaning of this?" Loravain shouted.

"Haven't you guessed that yet, Loravain? You must be a smart man. How else could you have become the Dark Master's favorite?"

Loravain glanced at his companions. He could see the fear in the witches' eyes. They had never faced creatures like this before. Without training, engaging the beasts in battle would be folly. Scanning the trees, the hunter searched for an escape route. He'd heard about these creatures before and they were nothing to be taken lightly. If he could find a way out, he'd take it.

"Retreating won't work," the man said, motioning to something behind them.

A fourth monster emerged from the cover of trees, effectively blocking all chances of escape.

"What do you want?" Loravain asked.

"Why do you ask questions you already know the answer to? Maybe you are not as smart as I gave you credit for. Nevertheless, I want you to know that unlike Dolan, I do not have orders to keep you alive."

Closing his eyes, the man on horseback seized, almost slipping from his saddle. As if sensing his imbalance, his hands shot out and gripped the horse's mane. Steadying himself, he opened his eyes, revealing only black.

"Na fut yamdlun," he choked as if his tongue was not accustomed to speaking the guttural language of the creatures he was addressing. "Indoit serum."

A crooked finger pointed towards Maggie. The nearest creatures immediately attacked, throwing their bodies at her in a crazed frenzy.

Loravain jumped into action as swiftly as the red-skinned demons did. He dropped his crossbow and slid a long-bladed dagger from the inside of his jacket. Not caring about showmanship, he hacked and sliced at the beasts' backsides, allowing Maggie time to escape. Sarah grabbed her hand and rushed her into the underbrush and out of immediate danger, leaving Loravain to face the four demons alone.

Loravain spun around to confront the other three creatures but only counted two, and they were closing in. He slashed at them, cutting them deep, but they showed no signs of injury.

"How is this possible?" Loravain asked after another round of ineffectual attacks.

The creatures were fast. Much faster than he was. Gnashing tooth and tusk, the demons feigned advances, testing him for weaknesses. Not only were they fast, but they were also smart. They had flanked him before he was prepared, yet they still hesitated to strike a killing blow. Or any blow for that matter. They were waiting for something. Loravain threw a nervous glance at the man on the horse.

"Are you only here to toy with me?" he asked.

"Their actions are not my doing. I can influence them and give them a target, but their tactics are their own. It's amazing to watch, isn't it?"

With his attention elsewhere, a third demon attacked from behind, knocking Loravain from his feet. He twisted around in the air and grabbed the charging monster. The festering, smoking wounds that pockmarked its skin stank of rotting flesh and brimstone, causing his eyes to burn with irritation. The sticky mucus seeping from its many wounds numbed his skin on contact. When he crashed to the ground with the creature, he threw it over his head and rolled back onto his feet. His left arm had lost all feeling, but the effects of the mucus wore off quickly.

Before another attack came, Loravain scooped up his fallen dagger and wiped the mud from the blade on his pants. The demons stared at him as if they weren't used to anyone lasting this long.

"Well, come on. I haven't got all day," Loravain taunted, swinging his blade in front of him.

A scream echoed from the woods behind him. It was either Sarah or Maggie, but that didn't matter. He was supposed to be protecting them. He needed to discover a way to dispatch these demons, and quickly.

The next attack came faster than Loravain could blink. Parrying with his dagger, it was all he could do to keep from losing ground. His only saving grace was that the creatures seemed confused. Their offense wasn't solid and they weren't working together. One used its own limbs as clubs and tried to beat him to death while another fell to all fours and swiped at his legs with bony elbows and tusks. The one facing him posed the most immediate threat. It slashed at his face with blade-like claws. He blocked a flurry of attacks, waiting for an opening, then darted in, burying the blade of his dagger deep in its chest. Thick black blood oozed from the wound, repelling the others. The demon took no notice of the dagger protruding from it and struck Loravain in the head with a mighty blow, sending him sprawling to his back. Hitting the ground hard, he rolled backward over his head and bounced back to his feet. With the other creatures gone, it was now one on one.

Not waiting for the demon to initiate the next attack, Loravain leaped into action, though his vision was blurry from the hit. He charged the demon and pulled his dagger free. The demon howled in anger as the blade slide from its chest, but Loravain kept moving. He spun around, ending up facing its back. He lifted the weapon high and brought it down hard, sinking the blade between its shoulders then down along its spine. That finally got its attention. Murder shone in its eyes as it spun around, screaming in fury, acidic saliva burning Loravain's face.

"What are you waiting for?" the man on the horse screamed. "Rip him apart."

While the demons were distracted by the man's outburst, Loravain made his escape. He fully expected the witches to be defeated or captured by now but was surprised when he crashed through the autumn brambles. They were faring better than he was, though they were both only facing one demon. Their tactic was simple. One would distract the beast while the other attacked from behind. It was a weak offense but effective. Soon or later though, their plan would fail.

Maggie moved with blinding speed. She was just as fast as the demon, if not faster. While Loravain watched, she stabbed the creature no less than five times. Still, the devil showed no signs of faltering. It continued as if nothing had happened.

Sarah was using her magic to try and subdue the beast. Each time it focused its anger on Maggie, Sarah would reach out for its head. When she got close, the demon would turn on her at the last second as if anticipating her tactics.

In an instant, everything fell apart. Loravain could sense the demon he'd stabbed behind him again, yet he never heard it come through the bushes. At the same time, Sarah tripped over a tree root. If he didn't act now, they would both die.

His dagger was wet with black blood and mucus. Mustering all his strength, he threw the blade at the demon advancing on Sarah. It hit home in the demon's neck just below the jawline but did nothing to stop the attack. It did buy enough time for Sarah to leap into the low-hanging tree branches above her and escape.

Pain blossomed through his muscles as another demon tackled him from behind, mucus smearing across his body. It seeped through his clothes as easily as water. He could already feel his arms growing heavy, and his breathing became shallow. This was it. If he couldn't fight back, he would die. He landed hard on his stomach, face bouncing off the compact dirt. The metallic taste of blood exploded through his mouth. Silently pleading with his muscles to respond, he cursed when he knew they wouldn't.

"Use your gift," Thanatos yelled over the tumult of screams, howls, and moans.

A glimmer of hope twinkled in his eyes. He'd been relying on his skills as a fighter to win this battle, forgetting he had another ability. Even if he couldn't move his arms, he could still breathe, and that was all he needed. Anger raged through him as he let loose a volley of embers. By will alone, they ignited across his body. The numbing effects of the mucus vanished as the flames engulfed him. Strength returned to his limbs. Pushing his fire out, it spread up the demon's body. In a moment of panic, the creature leaped into the air but soon fell calm once more.

"Did you think it would be that easy?" the stranger laughed. "The Master knows what you've been up to. These are demons from the deep. They were born of fire."

Still burning, the demon crouched to pounce. Loravain didn't have time to stand up before the punches came. Rolling over, he narrowly avoided a fist meant for his face. The beast's fist sunk six inches into the ground. The fire had increased its strength. With a wild kick, Loravain's foot connected hard with the creature's chest. It stumbled back but didn't go down, though it did give Loravain enough time to stand up. On his feet, he made a mental note of where everyone was. Sarah was climbing higher, trying to keep out of harm's way. Maggie was playing defense now that she was on her own but easily stayed out of reach. Thanatos was nowhere in sight but was most likely dealing with another one of the demons. The flaming demon was about to charge him again. His companions would have to manage without him for the time being. He needed to put this one down for good.

The demon finally attacked. At the last second, Loravain sidestepped as the monster careened past him. Stomping on the ground, Loravain tried to will the stone beneath his feet to come to his aid. If ever there was a moment he needed help surviving, this was it. Unlike his attempts on the mountain, he could feel the stone only a few feet below him this time. He pulled at it, but it refused to obey. Just like him, the stone was being stubborn. Only two choices were available now. Continue fighting for the stone to give in to his will or deflect the bony punches flying at his face.

The first punch landed squarely on his jaw, but he managed to dodge the next one and back-peddle out of reach of the knee that threatened his groin. He felt his fire magic begging to be used but he ignored it. He didn't want to give the demon any more power than it already had.

"Loravain? Thanatos?" Maggie called out. "I need help."

She was in danger. His fear for himself evaporated as he turned his attention to her. He had to keep her alive. If everyone else died, Maggie had to live. He could see her dark hair flashing in and out of view behind a patch of berry bushes.

"I'm coming," he yelled.

The burning demon blocked his escape, somehow keeping the flames ignited. It was feeding them with its mucus. The more mucus the demon expelled, the higher the flames rose and the taller it stood. Pus bubbled in the heat, giving life to the fire. But it also created . . .

"Smoke," Loravain exclaimed.

"What was that?" the stranger asked, amused.

Smoke was more like fire than stone. He might be able to persuade it more effectively. Reaching out to it, he expressed his desires. He needed to stop the demon and the only way to do that was by killing it. In essence, smoke was death magic. The smoke responded as quickly as his fire had. Directing the vaporous tendrils, they wound around the beast's neck then flowed into its mouth and nostrils. Thickening, the smoke prevented the creature from breathing. Panic set in. The demon collapsed and flailed on the ground, kicking and scratching at its face. The battle didn't last long. A few more violent kicks and spasms and the beast fell still. It was dead.

He barreled through the bushes. The demon Maggie was fighting was on all fours, hands and feet encased in large clumps of ice. It was fighting to break itself free. Behind it was more ice chunks, cracked and broken. This wasn't Maggie's first attempt.

"I couldn't think of anything else," Maggie cried out from above him.

She huddled next to Sarah high up in the tree. Sarah held her short sword at the ready. He motioned for it. It bounced off a few branches, but Loravain deftly caught it by the pommel. He returned to the trapped demon and quickly brought the blade down, severing its head from its body. Thick coils of dark smoke rose from the decapitated creature. It drifted into the air then shot downward, disappearing back into the depths below. He rushed over to the flaming demon, which still lie motionless on the ground. He dispatched it in the same way then watched it dissolve into smoke and vanish.

"What have you done?" the stranger screamed in anger. "You will regret you didn't let yourself be slain by my hand. You will suffer more than any man before you."

"I am sure I will," Loravain answered casually, wiping the blade on the grass. "Sarah?"

"Right behind you," she said.

"You know what to do."

As the man raised his hands to summon more demons, Sarah laid her hand on his knee. His body froze instantly, cutting off his reinforcements.

"It is no use, witch," the man said. "You may have prolonged your lives by days, but you will never get the information you seek."

"He's too powerful," Sarah admitted. "I can't get past his barriers. If I let go now, he'll be able to summon his creatures."

Loravain searched for his crossbow. When he found it, he loaded a bolt into its cracked frame and aimed it at the man's chest. "Can you silence him?"

"This witch may be able to hold my muscles in place, but that is all. She has no more power over me than that."

"Good. Now we can have that drawn-out conversation. If you don't answer in honesty, I will use you for target practice. And to prove that I mean it . . ."

He fired a bolt into his shoulder, just below the joint. The man's scream rang out through the forest.

"Do we have an understanding?" Loravain asked before he was tackled to the ground.

The man on the horse laughed. "You should have ensured all the creatures were dead."

Wiping his head back, Loravain collided with the demon, knocking it off balance. He rolled onto his back and ignited his hand. Flames trickled down his arms and engulfed his chest. As if eager for the strength that would follow, the demon threw itself at the fire. As it spread, Loravain caught the smoke as it tried to escape then quickly incapacitated the demon.

"They don't learn as fast as they should," Loravain said. The sword flashed forward and the demon dissolved. "Now, where were we?"

The man bit his lip, falling silent.

"Have it your way."

He loaded a second bolt into the crossbow and fired into his other shoulder.

"How about now?"

"Yes, yes," the man replied, sweat running down his face.

"What is your name?"

"Quinton."

"What did the Dark One offer you in return for completing this task?"

Quinton remained silent. His gaze shifted from Loravain to Sarah and then behind them. Loravain turned. Maggie stood at the far end of the clearing.

"Answer me," Loravain pressed.

Again, the man said nothing.

"Sarah, I would prefer not to waste another bolt. Can you do something?"

She nodded then set to work. Quinton's body twitched and convulsed as he watched.

"You will fail, witch. My mind will never be open to you," Quinton snapped, his voice trembling.

"I'm not searching for that part of your mind. It appears you are only protecting your memories."

A smile crossed her face as Quinton's paled. He screamed.

"Okay," he panted when he was able to speak again. "Stop. I'll talk. I was offered the Master's right hand and the power to raise enough demons to wipe the witches from existence."

"Why would the Dark One care if the witches were wiped out?" Sarah asked.

"War is coming. It is nearly upon us," the man said, managing a laugh at the back of his throat.

"When will this war start?" Loravain asked.

Quinton faced Maggie. "Once that one is dead."

"That will never happen. You have my word on that. You can let go of him now, Sarah."

As soon as she released her hold on him, Quinton toppled out of the saddle, his head hitting the ground hard.

"Is everyone alive?" Thanatos asked, hobbling out of the trees.

"Thanatos?" Maggie cried out. "Are you okay?"

"I will live," the wolf said. He was injured, blood flowing freely from his haunches. "We must make haste. The Dark One will continue to send assassins to finish the job. We will not find peace until we reach Priama. Even then, I fear our torment will not be long absent."

"Take the horse," Loravain told Sarah. "Load our things as best you can while Quinton and I have a little chat."

Loravain knelt next to Quinton, who was writhing in agony. Grabbing one of the bolt shafts, he twisted and leaned in.

"When you have the strength and courage, give the master a message for me. Unless he comes for me himself, his minions will continue to be sent back to him, just like you."

Quinton's face paled another shade. It was unclear if that was due to the pain, loss of blood, or the fear of having to return to his master knowing he had failed.

"Kill me now," he pleaded. "Do it quickly."

Loravain's knee creaked as he stood up, rising above the helpless man. The horse had been loaded and Maggie was tending to Thanatos' wounds. Blood and dirt were smeared across his fur, but he looked ready to travel.

"No, I will not be killing you today. Come against me again and that will be the outcome. As for today, your punishment is life."

CHAPTER 23

Silence prevailed after their encounter with Quinton. They had each come so close to death and were surprised they had made it through as unscathed as they did. The memories of the red demons still made Maggie shudder. She never knew such creatures existed. She didn't dare think about what other kinds of monsters might be out there. Glancing at her friends, she realized how lucky she was to have them.

Thanatos had taken the worst of it, but he seemed content enough trotting next to the horse. Sarah sat in the saddle. The toll of keeping that madman still for so long had been tremendous but she handled it well.

"Do you think she'll be okay?" Maggie whispered to Loravain.

"It's hard to tell. She has been exerting herself much more lately than she is used to. But magic is like a muscle. If you don't use it, work it out, it tires you easily. She just needs rest and more practice."

Maggie let herself fall behind the others so she could watch them. She missed her parents and her house. Being on the run was wreaking havoc on her nerves. She jumped at every sound, and with how sensitive her hearing was, that was often. Yet amid her sorrows, she was happy to be with Sarah, Loravain, and Thanatos. They hadn't been together long but she knew she would be lost or dead without them. Each of them had risked their lives for her when they didn't have to. As she walked, she watched Loravain catch and support Sarah each time she slipped from the saddle. He did it with such care and compassion. It hadn't been like that before Maggie had taken the poison dart to the knee. Something had happened while she was sleeping. She was curious but content to watch it unfold before her. Smiling, she chuckled to herself.

"What?" Thanatos asked, creeping up behind her.

Without thinking, she placed her hand on his neck, caressing his fur as they walked.

"What happened with those two?" she asked.

"Something that should have happened long ago," the wolf said. "He has punished himself for twenty long years. He needed some joy back in his life."

"They would make a smart pair."

"I'm not sure smart is the right word, but yes, they would be good for each other. Now might not be the best time for romance, though. With war coming, their happiness could be ripped away from them."

"I'm still confused about this war," Maggie said.

"As am I. There is still too much that is unknown, yet the signs are there if you know where to look."

"What do you suppose will happen once we reach Priama?" Maggie asked.

"What do you mean?"

"With them. I mean, I know change is coming. They each promised me they would help me reach Priama. But after we get there?" Maggie said, then faltered. "I'm scared."

"You will be queen. There is plenty to be nervous about, but you should not be scared. In the time I've been with you, I've seen him do things he never has before. He has shown a level of compassion I thought he was no longer capable of. But if there is one thing I have learned throughout my long life it is that love will find a way. It is more powerful than war."

"You're talking about him and Sarah?"

"No. He cares for Sarah, but you are his drive right now. You will be hard-pressed to be rid of him once we reach Priama."

Maggie smiled as the wolf trotted ahead, taking his place next to the horse again.

Afternoon came and went as they walked west, following the setting sun. When dusk approached, Loravain stopped their procession and lifted Sarah from the back of the horse. Carrying her over to a pile of dried, dead leaves, he gently laid her down.

"She needs better rest than she's getting on the horse," he said. "Maggie, gather some firewood. We'll camp here for the night. None of us would be worth anything in our condition should another attack come. We all need rest."

"Why do you coddle me so much?" Sarah asked him.

"Because you deserve it," he said, grinning at her. "And because I like to. Now, get some rest."

"Take what little rest you can get," a voice said from the trees. "You must reach Priama soon. The Queen's condition has become worse. Duncan fears she will not last the week."

"Who said that?" Maggie blurted out.

"Hold your tongue, girl," Loravain scolded. "You have no idea who you are addressing."

Taking that as her introduction, Gwendolyn the owl floated into view, landing on a broken stump of a branch reaching out of a tall, dead poplar tree.

"The future Queen of Priama is not for you to silence, human. Come, Maggie. Stand before me."

Maggie did as she was told. "Are you like Thanatos?" she asked.

The owl chuckled. "Our conditions are similar but we are not alike. I am only allowing you to speak to me out of the greatest of necessity. Thanatos has more love for humanity than I do. However, I have no desire to see them destroyed. Neither do I want to see the witches destroyed."

"Has the situation become that dire?" Thanatos asked. "Why would you worry about the destruction of man?"

Gwendolyn ruffled her feathers and turned her head. Her large yellow eyes stared at the wolf.

"The Dark One has been busy. The humans are readying for war. The soldiers of Mountain's Reach are slaughtering the covens in the marshes, who, in turn, are planning their retribution. As we speak, delegates have been sent to Priama to seek aid from the Queen. If Maggie is not pronounced queen before her mother dies, Alyssa will assume control. She will gain the Coven Seat and she supports the coming war."

"What must we do?" Loravain asked.

"Make haste to Priama. There is not much time left. Rest here until midnight and then go. My servants will provide you with means of transport. Thanatos," she said, turning her attention back to him. "Speak with Duncan when you arrive. He holds information vital to your cause."

Gwendolyn spread her wings and hopped to a higher branch. Turning back, she looked at Maggie.

"You alone hold the power to stop this war. You can prevent the deaths of hundreds of thousands of lives. Trust in yourself and your friends. You have a virtuous and pure heart. It will be needed."

The owl flapped her wings and was gone. Maggie's knees buckled beneath her, and she sunk to the ground. The words the owl spoke couldn't be true, could they? Loravain looked at her, sympathy clear in his eyes. He was the only one who understood what it felt like to be expected to do something impossible.

As night fell, a heavy tension hung over them like a wicked fog hiding more demons.

"How can any of that be true? How am I capable of doing what she said?" she asked herself once Loravain and Sarah had drifted off to sleep.

"The greatest warriors never ask for the battles they are fighting. They only rise to meet the challenge. You are like that. Thrown into a world you have no understanding of, yet destined to save it," Thanatos said from the darkness, startling her. His eyes glimmered in the fire-light. "You do not know it, but you are your mother's daughter. You have strength in you that the world has never known before."

"But will that be enough?"

"We can only hope," the wolf said.

Maggie sighed. She stared at Thanatos, who had dropped his head to his paws.

"What about you?" she asked.

"What about me?"

"I have so many questions about what or who you really are. I've never met an animal that could talk before, and you seem to know so much about everything."

Thanatos stared at her as if trying to decide how much to tell her.

"I am what I am," he said simply.

"But what is that?"

"This world is full of mystery. To grow and learn, we must accept that we will never understand it all in this lifetime. All you need to know right now is that Gwendolyn and I are here to help you. I promise more knowledge will come, but for now, we need to focus our energies on reaching Priama."

Maggie lay back, putting her hands behind her head, and stared up into the sky. The smoke and ash from the eruption were still spreading across the sky, but small pockets of moonlight appeared sporadically. She knew she needed to sleep, but she couldn't find it. Closing her eyes, she waited for the familiar haze of her dreams to shroud out her thoughts. When it didn't, she gave up. Rising to her feet, she stared at the fire. The light cast dancing shadows across the tree trunks, playing tricks on her eyes. Each time a log popped in the heat, she jumped, thinking another demon had come to take her away.

Fresh tears streamed down her cheeks and her knees shook. She'd tried not to think about what was happening. She only wanted to focus on finding her mother, but after this most recent attack, she couldn't help but long for Lakes Hollow. It was quiet there. No one was trying to kill her.

She held back a silent sob as she realized that if she had stayed there, she would most likely be dead already, along with her parents. By leaving, she had saved all of them. Taking a deep breath, she cleared the thoughts away. She was never going to find sleep with thoughts and fears running rampant through her head. Backing out of the firelight, she found a quiet, isolated place to sit. If she couldn't return home, the least she could do was make this place vanish, even if only for a few moments.

Clearing a flat rock of leaves, dirt, and grime, she sat cross-legged and began her routine. The wind was silenced first. It blew through the trees, rattling the dead leaves that somehow still clung to their branches. When that was done, she moved to the crackling of the fire. She continued until the only sound left was the breathing of her friends. Instead of shutting them out, she let the sounds grow. She listened to each of their breathing patterns in turn. Sarah was in a deep, relaxing sleep. That was good, Maggie thought. Her body was still recovering. Loravain's breathing was sporadic and shallow, indicative of a nightmare. She'd heard that enough from listening to her parents over the last few years. She never understood why they had bad dreams until now. Their lives had been littered with the fears they knew were coming. Those fears had been realized the day she left. They had been dreading that moment all her life. Finally, she turned her attention to Thanatos, who she discovered was not sleeping at all. He was breathing as silently as he could, but it was controlled and even. Was he watching her in the darkness? No matter. She let their breathing fall away.

Unlike other times, the eerie silence she'd created didn't have the desired effect. She wanted to escape but had ended up creating the perfect atmosphere for her fears to grow unhindered. They festered and dug deep into her subconscious, spreading seeds of doubt. She knew the future's safety depended on her, but she doubted herself and her abilities. The owl must have made a mistake.

When the negativity threatened to overpower her, her mother's words flashed through her mind. *"I mean that we can't be too sure about things sometimes. Take that spade for example. When you picked it up and saw that nick, you thought you would be able to grind it out and it would be as good as new. That's not always the case. We don't always see what is really causing the problem. And sometimes life can view you like you do that blade."*

Maggie was beginning to understand what her mother had been trying to tell her. Maybe her mother had experienced a harder time with life than she'd thought. Now, more than ever, she wanted to be comforted by her mother's arms and hear her words of wisdom. She knew her mother would tell her that she was doing what she was supposed to and that she needed to continue down the path fate had created for her.

She shook her head violently. These thoughts were getting her nowhere. If she continued this way, they would only cripple her. Straightening her legs, she fell back, supporting her weight with her arms. She dug her fingers into the dirt, enjoying the feeling. Growing up with herb farmers, she'd grown accustomed to the feeling of earth. She felt at home in the damp, cold soil. Wriggling her fingers, she created cavities in the ground. She almost recoiled when something wriggled back. It wasn't the familiar sensation of worms or insects. Her curiosity heightened, she kept her eyes closed and probed deeper. In a moment of fear, she realized what was happening. In a panic, she opened her mind, allowing all the sounds in the world to crash back in uncontrolled. She screamed out in agony as the deafening roar assaulted her mind. She'd always been so careful when reversing the process. She jerked her fingers out of the earth and jumped to her feet, frantically wiping her hands on her clothes. Something had crept around her fingers and up her arms. It was dry, coarse, and hard. Head pounding from exertion, she swayed, helpless to do anything else, and fell into the waiting arms of Loravain as she lost consciousness.

CHAPTER 24

"What happened?" Loravain yelled to Thanatos as he laid her next to the fire.

"I don't know. She was alone."

"How could she have been attacked if she was alone?"

The wolf shook his large head. "We don't know if she was attacked."

"How else would you explain this?" Loravain questioned.

"No one is out there. We were not followed. Still, even now, we are alone."

Loravain looked down at Maggie's body but could find no signs of injury. There was no blood, no cuts, bruises, or breaks in her skin. Turning her on her side, he examined her back as well.

"Nothing."

"I wouldn't say that," Thanatos countered after sniffing her hands. "Look at this."

Thin tendrils of plant roots were intertwined around her fingers. They were brittle and broke at the slightest touch, but had somehow managed to slither all the way up to her wrists and forearms.

"What could have caused this?" Loravain whispered. "Could someone do this from a distance?"

Thanatos had a troubled look in his eyes. "This is nature magic."

The wolf sniffed the air again and stared into the darkness. They left Maggie where she was, safe by the fire, and walked over to where she had fallen. Scouring the area, they searched for anything that might explain her current state. With a snap of his fingers, Loravain summoned fire to illuminate the ground.

"Your powers are growing," Thanatos commented.

"This is odd," Loravain replied, ignoring what Thanatos had said.

"What is it?"

"Holes near her handprints. Do you see these filaments?"

"They look like the ones around her wrists," Thanatos confirmed.

Loravain scanned the area but couldn't see anything else. The only place the roots were exposed was where Maggie had touched. He plucked a small handful of the roots free of the dirt and shoved them in his pocket.

"What do you make of it?" he asked Thanatos.

"I can think of only three possibilities, and none of them are likely. There could have been a witch or magician near enough to have done this. They would have had to be well hidden if I could not sense them. Second, this happened naturally, with no magical interference, which is near impossible. Or, the final explanation, and most likely of the three, Maggie is capable of nature magic."

"How would that be possible? She has never shown any signs of nature magic before and is well past the age of manifestation."

"Like I said, all three options are unlikely."

Loravain was stumped but there was no time to dwell on what might have happened. Midnight was fast approaching, and they would soon be on their way to Priama. They could continue their search for answers there. Taking another sample, Loravain freed some of the roots still attached to Maggie's fingers and put them with the others.

When he had done all he could for Maggie, Loravain hurried around their small camp and gathered their gear. He placed it near the fire, making sure to keep it all in order. Next, he removed the saddle from the horse and slapped its backside. Whinnying, the horse reared up and bolted into the woods, swallowed up by the night.

"Why did you do that?" Thanatos asked. "We could have used it."

"Anything Gwendolyn sends as transportation will be much faster than horses. If she means for us to make haste, she will provide suitable means."

"You show blind faith in the owl," Thanatos said. "Though well intended, it is not a good thing."

"I have learned that there are beings in this world who know a great deal more than I do. The owl seems genuinely concerned for the welfare of Maggie. I will trust in that."

"No being, no matter how powerful or intelligent, is perfect. Remember that Loravain. All beings have motives of their own."

"And you? Do you have motives I don't know about?" Loravain asked.

"Of course. Though at the time, they do not conflict with the course you have set."

Loravain stared at the wolf. "And when they do conflict?"

"Then I will do what I have to," Thanatos answered. "As would you if our situations were reversed."

Loravain watched Thanatos walk away and then finished his tasks and lay down next to Sarah. He closed his eyes for only a moment but was then back on his feet. An explosion rang out in the distance. Thinking it was an attack, he soon had a dagger in each hand. He waited for something to happen in vain. No attack came. As he listened more intently, he understood what he was hearing. Something large was crashing through the forest, ripping up trees as it went. As the sound grew louder, the ground began to shake. Tossing his daggers to the ground, he ignited his hands. Hot white flames danced around his fingers in anticipation. Taking a position to his left, Thanatos growled through bared teeth.

Neither of them were prepared for what came barreling into sight. Standing before them were two creatures Loravain had never seen before. His flames fizzled out as he took a few steps back.

"Anderins?" Thanatos exclaimed. "I thought they were extinct."

"You've seen these creatures before?" Loravain asked.

"I have. I knew that Gwendolyn would conjure up something impressive, but I never imagined anything like this."

"This is what she sent to take us to Priama? How do you know that? This could be another one of the Dark One's tricks."

"It couldn't be. Gwendolyn would never allow the anderins to be used for such a purpose."

"How can you be so sure of that?" Loravain asked.

"Because she created them."

Loravain stared at the massive anderins with renewed interest. Their heads were at least as twice as high as he was tall. Their faces were flat with small, black, birdlike beaks. Whiskers protruded from their cheeks, giving them an almost cat-like appearance. Their ears were large and stood on top of their heads, moving independently from one another like a horse's. Each leg ended with a set of razor-sharp talons or claws. It was hard to tell if the anderins were feline-like birds or bird-like felines. Their bodies were long and lithe and covered in light, coarse-looking fur. Each wore a different pattern, but the colors were similar. Light brown with streaks of yellow and orange. They were well matched for the flat plains they would be crossing to get to Priama. Their fur stopped at scaled tails, which extended straight out behind their bodies. Unlike a cat's tail, they remained motionless, pointing back the way they had come.

"We're riding these?" Loravain asked.

"You'd better wake Sarah. We have a long way to go," Thanatos said, then trotted forward to communicate with the two anderins.

Sarah was easily coaxed from her slumber with a few words from Loravain. She sat up slowly, trying to push the weariness from her eyes. Her gaze lingered on the dying fire until she heard the stamping and scratching of the anderins.

"What are those?" she screamed as she scrambled back, pressing her body against a tree trunk.

"That's how we're getting to Priama," Loravain answered, helping her to her feet. "They've proven to be quite docile so far."

"So far? What are they?"

"Anderins. I'm not surprised you're not familiar with them. Neither was I. Thanatos thought they were extinct," Loravain said, purposefully leaving out the part about Gwendolyn creating them. He still wasn't sure how that was possible.

"They have agreed to take you to Priama as quickly as they can. It will take them longer traversing through the forest, but once they reach the flatlands, they will be able to reach Priama in about half a day," Thanatos explained, silently padding up behind Loravain.

"How long until we're out of the forest?" Sarah asked, glancing nervously at the anderins.

"With riders, a day, maybe less. You will reach Priama within two sunrises."

"Why do you keep saying you?" Loravain asked. "Are you not coming with us?"

"I can't ride, and I am nowhere near as fast as the anderins. Not even Maggie could make that claim. I will get there as fast as I can. One will take the gear and one rider. The other will take the other two."

Loravain nodded. He picked up two of the bags at his feet and handed them to Sarah. When she took them, he picked up the rest.

"Help me secure these to one of them," he said, walking towards the closest anderin.

Sarah followed close behind and waited for Loravain to finish his work. He positioned the bags on the creature's back then motioned for Sarah to toss him a rope.

"We need to secure these tightly," he said.

"Not too tightly," Thanatos said. "The anderins need room to move. Whoever is riding this one can hold them steady. Once they get moving, you shouldn't have much trouble."

Sarah threw an end of the rope to Loravain. He tied it off on one of the bags.

"What should I do with this end?" she asked.

"Take it to the other side.

She began walking around the anderin but Loravain stopped her.

"No, you need to go under it."

"What? Why under? If that thing moves, I could die."

"Then be quick about it. We don't have any time to waste."

Huffing out a retort, she shimmied under the anderin as fast as she dared then lobbed the rest of the coiled rope up.

"That wasn't so bad, was it?"

"Just don't ask me to do it again," Sarah said.

"You have my word. You'll be riding up here with the gear."

"What?" Sarah screeched. "Why do I have to ride alone?"

"Something has happened to Maggie. She can't ride alone. I need to be her support."

Sarah spun around. Running over to Maggie, she placed a hand on the side of her head.

"Is it the poison again? Tell me exactly what happened."

Loravain told her what he knew and what Thanatos had said. He showed her the roots he'd collected. He finished with Thanatos' theory.

"It isn't impossible . . . ," Sarah said, then trailed off.

"What isn't impossible?" Thanatos asked, standing behind her.

"For a witch to manifest a third power later in life, especially after a traumatic experience."

"How long do you think she'll be like this?" Loravain asked.

"It's hard to tell. Without knowing if it was another power manifesting, or what type it was, I can't say. The best bet is to get her to Priama. They have some of the best healers in the world."

"Can you attempt to see what happened to her?" Thanatos asked.

"My power doesn't work that way. Anyway, I'm exhausted. Any more exertion might render me unconscious too."

"The risk will be minimal. In her state, she has no power to fight against you. Her mind will be like an open book. It will be like you aren't even trying. And you don't have to see what happened, just sense her emotions."

"Are you sure?" Sarah asked.

"Positive. The more information we have now, the better."

"If you say so," Sarah said, putting a hand on each of Maggie's temples.

It took a few minutes for anything to happen but Sarah slowly pulled her fingers away.

"I don't know what happened but Maggie is scared out of her mind. She wants to go home but she knows she can't. She worries that the Dark One will finish her off soon. She doesn't want to die."

"I thought you said you couldn't read minds," Loravain said.

"I can't, but her emotions are strong enough right now to paint a vivid picture. And Thanatos was right. I hardly needed to try."

"Her fears are valid," the wolf said. "All the more reason to get her to Priama as soon as we can."

"I agree. Help me get her on the anderin and we'll be on our way," Loravain said.

The hunter carefully scooped Maggie into his arms. She was breathing, but only just. Sarah raced ahead of him and scaled the side of the anderin using handfuls of its fur as handholds. Once astride it, she reached down and took hold of Maggie's arms. Together, Loravain and Sarah managed to slide her prone body into position. Once Loravain had climbed up and was seated, Sarah slid down and took her spot on the other one.

"There is not much time," Thanatos reminded them. "Maggie must reach Priama soon or all may be lost. Make haste. I will join you as soon as I can."

With a silent command from Thanatos, the anderins turned and fled the same way they had come. Leaning over, Loravain watched them run. Their claws curved in such a way that they slipped into the earth with ease, allowing them to push their bodies forward with great force. It was amazing to watch.

AFTER HOURS OF traversing through the forest, they finally arrived at the plains. The anderins sped up considerably when they didn't have to worry about maneuvering around trees. At times it seemed as if they were flying. They moved so fast it was more common to see all four legs in the air at once than seeing them touch the ground.

The anderins also needed little rest. They ran constantly, but the ride always felt smooth. Their tails supported their balance, swishing behind them only to make minor corrections to their course. The faster they ran, the more it felt like they were standing still in a heavy wind. At times, Loravain had to lean over Maggie to keep her from being ripped away.

After a long day of running, they reached the flatlands. No more hills or ravines for the anderins to avoid. Sensing they were home, they pushed forward with a speed they hadn't shown before.

"Are you okay?" Loravain yelled.

Sarah couldn't hear him over the rushing wind. Loravain chuckled to himself. She was going to kill him for making her ride alone as soon as they arrived in Priama.

CHAPTER 25

The hole in the hillside had been dug in a hurry. It was likely to collapse at any moment. But if this was the place his master had summoned him to, it would be secure enough for the time being. Ducking slightly to avoid bumping his head against the loose dirt, Quinton scurried deeper into the hole. He hadn't had any trouble pulling the darts from his shoulders, but by the time he'd regained enough strength to do so, his enemies were long gone. He knew he would be punished but never imagined the summons would come so soon. When the ragged little creature serving the master plopped down on the ground next to him to deliver his message, he knew that his life was over. But Quinton was a man of honor. He knew he had failed his master and would not run from his fate.

Making haste, he pushed plant roots out of his face and continued down the newly trodden path. The hole was much deeper than he imagined. As the trail steepened, he was forced to grip the wall to keep from falling. A fall here might kill him. Would that be so bad, Quinton thought? It would save him from whatever torture his master had planned. Wincing as his shoulder rubbed against the wall, he rounded a tight corner. The murky darkness that had been prevalent since entering was replaced by warm firelight. It gave the appearance of being swallowed by a gigantic, fire-breathing beast. With the light, the slope leveled out and the dirt walls changed to smooth black stone as he entered a natural cavern. His eyes slowly adjusted to the dim firelight, revealing immense columns rising out of sight above him, supporting an unseen ceiling. The workmanship of the pillars was astounding. He couldn't envision his master creating something like this just for their meeting.

"A beautiful room, don't you think?" a voice asked as if reading his thoughts.

The question floated through the air, echoing and reverberating off the stone surfaces. It was his master's voice, no doubt, but there was no telling where it came from.

"Yes, Master. It is quite impressive," Quinton answered as he fell to his knees in genuflection.

"I have been here for quite some time now admiring the beauty of it. And all along, I have been pondering about you. I have been deciding your fate. You, more than most, know that I do not reward failure, but your position raises a certain quandary."

"Forgive me, Master. I accept the fate you have chosen for me, and will do so gracefully," Quinton said sharply, no fear in his voice.

"I knew you would, hence my hesitation," the Master said, running a finger across Quinton's back, startling him. "You have been a wonderful asset to me. Almost as good as Loravain. With him gone, I can't afford to lose one such as yourself. But you must be punished."

"I understand your dilemma, Master."

"You are not like that quivering worm, Dolan, trying to impress me by taking credit for the deeds of others."

Quinton heard another man whimpering somewhere out in the darkness of the cavern.

"He has failed me too often, so I propose a challenge," the master said with a flick of the wrist.

Small sconces along the columns and walls burst into bright flames, illuminating the hidden areas of the cave. It was much larger than Quinton had originally suspected. A lone man, who he assumed was Dolan, lay on the floor near the center of the chamber. Strands of rope lay scattered around him.

"I am offering Loravain's position to the winner of this . . . ," the master said, then paused, choosing his next word carefully. "Venture."

The whimpering coming from Dolan stopped immediately but he continued to lay motionless on the floor.

"STAND!" the master shouted. Both men complied. "I require your most solemn oath that you will complete the task which I am about to present. Failure to comply, or to complete the task, will result in a fate much worse than death."

"I swear to comply to and complete the task you are about to set," Quinton said without hesitation, glaring at the man opposite him."

"I swear as well," Dolan replied with a faltering voice.

"The winner of this match will receive the honor of being on my right hand. I will need a strong commander, willing to do anything I ask of him in this upcoming war. Without the use of weapons, only the skills you currently possess, kill one another."

A smile appeared on Quinton's face when Dolan faltered and stepped back. He was about to surge forward when he was stopped by a hand on his shoulder. It was his master's.

"Kill him quickly and the world will never know of your failure."

The battle was over almost as soon as it started. Quinton rushed the smaller Dolan. Out of the corner of his eye, he saw the master weaving his way between the columns, taking his place on a large, ornate throne. A large black bird sat on the wooden back.

As soon as Quinton caught Dolan, he violently twisted his neck and dropped his lifeless body to the floor. With victory in his hand, he turned and faced the master, who was stroking the bird's head.

"I applaud you, commander," the master said, then turned his attention to the bird. "Tell Zane it is time. Instruct him to find our ally. Our quarry is headed right for her."

The bird flapped its inky wings and disappeared into the dark recesses of the hall.

"Come, Quinton. We have much to discuss."

CHAPTER 26

The flatlands were a blur and Maggie didn't stir for the entire ride. They hadn't seen anyone on their journey, but now that the sun had set and darkness was once again creeping in around them, they could see small pinpricks of light in the distance. When the anderins got too close to one, they would change directions, zipping off another way. The meandering path they took through the grass slowed them down, but it was safer. Loravain didn't want any unnecessary confrontations.

When the moon finally peeked out from behind the horizon, finally free of the ash, the anderins had been forced to change directions so many times that they came to a standstill. Ahead of them was the illumination of a larger settlement. The lights and fires they had avoided so far had been small and isolated. That wasn't the case anymore. The anderins refused to move ahead any farther. They fought against any prodding and lay down in the tall grass, giving their riders quicker access to the ground. Taking the hint, Loravain slid off the side of his mount with Maggie in his arms. He carried her a safe distance away then returned to help Sarah unload the other anderin.

"That was the most amazing thing I have ever done," she announced.

"Really? I thought you would have hated it. I was worried you were going to try to kill me when we arrived."

"I thought about it at first, but once you give in to it, it is exhilarating. I wish we could have ridden together."

"I know," Loravain agreed, placing his hand on top of hers.

They pulled the rope together, releasing its hold on the animal. When the anderin was free, it stood up and shook the bags from its back. As soon as they hit the ground, both creatures fled back in the direction they had come. Alone at last, Loravain pulled Sarah close and kissed her forehead. They hadn't had much time alone since before the Mountain of Fire. Things had been too hectic. Ever since he'd allowed her in his mind, they had been connected. They understood one another. He started to think he might be able to put aside his guilt for letting Camila die. He was opening himself up to love again after twenty years.

"We have to walk from here," Loravain whispered in Sarah's ear.

"You're such a romantic."

"How far do you think it is?" he asked, pulling away.

"Really? We're all alone and all you have to say is to ask how far it is?" Sarah snapped.

"We don't have time. You've seen the creatures the Dark One is sending after us. Once we can put all this behind us, then we can move forward."

Sarah sighed. "It shouldn't be more than two hours on foot. Those brighter lights are the outer rim of Priama. The capital itself sits in the middle."

"Two hours of carrying Maggie?" Loravain asked.

"Give or take."

Sarah stared at the gear spread around them. "What about all this? Do we make multiple trips?"

"Without Maggie to help carry it, we should only take what we need. With any luck, we'll be able to come back for the rest once Maggie is being looked after."

"Sounds good. Then we'll really have some alone time." Sarah winked at Loravain.

The hunter picked up a few loose items and placed them in his jacket then walked over and picked up Maggie, putting her over his shoulder. Sarah strapped one of the bags to her back.

As they walked, they discovered that most of the lights they had seen from the anderins were torches. They were spaced out across the plains, each one about two hundred feet from the others. They stood about twice the height of a man and didn't seem to serve any purpose. There were no houses, huts, or tents he could see. After carrying Maggie past three of four of them, Loravain stopped to rest. He studied the area but still couldn't find any logical reason for the torches to be there.

"What do you think these are for?" he asked Sarah, turning in circles to see them all. He counted twenty-four.

"I have no idea," Sarah answered. "I haven't been to Priama in a long time and I was never allowed out at night."

"They must serve a purpose."

"They do," a voice answered from the night.

A small woman walked towards them, hands extended in front of her. A faint aura of smoke and embers burned around her palms. Raising his hands, Loravain called out to her.

"We mean you no harm. Our friend here needs to be treated by your healers. She has fallen into some unknown illness."

The woman remained silent, moving warily forward. When she reached them, Loravain placed Maggie on the ground and he and Sarah stepped back to show they were not a threat.

"She is a witch," the woman said. "What is she doing all the way out here? Why is she not within the walls? What have you done to her?"

The woman jumped up, flames igniting around her hands. "Tell me or you will not live to see daylight."

Sarah stepped between the fire witch and Loravain. "Please, Maggie needs your help. She is a witch and so am I. I am her friend."

The flames faltered at her announcement but did not die out completely. The woman stepped forward to examine Maggie again. Only when she was satisfied did she let her flames fade.

"And the man? What of him? Is he friend or foe? Do not be afraid, Sister, you can answer me honestly."

"He is a friend. He has been protecting Maggie with his life. If not for him, we would both be dead."

"Where are you from, Sister?" the fire witch asked.

"I am from far away. We have come to seek counsel from the Queen. But before we do that, our friend needs attention."

The woman once again turned to assess Maggie's situation. Resting a hand on Maggie's head, she ran her other one down her spine.

"Verida, come quickly. Bring the sickbed with you," the fire witch snapped into the night, then returned her attention to Sarah. "I do not know what is wrong with your friend, but she does not appear to be in danger. We will carry her to the walls. Stay close to me."

A few moments later, a young witch, possibly Maggie's age, came bounding into the light. She dragged a long wooden stretcher behind her. The two witches took great care laying Maggie's limp body on it. When she was lying face up, the small fire witch lifted a finger to her lips and blew out a low, quick whistle.

"You will lead us, Verida. We must make haste. When Fabiola arrives, we will send her ahead with word that we are traveling with strangers. The way will be made safe."

"Yes, Harvest Mother."

Verida bent down and took hold of the wooden handles. The older fire witch waited for Fabiola to arrive before picking up her end.

"What is your name?" Sarah asked, making polite conversation.

"My name is Magenta. I am the night harvest leader. And since you were wondering, human," she said, directing her comment to Loravain. "The torches are here for us. We grow herbs here that can only be harvested at night. Even better under the full moon."

"Maggie will feel at home here then," he responded.

"Why should she not feel at home here otherwise?" Magenta asked.

"Her adoptive parents are herb farmers."

"Adoptive parents?" Magenta asked.

"Maggie was raised by humans," Sarah answered.

Magenta glanced down at Maggie with renewed interest. She was about to speak again when a young child came skipping into the light.

"You called, Harvest Mother?" she asked.

"Ah, there you are, Fabiola. We will be taking these visitors to the healer's tent. Please make sure the night watch and gate watch are made aware. Please hurry."

Taking her cue, Fabiola bounded back into the night. At her retreat, Magenta picked up her end of the stretcher and began walking to the gates of Priama. Loravain and Sarah followed behind at a distance.

Loravain studied the flames burning atop the torch poles. He watched the smoke rise into the air and disappear. Reaching out with his mind, he could sense each wisp and tendril. Now that he knew what it was like persuading smoke to move, he knew he could do it again. With a thought, the smoke wriggled around the flame like a transparent snake. It coiled lower around the pole then shot off into the night.

"Be careful," Sarah whispered. "You never know who might be watching."

He nodded silently when he noticed Magenta looking back at them.

"Please keep up," she called out. "If you get too far behind, I cannot guarantee your safety."

They picked up the pace, closing the gap between them. Magenta and Verida never spoke to one another, they just pushed on in silence. When the lights from the torches faded away, darkness swallowed them up.

"Curse this bed," Magenta cried. "I need my hands for light."

Without thinking, Loravain stepped ahead and summoned flame into his hand, casting eerie shadows through the bushes and grass. Magenta almost dropped her end of the stretcher. The look of shock on her face was enough for Loravain to kill his fire.

"Forgive me," he said. "I was out of place."

Managing to keep her pace steady, Magenta leaned over to him.

"How did you do that? Are you a magician?"

"I am no magician, I can promise you that."

"Then how have you come to know fire magic?" she asked.

"It was a gift," he answered, noticing Verida leaning back to listen.

Magenta's eyes grew wide with the announcement. Scanning the area around her, she prodded Verida to move faster.

"Keep up. We must hurry. No one else must know of what you can do. It is hard to tell who serves who nowadays."

"And who do you serve?" Sarah asked.

"Me? Why, I serve the true queen, Natalia the wise."

Loravain glanced at Sarah.

"We have heard that there has been some unrest in Priama as of late," Loravain said cautiously.

"As of late?" Magenta huffed. "It has been going on for years. That horrible excuse for a witch, Alyssa, has been trying to take the Coven Seat from the Queen. She has never had enough support though. Without support, a proper challenge cannot take place."

"What challenge?" Sarah asked, stepping closer to Magenta and taking Maggie's hand at the same time.

"You call yourself a witch?" Verida asked, speaking for the first time, a hint of venom in her voice.

"Watch your tone," Magenta scolded.

"No, it's okay," Sarah said. "I am a witch."

"Yet you do not know our customs? How can this be?"

"I grew up in one of the smaller covens near the southern marshes. They hold a different standard there. We didn't see eye to eye on many things. When I was old enough, I thought my life would be better lived away from the witches."

"Why come back now?" Verida asked.

"Because I made a promise to her," Sarah said, pointing at Maggie. "She freed me from a fate I was not keen on taking part in. As payment, I told her I would bring her to Priama."

"And you?" Verida asked Loravain. "Why are you here?"

"My reasons are my own and I will not betray myself to you."

Verida pouted at the rebuke and turned around. The conversation fell away. They exchanged only a few more words over the next hour and soon arrived at the great outer wall of the inner city. Braziers ran along the top of the wall, which had been constructed using wide tree trunks, sharpened to a point at the top. Loravain saw archers walking back and forth between the gaps in the timbers. The perimeter was impressive. At least fifteen feet high and built upon earthen mounds, the wall would be extremely difficult to breach. Taking the city by surprise would be near impossible.

The only entrance Loravain could see was protected by another short wall standing in front of it. Large cauldrons hung from the backside, most likely filled with oil or wizard fire. Unless granted access, no one could gain entry to the city un-assaulted.

"This is impressive," Loravain said as they passed the wall and entered the city.

"Priama is the greatest city in the land, though it may not be the largest," Verida said, leading them to the left. "The human city of Mountain's Reach is larger, but we hold the power."

"That is enough, Verida," Magenta said, hushing her. "Let's get them to the healer's tent. We must hurry back to our duties. We only have two more nights of harvest."

"Yes, Harvest Mother," Verida said, lowering her head. Her eyes, however, held a look of rebellion. She only seemed to be cordial under the constant constraint of Magenta.

A large building-like tent stood to their left. It was twice as long as it was wide and was wrapped in animal furs and skins. Its frame was comprised of long, flexible poles. Thin wooden planks lined the bottom of the tent, giving the structure more strength. Next to it, a massive building dominated what Loravain could see of the inner city. Five stairs led up to a thick set of double doors, which had been painted red. An intricate carving of a dragon's head had been affixed to the roof as if to ward off intruders. He turned his attention back to the healer's tent when Verida lifted open the flap, allowing the rest of the procession to enter. The smell of herbs and sickness assaulted Loravain's nose when they walked in. The air was stifling.

"Keep that closed," a voice demanded from the dim interior.

Verida passed the flap to Magenta, who closed it and crept inside with the others as they carried in Maggie.

"No, no, no. This will not do," the same voice said. "You two, out."

Loravain and Sarah were herded back outside by a large witch wielding a thick wooden spoon. When the flap fell shut behind them, Loravain paced in the cold night air. Everything had moved so fast that he hadn't had much time to feel the air until now. Breathing out, he watched a plume of frozen breath float away on the breeze.

"What do you think will happen?" he asked.

"They'll take good care of her. The witches here are different from the ones in the outer regions. At least that's what I've heard."

"I hope it doesn't take long."

"You really care for her, don't you?" Sarah asked.

Loravain looked at her. "I sentenced myself to death for her. I must see this through. It is the only way I can be redeemed for past sins."

He turned his back on Sarah and continued to pace, waiting for something to happen. He had promised Maggie's father he would keep her out of harm's way. So far, he'd done his best but she had still been poisoned, forced to outrun an erupting volcano, face a horde of fire demons, and now this. She had been anything but out of harm's way. And now, because of something beyond his control, he might fail.

"If anything happens to her . . . ," he began to say. "We're so close. Come on, Maggie. You have to pull through."

"She'll be okay," Sarah said, trying to console him. She moved behind him and wrapped her arms around his waist.

He relaxed a little and leaned into her. Lingering there, he enjoyed her warmth until his anxiety rose again and he broke free from her embrace. Walking in tight circles, he never took his eyes off the tent flap. When it opened, he was ready.

"How is she?"

"The girl will be fine," Magenta said. "You can go in and see her if you'd like. Verida and I must get back to the fields. Now, where did that girl get off to? Verida?"

Something wasn't right about Verida. Loravain had known people like her in the past and it never ended well. Apprehension crept up his spine, but he pushed it aside and entered the tent.

Maggie was lying on a low cot next to a central fire. Her head was wrapped in a white cloth and a brown and yellow flower sat on her chest. At least two dozen more cots surrounded her but only about five had occupants. A large fire burned in the center, a black cauldron sitting on top of the flames. The aroma wafting off it reminded Loravain of his childhood somehow but he couldn't pinpoint why. A square hole in the ceiling allowed the smoke to escape and provided a bit of fresh air to circulate around the tent.

"What happened to her?" Sarah asked the healing witch attending Maggie.

"She had what we call an overload. It is quite common among the younger witches, though I haven't seen it a witch her age in years."

"What causes it?" Loravain asked.

The witch stared at him in silence then glanced over at Sarah, who smiled and nodded assuredly, vouching for Loravain.

"An overload happens when a witch tries to do too much with her magic all at once. If we knew what she could do, and what she was doing at the time of the overload, we may be able to revive her faster."

"She can do this thing with sounds," Loravain said in a hurry, desperate to help.

"You're going to have to be a little more specific than that," the witch said. "And slow down. We have plenty of time. The girl is in good health."

"She told me it was like turning sounds off and hearing better all at the same time. She could hear my heart beating from a few feet away."

The healing witch looked down at Maggie, a smile crossing her face.

"She is an Audirium. Her mind processes sound differently than ours do. It is rare. Anything else?"

Loravain reached into his pockets and produced the roots he had taken from Maggie's fingers. "I found these wrapped around her hands after she collapsed. There were more in the ground around her."

"Plant roots? Has she ever shown any aptitude in nature magic before?" The witch took the roots from Loravain and examined them.

"Not that we know of," Sarah said.

"It is rare that she would manifest another power this late in life, but it is not unheard of. Has she been under any stress lately?" the witch asked.

Loravain remained silent and motioned for Sarah to do the same.

"If you do not wish to tell me, that is your business, but I cannot properly diagnose or treat her if I don't know what happened."

"Do what you can for her tonight," Sarah said. "We need her well enough to see the Queen in the morning."

The witch gave a small laugh. "That is not likely. Even if it was possible for a stranger to be granted an audience with her highness, the Queen is ill. She has been for some time. Even our best healers have not been able to halt her sickness. It is difficult for even the witches of Priama to meet with her."

"The Queen will want to meet with her, you have my word on that," Sarah affirmed. "Please, just do what you can for her."

"Does she know the Queen?"

"She did, long ago."

"We will do what we can though I make no promises about a meeting with the Queen. You can stay in the visitor's quarters for the duration of your stay. It is on the other side of the inner compound. If you don't mind, I must focus on my duties. Franklin will show you the way," the witch said.

Loravain nodded as a middle-aged man with a bald head appeared at his side. A dark yellow robe hung down to his calves.

"Please, come with me," he said, holding open the tent flap.

Outside, Loravain discovered that the inner compound of the city was much smaller than he thought. Most of the space inside the inner walls was open. By the looks of it, it was used mostly for gardening, training, and as a market. The center of the compound was filled with stalls and market stands. A large fire pit adorned the center of the market. Loravain could still sense the embers from the night's bonfire cooling in the night air.

"The visitor's quarters are just over here," Franklin said.

A tent twice as big as the healers' tent came into view as they rounded the market square. It was a mismatched concoction of rugs, hides, and furs that appeared to have no other use. Each piece had been sewn together at odd angles, but it looked sturdy enough.

"This is where you will be sleeping," Franklin said. "You will find all you need inside. Now, if you will excuse me, there are more pressing matters that demand my attention."

As he walked away, Franklin peered over his shoulder, suspicion in his gaze. When he was out of sight, Sarah sighed.

"Can you feel the struggle here?" she asked. "I can't even begin to know who to trust."

"I agree. The tension is thick," Loravain said then pushed his way into the visitor's tent.

The interior was just as he predicted. Identical to the outside. It was as if the visitor's quarter was created using material no longer suitable for anything else. Ropes hung from wall to wall with blankets and furs hung over them to separate the tent's space into smaller sleeping areas. At least it wasn't as hot as the healer's tent. The early winter air made the heat a welcome feeling though, Loravain thought.

A wrinkled old man sat on a small cushioned chair in front of them, smiling. His hair was white and he was clean-shaven. His gnarled and weathered hands held a stocky piece of wood he was whittling with a short blade.

"One or two?" he asked through a mouthful of missing teeth.

"One or two what?" Sarah asked.

"Two beds," Loravain said, earning a raised eyebrow from Sarah.

He had been thinking about what kind of relationship the two of them might have, but his past still haunted him. Giving his heart away was not something he did easily. He knew that just as easily as he could, it might be ripped away from him like it was with Camila. He knew Sarah understood that and appreciated that she never pushed the subject.

"This way," the man said, leaving his knife and wood behind. "Mostly empty this time of year anyway."

"Do you have a name?" Loravain asked.

"Of course, I have a name. What kind of fellow doesn't have a name?" he asked with a chuckle. "The name is Clinton."

"Nice to meet you, Clinton," Loravain said.

"Here we are. Sleep where you like, I really don't care. Just tidy up after yourselves before you leave," Clinton said as he turned on his heel to return to his whittling.

"Two beds, huh?" Sarah asked. "I remember a particularly chilly night where the lack of space between us wasn't an issue."

Loravain raised his eyebrows. He could not prevent the smile that slid across his face. "You were nearly frozen then and needed the warmth."

Sarah wrapped her arms around Loravain, clasping her hands behind him. "I'm cold right now. Keep me warm again."

The smile on Loravain's face faltered as his thoughts turned to Maggie. "When this is over we will continue this, I promise."

A pout appeared on Sarah's face as Loravain stepped away from her, but he needed time. Too much hung in the balance to let himself get lost in emotions.

CHAPTER 27

Her mind was cloudy when she woke up. The light, as dim as it was, pained her eyes. Groaning in discomfort, Maggie tried to shift her body. Something she was laying on poked into the small of her back. Each heartbeat throbbed in her head and pounded in her ears. Her throat parched, she tried to call out for something to drink but couldn't manage a sound. She grunted as best she could and turned slightly to the side, relieving the pressure on her spine.

"What happened?" she finally whispered, her voice rough and gravelly.

"You overloaded," a stranger's voice answered. "Do you remember what happened?"

A pair of hands slipped behind her head, lifted it up and placed a cup of water against her lips.

"Take your time." The voice was female, but it wasn't Sarah.

"Who are you?" Maggie asked.

"Drink now. It will help."

Maggie sipped at the water, savoring the cool liquid as it coated her tongue and trickled down her throat.

"More," she begged when she finished the cup.

Another one was waiting for her, which she drank more confidently this time. She breathed out heavily when she was done and looked around her. She wasn't where she thought she would be, and she wasn't alone. Several cots surrounded her and about half were occupied. A tall, lanky woman walked between them, checking on each person in turn. The woman helping her was young and refilled her cup for the third time. Maggie accepted it but held it in reserve.

"What's your name?" the woman asked.

"Maggie."

"Mine is Corina. I work as a healer. What do you do?"

"I don't understand," Maggie said, still taking in her surroundings. "Where am I? The last thing I remember was being in the forest."

"You've been brought to the healing tent. What is your job here?"

"I don't have a job here. I don't even know where I am."

"Can you tell me what happened to you before you lost consciousness?" Corina asked.

Maggie thought for a moment. She remembered speaking with Gwendolyn the owl. She could recall what had been said but everything after that was a bit fuzzy.

"I remember the owl and the fire," Maggie said, shaking her head to clear the cobwebs. "After that, all I remember is silence."

"Were you out there alone?"

"No, I was with my friends. I must have tuned it all out. I can do that. I can push sounds out of my head."

"That's right," Corina said. "You're an Audirium."

"What is that?" Maggie asked.

"It is what we call the witches who can do what you do. It is rare. Do you remember anything else?"

The more she thought about it, the quicker the missing pieces fell into place. She remembered the sensation of the ground wrapping around her fingers then slowly working its way up her wrists. She doubled over and grabbed her head at the memory. It was as if she was reliving the pain of the whole world rushing back in on her.

"It's okay," Corina said, holding her shoulders. "It's over now. The effects have worn off. We don't have to talk about it if you don't want to."

"Thank you," Maggie said, letting herself be pushed back down.

"Let me know if you need anything," Corina said as she stood up and walked away to check on the others.

When her head hit the blanket she was using as a pillow, the blindingly harsh white light of the morning sun invaded the calming dimness. Maggie looked around. By the looks of it, she was in a large tent. How had she gotten here, she thought? And where were Loravain and Sarah? Had they abandoned her? Looking back at the opening, she saw a tall woman with a bow slung over her shoulder silhouetted in the light. Even though she couldn't see who it was, Maggie knew she was important. She held an air of authority. The healers immediately rushed to her aid.

"My lady, what can we do for you?" the healers asked in unison.

"A young witch was brought in here late last night. Where is she?"

Maggie glanced around at the other cots and tried to make herself as small as possible. She didn't know where she was, or how long she'd been here, but she had the feeling that the woman was talking about her. Had Sarah or Loravain told them who she was?

"Over there," Corina said, pointing out Maggie as if afraid to displease the newcomer.

"Bring her and follow me. The Queen wishes an audience with her."

"In her state?" the older healer asked. "She is hardly in . . ."

"Did I mumble? Bring her."

The woman turned on her heel and walked outside, dropping the flap of the tent to the ground, shutting out the baleful light. The two healers rushed over to her, whispering in each other's ears.

". . . Is a mistake. Any kind of exertion at this point could prove fatal."

"There must be a reason for it. Let's just do as we're told. I don't want to be punished."

"When was the last time any witch was punished?"

"We're sure to be the next ones if we meddle in the affairs of the Queen. Hurry now," Corina said.

The conversation ended when they reached Maggie's cot. They lifted her to her feet and carried her out of the tent without dressing her. She was barefoot and only wearing a light sleeping gown. Shivering in the frigid morning air, she could tell she had nothing on beneath the gown.

"Where am I? Where are you taking me?" Maggie finally asked.

Corina hushed her and they continued.

"No," Maggie cried, trying her best to stop them, but she was still weak. They easily overpowered her. Giving in to the fact she could not get away, she tried to memorize her surroundings. They carried her between the tent they had just come from and a large log building. A tall wooden wall rose into the air in front of her. Where could she possibly be?

The healers quickly scurried along, half carrying, half dragging Maggie. Turning right at the end of the log building, a small, round yurt came into view. It stood on stilts, which lifted it off the ground a few feet. Two guards stood at the foot of a small staircase leading to the door.

"The Queen has requested to see this girl," Corina announced as the guards turned on them.

Saying nothing, one of the guards climbed the stairs and opened the door, letting them pass. The heat inside the yurt was brutal. It was at least twice as hot as the tent she'd just been in. A bed piled with furs and blankets had been pushed against the wall to her right with a small bedside table sitting next to it. A round table laden with vials, cloth, and a bucket of water stood in the middle of the room. A wardrobe taller than she was and three times as wide sat next to the double doors she had just come through. On the far end of the yurt, opposite the bed was an iron stove, a small stack of split logs, a chest big enough to fit her inside it, and a sturdy hutch with several shelves. Bundles of dried leaves and flowers hung from the rafters. If Maggie had enough time, she probably could have identified them.

"It helps ward off the infection," Corina whispered.

"What does?" Maggie asked.

"The heat. It is good for her sickness."

"Thank you, my dears," said a worn and exhausted voice. It came from the bed weighted down with blankets and furs. Maggie almost thought it was just that. "I wish to speak with her alone."

Corina helped Maggie sit down on the floor while the other witch watched.

"Thank you," Maggie said, doubting her strength to sit on her own.

Bowing to the bed, the two healers backed out of the room, never turning their backs to the Queen until they were outside. Maggie watched as layer after layer of bedding was pushed back. A face appeared first, then a frail and aged body.

"Can it be?" the Queen asked, tears forming at the corners of her eyes. "Have you come home?"

Maggie stared at her in confusion for a moment until the truth struck her. "Am I in Priama?" she asked.

"That you are."

"Then you would be . . . ?" Maggie started, close to an emotional break.

"Your mother," the Queen said, choking back the sobs threatening to silence her. "I knew you would come."

Maggie crawled across the cold wooden floor as fast as she could. She expected the planks to be warmer given the temperature, but it was a welcome relief. As she approached the bed, she noticed that her mother was not as old as she had first appeared. She looked no older than her adoptive mother in Lakes Hollow, possibly in her mid-fifties. Her hair was long but tucked into a tight bun on the back of her head. She only knew it was long because a few strands had escaped. Patches of gray had crept in but most of it was still dark brown. Even though her eyes were squinted, Maggie could tell they were similar in shape to hers, but she couldn't make out the color. Her skin was pale and glistening with sweat. Maggie reached out and caressed her face, which was freezing cold.

"What happened to you?" she asked, placing hands on both of her cheeks.

"My time is close at hand, my daughter," her mother responded, reaching out with a withered hand. "These last few years have not been easy. And now I have one more task to complete that I do not look forward to."

"What is that?" Maggie asked.

"I must bestow the Coven Seat to you before I die, and long before you are ready for it."

"What does that mean?"

"It means that you must become the Queen of Priama. You must take my place or else Alyssa will claim it."

"And she supports the war."

The Queen nodded then rolled onto her back. Her entire frame shook from the exertion of holding up her body.

"I don't think I'm ready for this," Maggie said, slumping her shoulders and falling onto the side of her mother's bed.

"I know you are not," the Queen said, stroking Maggie's hair. "None who become queen ever are. I wish we had been reunited under more desirable circumstances, but such is life. I must rest now. Belle will watch over you. She will prepare you and teach you what you must know to survive in this world. All will be well, my daughter. All will be well now that you are here."

Mere seconds after her mother fell asleep, the door to the yurt swung open, revealing the same tall, imposing figure she'd seen in the healer's tent.

"Are you Belle?" Maggie asked.

"Come. There is little time for talk," the woman said, holding the door open for her.

CHAPTER 28

The bed was much too soft for Loravain's back. For twenty years, he'd slept wherever he could, and it usually wasn't in a bed. After sinking in too deeply, he gave up and sprawled out on the floor. Dawn was breaking and he still hadn't slept a wink. He wasn't sure how long it would be before Maggie woke, but since the day he'd met her, his sleep had suffered. Tonight was no different. With her around, it seemed that danger lurked around every corner. Now that they were in Priama, he finally felt as if she was safe. So why was it that he couldn't find the relief he was hoping for?

He'd just gotten comfortable when the blanket posing as a door was thrown open.

"Can't I get any sleep?" he asked, dropping his head back down. "At least for a few hours?"

"No, you cannot."

He expected to hear Sarah reply, but this was not Sarah. The voice that responded held a lethal edge to it. He reached for his dagger as he jumped to his feet.

"Oh, I wouldn't do that if I were you," the voice said, a sweet, seductive charm woven under the words.

Loravain stood up straight as witches poured into the room, surrounding him. Three aimed arrows at his chest while another held the point of a sword at the base of his neck. Sarah had been taken against her will as well. She stood in the doorway, a dagger pressed to her abdomen and her hands bound behind her back.

"Okay," Loravain said, lifting his hand away from his weapon. "We'll do this your way."

"And no fire. We know what you can do."

"I knew Verida couldn't be trusted. She must have run straight to you when we arrived," Loravain said.

"She reported your arrival, but it was Franklin who first brought me word." The witch speaking finally showed her mask-covered face, stepping out from behind Sarah. "If you move to attack any of us in any way, things will not end well. Believe me when I say that I hold all the cards here."

"You might for the moment," Loravain said.

The witch pushed Sarah into the waiting arms of another who quickly bound her feet then knocked her to the ground. In the time that happened, Loravain had already assessed the situation. Three archers stood ready to fire. Two on his right, the other on his left behind his bed. A fourth witch was behind him holding the sword to his neck. One more was guarding Sarah. She brandished no weapons, so he assumed she was skilled in offensive magic. Then there was the instigator. Six against one.

"Here is how things are going to work," the witch said. "I am going to ask you some questions and you will answer them. It is as simple as that. If I like what I hear, you won't die. Well, not right away, anyway."

Loravain stared at her, searching for signs of weakness. She wore a thick but elegant robe. The mask covered most of her face though he could still see her green-tinted eyes. Something he would not soon be forgetting. With her came the heavy smell of flowers. Most likely the ones that were tied to her belt. He'd smelled that aroma before but couldn't place from where. A small voice in the back of his mind told him it was a bad memory.

"Why should I help you?" Loravain asked. "Who are you?"

"You are not in any position to be questioning me, but since we have some time, I'll let you in on a little secret," she said, sitting down on the bed in front of him. "I know who you are and what you have done. Well, more specifically, what you haven't done."

Loravain understood immediately. "You serve the Dark One."

"Serve is such a condescending word. We are partners working together to bring to pass a better world. Now that you have brought the girl here, I will finish the task you have failed to complete and be rewarded for it. I will earn a place on his council. Everything will work out in my favor."

"And what is your reward?" Sarah asked, fighting against her restraints.

"Why, the Coven Seat, of course."

"Alyssa," Loravain guessed.

"Well, well. You are better informed than I would have hoped for, outsider. I had wanted to keep that secret a bit longer," she said as she removed the mask from her face. "I guess there's no more point in wearing this silly thing."

Loravain knew that Alyssa had dark intentions, but he couldn't stop staring at her. She was beautiful. Her cheekbones were high and her lips were full and ruby-red. Her nose was thin and slightly upturned. He could see no blemishes on her skin at all, only a few freckles around her nose that gave her a youthful appearance. She looked nothing like the woman she was on the inside.

"Tell me, hunter, who is the girl you brought here?" Alyssa asked, running the blade of a dagger across her palm.

"No one of importance," he answered. "She just needed some help getting here. I'm afraid you've wasted your time."

Alyssa laughed. "Humans can be so stupid. I thought the time in the service of the Master would have taught you to lie better than this."

She lifted her dagger high above her head then drove it down with all the force she could muster, burying the blade deep in the meat of Loravain's thigh. He winced at the pain but managed to remain silent.

"I'll ask you one more time. Who is the girl?"

"Does it matter?" Loravain asked through gritted teeth. "You're just going to kill her anyway."

Slightly twisting the blade, Alyssa stood, leaving the dagger where it was. She paced the room, striding past Sarah without a glance. Her eyes flitted around the room, looking everywhere but at Loravain.

"You raise a valid point. I guess I don't need to spare your lives now," she said, motioning to the archers.

"No, wait. Please don't do this," Sarah pleaded.

"It seems that at least one of you has some sense," Alyssa said, backpedaling to Sarah, then kneeling in front of her. She caressed the side of Sarah's face with the back of her hand, slicing her skin with a fingernail. Bright red blood trickled down and dripped off her chin.

"Leave him alone and I'll tell you what you want to know," Sarah said.

"Give me one good reason I should listen to you, outcast," Alyssa said sweetly, laughing at Sarah's reaction. "You thought I wouldn't know who you were or where you came from? You forsook your heritage and became a mixed breed. You're worse than the humans. But no, I won't kill either of you. Yet. That will be my first act as queen. Executing the traitors."

"We are not traitors," Sarah yelled.

"As soon as I am crowned, you will be."

"You're crazy. What makes you think you can be queen?" Sarah asked.

"I was born for this. I can rule this queendom far better than that pitiful excuse of a witch currently sitting on the Coven Seat."

"From everything I've heard about Queen Natalia, you could never amount to half of that."

Alyssa spun around coming face to face with Loravain again, a wild look in her eyes. "TELL ME!" she screamed, hitting the pommel of the dagger with all her might, pushing the blade deeper into his leg. "WHO IS THE GIRL?"

"You'll find out soon enough," Loravain whispered. He'd managed to remain silent through the pain, but his body was starting to give in. A weakness crept through his veins and the room was spinning. A simple stab wound wouldn't do this. The blade must have been poisoned.

A dark memory floated through his mind. The smell in the room was getting stronger and he suddenly remembered why the aroma of the flower gave him a bad feeling. It was poisonous. His eyes flashed open with clarity, and he looked at the flowers at Alyssa's belt. Datura.

The white coned flower was immediately recognizable now. Alyssa noticed.

"You're quick. Now you understand the trouble you're in. I have the antidote. If you answer my questions, it's yours," Alyssa said, then nodded at the witch holding Sarah. "Do it."

The witch produced a short blade and ran it down Sarah's arm, biting into her skin.

"All or nothing," Alyssa said. "Either I get my answers or you both die. You know what the effects of the Datura leaf are. Do you want her to suffer through that? I'll ask you one more time. Who is the girl?"

Sarah answered. Tears fell freely from her face as she silently pleaded with Loravain to forgive her.

"Maggie. Her name is Maggie," she said, sobbing out loud. "She is the Queen's daughter."

Loravain nodded at her, a reassuring smile on his face. He guessed that Sarah had never had to endure torture before and didn't expect her to remain silent. The truth was going to come out sooner or later.

Alyssa stared at them both then turned to glare at each of her accomplices. She had not been expecting to hear that.

"It can't be true, can it?"

"If she is the heir, all could be lost," said the witch holding the sword to Loravain's throat.

"Nina, go. Find the girl in the healer's tent," she yelled then turned to another witch. "Take them to the hold."

In the commotion, Loravain attacked the witch behind him, taking her by surprise. They had made the fatal mistake of not tying him up, which would have done little good anyway. He quickly disarmed her with a sharp blow to her forearm. Picking up the sword, he swiped low, aiming at the legs of the archers, which they easily dodged. Still on his knees, he forced himself to move, dragging himself towards the fallen witch. The Datura poison was spreading faster now. Raising the sword to slay her, he froze as a pair of hands grasped the sides of his head. He couldn't move.

"Valiant try, hunter," Alyssa said from behind. "You forget that we are much more powerful than a human with little skill."

Loravain fought against the invisible force holding him prisoner but failed. He couldn't even wiggle his fingers. His mind worked just fine, however, but he could feel Alyssa trying to creep in. Taking a chance, he reached out to his power. He had the element of surprise on his side and hoped it would be enough. Breathing out, hot air escaped his lungs with the usual flutter of embers. Catching one on his lip, he willed it to burst into flames and spread across his scalp. He didn't stop there. Guiding the flames, they spread up Alyssa's arms, catching her coat on fire. He was about to intensify the heat when a blinding pain thundered through his head. Bright stars blinked into existence in front of his eyes as he lost consciousness and fell to the floor, darkness bleeding in around the edges of his vision.

CHAPTER 29

Belle handed Maggie a small vial filled with a dark green liquid. "Drink this," she ordered.

"What is it?" Maggie asked as she unstopped it and sniffed the concoction inside.

"A potion to help you regain your strength. I was told that you suffered an overload."

Maggie closed her eyes, put the glass of the vial to her lips, and tipped her head back. She expected the taste to be horrible but was pleasantly surprised. It tasted like apples. All the medicine her mother had ever given her when she was younger made her gag. The effects were nearly immediate. The weariness she had been feeling vanished and she pushed herself from the floor. She glanced at the empty vial and licked her lips.

"It wasn't what I was expecting," Maggie said. "Most medicine is terrible."

"First off," Belle said. "This is not medicine. It is a potion. Second, it must taste good or the young ones, who are usually the only ones to suffer overloads, would not drink it. Now come, we have much to do."

Belle rushed Maggie away from the yurt to an open area of the compound she referred to as the training grounds. A few small buildings and tents were scattered around the edges, but it was mostly a large, muddy field. Holding open the door to one of the buildings,

Belle motioned for Maggie to enter. Inside was a small pile of neatly folded clothes.

"Put them on," Belle said as she closed the door. "I'll be waiting."

Maggie quickly sorted through them, holding each one up to her body. By the looks of them, they had been specially prepared for her. Removing the borrowed nightgown someone had put on her, she carefully slipped into each piece. They fit perfectly but she had to call Belle on several occasions to learn how to put on particular parts. When she was dressed, she gazed at herself in the long, full-size mirror in the corner. She hardly recognized herself. Back home, she never would have been able to afford any of this. It was all beautiful, right down to the undergarments. She thought she was breathtaking. She looked the part of a queen, except for her face and hair. Those were still a disaster.

Out of everything she was wearing, she liked the boots the most. The dress's flowing red and purple fabric covered them, but they were soft and warmed her frozen toes. There was also a fancy pair of gloves but she couldn't bend her fingers while wearing them, so she slipped them inside her coat pocket. When she was finally ready, she opened the door, revealing herself to Belle.

The warrior witch appraised her with a few hums, tsks, and an ah-ha. "It's a start. Come, there is still much to do."

Belle turned out to be a brutally honest witch. She told Maggie precisely what needed to be done, how, and why. Nothing was left to the imagination and there was no room for guesswork. Belle was military through and through.

"You may be the daughter of my queen and the rightful heir to the Coven Seat, but you must look the part as well. If you don't look like a queen, you will be trampled on. There are witches here who wish to see the crown fall to another's head. You must show no signs of weakness here, even in your dress and appearance."

Walking away from the training grounds, they left the small changing room behind. The more Maggie walked, the more she appreciated the clothing. They weren't just for looks. Each piece served a purpose from correcting her posture to hiding weapons. And more importantly, they were warm. She could wear all her warmest clothes back home and wrap a blanket around her and she wouldn't be this warm. She didn't even notice the chilling bite in the air now.

"What's next?" Maggie asked.

"You are to be bathed. Grooming will follow. You reek of travel."

"But I just got into these clothes. Couldn't I have gotten dressed after the bath?"

"I needed to ensure they fit properly. A few minor adjustments will be made before the ceremony."

"What ceremony?" Maggie asked.

"Enough talk for now. Follow me."

Belle set a brisk pace forcing Maggie to jog to keep up. She led them to a large green tent. When they entered, Maggie was surprised to see a giant metal tub filled with steaming water. It was the most inviting thing she had seen since leaving home.

"I will take your clothes," Belle said. "When you're done, you will wear that robe. No dallying. We still have plenty to accomplish."

A white robe hung from one of the tent poles. Nodding, Maggie undressed again, doing her best to fold the clothes just as she had found them. When she was done, she dipped her body into the tub.

The hot water felt heavenly on her aching muscles. Her scrapes and cuts stung but she knew it would help them heal. She couldn't afford an infection right now.

"Stop dawdling in there," Belle called out. "There will be time enough for relaxing later."

"I'm coming," Maggie muttered, sad that she had to leave the warmth of the water so soon. She picked up a bar of soap and attacked her skin. When Belle had questioned her no less than four more times, she finally felt clean enough to call the job done.

Finding a towel, she dabbed at her body, meticulously drying every inch of her skin.

"By the nine, girl. Do you think we have all the time in the world?" Belle chided as she stormed into the tent. She grabbed the towel from Maggie and violently dried her body. "Put on the robe and follow me."

The shock of stepping outside nearly killed her. Each breath hurt and her skin burned from the cold. The robe did nothing to keep her warm.

Ahead of them was another line of buildings. They were much nicer than the changing rooms.

"What are those for?" Maggie asked, teeth chattering in her head.

"Were you raised by animals, girl?" Belle asked, exasperated. "Surely you know a market when you see one."

"Sorry," Maggie said, lowering her head and wrapping her arms around her chest. "Where is everyone?"

Belle sighed and calmed her voice. "Most of us do not live in the inner city. Our homes are in the outlining areas. You would never guess at our actual numbers. We come to the inner city for training, trading, and social events, among other things. However, no business will be conducted today. We must hurry. A witch is waiting for us who excels at the task we need to be completed. And if you don't get inside soon, we'll have an icicle for a queen."

"How long will it take?" Maggie asked. She was itching to spend more time with her mother.

"It will take as long as it needs to, and I don't want to hear any complaining. You are to be presented to the coven this very evening, and everything must be perfect."

"So soon?" Maggie blurted out through blue lips.

Belle stopped walking and faced her. "Have you not heard a single word I've been saying to you all morning? The Queen could die at any moment. You are her daughter. If the Coven Seat is not given to you, it will fall to Alyssa. There is no time left to wait."

They walked in silence until Belle found the door she was looking for. The building sat at the end of a long wooden boardwalk. Stalls and stores ran the entire length of it. It reminded her of the market in Lakes Hollow, though it was much bigger and nicer. She counted fourteen permanent buildings and a handful of tents scattered around the square.

"This is it," Belle announced, opening the door. "I will wait for you here."

Entering the room, Maggie came face to face with an old woman sitting on a padded stool. Her hair was gray and hung to her shoulders. It was straight and clean. Her eyes were dark brown and her face was wrinkled with age. She wore a beautiful necklace with a large polished blue stone hanging from it. Her clothes were nice but worn and patched in places. Maggie liked her instantly. A thick red pillow sat in front of her. The woman gestured to it, inviting Maggie to sit. A large bone brush was in her hand, ready for the task ahead.

"It is so nice to see you again, my dear," the woman said.

"Again?" Maggie asked. "But we've only just met."

"You don't remember me, do you?"

"Should I?"

"You were only a baby then, so I guess not. You have your mother's eyes, that's for sure," the old witch said.

Maggie sat down, allowing the woman to tug and prod the brush through her thick, gnarled hair. Her head kept bobbing back and forth from the incessant yanking.

"I was there when you were born," she continued. "I was one of the few witches your mother entrusted with her secret. To everyone else, you were dead."

"What? Why was everyone told that?" Maggie asked, shocked.

"That is not your place to fret about. It has been the burden of your poor mother for far too long. No sense in passing that down to you. You are finally together again."

"Why was I sent away?" Maggie asked.

"Haven't you figured that part out yet?"

"No, I haven't," Maggie sobbed, letting out all her pent-up frustrations about who she was. "I don't know why I was sent away or why I had to leave my home and family. The worst part is that people have been trying to kill me for it."

The woman stopped combing and wrapped her arms around Maggie as she cried. She rocked back and forth, humming a melody that was familiar yet somehow distant. Maggie tried to lose herself in the tune. When she started to relax again, she looked up into the old woman's eyes.

"Why did my mother send me away?" she asked.

"Because of love," the woman said, now crying herself. "She loved you so much but she feared for your safety. She is going to have to tell you the rest of that story herself. It is not my place to tell."

Maggie stared into her face, taking in every wrinkle and crease.

"What's your name?"

"Helena."

"Thank you, Helena," Maggie said, leaning into her.

"I would have been your godmother. I bet you didn't know that," Helena said. "I would have been the one to raise you while your mother ruled. It was as if I lost a daughter as well."

"Well, I'm here now. I'm finally home."

"You have been sorely missed," Helena admitted. "Your mother has spoken of you often during her most trying times. Oh, how she longed for today."

"And what of my father? When can I meet him?" Maggie asked.

"The story of your father is one even I do not know. Your mother keeps that secret hidden and locked away in her heart. All I can say is that she was needed elsewhere for a time and when she returned, she was pregnant with you."

"Where did she go?"

"These are questions you will have to ask her," Helena said. "For now, we have new memories to make together."

The two embraced each other tightly. They clung to one another until Belle interrupted them. She threw open the door, a look of grim determination on her face.

"I need you two to follow me. It is not safe here any longer."

"What happened?" Helena asked, pulling Maggie along behind her.

"I'll explain on the way. We must get Maggie to safety first," Belle said then handed Maggie a coat. "Put this on."

Three more witches joined them as soon as they left the market square. They were dressed identically to Belle. They circled Maggie and Helena as they walked.

"Is it Alyssa?" Helena asked.

"Yes. She has made a bold move. She means to take the Coven Seat by force today."

"Alyssa?" Maggie asked. "She is the one who will become queen if I don't?"

"Yes, but that is not all. She has taken your two companions prisoner. She has plans to publicly execute them as her first official act as queen."

"But she can't do that. She's not the queen," Maggie cried.

"No, she is not," Helena answered. "But that young upstart has been trying to weasel her way into the Coven Seat for years. Many of us blame her for the Queen's sickness."

"Us?" Maggie asked.

"Enough talk of conspiracies, old woman," Belle fired, cutting off the answer she was about to give Maggie. "We know what she is planning to do now. Chasing theories will do us no good."

"They are more than theories," Helena began but was silenced by a quick motion from Belle. They had rounded a corner and come into the open where a boisterous crowd had formed around a large, two-story building.

"The assembly hall," Helena whispered to Maggie as they skirted around it.

". . . Need Alyssa to rule. It is the only way to ensure our safety," a voice called out over the tumult of the mob.

"The Queen is not dead yet. She still rules Priama," another voice countered, causing even more arguing.

"We may need to proceed with our plans sooner than this evening," Helena said.

"I agree. If order is not restored, there may be bloodshed. Do you have any of her medication left?" Belle asked.

"Not much. Hardly enough for one last show of strength," Helena said.

"What are you two talking about?" Maggie asked.

They had been lingering just out of sight of the mob but now Belle led them past the healer's tent.

"We have a potion that, when brewed correctly, halts the spread of the infection invading your mother's body. It is not a cure by any means but it does grant her limited control of her body and powers, if only for a short time," Helena answered.

"Tanya, go rally support," Belle ordered. "Find everyone loyal to the Queen. Have them in here in two hours. The announcement must be made by then. Also, see if you can find out where they are hiding Maggie's companions."

One of the witches sprinted off into the crowd.

"Would your friends be able to help our cause?" Belle asked.

"Sarah is a witch who can do things to your mind," Maggie said. "And Loravain is an amazing fighter and a Fire Mage."

The group laughed when she said Fire Mage.

"What?" Maggie asked.

Helena leaned into Maggie and took her gently by the arm. "I know you have lived a life much different from ours so there are many things you don't understand yet. There are no more mages in the world. They died out hundreds of years ago. You must mean he is a magician."

"No. I mean he is a Fire Mage. The Fire Guardians gave him power over all three aspects of fire."

All levity fell from Belle's face.

"What do you know of the Fire Guardians?"

"Not much. I wasn't the one to meet them. Loravain was."

"And he told you about them?"

"All three of them. Fire, Smoke, and Stone."

"This would explain the reports I've heard. Get her to the Queen," Belle yelled. "She must be protected at all costs, as well as her friends. Once she is securely inside, no one gets in. And I mean no one. MOVE!"

Belle shifted her gaze to Helena and placed a hand on her shoulder.

"Helena, the Queen must know what Maggie has said. If it is true and a new mage has appeared, the lives of every witch here may hang in the balance. The Queen will understand my meaning."

Maggie and Helena were herded back to the Queen's chambers. The only thought spinning through Maggie's head was that she'd gotten herself in too deep.

CHAPTER 30

Pain shot through his head, bringing Loravain out of the darkness. Reaching up, he touched a wound just below his hairline. It was still wet with blood.

"I will make her pay for this," he said under his breath.

Taking a deep breath, the hunter took in his surroundings. The room he was in was like the one he'd slept in, only nicer. The furs hanging from the ceiling were full and beautiful. They were well maintained and cared for. The floor was wood, not dirt, and a masterfully crafted table stood in the center of the room. Candlelight flickered across the walls and ceiling, casting dancing shadows all around him.

He sat up, wincing at the dull pain in his leg, and felt a tugging at his ankle. An iron chain that was locked tightly to the floor had been wrapped around his leg. He pulled at it a few times to test its strength, finding it sound.

"This never would have happened with Thanatos around," he said.

Next, Loravain searched his body. His weapons had been taken, but that didn't mean he was helpless. As his hands ran along his legs, he was surprised to find that his wound had been treated and wrapped. He pressed his thumb against a small patch of blood, expecting pain to flair through is body but was relieved when it turned out to be only a small ache. A smile crossed his face as he continued. Power still burned through his veins, begging to be used. Whatever he did needed to be subtle though. He didn't want to get caught in the middle of the act.

The effects of the datura extract would be showing soon. Closing his eyes, he focused on controlling his breathing. If he wanted to prolong his life, he needed to slow his heartbeat, and in turn, hinder the progression of the poison through his body. When he was focused, he mentally reached out to the burning candlewick. A plan was already forming in his mind.

A prickling sensation built in his chest as he pushed his will across the room, asking the tiny flame to burn hotter. Something inside of him contracted, then began beating in time with his pulse. When he opened his eyes, the feeling slipped away. The candle, still burning, was nothing more than a stump now. Wax dripped onto the floor, forming a murky puddle. He smiled. He still had a long way to go before he could call himself a true Fire Mage, but this was a start.

With a wave of his hand, the light snuffed out, leaving him in darkness. He chuckled, then ignited one of his fingers, breathing light back into the room. As he stared at it, he imagined what he wanted it to do. He pictured a long, silken strand connecting his finger to the candlewick. Gently blowing, he envisioned the flame creeping its way along the imaginary filament, inching its way closer to the wick. He couldn't force it to obey, but he knew that the flame would be better off there and tried to communicate that feeling.

At his thoughts, the flame flickered and then slowly rose above his finger. Excitement flooded through him. He reinforced his desires, holding the image of the flame burning on the candle firmly in his mind. Confidence blossomed through his chest as the flame moved. The image faltered as his pride grew. As it did, the light flickered and died, plunging him back into darkness.

"Ugh," he grunted, slamming his fist on the floor.

On impact, sparks flitted out through the dark, which had never happened before. He struck the floor harder. Sparks erupted from beneath his fist. One of the tiny embers landed on the dry hairs of a hanging fur. Flames engulfed it in seconds. Loravain struggled to his feet as quickly as possible despite his wound and his legs being chained together. Pain flared through his abdomen, proof that the poison was spreading. Reaching out as he had with the candle, he attempted to smother the flames with his will alone. He managed to slow the spread but nothing else. It quickly reached the dry wood of the ceiling, illuminating the dark and hidden corners of his room. He was running out of options. There was no way he was going to be able to control a fire this large.

Escape was the only thing he could think of now, but how would that be possible while he was chained to the floor? Acting on impulse, Loravain dove through the burning fur, hoping to smother the flames in the process. The skin ripped free from the metal hooks holding it to the ceiling. It folded in on itself, burying Loravain and extinguishing the flames in the process. He rolled around on the ground to ensure the flames were out and then poked his head out. Alyssa was staring at him.

"Having a good time, are we?" she asked, holding a bucket of water in her hands.

Most of the fire had been smothered by his attempts to escape. The rest was easily handled. Alyssa doused the ceiling with the contents of her bucket, soaking Loravain in the process.

"Stop trying to escape. Don't forget, it's not just your safety you have to worry about."

Alyssa dropped the bucket to the floor and walked away, a look of disgust on her face. If he'd had his crossbow, he would have gladly put an arrow in her back. When she was out of sight, he lay down and cursed himself.

"What was all that about?" Sarah asked.

Loravain looked up in shock. She was sitting in a room identical to his. In his attempt to escape, he'd brought down their common wall.

"How long have you been there?" he asked.

"Hours. Haven't you heard me yelling?"

"I haven't heard a thing. I thought they'd taken you somewhere else."

"The dividing furs must be enchanted," Sarah said, running her fingers over the course hide.

"Well, whatever they've done to it, it doesn't change the fact that we have to get out of here."

"Escapes aren't really my style. I'm counting on you, handsome. Maybe you could burn us out of here?"

At her words, another idea began forming in the back of his mind. It was crazy, but that might just be what they needed right now to get out alive.

"I don't know if this is going to work," he said. "If not, it's better to die on our terms, right?"

"That's the spirit, but don't kill us just yet, okay?"

Loravain grinned at her. If Alyssa's quick response time told him anything, it was that he needed to do this fast.

"Stay here," he said. "When it starts, don't move."

"When what starts?" Sarah asked.

He stood and hobbled to the center of his room. Standing as tall as he could, he extended his arms. Closing his eyes, he sent a silent prayer to the Guardians for his plan to succeed.

His fire resided deep within him, and he desperately reached for it. When it responded, he pulled at it harder than he ever had before. The effect was minimal at first. Tiny flames arched between his fingers, drying his damp skin. It quickly spread to his hands then leaped up to his arms. The fire bit at his neck but he slowed the spread. Lifting his arms above his head, he willed the flames hotter. Turning white, they burned through his jacket.

"What are you doing?" Sarah yelled.

He ignored her and threw his arms out to his sides, balls of fire blasting from his outstretched limbs. They scorched through the animal skin walls, leaving smoldering holes in their wake. Exhausted from the exertion, Loravain crumpled to the ground and crawled back to Sarah as fast as he could.

"That was amazing," she cried.

Loravain put a finger to her lips, silencing her. "They'll be here any second."

On cue, Alyssa burst into the room, two other witches close behind.

"What have you done?" she screamed. "Flora, handle the blaze."

Flora, an ice witch, stepped in front of Alyssa and extended her hands. Icy tendrils pulsed from her fingers, slipping around the room. They attacked the fire, quickly extinguishing what Loravain had created. As the flames died, smoke rose into the air, pooling around the ceiling. Loravain smiled.

He lifted his hand and moved his index finger in circles, envisioning what he wanted the smoke to do. He needed this to work. The future depended on it. He breathed out a sigh of relief when the smoke began mimicking his movements. It swirled around the ceiling unnoticed by Alyssa, Flora, and the other witch, who were still trying to regain control.

"Get ready," Loravain whispered to Sarah, who nodded.

When Loravain was satisfied with the amount of smoke under his influence, he pulled his hands down, slamming them to the ground, throwing out another volley of sparks. Smoke flooded the room, engulfing everyone. The witches choked for air.

"What are you doing?" Alyssa shouted between coughs.

Loravain didn't reply. He pushed the smoke away from him and Sarah, holding it in place until he heard bodies collapsing to the floor. Releasing his hold on the smoke, it dissipated, giving them a clear view of the room. Three bodies lay face down on the floor. Flora had put out all the flames, but a few of the floorboards were still smoldering.

"Can you reach the keys?" Sarah asked.

Alyssa's body was just out of reach. Stretching out, Loravain could almost touch her boot. If he wanted to escape, he had to do something. Scanning the room, his gaze fell on his torched jacket. It would never be worn again, but it might serve a final purpose.

He tied the sleeves together and tossed it like a lasso. It landed on Alyssa's foot. Pulling as gently as he could, he slid Alyssa's body closer. The jacket quickly fell apart under the strain but it worked. Loravain could reach her boot now. Pulling hard, the witch's body was soon next to his.

Antidote and keys in hand, he turned to Sarah.

"Hurry," she cried. "We have to get to Maggie before they do."

CHAPTER 31

The Queen's yurt was just as frantic as the rest of the city. The Queen was lying on her bed still but there was a flurry of activity around her. Four witches were busy attending to tasks that were necessary to complete the ceremony. With her and Helena there as well, there wasn't much space to move.

"What happened?" Helena asked.

"Alyssa knows the time is close at hand. She is gathering her supporters so she can challenge the Queen. If that fails, she is planning on taking the Coven Seat by force."

Helena looked at everyone in the room, then at the Queen. "You haven't told them?"

The Queen shook her head. "There has been no time. Things have escalated much faster than even I would have anticipated. But I fear that somehow Alyssa knows. Why else would she try to force my hand at this moment?"

"It doesn't matter. We knew it was coming regardless. Drink this," Helena said, removing a small vial from her belt.

"The time has not come for that yet, but it will shortly. Gather everyone together."

Helena nodded and did as she was commanded. Calling for silence, the other witches gathered around the Queen's bed.

Maggie watched from the doorway. She was troubled and heartsickened by her mother's condition. She seemed to be in more pain now than she had been that morning. Taking a deep breath, she pushed her way through the bodies blocking her and knelt at the baseboard of her mother's bed.

"You are the girl we helped carry in last night," one of the witches said. "It is good to see you up and about, but what are you doing here? This is no place for a stranger to be."

Maggie turned to her mother for direction.

"Leave the explanations to me," the Queen said.

A memory suddenly flashed through Maggie's mind. It was the conversation she'd had with Gwendolyn the owl. She had told Thanatos to speak with Duncan.

"Mother, where is Duncan?" she asked quietly.

Her mother's laugh was kind but weak. "You surprise me. Even among my closest advisers, few people know that name. He is never far."

"We must speak with him."

"What are you talking about, child? Why are you addressing the Queen in that manner?" the same witch asked, then paled when she understood. "Can it be?"

"Soon," her mother said, answering her just as quietly, then turned her attention to address the room. "Yes, my dear Magenta, it is true. My daughter lives. Had I not done what I did all those years ago, she would be dead. She has finally come home to take her place by my side, and her rightful place on the Coven Seat."

The room exploded with excitement and disbelief. Each of them turned to face Maggie.

"Alyssa will not be taking the Coven Seat today, or ever," the Queen announced.

"I can see the resemblance," another of the witches said. "But Alyssa will never take your word for it. She will view this as a ploy to prevent her from becoming queen."

"After this afternoon, there will be no doubt that she is my daughter. There are many preparations to make. Belle is already doing her part and each of you knows what needs to be done. Go now. Time is short."

The room emptied except for Maggie, Helena, and the Queen. When the door slammed shut, the Queen fell back onto her pillows and laughed.

"My Queen," Helena said. "May I have a moment on your time? There are some things we must discuss."

"All in good time, Helena. I have precious few moments left in this life and I would like to spend them with my daughter."

"But," Helena began.

"Later. You are excused."

With pursed lips, Helena backed away and slipped out the door. The Queen still wore a grin on her face.

"Did you see their faces?"

Maggie stared at her. "Mother, are you not worried about what is happening?"

"I was. I truly was. But then a miracle happened. You appeared as if out of nowhere. Now there is no reason to be worried. Everything will be as it should be."

The Queen cracked her lips and produced a short, shrill whistle.

"Everyone sees me as the sick, frail queen that needs to be protected from the world. I let them believe that I am helpless, but I still hold a power that will save us all."

"But you are sick, Mother. I can see the toll this is taking on you. How do you expect to have the strength to use magic?"

"Have faith in me, my daughter. Before long, you will see the truth in my words. You will see something you have never imagined before."

Scratching noises echoed through the room. Maggie stared up to see where it was coming from. Above her head, a small hatch in the ceiling opened, allowing a slender raven to drop into the yurt. It landed on one of the bedposts. It cocked its head and looked from the Queen to Maggie, then back again. Maggie could see intelligence in its eyes. Her mother said nothing.

"Hello," Maggie said to the raven. It didn't reply.

Maggie took a deep breath and tried again. "Look, I know who you are, Duncan. Gwendolyn told Thanatos to speak with you, but he isn't here. I know you hold vital information about this cause. I need to hear it."

The raven looked at the Queen again, who nodded.

"You are the child then?" he asked.

"I am."

Duncan fluttered down to the floor and hopped around Maggie, appraising her. He circled her five or six times before flying up to a small perch set at eye level.

"I am impressed. Most beings, witches, humans, and a myriad of others, never meet with one of us, yet in a short time, you have met, and interacted with three. That is no small feat. One that I dare say few in history could claim. Fate must think you are important."

Maggie stared at him but said nothing.

"Alyssa is already making plans to kill you," Duncan continued. "She knows you are here and knows the threat you pose to her aspirations. As you may have guessed, Alyssa has allied herself with the Dark One. If you have truly spoken with Gwendolyn, you will know that if Alyssa is made queen, the Dark One will rise more powerfully than ever before. For this reason, you must become queen. To do that, you must prove to the witches of Priama that you are more powerful than she is."

"How am I supposed to do that?" Maggie asked. "I can hardly control my powers at all. I've hidden them away for most of my life."

"That, my dear, is where I come in," the Queen said.

CHAPTER 32

Loravain grabbed Sarah's hand and pulled her from the collapsing building. The antidote had already begun to work. The pain was starting to subside and his head was finally clear. When he was out in the open, he looked up at the imposing walls towering above him. They were no longer in the inner city. If they hoped to save Maggie, they needed to act quickly. Alyssa and Flora wouldn't stay down for long and it was more than likely that there were more of Alyssa's followers nearby. They needed a distraction.

"Stay in front of me," Loravain told Sarah as he limped forward.

"Why?" she asked.

"If they can see us, we'll be dead before we can reach the wall."

"I don't get how staying in front of you will help."

"Humor me."

When Sarah was in position, Loravain summoned fire into his hands. As it grew, it spilled from his fingertips. The late autumn leaves burned hot and fast. He hated the idea of causing a wildfire on purpose, but he had every confidence that the witches would be able to contain the inferno before it could do any real damage. His fire raced through the dry twigs, dead leaves, and other debris scattered over the ground. Smoke began to fill the air.

"Are you sure this is going to work?" Sarah asked. "They're going to know exactly where we are."

"They might know the general area, but they'll never see us," Loravain said, swishing his burning arms out in front of him.

Smoke billowed around them, rising high up into the sky. Snuffing out the fire closest to them, he added more smoke to fuel the barrier he wanted to create. Turning his attention to the smoke, he willed it lower, condensing it into a thick fog around them. Witches were already starting to fight the fire, but it only strengthened Loravain's cover.

"Find them." Alyssa's voice rang out above the commotion. "Forget about the fire. It's only a distraction."

"Is that what you were counting on?" Sarah asked.

"She's more intelligent than I gave her credit for," Loravain said, hurrying them on as he stepped in front of Sarah. "Let me take the lead now."

They surged forward blindly, hoping they were going in the right direction. Loravain had no clue where the entrance to the inner city was. To find out, he would have to leave the cover of the smoke. He would need to do that eventually anyway, but he wanted to ensure they were safe before that happened.

Extinguishing the fire burning in his hands, he pushed out with his mind, clearing the smoke in front of them, exposing a solitary witch.

"They're here!" she screamed when she saw them.

A rock soared past Loravain, striking the witch square in the forehead. A trickle of blood ran down her brow and she staggered backward into the smoke. Turning around, Loravain watched Sarah pick up a second rock.

"Forget it," he said, grabbing her arm. "We need to go."

Clumps of trees appeared out of the haze though most of the scenery they could see was bleak and flat. The farther they walked, the more distance the cries from the witches became. Loravain couldn't judge how far they had gone, nor if they were going in the right direction, but the effort of holding the smoke together was starting to wear on him. Sweat trickled down his face despite the nip to the air. His muscles ached in protest against his struggle.

"I can't keep this up much longer," he said to Sarah.

"Let it go. We don't even know where we are. Getting a decent glimpse of our surroundings will help more than this."

Loravain agreed. He knew it would put them in danger, but he released his mental hold on the smoke. It hung in place for a moment then began to dissipate. When they could see the walls of the inner city again, he realized why the sounds of pursuit had fallen away. They had been going the wrong way. Luckily, they were hidden in a small copse of trees and underbrush when the smoke cleared completely.

"This isn't any better than before," Sarah said. "How are we supposed to make it back without being seen?"

"At least we're not prisoners anymore," Loravain said. "Now we just have to focus on finding Maggie. That is our top priority. We don't know what kind of danger she's in right now."

From their hiding place, the entrance to the inner city was visible. It was a smaller opening than the one they had entered through the night before, but it was still well guarded. Three witches paced back and forth, two of them holding bows. A man leaned against the wall, watching the witches walk. He seemed vaguely familiar but Loravain couldn't place from where. He didn't recognize him but he had the feeling they had met before.

"I don't think we're going to get in that way," he said. "What do you think?"

Sarah looked around, concern written on her face. "We could try backtracking then going around the walls. They might not expect that."

"Or," another voice called out. "You could give up and walk in with us."

It was Alyssa. Sarah slumped her head in defeat as Loravain turned to face her.

"That was an impressive display of power. I've never seen anyone manipulate smoke before. It did make it easy to follow you, though," she said. "Next time you should take more time forming your plans before enacting them."

Alyssa stood confidently, hands on her hips. Two archers stood beside her, bows at the ready. Loravain was still uncertain of her powers, so he was hesitant to challenge her. Fighting her now would be foolish. He still didn't know what he was capable of. Alyssa whistled shrilly, signaling to someone at the gate. The lone man started jogging towards them.

"There is no use hiding anymore. As for your safety, if you were worried about that, you are still alive. Your attempted escape has done nothing to change my plans. Quite the opposite in fact. It has escalated them and reinforced my desire to execute you as traitors after you witness my triumphant rise to power."

"I don't care about your plans," Loravain said. "Can I give you a little piece of advice though?"

Alyssa laughed. "As if I would need to take advice from you. But I'll go along. Give me your advice."

"If you wish to survive through the day, you had better kill me now."

"Aren't you arrogant? Don't be so sure of yourself. You may be powerful, but you are outnumbered. Collectively, we are the strength here. Now mind your manners and come with me."

When their banter was through, the stranger was standing next to Alyssa. Now Loravain recognized him but couldn't remember his name. It was the same man who had summoned him to the Dark One the day he'd received his mission to kill Maggie."

"I have to say, Loravain," he said. "I never figured you for the type to turn your back on the master. Not when you were so close to being free of him."

"Zane warned us what you were up to and where you might be going. We were ready for you the moment you arrived, though we never anticipated it would be in the dead of night. You may have still been walking around causing damage had it not been for Franklin and Verida," Alyssa said. "Yet even Zane wasn't sure who the girl was, or why the master wanted her dead. Thanks to you, we know that now and I can ensure that I am the one to claim the crown and take the Coven Seat."

Loravain remained silent but trudged out of the underbrush, a smile creeping across his face.

"Don't get any ideas," Alyssa said.

"I wouldn't dream of it. You have nothing to worry about from me," he said, positive she hadn't seen what he just had.

CHAPTER 33

Belle's warriors had done well. Maggie pulled back one of the Queen's yurt's window flaps and smiled. A small army of witches stood guard, blocking the doors against the onslaught of angry protesters. If anyone thought they could break through that line, they were crazy.

Duncan and the Queen had explained the plan they had in store for them. The whole idea seemed insane to her, but she had lived in a human world her entire life. She had no idea what was normal, or even possible, in Priama. She paced back and forth, mulling over her part of the plan.

The Queen had fallen asleep again. She needed all her strength for what was to come. Still, Maggie had so many questions she wanted to ask her mother. Why had she been sent away? Why did everyone think she was dead? Who was her father? Would she ever meet him? She had tried to ask them all but her mother had urged her to sleep as well. There was too much excitement for sleep, Maggie thought.

She nibbled at the food that had been brought in for lunch. What she managed to eat was delicious. Soft bread, blue cheese, fresh fruits and vegetables, and a few strips of dried meat. Helena had told her to eat the meat sparingly as it would hinder her powers, but that it would help keep her warm. Her mother had told her that to become a powerful witch, she needed to learn balance in all things, including how she ate.

Helena surprised her when she burst back through the door carrying a bundle of clothes in her arms. She was followed by a young girl carrying a large basket.

"I don't think I'll be doing that again," she said as she dropped her bundle onto a chair. "No, I think I will be staying right here until all this is over."

"What happened?" Maggie asked.

"Those witches are out for blood. I have never seen it like this before. Alyssa has done a good job at causing dissension. The sooner this is over, the better."

The girl she was with looked visibly shaken as if she didn't know if she'd make it past the mob alive.

"I hope it is over soon too," Maggie said.

"Have you slept at all?" Helena asked.

"I tried," Maggie answered. "I don't know if I've ever been so tired but so awake at the same time."

Helena only nodded as if she understood. "Maggie, this is Fabiola. She was out in the fields with Magenta when you were brought in last night."

"Hello, Fabiola."

"Hi," the girl squeaked back.

"Get the water," Helena told her.

She scampered to the other side of the yurt and opened a large, wooden chest. Reaching deep inside, her feet lifted off the ground. When Maggie thought she would topple inside, she pulled herself out with a heavy jug in tow. Water sloshed around inside as Fabiola carried it back to the Queen's bed.

"The time is almost upon us," Helena said. "Belle has done her part well and Magenta is gathering the workers together. They are preparing for battle."

"And all because of me," Maggie said. "Will there really be fighting?"

"Trust me, my dear, this is not because of you. Priama has been divided for some time. One way or another, I anticipate some loss of life, though."

"That's horrible," Maggie cried.

"Such is the way of life sometimes. But be of good cheer. The children, young ones, and the sick and aging have been taken to the granaries to wait this out. They will be safe there. All who remain will be able-bodied witches and warriors."

"That is good to hear," the Queen said, frightening Fabiola. "I had hoped it would never come to this, but I pray we can prevent any unnecessary bloodshed."

Maggie hoped Alyssa would see that she had no claim to the Coven Seat after the announcement was made. She didn't want anyone to die because of her, whether she wanted to rule or not. However, with what she already knew about Alyssa, that was unlikely. Fighting was the outcome they were preparing for.

"Drink this," Helena said to the Queen, pulling Maggie's attention back to the present. "It is time."

"Let me get cleaned and dressed first, then I will take it."

Helena bowed and stepped back, giving the Queen space to sit up. When her feet touched the floor and she stood, the two embraced, eyes glistening with emotion.

"This is such a sad moment in our history," Helena said, tears running down her cheeks. "I wish it had never come to this. I wish there had been another way."

"Wish all you want, we all knew this day was coming. Your sister paid the ultimate price so we could prepare for it," the Queen said, motioning for Maggie to join them. "Without her sacrifice, there would be no stopping Alyssa. But my daughter has returned. We have hope that the Dark One will be thwarted."

Helena nodded and pulled Maggie into their embrace.

"It brings me joy for the three of us to be together once more," Helena said. "However, I do have other news."

Helena leaned in closer to the Queen and whispered in her ear.

"A Mage, you say?" the Queen replied, glancing at Maggie.

"You know the prophecy," Helena said.

"That I do, but it is of little importance now. That will have to be a discussion for another day. For now, my heart is full," the Queen said. "Come, let us continue."

Helena and Fabiola washed the Queen, preparing her body for what may likely be her last living act as queen.

When the washing was complete, the final touches were made to her garments. The dress wasn't long and flowing like Maggie thought it would be. In fact, it wasn't really a dress at all. The Queen wore flowing green pants with a dark yellow top. A long red jacket gave the outfit a more regal appearance without sacrificing her mobility. They had just finished dressing her when Belle burst through the door, a bloody gash on her arm.

"Your Highness," she gasped, nearly out of breath. "I fear we cannot hold them off any longer without taking lives."

"You have served me well, and I hope you will continue to serve my daughter. One way or another, this ends now," the Queen said, reaching out to Helena. "The vial."

Helena unstopped the small glass container and handed it to the Queen. With a deep breath, she drank the contents in one swallow. Maggie was shocked by the immediate results. Color returned to her skin, her muscles found their definition, and she stood with a royal strength. Her presence radiated her devotion to her position. Helena, Fabiola, and Belle knelt in front of her. Maggie was about to do the same but the Queen stopped her.

"You are the queen now," she said, a tear falling from her eye. "You bow to no one."

The Queen touched each of those present on the head then pulled Maggie into a rib-cracking hug.

"It brings me endless joy to know that you are back by my side. You will never know how many hours I spent thinking of you or how often I wanted to return to that doorstep. I love you so much, my Natalia. I know you have questions and I desperately hope I have time to answer them, but I fear I have reached the end of my life. You are the queen now and are destined to do great things with your life."

"There must be another way," Maggie cried. "I need more time with you."

The Queen kissed Maggie on the forehead. "We will have all the time we need in the next life."

"Highness," Belle called from the door.

"Helena, get Maggie ready," the Queen said as she released her daughter and moved towards the door. "This ends now."

CHAPTER 34

Crowds lingered at every turn, slowing their progression. Had Alyssa not been with them, they might have been brought to a standstill. At the sight of her, witches moved out of their way. Out of respect or fear, Loravain didn't know.

To his left was the visitor's quarters they had spent the night in. To his right was a large stable and blacksmith's forge. From the smell wafting past on the air, he assumed a tanner's shop wasn't far away. Alyssa led them past the forge and marched towards a row of narrow tents running along the edge of a large, open field.

"It is such a shame you aren't here under different circumstances, human. You would have done quite well here," Alyssa said. "We don't usually allow magicians to roam free, but we could have found a use for you."

A few of the witches walking behind them snickered at the comment, which only seemed to encourage Alyssa. She ran a finger down Loravain's cheek, eliciting a silent rise out of Sarah.

"We could have been friends, you and I. Perhaps more. But now we'll never know. You will be the first to die in the upcoming cleansing of the races."

Curiosity finally got the better of him. "What are you talking about?" he asked, eyes still staring forward.

"Oh, that's right," Alyssa said, self-importance dripping from her tone. "You were just the Master's errand boy. He never would have lowered himself enough to speak of such important things with you around."

"Do you think you are capable of prodding me into anger?" Loravain asked calmly. "I no longer serve that demon. Nothing you can say is worth my time or emotion."

"Not even the words of your dying bride?" she spat out. "I heard she begged for you to save her but you let her die."

In a single motion, Loravain grabbed Alyssa by the throat and lifted her off her feet. His rage at her speaking about his wife caused his fingers to unintentionally burst into flames, scorching her neck.

"You are unworthy to speak of her," he yelled before being attacked from behind.

He held on for a moment longer, relishing the look of helplessness in her eyes. His vision blurred when a sharp blow connected with the back of his head. He relaxed his grip and Alyssa fell to the ground. He smiled through his discomfort as he watched her claw at her throat.

"Do you think you're going to get away with that?" Zane asked, holding the blade of a short sword to Loravain's neck.

"No," Alyssa croaked as she struggled to her feet. "Leave him. Let him live now so that he may suffer a worse fate in the days to come."

Zane stepped back. Sarah tried to lay a reassuring hand on Loravain's shoulder, but he brushed it aside. He stood tall and glared into Alyssa's eyes. "That's twice you had the chance to kill me. I'm starting to get the feeling you want to die," Loravain said.

The look in her eyes betrayed the confidence she was trying to portray so she remained silent. Spinning around, she pushed her way through the crowd.

"Out of my way," she screamed.

A path formed in the sea of people. They flowed like water to let her pass. Zane pushed Loravain from behind until they reached the stairs of a large, round building. Immaculate carvings had been etched into the high doors. They depicted a scene of sorts, but Loravain was too far away to interpret it. Five stone steps lead up to the doors. Climbing to the top, Alyssa turned and faced the crowd of witches and servants.

"Witches of Priama," she yelled, demanding their attention. "Many of you here, if not all, have seen the lack of leadership Queen Natalia has shown over the years. Her lack of commitment to us has become our new way of life. We have abandoned the traditions we once followed. We have neglected our rule over mankind and their purpose here."

A roar of agreement exploded through the crowd, dying out when Alyssa raised a hand.

"We have adopted a more tolerant attitude towards our existence and lesser beings. But I still remember how it once was. How it should be once more. We once had years of prosperity that went unchallenged by our enemies. Years of plenty where no witch wanted for anything. All our needs were provided for. But now we are forced to till and work the grounds for ourselves like cattle. Like humans. This is beneath us. We have been granted power in this life, not the humans. It is our duty, our right, to use our power as we see fit."

Another cheer rose into the air. Angry voices replied in agreement. Loravain watched the poison Alyssa was promoting spread through the crowd like a disease.

"It is time for change," she said quietly, forcing the crowd to fall silent. "We are being held back from our true purpose by our so-called Queen. Even now she lacks the strength and courage to stop us. We have been granted this time to take back what we have lost. And I say we take it back by force. Our determination will be sealed by the blood spilled today."

The crowd was uncontrollable now. Alyssa had created an angry mob and she took joy in it. She had poured blood into the water and the sharks were circling. Loravain glared at her with contempt.

"The Coven Seat should be held by one who will represent witches and only witches. But they," Alyssa screamed, pointing at the guards forming a defensive line before the Queen's yurt. "They are standing in the way of the freedom we deserve. They mock us. And what have we done about it? What have we done?"

She stood in silence as she waited for an answer to come. When none did, she smiled.

"We have done NOTHING! But no longer will that be the case. No longer will we bide our time. We are ready to do something now. We will start by purging this city of the disease that is hindering us."

The crowd surged forward in excitement, threatening to pull Loravain and Sarah along with it.

"Up the stairs," Zane commanded, pushing them from behind. "Now."

From the top, Loravain surveyed the scene. Alyssa's supporters were crazed and waiting for violence. The royal guard, however, seemed to be doing their best not to spill blood. They were far better trained but incredibly outnumbered. Even with their weapons and magic, they would soon be laid to waste under the spell Alyssa had cast over the crowd.

All seemed lost. Tensions were high and still growing. When the doors of the Queen's chambers burst open, everything fell silent. The Queen stepped into view and in complete control of herself. Standing on her right, and looking just as regal, was Maggie.

"Sister of Priama," the Queen shouted, her voice carrying over the crowd. "I beg you to hear me. We can no longer afford to be divided. A much larger threat is upon us, and we must be united if we want to have any hope of surviving it."

"Do not listen to her," Alyssa countered, interrupting her speech. "These are only the feeble excuses of someone trying to hold onto her power. It will not work. We know of your ineptitude on the Coven Seat, Natalia. We know of the injustices you have wrought in our name for your gain, and we will accept it no longer. Give up your claim. Grant me the crown willingly and I will stop all of this. There won't have to be any unnecessary deaths weighing on your conscience."

The words flowed over Loravain. Her passion was mesmerizing, and she was beginning to make sense. Had the Queen done wrong?

"If anyone will be held accountable for the acts of evil done here today, it will be you, Alyssa. You have long sought the Coven Seat and it is not for the benefit of those you pretend to serve," the Queen cried.

The mob halted its attack. They were engrossed in the political debate taking place.

"Alyssa has conspired with dark, unknown creatures," the Queen continued. "She has done this for her own gain, and her gain alone. Once she has the Coven Seat, she will use it to destroy the race of man."

Loravain was confused. What the Queen said made sense as well. In a single moment of clarity, he understood. Alyssa was using mind magic. He'd heard about persuasion before, but it had never been used against him. Alyssa was powerful, but her lies could not counter the truth, no matter how much her magic influenced them.

"As is our right," Alyssa yelled back. "They were put here to serve us. If we deem them expendable, then that is what they are."

"But the bloodshed will not end there," the Queen said. "After man has been destroyed, the Dark One will turn his eyes to us. He will not be content to see us grow unchallenged. The witches will fall next. The Dark One will not share power."

Confusion flooded the onlookers, who remained silent. Their attention was still divided between the Queen and Alyssa. Persuasion was holding less and less sway over them as the truth was spoken.

"Oh, this is getting us nowhere," Alyssa muttered and nodded to Zane.

Zane moved silently around them, positioning himself in sight of the royal guard. When he was satisfied, he placed a hand on his temple and closed his eyes, much like Sarah did when she reached into someone's mind. Breaking his obedient facade, Loravain rushed him, hands igniting in flames, but it was too late. Zane's task was complete, and he crumpled to the ground.

It was pandemonium. The calm confusion that had fallen on the crowd turned into a sea of fury. A witch was on the ground, an arrow protruding from her neck. It was one of Alyssa's supporters. One of the Queen's guards was being unarmed and pulled back as well. That was Zane's doing. If things weren't brought under control, war was going to be inevitable.

The Queen was trying to calm the mob, but her words were drowned out in the tumult. She motioned wildly with her arms, but she was seconds away from being overcome herself. There was nothing Loravain could do.

"Can you do anything?" he whispered to Sarah.

Her face was pale from shock. She said nothing but shook her head.

Loravain was ready to jump down the stairs until someone handed the Queen a staff from inside the yurt. She grabbed it and slammed it down on the wooden balcony. A wave of solid air knocked everyone back, stunning them.

"I am still your queen, and you will listen to what I have to say," she yelled, once again holding the mob's complete attention. "The Coven Seat will never go to Alyssa. Look at what lengths she is willing to go to to take it by force. She is not fit to rule. The crown will be handed down to my daughter. The heir to the Coven Seat has returned home at last."

The gasp of unbelief was audible throughout the crowd.

"She lies," Alyssa screamed.

"SILENCE TRAITOR!" the Queen bellowed. "You have spoken your peace. As queen, I forbid you from speaking again, and as my subject, you cannot disobey. You will not rule."

"You have no proof that this is your daughter at all. With this ridiculous claim, I no longer see you fit to be my queen, so your will holds no sway over me," Alyssa cried in defiance as she descended the stairs. "You will give me the crown, or I will bring down torment and death on this people as has never been seen before. I will lay waste to all of you."

"You will do no such thing, you despicable child," the Queen said, reprimanding her, then turned her attention to her people. "Do you see what she is doing? If she does not get what she wants, she is willing to sacrifice you."

"I will," Alyssa cried. "Unless you, in all your wisdom and power, can stop me."

Alyssa walked past a tall witch, running a finger across her shoulder. The woman immediately turned and faced the Queen, a blank, unreadable expression in her eyes. Alyssa did this repeatedly to the people she passed, each one becoming a slave to her will.

The Queen stared at her for a moment before lowering her head. "I hoped it would not come to this."

"I thought so," Alyssa laughed, holding out her hand. "The crown, please."

As she passed, the crowd parted around Alyssa, afraid they would become unwilling participants in what she had planned. The Queen glared at her and reached out for Maggie's hand. Clasping fingers, they lifted their arms into the air. Maggie looked nervous.

"We have to do something," Sarah whispered in Loravain's ear.

"What do you have in mind? I don't know what we could do at this point."

It looked like Sarah wanted to say something until the ground shook. Thunder reverberated through the compound even though the sky was cloudless. Everyone froze, including Alyssa, who fell back a few steps. The sky continued to rumble as lightning appeared out of nowhere. Striking their outstretched hands, a powerful bolt of lightning connected with Maggie and the Queen. The force of the impact threw everyone from their feet. Loravain rolled out of the fall, helped Sarah up, then glanced over at Maggie. Her eyes were glowing brightly.

"I am the voice of the true Queen of Priama," Maggie said, her voice like thunder itself. "And I demand your attention."

Everyone in the inner walls of the city fell to their knees, witch and human alike.

CHAPTER 35

Maggie almost bolted when her mother reached down and took her hand in hers. She knew what was coming and she was scared. The Queen had explained how her power worked. She could open the mind of another, revealing their hidden potential. She said it was the only way for Maggie to understand what needed to be done. Duncan said it would also grant her full access to her powers, realized or not. Maggie knew this would be her mother's final act in life as well. If she could have done anything else to prevent this war, she would have.

The lightning didn't burn like she thought it would. It tickled a little when she felt the pure, raw energy flow through her body, cracking open her soul. Her powers rushed out uncontrolled and she became only a witness to what happened around her. She was being held prisoner by her own body. "I am the voice of the true Queen of Priama," she said in a voice that was not her own. "And I demand your attention."

She listened as this voice introduced her as the Queen. "I may only be a child, but I have seen what is out there. I have seen what is coming. The Dark One has specifically marked me for death as I am the only one who can undo what he has worked so hard to achieve. These attacks will not stop whether we are united or not. But, if we are united, we can survive. We can win. If we are divided, we will fall, and we will die. I do not expect you to believe in me by my word alone. I expect you to follow me by an example of my power."

Maggie let go of her mother's hand and watched her body crumple to the floor. From the corner of her eye, she saw Helena scurry out to attend to her. Her mind screamed out in anguish, and she tried to reach out to her, but she couldn't. She had no control over her body. She sobbed as she stepped over her mother, most likely dead by now.

The pressure that lived behind her heart swelled through her, flowing into the world around her. The air began to freeze. Every surface she could see iced over, including people, who turned white with frost. Her mind opened, allowing her to hear everything. She was aware of the panicked breathing all around her. She listened to their racing hearts. They were afraid and had every right to be. She was terrified for them. But as she listened, she began to hear deeper than she ever had before. She sensed the people's thoughts and desires. The witches of Priama weren't bad, they had just been manipulated by the power of another. The iciness retreated into her body when she realized this, taking the frost and bitter cold with it.

She turned her attention to Alyssa, who was still on her hands and knees, pushing herself back in fear. Maggie listened intently. Buried deep within her soul came the anguished cry of a tormented and corrupted being. She felt compassion towards her, which was the last thing she expected to feel. Alyssa had wanted to kill her. She had abducted her friends and tortured them. But there was a glimmer of light and hope buried inside, no matter how small it might be. It was a tiny desire to be the witch she had once been.

Maggie reached out to her. "It doesn't have to be like this anymore, Alyssa. The darkness can be purged from you."

Alyssa glared at her, hatred burning in her eyes. "Don't treat me like a sickness to be cured," she snarled. "ATTACK." All the witches she had touched and those still loyal to Alyssa converged on Maggie, taking her by surprise. One by one, they grabbed on to her, pulling her down. Maggie heard Belle issuing commands to her warriors, but the wall of bodies around her was too thick for them to reach her in time. The weight soon became too much for Maggie to fight against, and she fell. Alyssa rose above her.

"With Natalia dead, it will be so much easier to take my rightful place on the Coven Seat," she said.

"I can see the good in you, Alyssa, but evil has too tight a hold on your heart. I can't save you," Maggie said.

"I wouldn't worry your pretty little head about saving me. You should be worried about saving your own hide," Alyssa said with a chuckle then spun around. "Bring me the crown."

"I won't let you get away with this," Maggie cried, the light in her eyes starting to dim.

"Keep telling yourself that, darling. Before you know it, your head will be on the chopping block right along with your friends."

The witch pinning Maggie's right arm to the ground slumped forward, an arrow protruding from her back. Looking up, Maggie watched Loravain load another arrow into a bow.

"What are you waiting for?" he yelled. "Do something."

Reaching deep, Maggie discovered a new power inside her. She remembered sensing it for the first time only recently. It was a welcome feeling. As her fingers moved and twitched, roots broke free from the earth and twisted around Alyssa's ankles, locking her in place.

"What are you doing?" she screamed.

"This is for my mother."

One by one, the bodies on top of her slumped over. It took effort but she managed to push them off. She was relieved that Loravain was not shooting to kill, only to incapacitate.

Rising to her feet, Maggie glared at Alyssa. "You are a danger to every witch here."

Roots and vines had coalesced into a living cage around her, holding her in place. Once it was complete, the power that had surged through her body was gone. It was over. Maggie's body shut down and slumped forward. No one moved. They all stood frozen, watching Maggie, waiting to see what she would do next. As her abilities subsided, the only thing she could do was watch, feeling suddenly helpless.

Maggie searched the sea of faces for her friends. She needed to make sure they were still all right. When she found them, a smile formed on her face only to falter when a man she'd never seen before moved behind Loravain. Reaching into his jacket pocket, he produced a dagger. He rushed past Loravain and leaped off the balcony, charging at her.

"I will finish this once and for all," he cried.

She was helpless. She didn't have the power left to defend herself. She waited for the killing blow to come, but it never did. From the corner of her eye, a large black blur knocked the man over and savagely bit his neck, rendering him still and lifeless. Thanatos had just saved her life. Falling to her back, Maggie looked up into the faces of Loravain, Sarah, Belle, and Helena. They were all smiling at her. Then everything went dark.

CHAPTER 36

The assembly hall was filled to capacity. Word had spread quickly about what had transpired between the Queen and Alyssa. The passing of Natalia the Wise was hard for everyone to accept but they knew Maggie was to be crowned in her place.

After her show of power, Alyssa had broken free from her earthen prison and vanished. No one had been able to find her since. With her gone, no one was left to oppose the Coven Seat from being bestowed on Maggie. Helena, Belle, and Magenta helped console Priama for the loss of their beloved Queen and encouraged them to accept Maggie. With their endorsement, no one doubted that she was Queen Natalia's heir.

Before entering the hall, Maggie had attempted to convince Belle that she was too young to be taking on the mantle of leadership. Belle told her that not every situation was ideal. Maggie would have to learn to be Queen, and Priama would have to learn to love and accept another in place of Natalia. Realizing that nothing could prevent this, short of her running away, she sat in a small chair next to the ceremonial throne. She would not sit there until she had been officially crowned.

Loravain and Sarah were out in the hall somewhere, but she couldn't see them. After all they had been through, she felt exposed and vulnerable without them by her side. Before the ceremony started, they told her about their journey to Priama. She was sad she never got the chance to see the anderins. They sounded amazing.

Closing her eyes, Maggie waited for the ceremony to start. She reflected on how much her life had changed since leaving home. When autumn started, she was just the orphan girl who was adopted by two herb farmers. Now she was to be the Queen of all the witches. It was almost too much to fathom.

A bell chimed through the hall, and she opened her eyes. Helena sat to her left and Belle stood as her honorary guard at the foot of the throne. They were all beautifully dressed. Maggie wore a dark blue dress that had always been worn for coronations. It had to be altered to fit her as she was the youngest and smallest witch to ever hold the Coven Seat. Her hair was exceptional, thanks to Helena. She looked and felt gorgeous. She sat up a little straighter when the ringing sound fell away and the doors at the far end of the hall opened.

An ancient witch hobbled in, aided by two young children, one at each elbow. When they passed a designated point, the congregation stood, signaling the commencement of the ceremony. It was now only a matter of minutes before she would officially be Queen and take her place on the Coven Seat.

Sarah watched as the crown was placed on Maggie's head. The assembly hall erupted into boisterous cheers. A large feast would now be held in her honor. She was happy for her, but Sarah had now successfully fulfilled her end of their agreement. She had helped Maggie reach Priama. While congratulations were given and hands offered, Sarah excused herself and left through a small side door. She didn't want to draw any attention by using the large, main double doors.

The morning was cold and light snow blanketed the ground. She left a solitary line of footprints as she rounded the corner of the building, coming into view of the porch where she had been forced to watch the death of the Queen. She wasn't alone. Loravain stood there as well, leaning against the wall and looking out into the sky. Thanatos sat at his side.

"You couldn't stand it any longer either, huh?" she asked.

Loravain looked at her and smiled. "Too many people," he admitted. "I never did well around crowds."

Since coming to Priama, Thanatos had fallen silent around anyone but Loravain again, but he acknowledged her presence.

"What will you do now?" she asked.

"I will continue to fulfill the promise I made to her father. I will keep Maggie safe. Our fates are intertwined now."

"But she is the Queen. She has a Queendom of witches to protect her."

Loravain laughed. "And you saw firsthand how much dissension could come under the direction of one disgruntled witch. No, I am needed here. What about you?"

She didn't know how to tell him what she was feeling. She wanted things to evolve with him but after his reaction when Alyssa mentioned his wife, she wasn't sure that could ever happen. She was also getting nervous being around witches again. She had grown accustomed to the world of man, even though it was dangerous for her. It made her feel safer though knowing exactly what they were capable of. Witches were a different story.

"I don't know," she said. "I've been considering going to Mountain's Reach. I've never been there before."

"You'd really leave?" Loravain asked, taking a step closer to her.

She looked at her feet, not trusting herself to keep her emotions in check. It didn't help when he reached down and took her hands in his.

"I don't think this is the place for me," she finally said.

"How do you know that?"

"I've never gotten along with other witches very well," she answered.

"I'm not a witch."

Loravain pulled her closer and kissed her on the forehead. She was frustrated that that was all he would do and was shocked when he moved to her lips. Her knees went weak, so she pressed her body into his for support, getting lost in the warmth of the fire now living inside him. She wanted to stay like that forever. Maybe she could? He'd never actually kissed her before. Not like that. The sound of her heart pounded in her head, and she was sure her cheeks were flushed.

"What will I do without you?" he asked, then gently kissed her waiting lips again. "You have given me something I haven't had in many, many years. A lifetime really."

"What's that?" she asked, scared she was going to lose her composure.

"A purpose to live my life."

Tears welled up in her eyes as the large doors opened. Maggie stepped out into the early winter air to join them.

"What's going on here?" she asked with a giant smirk across her face.

Sarah laughed nervously, ashamed of her weakness. "Nothing," she said, wiping away a tear. "We're just talking about our futures."

"Good," Maggie said. "That is what I wanted to talk about too. I need you here with me. All of you. We're family now."

Maggie embraced them both, holding them tightly until Loravain gently pushed her away.

"My life is yours to command, your Highness," Loravain said, kneeling in the snow.

Maggie laughed and begged for him to stand up. Against her better judgment, but doing what she felt was right, Sarah joined Loravain and knelt in front of Maggie as well.

"Then I guess mine is too," Sarah said.

With a glance over at Loravain, Sarah smiled. He smiled back. Thanatos silently nodded his approval.

ACKNOWLEDGMENTS

This book has been a long time in the making, and there are so many people who were pivotal in its creation and helping me make it what it is now. They say that writing a book is like raising a child. It takes a village. Okay, no one says that. I just made it up, but it sure feels true, and I want to take a moment to thank my village.

First and foremost, I want to thank God for the stories He has given me and the ability I have been given to get them down on paper. Storytelling is a gift from heaven, and I am thankful for it every day.

My wife, Laura, has shown so much patience with me in this process. I started this story before I knew her, and we have been married for thirteen years now. She has pushed me, pulled me, and told me when things were getting too crazy. She encouraged me to write, even though I think she regretted it for a time. But now that the fruits are showing, she could not be prouder.

My daughter, Celeste. You are just a baby. You have no clue.

To my first readers. You have been invaluable to me, and the feedback you have provided has been instrumental in telling this story. I list you in no particular order: Taylor Morrison, Elizabeth Drysdale, Bekah Rowell, Tyler Thiessen, Stephanie Islas, Mandy Price, Amy Simmons and family, Alexis Fillos, Travis Coleman, Jenny Furse, Joe Furse, and many more. If you read for me and I didn't mention you, call me out and you will be in my next book. I promise. (Unless I forget. Again.)

Elizabeth Drysdale, you get your own line here, and not just because I got my own line in your book. You pushed me to submit this book to Cedar Fort even after I had doubts. If not for you, this moment may not have happened. You are a great friend. And readers, if you made it this far, check out her books, *Curse of the Forgotten* and *Out of Time*. We are publisher siblings. Hooray, Cedar Fort!

To my team at Cedar Fort. I used to read the acknowledgement of authors I aspired to be like and wondered what it would be like to have a great publishing team backing me. Now I know. Thank you all for your hard work and willingness to put up with all my questions. Angela Johnson, thank you for having the faith in my story and giving me a chance after I was probably awkward on our first call. Well, on our only call. Rachel Hathcock, thank you for being my first real editor and helping my story become what it is. It is now worthy of its cover. Speaking of the cover—Shawnda Craig, you made a beautiful one for me. Thank you for being willing to take all my suggestions and for putting up with me. Because of your work, more people will be willing to pick up my book and read the back. We preach how we should not judge a book by its cover, but we all do it. Every day. Now *The Clandestine Queen* has a cover worthy of being picked up. And to anyone else at Cedar Fort who I did not get a chance to work much with, I hope we will have plenty of opportunities to get to know one another.

To my writing group—you know who you are. Thank you for all the hours of non-writing gossip mingled with the occasional word sprint. I wish I could take the time to list all your names here, but let's be honest, I don't remember them. How often do you remember me calling you by name? Right, never. Because I never knew them, but I loved you all the same. I still love you. Thank you for everything.

Finally, a thank you to Richard Paul Evans. I had the huge opportunity to join his mentor program and to learn so much about the writing process. He has been a supportive voice to my work and the works of all the other authors he works with. He is responsible for the amazing Author to Watch Award on my cover. He had enough faith in me and my work to put his stamp of approval on it.

And dear reader, do not make the mistake of thinking this is all. No. Maggie, Loravain, Sarah, and Thanatos will be back. More stories are coming, in and out of Priama. Keep reading, keep dreaming, keep being wonderful. Authors would not have an audience without you. You keep us in business. Or at least busy. We give our time and energy to entertain you, and we love it.

I love you all dearly. Except you, Dave. You know what you did.

ABOUT THE AUTHOR

Photo: Jennifer Bryner

BRANDON J GREER is second and third oldest in a family of ten. (He was second oldest until a new marriage brought a new child that bumped him to third.) To set himself apart from so many siblings, he discovered the arts. Drawing, acting, and writing pulled him in at a young age. His first book, *Around the World in About a Year*, was completed in the sixth grade and was complete garbage, but it won him a place in an arts competition at the local university. Now living in northern Utah with his wife and daughter, he travels as much as he can.

Scan to join the author's mailing list

https://forms.gle/6iQGzZ3JpGbYw54s9